D0180030

Mad Maria's Daughter

—— *and* ——

The Genuine Article

Patricia Rice

A SIGNET BOOK

SIGNET
Published by New American Library, a division of
Penguin Putnam Inc., 375 Hudson Street,
New York, New York 10014, U.S.A.
Penguin Books Ltd, 80 Strand,
London WC2R 0RL, England
Penguin Books Australia Ltd, 250 Camberwell Road,
Camberwell, Victoria 3124, Australia
Penguin Books Canada Ltd, 10 Alcorn Avenue,
Toronto, Ontario, Canada M4V 3B2
Penguin Books (N.Z.) Ltd, 182–190 Wairau Road,
Auckland 10, New Zealand

Penguin Books Ltd, Registered Offices:
Harmondsworth, Middlesex, England

Published by Signet, an imprint of New American Library,
a division of Penguin Putnam Inc. *Mad Maria's Daughter* and
The Genuine Article have previously been published separately
in Signet editions.

First Printing (Double Edition), March 2003
10 9 8 7 6 5 4 3 2 1

MAD MARIA'S DAUGHTER

ONE

"You want to what?" Daphne's voice broke on a high note with the last word as she stared incredulously at the gentleman holding her hand. Only her awareness of the crowd behind him kept her nervous question from reaching a shriek.

"Marry you." Albert's cheeks reddened behind his military whiskers, but then, his normally ruddy color prevented anyone but a close observer from noticing.

"Marry me?" She sounded like a shrieking parrot despite herself, and heads turned in the ballroom behind them. This alcove certainly did not lend itself to an intimate setting.

Daphne read the uneasiness in his eyes easily as they shifted from her face to the velvet draperies and then to the floor. He was thanking his stars he'd had the sense to propose in a crowded room, and at that thought, Daphne took a deep breath and tried to control her soaring temper. She wouldn't let her temper fly. She wouldn't.

"Don't be absurd," she answered sharply, lowering her voice an octave.

His ruddy cheeks grew redder, but a stubborn line marred his mouth. "Absurd? What other offer have you?"

Control. One. Two. Three. Daphne squeezed her eyes shut to eliminate the staring crowd. Why did they always stare? She wasn't her mother. She wasn't. She chanted the familiar refrain to cool her ire. She was perfectly normal, and this absurd little man wouldn't prove her wrong.

"We don't even know each other," she offered reasonably, although her legs felt as if they were shaking beneath her. She needed to sit down. It had been four years, but sometimes . . . She shut out that thought along with the crowd.

"We've known each other forever," he remonstrated.

"We've danced one dance at each occasion we've met since you came home from the.Continent." She couldn't believe this was happening. Just as she had made up her mind to leave London and set herself on the shelf, this abysmal little man had to come along and shake her newly won confidence. Why did he have to do this to her?

He stared at her as she stood there with her eyes closed, her hands clenched in fists at her side, and he glanced cautiously to the people behind him. They were staring. He coughed slightly to gather his courage and tried again. "Surely that is sufficient to judge we suit?"

Daphne heard the meaning behind the words. That was "sufficient" to know she wouldn't have hysterics in public as her mother had been apt to do. That was sufficient to know she wouldn't cause any public scene as had been rumored she might. He'd been in Spain when she first came to London. He hadn't seen her stumble awkwardly across the dance floor, or fall attempting to enter a carriage. Most of all, he hadn't seen one of her uncontrollable rages when these things happened. But he'd heard, as he had heard about her mother. Instability ran in the family, it was whispered. One had only to remember her grandmother Pierce, who proclaimed pigs were superior to men in every way. And there was her Aunt Agatha, who lived the life of a recluse in the backwaters of Devon. And of course, there was always her mother, her dashing, lovely, charming, and very dead mother.

No. It wouldn't do. She had been right to decide to leave London, where her mother had left such an indelible impression upon society. Daphne had tried to eradicate that impression, but she had her own flaws to cope with; she couldn't hope to cover her mother's as well. The memories of her mother's dramatic departure from this world and its effect on her daughter's life hadn't faded from the petty minds of society, would never fade as long as Daphne was available to remember them. She had been young and foolish when she had come to town. She no longer had that excuse. They would never forget, and they would never let her forget.

Daphne opened her eyes and commanded her suitor's

attention. He shifted nervously from foot to foot. "No. I will not marry you," she stated calmly but without the requisite murmurs of honor and flattery. His proposal had just barely been honorable and certainly not flattering.

Albert looked vaguely startled. "Of course you will. What other choice have you?" he repeated.

It was really quite the last straw. She had forgotten that the hand he didn't hold was also occupied. Until now. Lifting the crystal cup of punch, Daphne poured it gently and carefully over his elegantly combed gray hairs. Sweetly, she replied, "This," then handed him the empty cup and strode off.

Clutching her reticule in her lap, Daphne stared out at the growing darkness beyond the carriage window. It had been kind of Lord and Lady Lansbury to loan the use of their carraige to take her to her aunt's. But then, everyone had been so kind and sympathetic—once she had announced she was leaving. And relieved. She shouldn't forget how relieved they were at her departure.

Daphne bit her lip and tried to retrieve her straying thoughts from the debacle that had capped her stay in London. She was almost at Aunt Agatha's. There seemed no purpose in stopping for the night despite the driver's protests. He could travel on to the Lansbury estate in the morning. The carriage had to come this way anyway. The Lansburys had merely been offering a minor kindness, after all.

Clutching her gloved fingers in the lap of her wool traveling gown, Daphne wrestled with the twin devils of ingratitude and cynicism. She could have taken a post chaise like anyone else. She was not helpless. She was not even incompetent. She was actually quite intelligent. Not that anyone cared. Biting her lip, she watched the road to her voluntary exile go by.

In a society that demanded perfection, she lacked the essential requirement, though she was not to blame. She supposed she looked well enough. Friends and family had assured her that her brunette curls were just as they ought to be, that her features were quite well-formed, even to the point of prettiness and past. They even claimed that her eyes were a most extraordinary green, and if they seemed a trifle hazy and mysterious at times, that was more to her account than not. The fact that they were her mother's eyes created the problem. Part of the problem, she had to admit. The rest of the problem she created herself.

Biting her lip and clenching her fingers, Daphne fought back the tears and forced her chin up. She had been green enough at first not to realize why the young gentlemen passed her by for flighty, less presentable girls. Oh, there was always someone's kind relative to bow politely and ask if they might fetch her some punch or to exchange meaningless gossip through a dance set or two. She was never left to feel alone and neglected, but she was seldom asked for more than one dance, either. Once was daring enough. Twice would have been foolish. After all, what if she took leave of her senses in the middle of the dance floor? Not that her mother had ever committed such a social solecism. She had been very polite about her madness. If her effervescence sometimes reached the heights of hysteria, or her dismals became black whorls of discontent, no one paid them any mind. That was just Maria. Charming, ever-maddening Maria. Even her suicide had been committed with exquisite care to make it look an accident. It was only by pure, horrible chance that she had been discovered.

Daphne closed her eyes against that long-ago pain. She could remember her mother as sweet and smiling and ever gentle. Why could society not remember her that way, instead of as the lady who had suddenly driven her carriage off a cliff one dark night, in full view of her only daughter? The period of mourning for her mother had long passed, but the *ton* continued to look at Daphne askance, waiting for her to show signs of her mother's instabilities, finding them all too frequently in the sharp lash of Daphne's temper, her cool withdrawal when anyone approached the subject dominating their minds, and in her inability to be one of the crowd. They would nod their heads sagely and give each other knowing glances, then treat her to saccharine smiles and insipid pleasantries until they could make their escape. After all, who wouldn't be unstable after such an experience?

At times, Daphne felt as if the *ton* resented being reminded by her presence that the world outside their hallowed halls was not a perfect one. Perhaps if they knew how imperfect she was, they would turn their backs on her completely. As it was, Daphne had persisted, refusing to believe all of society could be so shallow and thoughtless as to disregard her because of her mother's tragedy. Besides, she had no where else to go, naught else to do unless she wished to play the part of sheltered invalid in her father's house. And then she truly would go mad. For four long years she had determinedly beat her head against society's thick walls. Now, she had given up. She would not go back.

Gazing blankly out the uncovered carriage window, Daphne tried not to imagine what her future would bring. Like any other young girl, she had set out in society with the dream of finding a young man who would understand and care, someone she could share her thoughts and her life with. She certainly hadn't set any higher goals than that. Considering her imperfection, it mattered little to her if the man of her dreams were handsome. She had a secure competence from her mother's estate, not a wealthy one, but sufficient for a comfortable life, so she didn't require great wealth. She didn't even need a title. Her father was only the younger son of a relatively obscure north country title. Titles meant nothing. But she had expected to be found pleasing by someone, somewhere. It was not as if she were a complete antidote, after all.

But, as it turned out, apparently she was. After four years on the Marriage Mart, despite the kindness of all her relations, she had received only that one proposal of marriage, and it had been an insult. She had scarcely known the man. Albert wasn't the sort her very protective relations would normally allow near. Bankrupt and twice her age, his offer had been made out of desperation. If that was the best she could do, she was better off remaining unmarried. Society could pity her little more for her unmarried state than it already did for her mother's death.

Her maid snored slightly, jolting Daphne back to the present. Aunt Agatha's house couldn't be far. They had just come through the village a little while ago. It had been a long time since she had come through here. She had forgotten how steep this road was as it wound down to the riverbank. Or perhaps she had never known. She had probably been just as soundly asleep as her maid the summer she traveled here with her father.

The world outside seemed darker. Daphne looked up, trying to tell if clouds were covering the moon that had just risen. From the varying shades of darkness, she surmised the bank down to the river was overgrown with trees. The road appeared to travel along the river a little way before the bridge, and there must be trees all around. She would have to ride here one day and investigate. It ought to be a lovely place on a sunny day.

If Aunt Agatha would allow her to ride. Throwing herself back against the seat in disappointment, Daphne had to consider that possibility. With her brother's reluctant assistance, she had escaped her father's home because he had insisted on watching her every minute, forbidding her the stables, insisting that she be accompanied every time she ventured out of the house, all but ordering her to remain inside for fear she would be lost to him as her mother had been. She had been unable to tolerate the restrictions. If he had written Aunt Agatha with those same orders, would she obey?

Her mother's relations in London had been more under-standing, but that had been London. She had been accompanied everywhere by her cousins and footmen and maids. The size and sounds and smells of the city had intimidated her and she had accepted the fact that a lady could not travel alone, so she had not protested the limitations there. But the country was different. She used to love solitary walks with nature, and she had learned to ride as soon as she could walk. She did not wish to abandon those pleasures altogether to please her grief-stricken, anxious father.

For all that mattered, Daphne thought petulantly, she didn't see why she couldn't learn to navigate the streets of London just as well as a garden path, if only people would leave her alone. There had been so many exciting things around her, places she would have liked to linger, people she would like to know, but she was limited to those her family chose to visit. Now that she was older and more sure of herself, she resented their interference. She was not likely to go berserk or collapse in the middle of a busy street in broad daylight.

But she would never have the opportunity to explore London now. If she and Aunt Agatha rubbed along well, she would in all likelihood spend the rest of her life in splendid isolation in the rugged wilds of Devon. Relatively speaking, of course. She had heard of the mountains in Scotland and Wales, and learned of the magnificent scenery of Europe and America from her tutors, but unaccompanied, she wasn't destined to see them. So she really ought to make the most of this rough bit of coast and moor. She and Aunt Agatha would just have to come to an understanding.

A shout outside the carriage shocked Daphne from her reverie. What on earth was the driver doing? She grabbed the strap as the carriage swayed and pitched forward wildly. The horses' neighing protests as the carriage rocked to an abrupt halt drove a sharp spike of fear through her. Had the bridge gone out? Had a wheel broken? What was wrong?

The instant the carriage came to a full halt, Daphne shoved open the door. Behind her, her awakened maid wailed a protest, but she wasn't going to calmly sit here and wait for someone to inform her that they were about to fall off a precipice or something. Memory sent a *frisson* of fear through her, but she refused to retreat in the face of her cowardice. The shouts outside sounded like several men. Had there been an accident?

A dark shadow veered close to the Lansburys' elegant landau. Daphne recognized the sound of horse's hooves and before she knew it, the shadow of a horseman loomed before her. Cast in darkness outside the carriage lamps, he presented an otherworldly appearance. The specter made a gentlemanly bow and doffed his hat.

"What is happening? Has there been a mishap?"

The interior lamps she had insisted on lighting when it grew

dark illuminated the warm ivory of a delicate face etched
in worry. The horseman smiled against the darkness. "I have
only come to relieve you of a few baubles, my lady, and
any coins you might have in your reticule. Consider it a
contribution to charity, if you will, and you will soon be on
your way."

Thieves! That was impossible in this day and age. Highwaymen had been long banished to . . . The wilds away from
London where there was little or no law, Daphne finished
the thought belatedly. Still, she could not just give up her
entire quarter's income at his request. She leaned out to pull
the door shut again.

At that moment, a shot rang out farther down the road,
and a scream of warning vibrated through the cool night air.
From a distance, someone shouted, "Soldiers!" and closer
to hand, the mounted highwayman muttered, "Damnation,
a trap!" Before Daphne could jerk back out of reach, he
leaned over, hooked his arm around her waist, and hauled
her over his knees.

She screamed a terrified protest. Her maid wailed in a
soprano crescendo that pierced the ears. The highwayman
merely kicked his horse and sprinted off into the darkness,
one hand holding his prisoner safely in place.

"Cease the caterwauling and you'll be safe," he ordered
as the horse leapt a small hedge and dashed through a clearing
between the trees. "Continue, and you'll live to regret it.
I mean only to keep you hostage until the soldiers are gone."

Daphne was silent, more from lack of breath than
obedience. The horse's rough gait jarred knees against ribs,
and to her utter humiliation, she found herself clinging to
a very masculine leg from a very intimate position. Still, she
felt as if she would slide off at any moment.

She strained to detect any sound of pursuit, but her blood
was throbbing in her ears and panic clouded her senses.
Never in all her years had she been subjected to this kind
of ill treatment, and to think, she had thought he sounded
a gentleman!

They splashed across a river, soaking her woolen traveling
gown at the hem and spraying water up the back of her

heaving pelisse. She shivered as the icy water soaked through, and the horseman adjusted her more comfortably.

"Not far now. You'll be fine."

Daphne scarcely considered his promise reassuring. What did the highwayman consider to be fine? She was already soaked, cold, and humiliated to the marrow of her bones. She couldn't wait until she had breath to release the outrage choking in her throat.

The smell of his boot leather filled her nostrils, and she became gradually aware of other scents besides that of damp vegetation. The faint scent of bay rum mingling with masculine perspiration confused her. Did highwaymen wear bay rum? It was an odor that choked the ballrooms of London, but out here in the desolate countryside it had an almost pleasant scent. Perhaps it just reminded her of civilization.

The horse reared abruptly, and the thief chuckled as Daphne's fingers dug into his leg and creased his trousers. A hard arm lifted her with casual ease and slid her to the ground as a shrill whistle in the distance cut the air in a vague resemblance to a bugle's all-clear. He released her in obvious response to the signal. "My men should be safely away by now. You'll find a short walk down this path will lead you to a cottage where a very kindly widow and her servants live. If you'll hand over your trinkets, I shall leave you alone."

Now that her feet were back on solid ground and the breath was returning to her lungs, Daphne stared up at the immensity of the man and beast and the old, familiar anger struck again. She had promised to learn to control her temper, and she had honestly tried, but this was more than any one person should have to bear. Anger was better than fear, in any case, and she unleashed it without thought upon this masked stranger.

"You can't do this! This is an outrage! How dare you desert me like this! You must take me back to my maid and carriage at once. You cannot leave me out here miles from civilization. What kind of gentleman do you purport to be to thus treat a lady?"

The highwayman leaned over slightly in the saddle to study

the angry face beneath the disheveled bonnet. He had been quite prepared for her to faint and weep and plead for mercy. This mixture of rage and haughtiness from one so delicate caught him by surprise, but the fury underlying her words held something else. If she were afraid of him, wouldn't she use her anger to run? What kind of woman would demand that a thief linger to return her to her maid?

"The carriage is further than the cottage, miss. Did you enjoy our ride so that you wish to repeat it?"

The taunting mockery of his words drew blood into her cheeks, and Daphne had to clench her fingers to restore the proper decorum she had almost lost. "I am not familiar with these woods, sir. I could be lost for days. If you will not return me to the carriage, you must take me to the cottage." She said it as firmly as she could manage through chattering teeth. The icy river water was responsible for only a small part of the chill, she feared.

Beginning to lose his patience, the highwayman leaned over to wrap his fingers around the gold locket at her throat. "Are you so rich you have forgotten how to walk? Then you won't mind if I relieve you of this feeble trinket. I daresay Lansbury was too smart to bait a trap with real jewels."

Daphne smacked at his gloved hand and stepped backward. Her foot slipped on the damp moss and her weak leg betrayed her. The aching cold of the river water had done its damage, and she would have fallen had he not dropped to the ground and grabbed her. She righted herself hastily and attempted to elude his grasp, but the thief's fingers kept their grip on her shoulder.

"I don't know what you're talking about. Let me go." Daphne tried to disguise her fear. Now that he stood before her, she knew her abductor to be very tall, and the broad shadow of his shoulders conveyed his strength, even if his grip had not already warned her. Gentlemen were supposed to be languid and incapable of such violent swiftness of action. He could not be the gentleman her other senses said he must be. Yet she could not run from him if he showed himself to be scoundrel.

Her air of fear and defiance puzzled him, and instincts ever alert, the thief pursued his curiosity further. If she truly were Lansbury's bait, then perhaps she did not know what he was talking about, but surely even Lansbury wouldn't send a lady out to trap a highwayman without warning her! That meant she had to be some common trollop off the streets eager to earn a few coins in any way she could. That thought lasted no longer than it took to breathe in the scent of his captive's expensive French bath salts and to hear the aristocratic accents of authority in her bell-like voice. The quality of the fine woven wool beneath his fingers and the delicacy of the bones beneath his grip put the lie to commonness. She had to know of the trap. His fingers tightened.

"Lady, I'm willing to be fair with you. Lansbury won't miss these few baubles, and I'm certain he didn't intend for you to risk yourself in this attempt. We weren't pursued, so you cannot hope to be rescued at any moment. Had you paid any attention at all, you would have noticed the soldiers were on foot. They don't send cavalry after thieves."

"I know we're not being pursued or I would have told you to be on your way." Retreating behind the mask of dignity she donned when she betrayed her weakness, Daphne took the offensive. She dusted down her gown and pelisse and took another step away from his overpowering presence. "I cannot imagine why a gentleman should resort to terrifying ladies, or what Lord Lansbury has to do with any of this since he is exceedingly occupied in the government right now and not inclined to worry about wayward gentlemen . . ." She stopped, trying to remember where this thought was supposed to lead. She was chattering like a nervous magpie, but this man's presence had unnerved her as no other had. She gathered her scattered wits and tried again. "I have no wish to do anything but reach Aunt Agatha's safely, and I cannot do so if you desert me in the middle of the woods. And you can't have the locket. It belonged to my mother and is worthless to anyone but me. I have a few coins in my pocket, you may have those. And this silly ring that Cousin Sally insisted I must wear." She pulled off the despised object and joined it with the coins she carried so that her footman and driver could enjoy the occasional draft of ale, thankful that the reticule with her allowance was still in the carriage. "Now, take me to the cottage, please, and you may be on your way."

This was most extraordinary. He generally didn't stop unaccompanied young ladies, but her pensive face in the window had lit a wicked bit of mischief in him. He hadn't meant to do more than relieve her of a few coins and compliment her beauty. Lansbury was wealthy enough that he could afford to replace a few stolen coins. But in the few months since he had taken up this life of crime, he had never met so self-possessed a victim, even if she were as barmy as a Bedlamite. He almost felt inclined to obey her commands. Almost.

He pocketed the trinkets and reached for his horse. "The cottage is straight ahead. You cannot miss it. Good night."

Fury overcame dignity at this certain desertion. She had been scarcely left alone for a moment these last five years, and certainly never in a strange place. Her knee throbbed with pain and threatened to give out under her. Refusing to admit to anything so telling as terror, Daphne stamped her foot and grabbed the thief's coat sleeve. "I'll not be left alone like this, without even a lantern to light my way. I will not, do you hear? Show me to this cottage if it is so close by."

Astonished at her behavior, the highwayman took his boot from the stirrup and turned to stare at her. No one had ever spoken to him in such a manner. Obviously, she was badly spoiled. Or was she? Did he detect a trace of something else behind the fury of her soft voice? She did not strike him as the shrewish type. The memory of her lovely face in the window worried at him. He caught her chin in his fingers and raised her face to study it.

"And if I don't?"

She had been leading a sheltered life much too long. She had faced down other fears; it was time to conquer still one more. Closing her eyes to control her temper, Daphne summoned her flagging courage to reply with the arrogant flippancy of her cousins. "Were I still in London, I would have my groom flog you. Since I must now adapt myself to country ways, I suppose I shall have to hunt you down myself and shoot you.''

A hint of amusement laced his voice. "You are quite mad, you know.''

Daphne heard none of the amusement or admiration in his voice. She heard only the word "mad" and her temper soared beyond the boundaries of reason again. Ignoring her aching knee, she swung from the thief's grip and struck off blindly in the direction he had indicated earlier.

No one had ever spoken to her as had this wretched thief, confronting her with her worst fears. They had whispered about her mother and voiced their suspicions behind her back, but never had she been forced to face their accusations directly. "Look at the eyes," they'd say. "Just like her mother's.'' That epithet was the one that terrified her the most. Perhaps she was mad. Perhaps her mother's madness had started this way, with fears she could not control. Daphne tried not to think it, but the stranger's words cut through all pretense. She would rather risk falling on her face than plead with him again.

Watching her limp as she proudly walked away, the thief cursed. He was as mad as she, but he could not leave a lady in distress. Stepping forward, he caught her hand and placed it on his arm. "I am sorry. I had not realized I injured you in my haste.''

Daphne grasped this support with a shudder of relief. The pain had been sufficient to cool her temper. In a little while, it would go away, but she was too terrified of disgracing herself by falling to turn away a helping hand. At the concern in his voice, she answered honestly, " 'Twas not your fault but the water's. And the cold. Just call it an old war wound, if you will.''

At the pain in his victim's voice, the highwayman let her comment go by unquestioned. Old war wound? His gaze surveyed her slender figure consideringly, wondering what to make of that. "You are come to stay in these parts?" he questioned randomly, leading her a little farther down the path, watching carefully as she fell into step beside him.

"With my aunt, Lady Agatha Templeton. I can only be thankful she will not worry when I do not arrive tonight. She does not expect me until tomorrow."

It was very probable that the carriage had gone on to Lady Agatha's by now, and the entire household would be in an uproar, but he did not tell her of that. He was beginning to feel very ashamed of himself for frightening a mere woman and a harmless old lady for the sake of a coin and a pretty. face. A hell of a highwayman he made.

"I will take you to the widow's light. I dare not go too close to the cottage, for the widow's sake as well as my own. If the soldiers are still about, they may think her an accomplice."

Daphne grasped the warmth of his arm haughtily. "It is absurd to thank you after the harm you have done, but I do know you could have left me. I am something of a coward when left alone." That was an understatement, but she didn't enlarge upon it. "I will thank you for this small kindness."

He could have done a great deal more than leave her there, but such topics did not come easily to a lady's mind, and he certainly wasn't one to introduce them. It had been a few months since he had escorted a delicate female about, and he was rather enjoying the moment. She smelled delightful, although anything clean would smell delightful after months of living with unbathed villains. Now that she had his arm, she moved gracefully and with some assurance at his side. He could not discover any sign of limp or injury now. Actually, he could almost believe he was calmly walking down Bond Street with a beautiful companion for all she showed any fear of the situation now that he had accepted her company.

"Shouldn't you be afraid of me?" he asked out of curiosity.

She tilted her head to look up at him. "Utterly terrified," she assured him.

"You're roasting me."

His reply was so decisive and so much the gallant chatter of London that Daphne smiled. "My word, sir, how you do go on. Do you doubt my sincerity?"

He chuckled at the mimicry. She sounded just like one of the lovely Toasts of the Season he had briefly flirted with many years ago. Things hadn't changed in London then.

"I shall try not to in the future. I fear I would lose any battle of wits with you. Can you see the light now?"

The welcoming gleam glittered not too far off. Daphne gave a sigh of relief and released his arm. Any light at all was welcome in this darkness. She preferred company against the night terrors, but even she wasn't mad enough to believe this man was safer than the light ahead. Still, the light was a long way off. "There are no surprises between here and there?"

"Just lawn. I wish I dared lead you closer. . . ."

Daphne waved a hand in dismissal. "I shall be fine. This is all very adventurous. I think I shall enjoy the country more than I suspected." She offered her best imitation of courage. "Shall we say good night, then?"

It was utterly preposterous, but he bent over her hand as if he had just escorted her to her townhouse and delivered her safely into the hands of her servants. He felt a light squeeze, then she stepped out onto the lawn, tentatively testing the uneven expanse of ground before proceeding haltingly toward the cottage.

The highwayman stepped back into the shadows, wishing he could at least have had her name.

TWO

"I regret that you had to meet with such an inhospitable welcome to our neighborhood, Miss Templeton." The tall gentleman settled into the seat across from Daphne as her aunt handed him a cup of tea.

He smelled of fresh air and faintly of horses, not of bay rum, yet his voice . . . Daphne held back her frown as she accepted the cup given her. "Actually, it was the most adventurous night of my life, though I know I shouldn't say that." She was twenty-three years old and about to embark on an independent life of her own. People would have to begin accepting her as she was, she vowed. No more would she keep her tongue still for fear every word would be held against her. The man across from her was in all likelihood considered very eligible, he spoke with that kind of confidence, but she had no intention of trying to impress him.

"Adventurous? Surely not. Your poor aunt can only be relieved that you came to no harm in such an adventure. It was a reckless, heedless thing to do, and I am quite grateful no more came of it than this. Until now, the man and his band of thieves have harmed no one, but if he continues, I fear we will find the village and its environs overrun with soldiers."

Daphne sipped her tea and tried to puzzle her way through the variety of clues the man's words seemed to leave unsaid. His voice still bothered her. He had been introduced as Gordon, Lord Griffin, and his cultured accents evidenced his claim to aristocracy. The squareness of his strong face and the burnished gleam of his golden-brown hair gave her no clue, however. She had never met the man before—not to recognize, leastways.

But his voice revealed a strong similarity to the highwayman's. There were differences. Lord Griffin's voice was quieter, his accents a little more refined. Of course, he spoke in a lady's drawing room. A gentleman would more likely speak with gentleness there. Yet, the thief's voice had the ring of command to it that this man's did not. And she remembered a hint of amusement behind many of the thief's words, while this gentleman seemed all that was proper and concerned.

His words, too, were odd. Who was reckless? She, or the highwayman? She didn't think highwaymen were supposed to be anything but reckless. Did this area breed cautious thieves, then? The idea made her lips turn up in a smile, and lost in her own thoughts, Daphne didn't notice the suddenly smitten look on the young man's face as she turned that smile and her brilliant eyes in his direction.

"I should think the government would find better uses for its men than combing the countryside for a gentleman thief. Is there some reason for your concern over a sudden inundation of handsome soldiers? I should think the ladies in the area would be delighted."

The viscount lowered his cup and his usually serious mien offered a tentative smile. "You are quizzing me, Miss Templeton. I do not fear the competition of a company of soldiers. In fact, it might be a great relief to my social obligations. No, I fear the havoc such men can wreak in our peaceful village. I have no liking for guns in an area that previously knew only contented sheep and cows. As you saw last night, the presence of the military resulted in near catastrophe. I am convinced the highwayman would never have harmed you had those soldiers not appeared."

How very extremely odd. He seemed to be defending the highwayman. Most men would have blustered and declared all thieves should be hung or transported. Was he laughing at her as people so often did behind her back? Could this be the highwayman sitting right here in her aunt's drawing room, laughing at her? She didn't like to think so.

"You are exceedingly considerate of your resident thief, Lord Griffin. Wouldn't it be more proper to be out hunting him down?" There, let him see that she doubted his sincerity.

It was her aunt who answered. "Oh no, you don't understand, at all, my dear." Lady Templeton wasn't much taller
than Daphne, but her regal carriage gave the impression of
height. Exceedingly slender to the point of thinness, she
dressed in the full skirts and whalebone of an earlier age,
and her petticoats rustled as she moved. "Our highwayman
apparently pictures himself as something of a Robin Hood.
He only robs those wealthy enough to afford the loss. He
is always exceedingly polite. And the next day, some poor
unfortunate in the area is blessed with those things he needs
most. If there is illness in the house, a physician is paid to
visit. If the children are without shoes, several pair
miraculously appear on the doorstep. He seems always to
know who is in the most need. It is tremendously exciting
to the villagers, of course, although a few passing nobles
may have a different view on the sport."

Daphne was beginning to like her Aunt Agatha better and
better, despite the whispers of London gossip about her. Her
aunt possessed a sharp mind and a blunt tongue. She could
well picture the dismay of certain drunken gentlemen
galloping through the countryside being brought up short by
the reckless highwayman or Robin Hood. But still it was
wrong.

"It would be much more sensible did he find decent
employment and share his earnings for charitable purposes,"
Daphne announced determinedly. "Frightening people in the
dead of night is not the work of a gentleman."

Lord Griffin spoke firmly in agreement. "You are quite
correct, Miss Templeton. He must be stopped." He set the
incongruously small teacup aside and rose to his towering
full height as he bowed politely over her hand. "I regret that
I cannot linger. I only wished to see for myself that you
escaped unscathed. You are a very brave lady. I hope I can
expect your company at a small entertainment I will be
holding on Friday?"

Daphne smiled acceptance, and he departed.

Agatha watched her niece's dazed stare follow the viscount
out, and she smiled. "He is a handsome, polite young man,
is he not? How very fortunate that he chose to live here this

summer instead of returning to his grandfather's estate. His father only died last year, you know."

"Did he? How very sad. Were they close?" Daphne picked up her teacup again and feigned disinterest. There was a mystery here, she was sure of it. Two voices could not be so similar, and the viscount seemed almost the exact same height and size as the masked highwayman.

"I do not know if they were close. They seldom resided here except when the boys were younger, for a summer or two. They seemed happy enough, as lads do. Poor man, hard on the heels of his father's death, he lost his brother, too. Very tragic. It is strange he is not still in full mourning. He has been very brave about all this."

"Brother?" Daphne forgot to show disinterest as she turned to her aunt. "Older brother?"

"No, younger. He was quite distraught. I cannot believe they've been close these past years since Evan has been overseas in the military, but as boys, I believe they were. It is a pity. He is such a nice young man. And he seemed quite struck with you, too. I cannot imagine why you have not married before this. In my day, the gentlemen would have been at your door on bended knee in your first Season."

"Perhaps, dear aunt," Daphne replied, smiling sympathetically, "Lord Griffin was so kind because you have not yet informed him of my history. That was thoughtful of you, but someone is certain to tell him sooner or later."

"Fustian! What your mother did is no reflection on you. You are quite as sensible as I am. And you don't appear at all the invalid. My brother was simply much too protective of you. I can understand, you are his only daughter, and he wanted what was best for you, but men are so extremely foolish sometimes. I will rely on your own good sense to decide what you wish to do and how much you wish to tell to whom. I'm just too happy to have your company to complain."

Since her aunt had never married and had happily lived here the better part of her life without any sort of a companion, Daphne felt there might be a modicum of insincerity in this last, but she appreciated the thought. Leaning over, she kissed her aunt's cheek and rose to leave.

"You must tell me when I become an awful nuisance. I am grateful for your invitation, but I do not wish to be a burden."

"Off with you, then. I can see you are spilling over with energy and the need to be about. Oh, to be young again," she sighed, and casually dismissed her niece.

Daphne hurriedly departed for the gardens. She had missed having her own garden in London. Perhaps her aunt wouldn't mind if she dabbled a little in this one.

A few days later, feeling bolder, Daphne borrowed one of Lady Agatha's placid carriage horses to begin exploring the lines of the property. A groom offered to accompany her, but as she had no intention of going any distance, Daphne politely declined. She wanted to try being alone again, to learn living with herself without critical eyes following her every action.

The horse made an excellent guide. He willingly responded when she noticed the line of trees along the riverbank and turned toward them. She hadn't realized this area was so close to her aunt's house, and curious, she wished to explore.

Not familiar with the terrain, Daphne found an old tree stump to use for dismounting, and trailing the reins in her hands, she methodically began to find her way into the grove. To her, it seemed a vast, lonely forest of towering limbs and trunks, but she suspected it was merely a rough piece of land unsuitable for farming. She heard the rush of water and felt the downward slope and knew the river was near, but judging from the distance she had been carried from the place the highwayman left her until she reached her aunt's, this was a different part of the river than she had seen that night.

The day was warm and the shade felt deliciously cool. She hated the restriction of her heavy riding habit, but she was not yet brave enough to discard appropriate attire in public. Alone here, she unfastened the jacket and threw it over her saddle. A breeze whispered through the linen of her shirt and ruffled the jabot, and she smiled in delight at this small freedom. It was good to be herself again.

The horse whickered nervously, and Daphne hesitated, looking cautiously around. She could see the tree trunks sloping gradually downhill. There did not seem to be any dangerous precipice. All was quiet around her except for the crunch of her feet in the dried leaves. That was when she realized it was too quiet.

In the field she had crossed, birds had been singing. It was spring, after all, and the trees should be full of bird song. Perhaps her presence had intruded, but it had been quiet even before she entered the grove. She stood still, waiting to hear the sounds of scampering feet or rushing wings that she remembered hearing when she stood quietly in the woods of her home.

Nothing. Not a sound. A ripple of fear coursed down her spine, but Daphne proceeded onward, more determined than ever not to be frightened. It was broad daylight. There was nothing to fear of the day.

A moment later, she had the distinct impression of being watched. The hair on the back of her neck prickled, and she frowned in concentration, trying to find the source of the sensation. She could see nothing but trees and shrubs. No movement caught her eye, yet the feeling was all around her.

Annoyed at herself, refusing to admit her fears were becoming irrational, Daphne looked up, trying to scan the density of the branches overhead. A patch of blue appeared where she didn't think there ought to be sky, and her heart gave a nervous lurch.

Determined to conquer her fears, she announced firmly, "Whoever is there, come down at once. I do not like being spied upon. It is impolite and cowardly."

A chuckle and a rustle followed her words, and before she could jump back, a tall, lithe form fell from the branches to land at her feet. The scent of bay rum was stronger this morning, and she scowled ferociously.

"You! I should have known. I carry no jewels or money today. What is your purpose in frightening me this time?"

Pulling his hat farther down over his face, and relying on

the obscurity of the dense shade, the intruder caught her elbow and began to turn her back the way she had come. "I don't think anyone or anything is capable of frightening you, Miss Templeton. I think it is all a hum. Where is your groom if you fear walking on uncertain ground? You shouldn't be wandering about alone."

Daphne shook her arm free and halted their progress. "Do you tell all the ladies to stay at home where they belong? Fie on you, sir. And how do you know my name?"

She could see his broad shoulders in the fitted blue coat lift in a shrug, but she could not see his face. "This is a small village, Miss Templeton. Everyone knows everything. And any young lady of good breeding should be accompanied. There are brigands living along this river whom you wouldn't like to meet."

"Obviously," she replied, her voice tinged with irony. She feared to look too closely at his features, and the broad-brimmed slouch hat he wore pulled low hid him well.

"I have answered your questions, Miss Pert. Now tell me what you are doing here and how you recognize me. It is not at all healthy for either of us for you to know me."

Daphne gave a supercilious sniff. "I am merely exploring my aunt's property. And I cannot think that many thieves wear bay rum. It is hard come by outside of London and not generally worn by any but gentlemen familiar with the clubs of London."

His grin was one of wry mockery at himself. "I see that I shall have to grow a beard and cease bathing to better blend in with my surroundings. You are too sharp by far, Miss Templeton. I would advise you not to let anyone know that you can recognize me. It would cause both of us some difficulty."

"I can imagine it would cause you a few sleepless nights," she agreed with alacrity. "But I do not think anyone would believe me if I told them. You overestimate the general populace. Now tell me how it is that the Hanks girl received only sufficient fare for a coach ride to visit her ailing mother when that ring you stole was worth enough to pay her fare by post chaise all the way?"

The highwayman leaned one arm across the horse's saddle and stared down into her intrepid expression with amusement. Her face was all frail bones and delicate angles, dominated by the largest, most vibrant green eyes he had ever had the misfortune to encounter. Long, dark lashes swept upward as she stared back at him angrily, and he had the sudden urge to kiss that rosy flush on her cheek to see if those lashes would close in pleasure. It was an insane urge and he resisted it.

"Thieves have to live, too, Miss Templeton. Did you think those men I had with me that night robbed carriages for fun? What I do with my share is my business, not theirs. They have naught else to live on but what we steal. It is a sad state of affairs that the men who fought so bravely to save our country from Napoleon's maw must be reduced to thievery to eat, but you need not understand that."

"No, I need not." Furious, but more because of the unsettling effect his proximity had on her than by his words, Daphne took the offensive. "They could work like honest men. You do them no favors by encouraging them to an occupation that only can lead to the most violent of deaths." She did not know where she got the assumption that he was their leader, but he had a commanding air about him that could not cause her to think otherwise.

His laugh was short and bitter. "What kind of occupation do you think they had in the army? They are hardened to the inevitability of death, and a violent one is preferable to slow starvation. Look around you, Miss Templeton, and try to imagine who would employ crippled men whose only skills are to shoot other people? It is a wonder England is not overrun with cutthroats and thieves now that this war is over. I, at least, keep them from violence."

Daphne knew first hand the prejudice society held against the unfit. It didn't justify wrong, but she certainly was not one to hand out advice on how to combat it. She wrapped the reins more tightly around her gloved hand and began to search for a fallen tree that might serve as mounting block.

"I am sure you are to be commended, sir," she replied haughtily. "Just know it is on your head if anyone comes to harm. Lord Griffin seems most upset by your escapades, and he has vowed to see them halted."

"Has he now?" Amusement laced his voice as he lifted her forgotten jacket from the saddle and handed it to her, then calmly caught her by the waist and threw her up on the horse before her faltering attempts at mounting could become an embarrassment. "Well, I shall certainly take that into serious consideration. Does he come calling often, Miss Templeton? A viscount makes quite a handsome catch."

"You are insulting, sir." Whipping the reins from his protective grip, Daphne spurred her horse into motion. She did not have to endure the insinuations of a thief, gentleman or no.

"Don't come back here, Miss Templeton!" he called after her as she rode off toward the beckoning sunlight. For his own peace of mind, don't come back here, he thought as he watched her proud back ride away.

It had been a long time since he had held and been with a lady. Too long, if he was beginning to look fondly on a brittle termagant like that. He must have jelly for brains to even consider it.

THREE

That Friday evening, garbed in what she considered a modest costume of green sprigged batiste with the new flounced hem, a wide green satin sash, and long sleeves ending in a small ruffle, Daphne entered Lord Griffin's home accompanied by her aunt. The mounting whispers as she entered the salon caused her to stiffen. Assuming they were the usual rumors and speculation about her mother's death and her own involvement, Daphne held her chin high and barely touched Lord Griffin's arm as he led her to a chair.

Before she could be seated, a young lady all in white with the puffed sleeves of several seasons ago hurried to join them. "Lord Griffin, please, introduce me before Mama comes back in the room. I have never met someone who's talked to a highwayman before, and I have so many questions to ask."

Daphne heard the warm amusement in the viscount's voice as he made the introduction. Judging by Miss Jane Dalrymple's breathless forwardness, she was considered the town beauty. It seemed that only attractive people could get away with such behavior.

"Please, Miss Templeton, do not think me encroaching. I have so wished to meet you. You are the only lady hereabouts even close to my age, and you have such a dashing reputation, I just thought I would die should we not be introduced."

Dashing reputation? Daphne's brows rose and she heard Lord Griffin's chuckle, but she managed a polite smile. "Then we must get to know one another, Miss Dalrymple. It will be good to have someone of my own age to converse with." She was quite certain she was at least five years the girl's senior, but she would not quibble over age differences.

If the girl wished to consider her reputation dashing because her mother had comitted suicide, standards were considerably different between town and country. Or did her conversation with the highwayman truly rate that ranking?

"Oh, I knew you would be all that is proper. Mama would keep me hidden under a stone if she could. Imagine, thinking you fast simply because you have talked with a highwayman! I think it ever so exciting, don't you?"

Dashing, now fast—what kind of reputation had she developed in these rural circles? Daphne sent her host an inquiring look, but he merely squeezed her arm gently and released her.

"I shall leave you safely in the company of Miss Dalrymple, shall I? I must see to my other guests." Lord Griffin strode off, leaving Daphne momentarily stranded in a strange room with only this frippery female for company. Lady Agatha had already wandered off to gossip with her own cronies.

Cautiously, she took a chair. Miss Dalrymple eagerly took the next one. Daphne was about to begin on the polite series of questions she had learned to fulfill her social obligations when Miss Dalrymple made an expression of annoyance.

"Dash it all! Here comes Mama. She will drag me away, I know. Please say you will come riding with us Monday. Mama cannot complain if I say you are of Lord Griffin's party."

Having been an object of pity and suspicion, and a nuisance to be politely invited along with her cousins for the last years, Daphne found it extremely irregular to suddenly be considered a fast woman not to be met in polite company. She made a wry smile and a murmur that could be considered assent before the protective matron arrived to snatch her daughter away.

"Come along then, Jane. You must not be occupying all of Miss Templeton's time. There is Mr. Riggs just come in. Let us greet him and thank him for the lovely seeds his gardener sent over last week."

Daphne thought herself suddenly abandoned only to have a voice intrude upon her from behind. The familiarity of the accents sent a chill down her spine until she realized it was Lord Griffin. She mentally shook her head over the lapse in her perception and turned to give him her attention.

"You must forgive Mrs. Dalrymple, Miss Templeton. She has lived all her life in the country and abides by the rules of another age. She will come around soon enough, but you must expect to be a stranger here for a while. London ladies seldom visit these environs, particularly not ones as lovely as you." He took the chair that Jane had just recently vacated.

Such flattery did not often come her way, and usually then only in the most perfunctory of manners. Lord Griffin's charm had an immediate effect, and Daphne relaxed in his company.

"I shall be quite overwhelmed momentarily, my lord, if you continue so. How is it that London ladies do not visit here but you seem very much at home? I cannot believe that London has not been your life for some while."

"For a number of years it was, but I grew bored of it early. I have spent most of my life learning my grandfather's estate. One rural neighborhood can be very much like another, I suspect."

The call came for dinner then, and they were interrupted. Daphne found herself led to the table by the local squire while Lord Griffin escorted her aunt. It seemed very strange to be considered part of the social hierarchy after years of playing the part of everyone's dependent, invalid cousin, but she was not certain she enjoyed her new status any more than the old. She was assigned a place and expected to stay there without anyone's consulting her wishes, as if knowing where she belonged was the same as knowing who she was. Being Lady Agatha's dashing London niece was no more her style than being her mother's family's peculiar relative. What would it take to make these people see her as herself?

After dinner, when the gentlemen rejoined the ladies, the company formed foursomes for whist. Not appreciating the niceties of this social accomplishment, Daphne politely bowed out. To her surprise, Lord Griffin also declined. His tall form loomed beside her a moment later, and he extended his hand.

"I have a flower in the garden that seems only to bloom at night. Would you care to help identify it for me? Lady Agatha tells me you enjoy gardening."

She was twenty-three years of age and not some schoolroom miss. Daphne saw no reason why she should not accompany a gentleman alone into the garden. If her reputation was already fast, she might as well enhance it. Besides, she much preferred the cool night air to the stuffy confines of a salon of cardplayers.

She accepted without hesitation, taking his offered arm and following him through the French doors to the terrace beyond. It did not take many steps into the garden to recognize his night-blooming plant just from the scent, but Daphne refrained from announcing it immediately. She rather enjoyed the opportunity to stroll privately on the arm of a handsome viscount. Such opportunities never occurred in London.

"I understand your aunt allows you to ride alone, Miss Templeton." He spoke with a certain hesitation, as if fearful of giving offense.

Not knowing if he objected in general or because he recognized her slight lameness, Daphne replied calmly. "My aunt's properties are not so large or dangerous as to give me reason to do otherwise, my lord. After London, the privacy is most welcome."

He shook his head and sent her a puzzled look. "Surely by now you must know your loveliness can attract more than flattering attention. Even the plainest of ladies would do well to ride accompanied now that our woods seem to be filled with unsavory characters. I should recommend a small army to keep you protected from unwelcome attentions."

Daphne laughed at the seriousness of his words. "You do that very well, my lord. I was not even expecting it. An army! Well done, I congratulate you. I am most flattered. Although, as I understand it, it is a piece of the army who lives in those woods. I should think my own company better than theirs. Is this the plant you brought me to see?" She touched the round white blossom in the darkness. A sweet scent exhaled upward, perfuming the air around them.

"Not the most attractive of blooms, perhaps, but it is rather magnificent in the dark, is it not?" He pinched a branch to give to her. "And I was not offering gallant flattery, Miss Templeton. These are dangerous times. You almost came to harm your first night here. I would not have it happen again."

Daphne touched the blooms in her hand. Magnificent in the dark, how well he said that. Had she finally found someone sensitive to her pain, who understood that she was herself and not her mother? She desperately wanted it to be so.

"It is a night-blooming nicotiana, my lord, a tobacco plant. How extraordinary to find it here. Did your father travel a lot to bring this home?"

She was diverting the subject without giving him the reassurances he desired, but Gordon made no objection. She did not wear her hair in a fashionable frill of curls, but small wisps of light brown had escaped her coiffure, and his fingers ached to smooth them back from her face. There was something frail and vulnerable about her that he longed to protect, but he could only do that by keeping his hands to himself.

"Yes, he traveled almost constantly after my mother died. There are times when I think he never intended to live long enough to take his title and place in society. It feels very odd to be the Viscount Griffin now, when that is how I thought of him all those years."

Responding to the sadness in his voice, Daphne touched his sleeve with gentle fingers. "My aunt told me he died only a year or so ago, and that you lost your brother not long after. I am so sorry, my lord. I cannot even begin to imagine two such losses. It must be very difficult for you."

Something seemed to snap shut between them at these words. Without replying to them, Gordon formally placed her hand in the crook of his elbow and turned toward the house. "You will be missed inside, Miss Templeton. It was rude of me to keep you from the company for so long."

She didn't know what she had said to cause this reaction. Was it wrong to offer sympathy? Had she somehow overstepped the bounds of propriety? She hurried along at his side, abysmally defeated by his rejection so reminiscent of her days in London society.

"I apologize if I have offended you, my lord," she offered, feeling all the old hurts flooding back at the potential loss of this new friend. "I do not usually gossip, but in the country, everyone just seems to know everything. I will mention the subject no more."

He halted on the terrace and gazed down into her bewildered, pained expression. He had not meant to be so abrupt as to cause her consternation. Damn Evan into eternity, but he did make things difficult.

"I am not offended, Miss Templeton. It is a subject I still find difficult to discuss. Perhaps, one day . . ." Gordon's voice trailed off as he stared down into the lovely mist of her eyes. A man could lose himself easily in those eyes, and his thought halted, only half-formed.

Slightly giddy from the intensity she sensed in his voice and gaze and from the flood of relief that he did not reject her, Daphne touched his arm. "You will find I am quite easy to speak to. Come, let us go in, my lord. Your guests will wonder at your neglect."

She had much to think about when she went home that night. Lady Agatha's chatter about Lord Griffin's flattering attention verified what she had felt herself—he did seem to single her out above the other ladies present. After all these years she was unwilling to allow herself to believe someone would be interested in her as herself. She thought there very well might be a different explanation, and that the local Robin Hood might somehow be involved.

That was a dismaying thought, for she found the viscount to be a charming and attractive man, much more so than any of the other gentlemen of her acquaintance. Why was it that she could not be allowed a small flirtation like other ladies had with regularity? Just a flirtation, something to soothe her confidence before she made him aware of her background. He would lose all interest then, she knew, but it would be pleasant to have a beau just for a little while.

Only it was too difficult to believe that he would seek her out just for herself. She had too much experience at being ignored to believe she had the kind of beauty or charm to attract wealthy, titled gentlemen. And there was something decidedly odd going on around here. She sensed it. She just could not put her finger on it.

Why would Lord Griffin not talk about his brother? He had talked willingly enough of his father, but he had closed up abruptly when she mentioned his brother. How was it that Lady Agatha had said Evan Griffin had died? She hadn't. She hadn't mentioned how his father died, either. She really could place no consequence on that. Yet the coincidence of their voices . . .

The viscount had warned her away from riding alone. The man in the woods had warned her away from his hiding place. What were they trying to keep from her? It would be much wiser to puzzle that out than to think of the viscount's haunting sadness and the way he held her hand.

Next morning, Daphne set about to discover a few facts. It couldn't be too difficult. Judging by her conversation with the highwayman, everyone knew everyone else's business around here. She had only to ask the right people, and they would tell her.

She found Lady Agatha taking tea on the terrace. The day promised to be another warm one, but the sun had not quite reached this part of the house yet, and it was pleasantly cool. Garbed in a white muslin morning dress with short puffed sleeves and eyelet at the hem, Daphne considered fetching her shawl but settled for moving her chair toward the sun. It seemed a shame to wrap in wool on a day like this.

"Good morning, my dear. Lovely day, isn't it? I take it you are not riding today." Lady Agatha set aside the letter she was writing to look up expectantly at her niece. In that flimsy gown with only a bit of ribbon to frame her face, Daphne really was quite fetching, and Agatha nodded approval. This business about her mother's death and fears for her state of mind and health was a lot of faradiddle. The

girl had good sense, good looks, and a plump pocket; no
gentleman in his right mind could ignore that combination.
Her mother's relatives had to be all about in their heads to
discourage her. Agatha wagered the cousins looked like
mudhens and the aunts had mush for brains. She really should
have stepped in sooner, but the young so seldom appreciated
the isolation of the country. It was much better that she had
waited until the young viscount was in residence.

Daphne poured a cup of tea and added a piece of sugar.
"I thought I would try walking into the village today if you
would spare a maid to accompany me. Tillie is unfamiliar
with the roads, and I am not yet ready to attempt strange
places alone."

"Of course, take Marie. You must think of her as your
own. She is useless to me. I have too little hair anymore to
bother over and can arrange it just as easily, if not better,
than she can. But she does very well for you, I see. You
are quite in looks this morning. If you intend going into the
village looking like that, it might serve you better if I sent
a groom and a footman with you."

Daphne looked down at her outmoded gown in bewilderment. "But what is wrong with how I look? I realize the
simpler styles are not out of favor in London, but I thought
surely here . . ."

Agatha laughed, her proud gray head tilting backward to
regard her niece with fondness. "Child, there is not an ounce
of conceit in you. Your new French fashions have not reached
this rural outpost, if the whispers when you entered the room
last night did not tell you. No one here will know the gown
is outmoded. They will see only your bare throat and short
hem and how very dashing you look and every female tongue
will flap and every male one will pant. Do you not have a
suitable walking gown that trails in the dust and covers you
all over?"

Daphne drew her brows down in a pucker. "But that would
be so very warm and it is such a lovely day. I shall carry
a shawl and a parasol and gloves and surely look all that is
proper. I did not think I must be on display every minute."

"Oh, but you are more so here than in town, my dear," her aunt laughed. "But if you do not mind the biddies clacking, I do not. Wear what is comfortable to you. Do you have some errand in the village?"

"I hoped I might see Miss Dalrymple. She mentioned a riding party but I never had time to learn the details."

"I should avoid her mother, then, were I you. She is a monster of propriety, though it is said dear Jane was born but eight months after the wedding."

It was Daphne's turn to laugh at the thought of the plump and toplofty lady dallying before the wedding. The wry twist to her aunt's noble lips encouraged further confidences. If she went to a bad place for gossiping, it might as well be for gossip worth having.

"You mentioned the other day that Lord Griffin had a brother who died not long ago. He seemed reluctant to speak of it last night. Did I do wrong to mention it? Shall I hold my tongue in the future?"

Lady Agatha looked thoughtful as she refilled her cup. "There is nothing for him to be ashamed of. It was an accident, pure and simple. The boy had bought out of the cavalry after his father's death and was returning home as I heard it. He apparently rode too hard for too long in his haste to be home. As best as anyone could tell, his horse stumbled on a bad plank at the bridge and he fell in the river and drowned. They recovered the horse, but they never found Evan, just his coat and such where he must have tried to swim. The river is quite high in the spring, and I understand the current is strong. It was a great tragedy. Lord Griffin was so grief-stricken that he refused to have more than a private funeral. It was said he did not leave his room for days. Perhaps he still has not learned to bury his grief. I would leave it up to him to mention the subject the next time."

Oh, yes, she most certainly would, Daphne vowed grimly as she contemplated the impact of this story. Perhaps she was jumping to hasty conclusions. She really had no right to be so suspicious. Lord Griffin had never done anything to her to excite such cruel thoughts. But their local Robin Hood had.

Casually, she probed for further facts. "You said he was a younger brother, but he could not have been too young to be in the cavalry. Were they much alike, then?"

Lady Agatha finally sent her niece a sharp glance. "What is all this interest in a dead man? Evan Griffin was only a few minutes younger than Gordon, and yes, they were much alike. They were identical twins."

Daphne set her cup down and stared blankly at the rolling front lawn. Twins. Of course. How very stupid of her.

FOUR

The maid Marie was a silly widgeon, but as Aunt Agatha had said, she had a decided talent for arranging hair. Pity that she had no talent for intelligent discourse. The walk into the village was long and dusty and even the marvelous scenery could not distract from the prattle of the maid. The slight ache in Daphne's knee was a minor inconvenience in comparison.

Perhaps she ought to learn to drive a curricle. How difficult would it be to guide a pair of horses down this open country lane? It was not as if it were crowded with vehicles. Large ruts like the one she skirted now might be a problem, but if she drove slowly, she could not do much damage even if she hit it. She must learn to go about on her own. She forced the memory of her mother's wildly careening vehicle out of her mind with determination. She had to go on with her life.

The thought of driving her own vehicle buoyed Daphne up for the last leg of their journey. She would have to buy it with her own funds. She felt quite certain Aunt Agatha did not have so frivolous a means of transportation as a curricle. Where did one go about purchasing carriages out here? Perhaps she should write to London, but the image of the horror on her relative's faces at the mention of her driving instantly quelled that notion. Perhaps Lord Griffin might help her.

The walk was much longer than she had thought, and they arrived hot and dusty in the little stone village. The foxglove and campion in the hedgerows had been lovely to look on, but these old stone buildings built on the road with only a fringe of flowers for yard fascinated Daphne. She wondered how many generations of families had lived behind those ageless walls. Such stability amazed her after the frantic pace of London. A lazy cat sunned itself on a spotless doorstep. A sturdy matron stepped from the greengrocer's with her shopping basket and strode briskly toward the butcher's. Two children rolled and giggled in the dust, their homespun breeches coated with the thick dirt. The tranquility soothed the mind.

To the right a two-story inn sat slightly apart from the connected houses of the village. Paned windows of a century ago glistened in the sunlight, and a picket fence concealed a riot of color beyond the gate. Daphne lifted her skirt from the dusty street and hurried to investigate the garden in the inn's side yard.

The alley on one side of the inn led back to a stable, but on this side some industrious person had mixed a kitchen garden with a love of flowers. Admiring the lovely colors, Daphne looked around and seeing no one to object, she slipped the latch from the gate, and strolled onto the stone path, leaving her maid on the street flirting with some stable lad. Perhaps this pleasant garden might only be for patrons, but surely the owner could not mind an admirer when there was obviously no crowd of patrons to fill it, and she badly needed to sit down and rest her leg.

June was always her favorite month. Finding a stone bench, Daphne perched upon it and gazed around admiringly. Rambling roses spilled up the stone side of the inn and across the stable in back. Larkspur bounced and danced in the wind, and the last of the rhododendrons filled a far corner by the fence. Daisies and poppies brightened the rows of vegetables, and the effect was so cheerful, Daphne just sat among the dancing heads and admired.

It was a minute or two before she noticed the voices coming from an open window at the back of the inn. She really would never have noticed them at all had there not been a familiar cadence to one that caught her ear. She hesitated, wondering if she ought to just slip out of the garden and be on her way, but the idea of a known criminal's taking his ease in such a pleasant village, endangering the inhabitants, roused angry instincts and dispelled any need to rest.

He had no right to be here, none at all. She had stayed away from his turf, now he must learn his place. Perhaps she ought to find a constable or soldier or someone, but not knowing of a certainty the connection between viscount and Robin Hood, she hesitated at going thus far. Perhaps if she accused him of her suspicions he would see the error of his ways and depart. Then Lord Griffin could relax and be happy again.

Summoning up her small courage, Daphne lifted a gloved hand to her face and made a small moan. She had seen enough vaporish ladies in London to mock their actions now.

Marie instantly came scurrying to her side, and Daphne rose and rested her hand on the maid's shoulder. "I feel frightfully warm. Is there a place inside I might sit a spell?"

"Oh, yes, mum. It is a most respectable place. My mum once worked here. Let me see you inside."

Daphne allowed herself to be guided through the small side entrance nearest at hand. The shadowed coolness of the white-washed interior was refreshing, but she wouldn't let the maid know that. She settled on a rough wooden bench just inside the door and closed her eyes and leaned her head back against the wall. "Some water, Marie, please. I feel quite faint."

She ought really to despise herself for such dramatics, but she could not let the poor maid come face-to-face with the notorious criminal. She had done it herself twice now and come away unscathed, but she was certainly trying her luck with a third time. It made no matter. Now that she was here, he would have to change his vagrant ways. It was unfair to the kind Lord Griffin to be saddled with this Robin Hood's treacherous antics.

As soon as the maid disappeared around the corner, Daphne leapt to her feet and allowed the low murmur of voices to guide her. The room she wanted was right beside the door they had entered. She need only find the door to the room . . .

Her hand hit upon it almost before she recognized the rectangular irregularity in the wall. Without a second thought to what she might find behind it, she shoved open the door.

She had enough sense of self-preservation to know the gentleman thief would not harm a lady. She needed no other weapon but her womanhood.

The two men inside jumped to their feet as she barged in. The taller, broad-shouldered one in shirt sleeves and slouch hat immediately relaxed his stance at recognizing the intruder. The slim young man in livery remained at stiff attention, however, as Daphne's gaze swept consideringly over him. She did not need to recognize the servant's face. The discreet gray and black of the viscount's household told all.

Her scathing glance brought a shrug from the thief but he dismissed the footman before the diatribe that would undoubtedly follow. "Fetch the lady a lemonade, Michael."

The servant sent a nervous glance to Daphne but hurriedly did as instructed. As the door shut quietly behind him, Daphne bent her lips in a straight line that did not quite suit her femininely frail lace-edged attire. The highwayman surveyed her slim figure admiringly even as the storm broke from her lips.

"How dare you treat your brother this way?" she demanded. "What can he have done to you to deserve this treatment? Would you have him hanged for your misdeeds?"

That wiped the admiration from his face quickly enough. He straightened his long, lean figure to gaze piercingly at her. "How does a coward dare repeat such slanders, Miss Templeton?" he threw out defensively, searching for some means of stemming this attack.

"Coward I may be, but stupid I am not. The similarity in the voices is telling enough, but you cannot believe there are two men of the same height and breadth with the same cultured accents in this remote area, can you? Take off your hat and tell me I am wrong. Do you mean to embarrass your brother, sir, or is your scheme more nefarious than that?"

He swept off his hat and made a courtly bow. The resemblance was startling to a high degree. Golden-brown hair fell over a high, intelligent brow, accenting the lively snap of thick-lashed brown eyes and the aristocratic lines of a long nose and angular cheekbones. When he spoke, his voice was suddenly softer and more refined. "You have caught me out, Miss Templeton. Please do not speak of this to anyone. I am attempting to find my brother Evan's murderer, and I cannot do it in the role of viscount. No one must know of my charade. You will help me to keep my secret, will you not?"

She faltered uncertainly. She had been so certain that they were two different men. Could Lord Griffin truly be playing the part of coarse ruffian? It seemed highly improbable, yet the accents had changed from military to refined, and she was not yet familiar enough with his features to discern any physical differences. The golden hair glittering in the sun seemed the same as the man's who had walked her through the garden in moonlight.

A breeze from the open window brought a faint whiff of bay rum, and Daphne's back straightened angrily. "Do not give me that flummery, Evan Griffin. Perhaps others are fooled by your physical resemblances, but I know how to rely on my other senses, and they tell me you lie. You are a rogue and a thief, and I would have one reason why I should not turn you over to the law."

"Because it is none of your damned business?" He stalked toward her, his hands on his hips, his expression threatening. "Why don't you go back to London where you belong, Miss Templeton? This isn't a game and you can't play in it."

She refused to retreat before his fury. "I don't intend to play, Mr. Griffin. I wish only to see justice done. You may hang for all I care, but consider the effect on your brother, unless you are beyond all conscience."

Staring into her lovely, outraged face, Evan Griffin growled something irascible and stifled his temper. In that white gown with the frilly parasol, she appeared some avenging angel, and he certainly looked the part of devil. Thoroughly ashamed of his disreputable appearance, he rubbed a hand over his unshaven cheek and glared at her for her interference.

"You are almighty considerate in his defense, Miss

Templeton,'' he said mockingly. ''Have you decided you would make the ideal viscountess for poor, harmless Gordon? Why don't you go turn your sharp tongue on him?''

Red rage overwhelmed her. She had spent years perfecting an image of grateful courtesy as suited her dependent position, but that shield evaporated under his harsh attack. Never had anyone spoken to her like that. She would not have it. Without even thinking, Daphne reached for the pewter mug of ale on the table. It only took a little extra effort to reach high enough to dump the contents over his swelled head. She had been expelled from London for just such behavior, but it seemed satisfyingly justified this time.

Evan Griffin spluttered, opened his mouth to bellow with rage, and closed it swiftly with the sound of a light tap and a voice at the door.

''Miss Templeton?'' The maid's voice hid a nervous quaver. ''Are you in there? I have your lemonade.''

Streams of strong-smelling liquid slid from the thief's hat to drip on his shirt sleeves and smudge the dirt on his face. Daphne sent his frozen stance a quick glance and shivered. He was not only furious, but trapped. She sensed the danger as swiftly as he. The last time this had happened, she had been the one to suffer. Not this time. Wordlessly, she pointed at an ancient wooden cabinet teetering against the wall. She didn't care if he had to fold himself like a piece of linen to fit on the shelves. She didn't intend to be caught in his presence.

As Evan pried open the warped cabinet doors and disappeared from view, Daphne settled onto what appeared to be a comfortable chair and answered vaguely, ''Yes, Marie, do come in.''

The door swung open and not only did the little maid stand there, but a soldier in a red coat with gold trim about the shoulders and sleeves. Daphne gave a silent shudder, then lifted her head and held out her hand to her maid.

''You have found some lemonade? How thoughtful you are.'' Then frowning as if only just discovering the stranger, she inquired, ''What is this? Marie, you cannot keep company—''

Her words were cut off by the soldier's polite bow. "My apologies, Miss Templeton. Your maid was concerned by your disappearance from the hallway, and when she thought she heard your voice," he glanced carefully around the room to reassure himself she was alone, "and that of a stranger, she was worried. I was nearby, and knowing me to be an acquaintance of your aunt's, she naturally summoned my services."

She had not expected such perspicacity from the silly maid. Daphne smiled in genuine fatigue as she tried to imagine how to rid herself of this very proper servant of His Majesty while concealing a thief in a closet. It was all very distracting, to be sure. She took the lemonade offered and sipped gratefully.

"An acquaintance of my aunt's? I am sorry we have not been introduced . . ." Her voice trailed off. How did one address a soldier? Officer? Sir?

"Captain Rollings, ma'am. Are you quite all right? The countryside has been beset with brigands of late. I would not see you harmed." His gaze roved to the large cabinet.

Daphne didn't need to open her eyes to know where his attention had wandered. Smiling cheerfully, she rose, and twitching her short skirt hem to draw his attention back to her, she patted her hat in place and twirled her parasol. "How very kind of you, Captain. I have foolishly caused myself some fatigue in this heat, but I can assure you that no harm comes from a little overexertion. Do you by any chance know the way to the Dalrymples'? I was on my way to visit Jane, and I would be glad of an escort."

It would be exceedingly ungentlemanly to shove a lady out of the way to inspect what was in all probability a linen cabinet, and the soldier bowed his acceptance. "I know the house, but I have not had the pleasure of being introduced. I have only been in the area a short time."

Daphne lay her gloved hand against his sleeve and determinedly started for the door. "I am certain Jane would be delighted with the introduction. I shall presume on your acquaintance with my aunt, if I might, and insist that you accompany me."

She thought she heard a muffled noise from the cabinet,

but ignoring the dratted thief's discomfort, Daphne proceeded out. Let Evan Griffin stew in his own ale for a while. With any luck at all, the cabinet did not open from the inside. See if he could find his way out of that one.

Some time after the soldier was well out of sight, the terrified footman crept back into the parlor and darted nervous glances all about. A muffled curse drew his attention to the cupboard, and he jumped back, startled, as a knife protruded through the crack between the doors and began to saw at the latch. Hastily, he closed the parlor door and twisted the latch to open the cabinet.

Evan tumbled unceremoniously to the floor. His hat reeked of ale, and the disgruntled expression on his handsome features clearly revealed his state of mind. The footman hurriedly reached to help him to his feet. Being new to his exalted position and uniform, the servant did not dare crack a smile as the gentleman began a series of curses on the perversity of the female sex as he straightened his decidedly rumpled and odoriferous clothing.

Finally recovering some of his self-possession, Evan cast a glance to the closed door and then back to the nervous footman. He muttered a pithy curse and ran strong brown hands through already rumpled golden-brown locks. "Deuce take it, Michael, have the ladies changed so much while I was away? They never used to be so damned clever."

"No, sir." Michael shifted from foot to foot, uncertain of the proper reply.

"Well, you'd better inform his lordship that we have been caught out. He'll not be happy. Mayhap if he wore cologne like any civilized man, we'd not be in this now. Persuade his valet to douse him in bay rum in the next time Miss Templeton calls. That ought to muddy the waters a while longer."

Not having the least idea of what the gentleman was talking about, Michael merely nodded and tried desperately to memorize the message.

Evan wrung out his hat, sniffed it disagreeably, then shoved it back on his head. Producing a large coin, he handed it to the servant. "Give this to Beckworth for the use of his room. I'd best slip out the side way. Give me a warning if there are any strangers about."

Evan grimaced wearily as the footman left. Subterfuge wasn't his strong point. Miss Templeton had made that savagely clear. Remembering those furious green eyes in that delicate face, he stalked for the exit and the safety of the woods. Lud, but Gordon had all the luck. It didn't seem quite fair that his brother got to sleep between clean sheets and enjoy the company of lovely damsels while he had only the hard forest floor to comfort him.

But it had been his own suggestion that had put him there. He had no one to blame but himself. At the time, it had seemed the smartest thing to do. His brother had no knowledge of how to survive in the wild. But he certainly did have an ability to tame the ladies. Cursing, Evan searched the inn yard and slipped out the back door to the riverbank beyond.

He would like the pleasure of spending an evening or two in the company of one Miss Daphne Templeton. He owed the lady either a sharp setdown or a thank you, and he wasn't at all certain which he would administer.

Why had she hidden him from the soldier?

FIVE

Evan Griffin spread his long legs across the entrance to the cave overlooking the riverbank and watched as the man outside whittled away at a thick branch of pine. The whittler sat sprawled against a slender sapling, his good leg tucked under the bad one, whistling a tuneless song, and tapping the wooden stump where his foot should be in time to his own music. His thick dark locks fell across a craggy face dark with exposure and the heritage of his Welsh parents. Evan grimaced as he noted his comrade's disreputable rags of clothing and glanced down to his own.

He had tried to rinse the stench of ale from hat and shirt, but he greatly suspected the lady would be able to identify him henceforth from that odor instead of bay rum. He grimaced at the mass of wrinkles his shirt had become. It was no worse than the grass- and mud-stained wreck of his trousers.

It was time he sent for a change of clothing, but Rhys down there had no such source to call upon, nor did the others. They all knew bits and pieces of Evan's story, knew he was a pretender, but he had difficulty accepting the fact as easily as they did. To offer to send for new clothes for all of them when the servants brought his would humiliate them, but donning a new wardrobe when they wore rags was worse. He should have considered a few more of these prosaic factors when he made this choice.

Chewing a piece of the unpalatable leather that passed for their evening meal, Evan stared up at the darkening sky. He had lived like this in Spain for years. It wasn't anything new. Odd, though, he had thought when he came home it would be to the life of luxury in which he had grown up. He had envisioned crowded ballrooms filled with lovely dancing

beauties, their diaphanous gowns tempting him, their soft
perfumes and moist lips and laughing eyes giving him a
choice of ecstasies. He had dreamed of soft beds, soft bodies,
weeks of sleep, and hours of wine and food, not necessarily
in that order..

But first there had been the army of occupation, and at
the request of his superiors, he had agreed to stay a while
longer. That life hadn't been unpleasant, but it hadn't been
home. He had begun dreaming of green trees and fog and
rocky shores. Then Napoleon had escaped and it had been
back to the camps again, training new recruits who would
undoubtedly be mown down the first day of battle. By the
time Waterloo had ended, he was heartily sick of the glorious
career he had envisioned. Still, it had only been word of his
father's death that had brought him home, and that, months
after the fact.

Evan swallowed the unpleasant bite of meat and grimaced.
There really had been no excuse for the message to be
delayed that long, just a string of bad luck as it kept arriving
at places he had just left. By the time it reached him, he had
recovered from his injuries but there were dozens of his men
who had not. He'd managed to get as many as possible onto
the hospital boat, but there were some who were well enough
to travel with nowhere to go. He had left them his direction
and fled in response to the message, never dreaming what
he would be leading them into.

As he threw away the bone he had been gnawing on, Rhys
looked up and gave him a grin. "Did the pheasant not please
you, milord?"

"Oh, shut up." Growling, Evan didn't disdain to give his
loyal friend a glare. Rhys had been with him long enough
to be called brother. There were no secrets between them.

"You don't stop thinking about that woman, you won't
be worth a ha'penny tonight. What's she got that the others
ain't, I ask you?"

Before Rhys could begin a graphic catalog of womanly
assets, Evan interrupted impatiently. "The damned female
has nothing to do with it. We've run out of time, and you
know it. I'd have thought he would have acted by now."

"Maybe it's all in your head, after all. That plank could have been loose, you said so yourself."

Evan closed his eyes and leaned back against the hard rock behind him. He remembered that night all too clearly. The plank might have been loose, but it wasn't the plank snapping that had sent his horse rearing into the air and into the river at its most dangerous point. He'd been at war far too long to mistake that sound.

He transferred his thoughts to the interfering female Rhys had accused him of daydreaming about. Why in hell he had stopped that carriage that night was beyond his capability to imagine. He never stopped females. They were more trouble than they were worth. Even under civilized circumstances he tended to avoid the respectable kind. They expected him to make elegant comments and come when they giggled and fluttered their fans. That wasn't his style and never had been. He'd always left the wooing to Gordon, who was the heir after all and was expected to make a proper match. He'd spent his time with the Fashionable Impures who might sulk if he didn't compliment them, but smiled happily enough when he presented them with baubles. That was the kind of transaction he understood.

The only reason he thought of Daphne Templeton at all was that she was the only person who could reveal his identity. He couldn't trust such knowledge in the hands of a female. Gritting his teeth, Evan swung around and contemplated the campfire Rhys was starting.

"I'm damned sorry I started this. I've solved nothing."

Rhys shrugged with his usual fatalistic nonchalance. "You didn't have much choice. You intending to rise from the dead now? That should be a show to be seen."

Restlessly, Evan skittered a pebble across the dry leaves. "I can't rely on Gordon to convince her we're one and the same. She has him wrapped about her finger already."

His former sergeant raised a skeptical eyebrow. "What makes you think that?"

"He's read me the riot act twice now, and his choice of adjectives is revealing. Miss Templeton is by turn a 'delicate' lady, 'too sensitive' for my crude behavior, and 'too kind and gentle' to be treated rudely. I wonder that he thinks he's wooing some saint instead of the fire-breathing termagant she is.''

Rhys snickered. "You're the one sitting in trees watching for a glimpse of her. Are you afraid she will catch you unawares again?"

Remembering how the female in question had looked when she shed her jacket with a gleeful smile and threw her head back to allow the sun to bathe her face, Evan warranted he had good excuse to spy. He couldn't decide whether he liked the sight of her better in tailored linen with her breasts pushing at the fine fabric and her hair caught in tight pins waiting to be plucked, or in lacy batiste with wisps of curls and feminine frills to tease his eyes. She was a torment and a temptation, and he would be wise to keep an eye on her.

"She's too sharp by far," Evan admitted irritably. "Coward, she calls herself, but she identified me faster than my own brother."

The sergeant's grin grew more wicked. "Doesn't that tell you anything, Captain? It's coward you are yourself, if it don't."

Evan scowled. "It tells me she has a nose for trouble. Why else would she follow me into a common inn where no respectable lady goes?"

Rhys chuckled and gave his friend an almost affectionate glance. As an officer, Evan Griffin was a hard man and a demanding one, but as a friend, he was generous and loyal beyond the bounds of friendship. Unlike those of the other officers, Evan's hands bore the calluses of hard work, and his noble features wore the evidence of harsh weather as much as those of his men, though much had faded with the passing of time and circumstance. He was the kind of leader who demanded loyalty by his actions, not his words. He had personally saved the lives of several of the men here, risking his own in the process. Rough lot that they were, there wasn't a man among them who wouldn't lay down his life for Captain Evan Griffin. And that bold and brave officer sat there like a besotted fool, not knowing what had hit him. Rhys chuckled again.

"Why else, indeed?" his friend repeated cheerfully, adding a bit of kindling to the fire. "Why does any young lady follow a gentleman except to get him into trouble? You have her pegged, indeed, Cap'n."

"You're a mincing fool if you believe that, Welshman. She was protecting my brother. Females do the strangest things in the name of love."

"Aye, and they do that. That's why she dumped the ale over you, ain't it? In the name of love?"

Evan threw a stick at the fire and stood up. "In the name of loathing, I should say."

Before his friend could stride away, Rhys threw in the last word. "Aye, and in the name of loathing, she hid your hide from the soldiers, didn't she?"

Not deigning to reply, Evan stalked off into the protection of the trees. Who was he to know the mind of females? All he knew were their bodies, and damned if Miss Daphne Templeton didn't have just the body he had dreamed of all these long and lonely nights.

Coward, indeed, he snorted as he made his way to the roadside. Had she full courage, she would be a lethal weapon. All he could see in his mind were those flashing green eyes, the impertinent dimple at the corner of those luscious lips, and those delicate, fully feminine curves that beckoned a man's hand. He didn't even want to go into what his other senses told him. He was already in well over his head.

Jane Dalrymple seemed to prance as excitedly as her horse as she rode up next to Daphne. The swooping feather of her hat bounced pertly and her blue eyes danced with laughter as she whispered, "Have you ever seen such handsome gentlemen as Captain Rollings and Lord Griffin? I cannot decide between them. The captain is so dashing in his uniform, but there is something about a title . . ."

Daphne laughed at this nonsense. It was very easy to see that Jane was a mischievous minx, but there was no harm in her. Freedom from her mother's overprotective presence had only released her high spirits. She glanced at the two men riding ahead and smiled. To her, from this distance,

they were merely a scarlet coat and a blue one. Both rode
exceedingly well, with the aristocratic grace of hours in the
saddle. Lord Griffin was noticeably taller, but Captain
Rollings appeared broader in the shoulder. Perhaps that was
just the uniform.

"Why don't you choose on the basis of color? Lord
Griffin, I have noticed, favors blue that looks well with his
light-colored hair. The captain, of course, wears scarlet and
looks quite dashing since his hair is so dark. I should think
you would favor the captain since he provides such a striking
contrast with your own light coloring," Daphne announced
judiciously.

Jane's peal of laughter brought both men to a halt. Allowing the rest of their party to ride ahead, they waited for the
two slower horses to catch up. No one questioned Daphne's
cautious pace. The party had alternately slowed and spread
out so that she was not always alone or in anyone's particular
company. Their graciousness endeared them to her, but she
was still wary of it. Had the rumors yet circulated about her?
Aunt Agatha swore they hadn't.

Lord Griffin gave Jane a mocking grin of familiarity. "Are
you saying shocking things to Miss Templeton, Jane? I'll
not have her thinking badly of us already."

Jane wrinkled her pert nose at him and turned to the more
serious mien of the soldier. "Do I look the sort to say
shocking things, Captain?"

Having only just met the lady a few days before, the captain
was extremely reluctant to put his foot forward. He took only
the most cautious of steps where the blonde handful was
concerned, but his dark eyes shone with admiration as he
replied. "You could never be anything but what is proper,
Miss Dalrymple."

Daphne grinned. "Then saying shocking things must be
proper, and we must all indulge in it from now on. Am I
correct, my lord?" She threw Lord Griffin a laughing look
that brought a twinkle to his eye as he drew closer.

"Undoubtedly, Miss Templeton. Shall I begin by calling
you Daphne? It is a most enchanting name and one I have
been eager to use."

He was swift on the uptake; there was no doubting that. Before Daphne could reply, the remainder of the party swarmed down the hill, shouting with excitement, and she was saved the need of response.

Despite Jane's protestations to the contrary, the neighborhood did boast a number of young people. Some were not old enough to be out yet, and some were already married and looking for diversion on a sunny day, but they made a group of nearly a dozen. Captain Rollings was the only officer in the area, and his introduction to the group had resulted in a number of spontaneous invitations to impromptu routs and entertainments. At the moment, the boisterous riders inundated the laggards, demanding a race across a nearby field to the clapper bridge in the field beyond.

Daphne froze at the thought of racing an unfamiliar path on a strange horse or of straggling cautiously along behind. As daring as she might be on some occasions in her attempt to return to normal, even she knew the dangers of racing when she did not know the terrain. But to refuse to join in would be humiliating. She was not yet certain enough of her mount or her ability to control him with her weak knee to know which choice to make.

The decision was easily taken from her by Lord Griffin. "Line up on the hill there, and Miss Templeton and I will give you the signal to start. We should be able to judge the winner from that height."

There were protests that they did not join them, but only half-hearted ones. The Griffin stables sported some of the finest horseflesh in the shire, and the outcome would be a given should Gordon join in. If the race had been a malicious design by some prankster to draw the London lady into a pratfall, no one stepped forward to complain of the ruin of their plans.

Under Gordon's direction, they lined up and dashed off at the drop of his crop. Daphne couldn't help but feel superfluous. Lord Griffin didn't give her time to feel that way for long. When the others had set off, he moved his restless mount next to hers and took her reins.

"I daresay we can judge the winner while resting in the shade of that hedge, don't you agree?"

Daphne suddenly felt nervous that Lord Griffin had singled her out to this degree, and her mind worked feverishly to discover the reason, but she acquiesced when he dismounted and lifted her off to stand by his side. A sapling sprouting from the hedge gave adequate shade, and they could easily see the entire field spread out below them. Daphne wasn't certain she could discern the narrow wooden clapper bridge, but she could see the riders galloping wildly toward it.

"There is room for only one horse to cross the bridge at a time. It will be easy enough to judge the winner without our help."

His warm voice murmured startlingly close to her ear, drawing Daphne from her daze with a jolt. The accents were so much those of the highwayman that she had difficulty separating the two, and for the first time, she caught a faint scent of bay rum. Her mind froze, and she stared up at him with the frightened eyes of a trapped rabbit.

Gordon had the urge to apologize for his similarity to his brother. She had the fairest skin, with just a touch of color from the sun despite her fanciful hat. Beneath the curled beaver brim, a pair of terrified green eyes stared back at him, and he had to wonder at the depth of their terror. Gently, he brushed back a wisp of curl on her cheek.

"I did not mean to startle you, Miss Templeton, or may I call you Daphne? It would give me much pleasure to hear you address me as Gordon. I still think of 'Lord Griffin' as my father."

Said that way, she could scarcely refuse his request. His proximity was beginning to unnerve Daphne as much as his brother's, if the Robin Hood of the woods were his brother. Now was the opportunity to find out, and she sent him a hesitant look before staring resolutely back to the riders in the distance. It appeared the scarlet coat was in the lead.

"I'm not at all certain that is proper, my lord. Our acquaintance has been very short. I daresay you will be returning to your grandfather's estates before long and would find it dismaying to be on terms of such familiarity with a country miss such as I intend to be." That wasn't at all what she had wanted to say. Daphne bit her lip and cursed herself mentally. She never used to be so backward. London life had diminished her more than she had thought.

A firm hand gently touched her shoulder, causing her to look up to him in startlement. He was not so very tall that she could not see the mobile curve of his mouth as he gazed down on her.

"I am not planning on leaving Devonshire any time soon, and even if I should, I would be honored to call you friend. Perhaps our acquaintance has been short, but I think we are both mature enough to recognize a friend when we see one."

A friend. Yes, that would be right and proper. One did not have this easy companionship with a suitor. Daphne had seen that from observation of her cousins, not from any experience of her own. Courtship was a stiff formality with one intent in mind. Friendship was a freer flowing feeling, an easiness and a familiarity that she felt in the company of Jane Dalrymple, or Lord Griffin. Relaxing, she smiled up at him.

"You are very persuasive . . . Gordon." She tried the name cautiously, waiting for some sign of repulse from the charming man beside her.

"I can be when I know what I want . . . Daphne." He paused before her name for emphasis, smiling as he lifted her gloved hand and bowed over it.

Now. She should act now. Ask if he knew his brother were alive and well and stealing from the rich and giving to the poor. Or perhaps that wasn't Evan Griffin in the woods, but this man. The scent of bay rum confused her. How could she insult him by asking such questions? How could they be friends without knowing the answers?

There was no time to find out. The shouts and yells from below declared a winner, and with a gentle squeeze of her hand, Gordon assisted her back into the saddle.

The thought came to her then that she could be riding beside a thief, an imposter, and once again, fear and confusion froze her into silence.

SIX

This way lay madness, Daphne declared to herself as she urged the young pony down the lane.

Her aunt had remembered a long neglected pony cart buried in the stables and the grooms had dragged it out, repaired it, and given it a fresh new coat of green paint. It wasn't fashionable, but Daphne had little use for fashion. Going to the village in the pony cart was much more comfortable than walking, and the road was less fearsome from its lower height than from a carriage. She had already made the journey once without mishap, so she was feeling fairly confident.

It wasn't her trip into the village that was madness, but her tumultuous thoughts about the viscount and his wayward brother, or the two of them as one, whatever the case might be. She had gone so far as to return to the woods and river in hopes of discovering the elusive Robin Hood, and now she was making spurious trips to the village in hopes of finding him there again. She had to get to the bottom of this mystery, although why, she couldn't say.

The thief had struck again last night. This time, Squire Dalrymple had been the target, and this morning the countryside was in an uproar. Captain Rollings had already been out to the house inquiring if anyone had heard or seen anything unusual during the night. The blasted thief had set his trap practically at their front door.

How dare he! Daphne gritted her teeth and lashed the reins to speed the pony's progress. He had to have escaped through their side lawn, practically under their windows. If she could only lay her hands on that man . . .

Madness. What could she do with a man twice her size? Curse him? She should have let Captain Rollings have him

that first time. For all the world she could not imagine why
she had not. That would have solved the mystery and she
would have been able to live in peace. As it was, she kept
waiting for the devil to show up every time she turned her
back.

As they clattered onto the cobbled road of the village,
Daphne slowed the pony. The maid beside her let out a sigh
of relief and released her death grip on the side of the cart,
but Daphne gave her little notice. She concentrated on
avoiding the unusual number of strollers in the road this
morning.

"Out! Away with ye! We don't take to beggars in these
parts!" The woman's harsh voice caught Daphne's attention.
Halting the cart in front of the millinery, she glanced about,
trying to locate the source of the commotion.

"I'm not begging. I'm just looking for a bit of work. Do
ye not need your garden spaded or your steps scrubbed? I'll
do aught for a coin or two."

It took Daphne a moment to realize this plea came from
a young boy a few yards away. A young man, she amended
as she recognized the tattered remnants of his uniform.

"Aye, and how ye expect to do that?" The woman's voice
asked scornfully. "Be gone with ye now. This is a poor place.
We have naught for the likes of ye."

The thin young man turned away, and it was then Daphne
realized one sleeve of his jacket blew in the breeze. Anger
raged hot and cold through her. Perhaps she ought to feel
pity or sorrow for the lad's plight, but she only felt escalating
fury at the villager's treatment of someone who honestly
wished to work despite his infirmity. Evan Griffin's words
came back to mock her, but she refused to let him have the
right of it.

Before she could climb down from the cart, she noticed
another man stepping from the tavern door. She tried to see
the reason for his uneven gait, fearing to become embroiled
with a drunkard this early in the day. But the sound of his
wooden leg on the cobbles dispelled that notion. She gathered
her narrow skirt in one hand and stepped out.

"I told ye, lad, there's none to be had in these parts. Come with me, and I'll see you fed, leastways." The peg-legged man raised his hand to the young boy's shoulder, but his words came to a sudden halt at the sight bearing down on him.

Wearing a fetching green spencer and straw hat with matching ribbons streaming behind, the delicate eyelet overskirt of her walking gown catching and blowing in the wind to reveal a frail muslin gown and kid shoes, the lady hurrying toward them did not appear the fire-breathing dragon that she obviously thought herself. The two men gaped at this vision of loveliness, hastily reached to doff their hats, and stared in open-mouthed astonishment when she stopped before them.

"You are looking for work, sir?" Daphne snapped crisply, addressing the younger man while holding on to her straw hat in the brisk breeze.

"Yes, mum, milady," the lad answered nervously.

"Then come with me. We will find you work." She started down the street, but the older man's polite cough caused her to halt and raise a delicate eyebrow. "Yes?"

"Perhaps you ain't noticed, milady, but he ain't got but one arm. You might want to . . ."

Daphne's stare froze him into silence. "And you have but one foot and you still walk, do you not? I do not believe it is necessary to state the obvious. The gentleman wishes to work. It is up to him to devise a means of doing it." She turned to the lad who could not be older than herself, perhaps even younger. "If you are asked to do something that you do not feel capable of doing, you must speak out. It is very hard to do, I know from experience, but you surely must have more courage than I. You have been a soldier. If you can face cannonballs, you can face a blustery squire. Do you wish to come with me or go live with those other layabouts in the woods?" She sent a disdainful glare to the unbathed scoundrel with the wooden leg.

Rhys pursed a silent whistle. Beyond any shadow of a doubt, this was the termagant who had turned his captain into a haunted ghost of himself. No other lady in town would have knowledge of the handful of miscreants living off the land, nor would they have spoken of having experience in facing their limitations if Evan's speculations about her lameness were true. Besides, only a lady as lovely as this could have turned the captain's head so easily, and he hadn't seen another like her, ever. By the devil, he could easily understand Evan's problem, but the solution wasn't so easily discovered.

"If you're handing out jobs, miss," Rhys hurriedly replied, "I'm as willing as any man to work. There's just not many as takes to my looks."

Daphne could see why. Coming out of the tavern in those disgraceful clothes with a week's unshaven beard, he appeared no better than a rum-soaked old reprobate, but she should not judge by appearances, she reminded herself. Unfortunately, if he looked that disgraceful to her, what could he possibly look like to someone else? The thought did not bear dwelling on.

"Very well." She frowned. The squire had needed someone to help with the clearing of old shrubs and debris in an unused section of his park. Perhaps he could hire two men to do it, but that would leave both men with half the expected wages. It would be better could she find two jobs, particularly since she found it highly improbable that Squire Dalrymple would wish to have anyone as disreputable as this near his family. Her frown cleared and she pointed at her pony cart. "Stay here while I take . . ." She turned to the young soldier. "Your name?"

"David, mum, David Stone." He twisted his battered hat nervously between the fingers of his one hand.

"All right, Mr. Stone, we will go to Squire Dalrymple." She turned to the peg-legged man. "Your name?"

"Rhys, milady." He hesitated before offering his whole name, but in for a penny, in for a pound. He shrugged. "Rhys Llewellyn, milady."

The name as he said it had a noble ring to it and Daphne looked momentarily startled, but occupied with other thoughts, she merely nodded. "Very well, Mr. Llewellyn, if you wish to work, wait for me by the pony cart." She threw the sturdy vehicle a nervous look, but her maid had already wandered off on her errands. That was why she had brought Marie; the little maid always left her alone.

Having arranged everything to her satisfaction, Daphne set out for the modest Dalrymple house at the edge of the town. It boasted a small fenced park with an overabundance of trees and very little landscaping since none of the squire's family had any interest in gardening.

As she had feared, it took some persuasion to convince the squire that a one-armed young soldier might take on the arduous task of cleaning out one of the long-neglected corners of the park. The innocent mentionthat the young man might otherwise fall in with the band of thieves in the woods brought him around with reluctance.

"You won't regret it, sir," Daphne assured him. "After all these poor boys have done for us, keeping Napoleon from our doors, we can only do our best to see them taken care of when they return home. I am certain Lord Griffin will commend you for your patriotism."

That was a compelling argument, and the squire finally nodded doubtfully and glanced at the young man. " 'Tis a pity we cannot replace the uniform and give him a gun. With thieves swarming about, a bodyguard is what we need."

David straightened his shoulders and met the squire's eyes. "I can still shoot straight, sir. If you have a weapon, I can ride behind your carriage."

To Daphne, that was an alarming thought, but the squire brightened perceptibly, and she dared raise no objection. With a few parting words, Daphne left them discussing the war and hastened back toward her pony.

The wooden-legged man was leaning against the cart as she approached. He straightened at the sight of the faint frown on her pale brow, but politely he did not speak until spoken to.

Coming up against her next project, Daphne regarded his revolting clothes with a shudder and glanced around for some sign of Marie. She found the maid huddled nervously in the doorway of the notions shop, staring at the vagrant whose unkempt form had usurped their vehicle. Daphne gave a sigh of exasperation and turned back to the odoriferous Mr. Llewellyn.

"You will have to bathe before I can take you with me," she announced severely, refusing to acknowledge her creeping embarrassment at speaking so to a stranger. "Ask the innkeeper the cost of a bath and I will advance you the funds."

Rhys glared at her in astonishment, then growing amusement. She was red about the ears, and he had to acknowledge the justice of her decision. "The boy, milady?" He persisted in using the title even though he knew she didn't possess one. "Did he find a place?"

Daphne looked even more uncomfortable. She worried about the idea of placing an eager young soldier with a gun on a private carriage. It didn't seem at all wise. She wondered if there were any way of warning the thief; then she wondered why she should care.

Her concern came out in her sharp reply. "He has a place, and if the squire has any say in the matter, he'll be riding as an armed bodyguard as well as working in the yard."

Rhys hid his alarm. "I've had enough shooting, ma'am. If that's what you have in mind for me, I'll be going now."

Daphne sent him an exasperated look. "That's not what I had in mind for anybody, but Mr. Stone is no longer our concern. Will you follow my suggestion or shall I let you wander back to your pig sty?"

Rhys had half a mind to stalk off and leave Miss-High-and-Mighty to her busybody ways, but the blow to his pride wasn't as strong as his sudden desire for a real bath or his curiosity as to what she had in mind for him. He made a slight bow. "I'll make inquiries, milady, but the clothes will have to bathe with me."

Her flush at that remark served to bolster his sagging pride to some small degree.

She really had bitten off more than she could chew this time. This wasn't any grateful or subservient creature eager to obey her every word. He was a grown man, probably a career soldier who had seen a good deal more of this world than she. Whatever on earth had given her the notion that she might redirect his wayward habits? And he was undoubtedly right. He would have to have clean clothes before a bath would benefit him. She wished heartily that she were anywhere else but here.

Sublimely unaware of the other splashes of color passing her by or idling in doorways watching this scene, Daphne didn't recognize the horse and rider coming down the street until she heard the excited whispers of a couple of the housewives behind her.

"It's his lordship!"

"Ain't he grand? Look at them boots. Wager some poor bloke had to spit and polish for a week to make them shine like that."

"Do you think he'll . . ." The whisper trailed lower to a voice Daphne couldn't hear, but she had heard enough. She lifted her head to the sound of hoofbeats and found the navy coat and immaculate breeches that identified Lord Griffin. She sighed in profound relief.

Rhys followed her gaze and frowned as the viscount approached. Insolently, he leaned back against the cart again and waited for the handsome lord to discover this little tableau. It didn't take long. The street was short and narrow, and Miss Templeton stood out like a rose on a mud flat against the backdrop of dreary stone.

"Miss Templeton." Lord Griffin dismounted and came forward, shooting the shabby vagrant at her side a quick glance which turned to one of astonishment and then vanished as he bowed and returned his gaze to Daphne. "Well met. I thought to take some tea and persuade Mrs. White out of some of her delicious tarts. Would you care to join me?"

Not catching the swift exchange of glances between the two men, Daphne smiled welcomingly. "That would be lovely, but first you must rescue me. I have promised Mr. Llewellyn that I could find him employment so he need not live in the woods any longer. We have not had time to discuss his skills, but surely there must be some that can be put to some use in an estate as large as yours."

Amusement curled the viscount's lips as he turned to the

insolent ex-soldier leaning against the cart, glaring at him.
"To be sure, Miss Templeton. If you vouch for the man,
I'll be certain to find him a place. Mr. Llewellyn, is it?"
He removed a gold piece from his pocket. "Take this coin
and tell Beckworth at the inn to provide you a bath and change
of clothes. We'll discuss employment after Miss Templeton
is on her way."

The filthy vagrant made a sardonic obeisance and caught
the coin flipped to him. "Certainly, milord."

As he walked off, Lord Griffin offered Daphne his arm.
"I'm surprised at you. How do you come to be speaking
to creatures such as that?"

Still irritated and flustered by the incident, Daphne
answered curtly. "We are all God's creatures, my lord. Who
am I to judge between them?"

The laughter in his voice hid the look of concern in his
eyes as he glanced at her proudly held head. "Well said,
but whatever happened to calling me Gordon? I shall have
to remind you until you realize I mean it. We must be friends,
my dear Daphne, if you are to go about rescuing the countryside. Do you have plans for our resident Robin Hood as yet?"

There it was again, that hint of amusement that said he
knew more than he revealed. Daphne clenched her fingers
and bit her tongue. How was she ever to persuade him to
tell what he knew?

With a crisp smile that said everything and nothing, she
replied, "Of course, my lord, Gordon, I mean to bring him
around the same as you. The two of you are very much alike,
you know."

To his credit, the viscount only made a startled jerk before
reaching to open the door to the tea shop. His thoughtful gaze
fell on the smiling uplifted face of the daring Miss Templeton as they entered the shop, and he experienced the sinking
feeling that he had met his Waterloo as she stepped inside
in a swirl of skirts.

How could one slender, interfering female wreak such
havoc in so short a time? Thank God she wasn't working
for the enemy.

Even as he thought it, he watched the scarlet coat of Captain Rollings rise up from the table inside and bow in greeting.

By all that was holy, they were in for it sooner or later.

SEVEN

"Have you taken leave of your few remaining senses? Of all the caper-witted, maggot-brained . . ."

Rhys dusted an invisible mote off his new broadcloth coat. It was a servant's plain brown sack coat without an ounce of fashion to it, but it was blessedly clean and whole. He was rather proud of it for the moment, and he gazed at his friend with more amusement than concern.

"She's a rare dragon, that, you know. A golden dragon with wings of gossamer. While the two of you battle over her, I think I'll steal her away."

Evan swung around and aimed a furious punch at the Welshman's nose. Rhys ducked, and the fire died out of Evan just as swiftly as it had flared up. He shrugged his own filthy coat back on and stared out over the sloping riverbank. "She's not for the like of either of us. Gordon's welcome to her. She'll beat the countryside into shape in no time. And when she's done here, she'll be a grand countess with an entire earldom to reform. We need to put our minds to ensuring that will come about."

Rhys gave a disdainful snort. "That means keeping both of you hale and hearty. Now what's the chance of that? And if the lady becomes involved with either of you . . ." He gave another shrug. "She'd be better off with me."

Evan gave an explicit curse as to the origin of his friend's birth, then grimaced in recognition of the truth of his words. "How in hell are we going to get her out of here? Damn Gordon for encouraging her! Had he not thrown his cap over the windmill, she might have grown bored with the countryside and left."

Rhys threw another branch on the fire and crouched warily on a log. His new trousers were a trifle tight, and he didn't wish to ruin them. ''Had you not stopped her coach, she might never have met either of you, and Rollings would be the lady's only concern. Looking back is to no advantage. How are you going to get rid of her? Scare her off?''

Evan clenched his fists and glared at the dying light of the sun behind the trees. He was being an imbecile. This was no time to be arguing over women. Damn, but he was out of his mind to even be thinking of a woman he had only met three times, and then under the worst circumstances. Rhys was right. They had to get her out of here. Maybe later, long in the future, he could contemplate wooing and winning her.

''Give me time, I'll think of something,'' he muttered, and stalked away.

Rhys stared after him, wondering if it wouldn't just be wiser to go to the lady and tell her the truth. She was the first female he had encountered who hadn't looked at his mutilated foot in pity or horror. She might be sensible enough to handle the truth. But it wasn't his story to tell. Kicking at the fire, he settled more comfortably on the log. Lord Griffin knew better than to expect him to sleep in the stables.

Evan stared up at the darkened windows of the house. He had watched as candles flickered out until only one burned behind the heavy draperies, then went out a brief while later. What was someone as lovely as she doing in an isolated village like this? Why had she never married? What was the story behind her real or imagined cowardice? Or lameness? What was there about her that drew him like a moth to a flame? There were so many questions he would like to ask, but he had no right to speak of any of them.

How did one go about scaring off a lady as intrepid as Miss Daphne Templeton? Imagine finding employment for a villainous looking character like Llewellyn! She was beyond the bounds of reason, on a plane all her own, evidently. Perhaps she compensated for her fancied cowardice by being fearless in all she did.

Frowning, Evan glared upward. He could try reason, but he daren't endanger her with the facts. Well, then, he would have to make it clear that she was in danger without giving explanations. He stroked his jaw thoughtfully, wishing he hadn't just shaved. He ought to look the part of ruthless mercenary, at least. Remembering her treatment of the disreputable Rhys, Evan grinned. Looking the part wouldn't aid his cause. In all probability, she wouldn't even see him in the dark. He needed to smell the part.

He had just bathed in the river, but at least he had refrained from dousing himself with his favorite scent. Drawing a silver flask from his pocket, he took a quick gulp, then sprinkled the contents liberally over his already ruined clothes. The ale had faded out after several washings. He would see how well brandy worked.

The next task was tricky, but not difficult. Mounting his horse, Evan rode quietly to the shrubbery beneath the portico. It was a moment's work to grasp the arch between the Corinthian columns and swing his long legs to the flat roof. He then need only find a foothold in the vines and stones beneath the open casement . . .

Evan swung onto the window ledge, one leg in, one leg out as he halted to survey his position. Through a partial opening he created between the draperies he could see only the shadows of an armoire and one post of a curtained bed in the heavy darkness. Miss Templeton would undoubtedly be lying in that bed, and he tried not to allow his imagination to roam over what might be revealed had he a lamp to light his way. His intent was to terrify, not admire.

He hadn't completely thought this through. Should he make this a verbal attack? A physical assault to her belongings? Both? Perhaps he should have just brought a written message warning her away. Too late for that now. He was here and he'd have to make what he could of it.

Evan swung his other leg into the room and was met with a solid blow to his stomach just as he straightened. With an "oomph," he staggered slightly backward, catching himself on the window sash. A second blow lashed out, and he found himself grabbing at billows of silk and bits of whalebone in the darkness. Caught by surprise, he let it go, and the weapon made a third and equally silent strike. Finding himself in great

danger of falling backward out an upper story window, Evan
wielded his forces a little better this time, and his hand filled
with the silken stuff and didn't let go.

A muffled cry of frustration followed this ruse, and Evan
felt a chuckle rise in his throat. He stifled it, and tried to
sound gruff as he jerked the flimsy parasol from her hands.
"It ain't particularly smart to go after them that's bigger than
you are." He thought the false accent a particularly fine
touch. He flung the parasol into the bushes below and stood
to his full height, looming over the delicate maiden in her
long nightrail and braid.

Instead of giving a cry of fear and trying to escape, Miss
Daphne Templeton merely gave a sound of disgust and
stalked away, muttering, "You! I should have known."

Evan stared after her in astonishment. She couldn't
possibly recognize him. It was dark. He had disguised his
voice and his accent. How the devil could she know it was
him? It had to be a bluff.

"You expectin' someone else?" he asked in his most
churlish tones, moving threateningly after her.

Daphne removed a robe from the armoire and tugged it
on, struggling with the bits of ribbon that tied it beneath her
breasts as the ungallant Robin Hood advanced into her room.
Perhaps she ought to be terrified. He smelled to high heaven
of brandy and was most probably drunk, but she didn't think
real miscreants went to the trouble of disguising their voices.
She finally managed to knot the ribbon and took up a stance
on the far side of the secretary, using it as a barrier to his
progress.

"You could certainly have found a better way to talk to
me than this. It is most improper. Have you come to say
you're taking your criminal services to other parts of the
country? Or are you going to offer some ridiculous explanation of this masquerade?"

Her prim, knowing tones infuriated him. Frustrated, Evan
stood with hands on hips and glared down at his daring
antagonist, wishing he could shake her. He didn't overlook
the fact that she had a silver letter opener and a solid brass

inkwell within inches of her fingers. Couldn't she at least act vaporish at this intrusion?

"Miss Templeton, you are the most irritating female I have ever had the misfortune to encounter. How the deuce can you know who I am?"

She hadn't realized how thoroughly frightened she had been until his familiar accents rang in her ear and the muscles in her back and shoulders seemed to melt with relief. She caught the edge of the desk and glared at him.

"Who else would be mad enough to crawl in my window in the middle of the night? Honestly, will you never grow up? I have half a mind to scream for the servants and put an end to your foolishness forever."

Never grow up? Here he was trying to save her bloody life, and she accused him of a child's game! He ought to wring her pretty neck, but instead, Evan grinned and leaned his hip against the secretary, crossing his arms across his chest as he looked down on her thick, silken tresses. She was severely out of charity with him, and he ought to be berating her soundly for a half dozen causes, but all he could think of was how sweet she smelled now that he was this close. He could have her in his arms in a minute, but he rather imagined she would scream the roof down should he try. That thought led to even more interesting images, and his grin grew broader.

"We should be thoroughly compromised if you utter so much as one tiny moan, Miss Templeton, but I'll not object to that. Scream, and let us see who regrets it later."

Fury washed over her. She wanted to scream and shout and beat her fists against his arrogant chest and kick his shins and make him regret his insufferable attitude. At the very least, she ought to scratch his eyes out, but the thought of reaching up to accomplish such a thing stirred far different emotions, and she managed only a "Conceited oaf" before retreating further into the corner.

At Daphne's retreat, Evan advanced, keeping only a few feet between them. He had meant to terrify her, but instead, he was having more fun than he'd had in a long time. What a dance she could lead him if they were only in different circumstances. He had never paid much attention to ladies before, but beneath that frail exterior, she was as much a soldier as he. Conceited oaf, indeed. He smiled. "I'm only here to warn you, Miss Templeton. Anything else is on your head."

"You could have found a more decorous means of sending a message, Mr. Griffin. This is highly improper, and that was my best parasol you flung in the bushes. How will I ever explain that?"

"Tell them you were experimenting with flying. I should think more modern witches might try parasols rather than brooms. I don't care what you tell them, Miss Templeton, just heed what I have to say."

She wished she had taken the parasol to his head. He was too close, and she could not retreat farther. He filled her senses, his broad shoulders blocking out all view of the room, his masculine frame overpowering her slight one just by standing there. The brandy fumes helped keep her perspective, but only slightly. "Then speak and be gone," she declared boldly.

Momentarily stunned by the proximity of all this dainty femininity challenging him with more than words, Evan did not immediately reply. It had been so long since he had held a woman, heard the rustle of silk, felt the velvet smoothness of a woman's hands, that he ached with the need now. Just a step closer . . .

He resisted. Forcing his mind to overrule his body, he replied dryly, "You have a remarkable propensity for getting yourself in and out of trouble that I can only applaud, Miss Templeton, but you have no idea of the immensity of the danger you are placing yourself in by interfering where you should not. I would recommend an immediate return to London if you value your life."

He was much too close, and the room was so dark . . . Daphne had the insane thought that her most immediate danger was this man filling her field of vision. The desire to be taken into his arms and be held against him fogged her senses, and she could only grasp the wall and pray for rationality. What was there about this commanding Robin Hood that impelled her to him rather than away, as all good logic would demand? She forced herself to remain aloof.

"Are you threatening me, Mr. Griffin?"

Her quiet question nearly broke his control. Evan lifted his hand to bring her closer, then dropped it as if burned. "Forces beyond my control are threatening you, Miss Templeton. For your own safety, you must go away. Not forever, perhaps. Just a little while, just long enough for matters to be settled."

He sounded almost unhappy at the thought of sending her away, and Daphne regained a little more of her confidence. She straightened and drifted an inch closer, wishing she had a candle. There had to be some way of differentiating him from his brother. Instead of questioning his words, she impulsively drew her fingers across his cheek, seeking their differences. She found the same rugged cheekbones, traced them downward to a strong jaw, almost square in its breadth, with a rounded dent in the chin. Her fingers moved upward, exploring the chiseled, mobile lines of his mouth that remained tense and expectant beneath her touch. She found the harsh blade of his nose and reached to stroke the golden thickness of his brows and outline the high plane of his forehead, wrinkled now in a frown of concentration. Her fingers briefly entangled in the warm strands of his hair before quickly retreating.

Somewhat taken aback by her forwardness, Evan struggled to remain still throughout her examination, but when she was done, he expelled a soft sigh. "Can you tell I am not Gordon? Will you believe me now?" He didn't dare put any other construction on her actions, or her proximity. She was close enough to enfold in his embrace, and he struggled inwardly to keep from doing so.

"It does not matter," Daphne answered simply, retreating another step. Her hand tingled from touching him. She had been dying to explore the viscount's handsome features but had been unable to summon the courage to admit her need to do so. How was it that she could be so bold with this man? "I cannot return to London. This is my home now."

Evan gave a hiss of surrender and grabbed her shoulders. "What do I have to do to convince you?" His fingers kneaded the soft flesh beneath her thin robe and without thought, he drew her closer until her hair brushed his chin. "Leave, Daphne, before you distract me from my purpose."

She raised her hands to his chest as she had wished to do earlier. She could feel his heartbeat, sense his tension, and knew a strange desire as she braced herself against him. This wasn't a lover's embrace, she knew, but a contest of wills. She struggled to maintain her superiority.

"Let me help," she implored, not knowing what she asked.

He muttered a curse, and she thought he brushed his lips against her hair, but then he shoved away and strode to the safety of the far end of the room. "Why can you simply not accept the fact that there is danger here and that you are jeopardizing your own life as well as others' by staying? I am not asking it to be forever, just long enough for me to straighten out a few matters."

"And I am supposed to take the word of a common criminal, a thief who must sneak in windows and molest ladies in the middle of the night? Why should I believe you? Why should I not suspect you are after your own advantage in this? What proof can you offer me?" Daphne demanded, recovering her senses now that he was not so dangerously close.

"Do you need to be shot at and thrown in the river to believe me?" Angrily, Evan stalked back to the window. She had neatly set him in his place, and he could not help but feel resentful. Let Gordon deal with her. He was the one who knew how to deal with ladies. For himself, he preferred a horse and rifle any time.

"You are being absurd! The only ones with tendencies toward violence around here are you and your merry band of thieves!" Daphne followed him to the window so she need not speak her accusations in more than a whisper.

Half in and half out the window, Evan turned back and said, "Go talk to my esteemed brother if you believe that!

Good evening, Miss Templeton." He dropped out of the window and out of sight.

Daphne ran in terror to see where he had gone, only to find him landing on the portico roof below. "So you admit you have a brother, Evan Griffin?" she threw after him.

Evan glanced up to her white-draped figure in the window above, her long braid hanging past her waist, and he cursed vividly to himself. "Tell that to the world and see how long he lives!" he threw back at her before determinedly striding out of hearing.

Daphne waited in the window as he disappeared from her sight. In minutes, she heard the sound of hoofbeats and knew he was gone. Slowly, she retreated from the casement and into the safety of her room. What had possessed him to come here like that? Could he truly mean she was in danger? She could not see how—except from him. He was definitely a danger—to her sanity, if nothing else.

Remembering his fierce touch, the brush of his lips against her hair, Daphne retreated further, staring at the empty window where he had sat a few short minutes ago. He could not have meant any of those things she had thought she heard and felt. They must be at cross-purposes. She was unaccustomed to dealing with men. Men said things that could be interpreted too many different ways. He was a complete stranger. He could not be concerned enough about her to risk his neck by coming here like this to warn her. He must have meant to rob her but she caught him by surprise.

That made sense. Relaxing a little, she returned to her bed and sat down upon the turned-down sheets. He had thought she would be asleep. Perhaps he hadn't even known this was her room. His hastily invented lies were meant to frighten, that was all. And then she had foolishly encouraged him by touching him. Shame swept through her as she realized how her curiosity could be misinterpreted. Lud, but she was glad she would never have to meet with him face to face again. How could she have been so brazen?

Still, as she leaned into her pillows and sought the elusive clouds of sleep, she could not help but remember the strong force of his fingers pulling her close, the steady heartbeat beneath her palms as he bent over her, and the aching dreams such a touch elicited.

She had denied herself London and the world. Must she deny herself any chance of love as well?

EIGHT

Nervously, Daphne watched Lord Griffin speak to Jane Dalrymple and lead her out into the small, cleared area in the main salon that had been transformed into a dance floor. It was just a small informal gathering of friends, with Mrs. Dalrymple playing the pianoforte and an elderly neighbor wielding a lovely violin. She had no reason to be nervous, no reason for her palms beneath her light gloves to grow moist.

When Captain Rollings came to bow before her and request this dance, Daphne nearly fell from her seat in startlement. Men seldom asked her to dance, but of course, the captain knew nothing of her defects. She was quite certain she could manage that small dance floor, but it had been years since she had actually waltzed around a schoolroom with her dance instructor. She was not at all certain she was prepared to make a cake of herself yet.

Politely declining, she asked if she might have another small glass of sherry. When the captain returned, he remained at her side while several more couples maneuvered around the room's center. "Have you been enjoying your stay in Devonshire, Miss Templeton? It is somewhat remote from London, wouldn't you agree?"

"No more remote than where I grew up," she replied easily. Captain Rollings was one of the reasons she was nervous, although she knew she had no reason to be so. He was polite and respectful and a good deal more civilized than the Robin Hood he sought. She just couldn't help feeling guilty whenever he was around. She was harboring knowledge of a known criminal. Could he have her arrested for that? She felt quite certain he could.

She tried to keep the subject light. "London is exciting,

and there are many things I enjoy doing there, but the country has always been my home. I enjoy small groups over large crowds, and I have a long-standing interest in gardening. I'm quite comfortable here, Captain. And you?"

His gaze followed the blond, lithe figure of Miss Dalrymple as she swung about the floor in the viscount's arms, her laughter keeping time with the music. "I have learned to be comfortable wherever I go. I cannot think that there is any place in England that isn't an improvement over the Continent, however."

"You were with Wellington?" she inquired politely. Daphne had gleaned what information she could of the war by eavesdropping on the conversation of gentlemen and scanning the newssheets daily. The awe in which they held the great general had impressed her, and his name came easily to mind.

"Nothing so brave, I fear. My father has seen to it that I am employed only in minor diplomatic posts and domestic situations. Being the eldest son has its drawbacks."

"So has being an only daughter," Daphne said wryly. "Now that the war is over, have you considered resigning your commission?"

He gave her a perceptive look. His dark hair gleamed in the brilliant candlelight, and there was a glint of determination in his dark eyes as he gazed down at her. "I have considered it, but I should like to leave with something to show for my efforts. That was why I volunteered my services to answer the complaints of your local Robin Hood."

Daphne prayed her courteous smile didn't falter. "I cannot find it in me to judge him harshly. He has harmed no one and helped many. Catching a harmless eccentric cannot be much of a feather in your cap."

"A harmless eccentric does not rob gentlemen at pistol point nor abduct young ladies from their carriages. It is only a matter of time until someone is hurt." His voice was harsh. "Surely you cannot sympathize with a man who must have caused you a great deal of terror."

Daphne shrugged blithely. "I saw no pistol, and a horse ride at twilight after a tedious day's journey was rather adventurous. He allowed me to keep my mother's locket and only took what I offered him. I repeat, he seems harmless enough."

She didn't know why in the world she was defending him. She must be quite out of her mind. She ought to tell Captain Rollings everything she knew and be done with it. But first, she needed to speak with Lord Griffin. She turned her gaze in the viscount's direction, but his back was turned to her. She wished she could see his expression. Was he looking at Jane with delight and admiration? Remembering her fantasy of several nights ago with the irritating thief, Daphne quenched a wave of embarrassment. A person was allowed to make a fool of herself once or twice in life. It was good for the soul. She just didn't wish to make it public.

The music came to an end then, and the laughing, chattering couples left the floor. Lord Griffin led Jane to the corner where the captain and Daphne waited. A brief hint of suspicion darkened, then disappeared from the viscount's eyes as he watched them together. His smile was its usual affable curve by the time they reached the corner.

"That was so enjoyable, I would like to do it again. We shall have to switch partners, though. Daphne, would you care to join me?"

Oh, yes, she would, but Daphne refrained from blurting out such eagerness. Besides, she had more important things to do than dance with the viscount and make a cake of herself. She needed to speak with him, and if she did not do it now, she might never have the courage.

"If you do not mind, my lord, it is a trifle warm in here. I would be happy to step outside just a minute and return you to Jane and the other ladies when the music begins again." She sensed rather than saw his tension as he placed her hand on his arm and made a dignified bow to their companions.

"Of course, Miss Templeton. Jane, you are not to speak any wickedness to Captain Rollings while we are gone. It can only be done when we are all together," he admonished her, laughter concealing any of his concern.

They made the circle of the room, politely chatting with

neighbors and friends, declaring their intention of walking out briefly so none would remark their disappearance and put other connotations to it. Daphne was both grateful and chagrined at this attention. Did he think she would deliberately compromise him should they be alone together too long? It was a dampening thought and just one of many she seemed to be having lately. Perhaps she ought to just come out and tell everyone that she was not marriage material and they had no need to worry. In London, she had not been considered eligible enough to worry over such complications.

Once having run the gamut of their neighbors, they stepped out the open terrace doors with only a minimum of whisper and speculation stirring the air behind them. Gordon still seemed stiff and uneasy as he led her toward the wall separating the large, circular terrace from the gardens. Dark did not come early this time of year, and Daphne could still see the rigid set of his shoulders when she looked up at him. What was it he expected her to say that had him as nervous as she?

"You are looking particularly charming tonight, Daphne. That shade of rose becomes you."

"While your compliment is very flattering, my lord, your dissembling is not. Do I appear the sort to need compliments to still my tongue?"

Gordon laughed softly and turned her to face him. "No, not at all, and whatever happened to calling me Gordon? Am I sunk so far in your esteem that you must scorn me with politeness? I hope we know each other better than that, Daphne. You are very easy to know. I have not felt so with any other woman of my acquaintance."

And he spoke the truth, he realized. There was something so vulnerable about her that he longed to envelop her in his protection. At the same time, she was more forthright and honest than any woman he had ever known. Somehow, she also managed to be loyal and brave, but he was afraid he was about to become a victim of those attributes. Taking the initiative, he offered the opening she sought.

"Did you simply wish a turn about the garden or was there something else behind this request? You realize I do not flatter myself into thinking it is my company you seek.''

Daphne managed a small smile at his kindly face. He really was a very nice man. She just wished she didn't have to be the one to open the unfortunate subject. ''Perhaps, after all, it is, my lord. Your company is very pleasant and I do not wish to be denied it, which is why I hesitate to speak.''

''Call me Gordon and I shall forgive you anything you say,'' he offered magnanimously.

Daphne laughed. ''Now you are opening yourself to Jane's wickedness. I could name you every sort of villain and you would be forced to forgive me . . . Gordon.''

He caught her arms and forced her to continue looking at him. ''Tell me what's on your mind. I cannot stand the suspense any longer. Is it so bad that you cannot say it?''

She looked very worried and his heart froze in his chest, but he refused to give in to his fears. He would have this in the open and pray that she would still speak to him when it was done.

''I cannot say if it is very bad or very good. I cannot know how you feel about your brother. You never speak of him. Surely you must know he is still alive?'' Daphne allowed the words to spill from her lips without thinking. She had to talk to someone. She couldn't contain it any longer. Gordon seemed he only logical person to speak to, but she couldn't help feeling a twinge of disloyalty at this small breach of confidence. Why did she feel it necessary to protect a thief?

Gordon took a deep breath as the secret spilled out and filled the void between them. Just the same, he could not speak the truth, even should he endanger the slight harmony that was building between them. The urge was there, but he could not give in to it.

With a wry twist of his lips, he asked, ''Can you not believe it even yet? I have tried to make it clear so you would stay away from danger. Evan is quite dead. I am the one you must scorn.''

A shiver coursed down her spine at the impact of his words. This wasn't the rogue in the woods lying to her, but Lord Griffin. Could she really be so wrong? Was he truly so superb an actor as to make her believe he was two different people?

"Why are you doing this to me?" she whispered, not at all certain what "this" was. He couldn't be the highwayman. She wouldn't believe it.

"I am trying to protect you, Daphne," he murmured near her ear, his lips brushing against her hair. "Do not ask me to explain just yet. Give me time and all will be known, my word on it."

No, it wasn't. It couldn't be. Before she could utter any of those protests, Gordon lowered his mouth to hers.

His kiss was very soft. And warm. His lips caressed hers with respect, but were quick to take advantage when given no opposition. They plied her mouth slowly, delicately, telling her with action and not words that she wasn't to worry. His hands on her arms slid lower, caressing, reassuring, until Daphne raised her hands to his chest and turned her head to gasp for breath.

He held her there briefly before saying, "We had best go in." He cupped her elbow, giving her time to recover. "I will not apologize, Daphne. I have been waiting to do that for days. But I hope you will be more patient than I and wait until I can give you explanations before condemning me."

Daphne was too stunned to do more than follow Gordon's lead. She had never been kissed before. Really kissed. There had been a few young gentlemen who had attempted to steal more than she was willing to give and had hastily retreated when she made it clear she did not take their attentions lightly. This wasn't the same at all. She didn't know what she had expected, but it hadn't been this.

She felt the kiss all the way down to her toes. Obediently, she followed him. She didn't have any answers, only more questions. She couldn't afford to ask more questions just yet.

In the shadows of the shrubbery, a figure watched them go with a curse on his tongue and pain in his heart. This wasn't how it was supposed to be. He didn't want to fight, but it didn't look like he had much choice.

With resolution, he crept back through the shrubbery toward the side of the house.

* * *

Violin music filled the air as the guests indulged in a late supper. Daphne brought her aunt a fresh glass of sherry and exchanged comments on the delightfulness of the evening with several of her aunt's companions. Before one of the young bachelors could push their way from the buffet to rescue her niece, Agatha requested still another errand.

"Lord Griffin says he left a volume of *Emma* on the library table for me. Will you fetch it so I will not forget it before we go?"

"Of course." Daphne gave her empty plate to a servant and slipped out a side door to make her way to the viscount's male-oriented library. She could not imagine why he should have a copy of Austen's *Emma* other than out of curiosity, since the Regent had requested it be dedicated to him, but she didn't mind the diversion from the crowd in the other rooms. Ever since that stroll on the terrace she had desperately wished for a moment alone, time to think and make sense of what had happened, but she had been kept busy smiling politely and chatting to neighbors and friends as if nothing momentous had happened. She took a deep breath of cool air in the deserted hall and pushed open the library door.

She sincerely hoped Lord Griffin had left the volume in a noticeable place. No candles had been lit in here since the sun went down, and she doubted that she could linger long in this overwhelming blackness without succumbing to the urge to dash for the well-lit hall. It would be exceedingly embarrassing to come out with a volume of world history or Latin essays.

Before she could reach the library table, a figure stepped out of the shadows at the rear of the long room. "Daphne," a familiar voice entreated.

She looked up in surprise at the familiar blue frock coat and white embroidered waistcoat of Lord Griffin. Had he known her aunt would send her here? She took a step backward as he approached, then stood firm. She had nothing to fear but herself. "Gordon?"

Evan Griffin hesitated, regarding her slight figure with

trepidation now that he had her here. He had wanted to stand before her on the same grounds as his brother, scrubbed and decent and looking like a gentleman. Out of habit and in the interest of concealing his identity, he had donned a coat from his wardrobe that matched his brother's. It had not occurred to him that the one time he wished her to recognize him, she would not. That presented interesting, if ungentlemanly, possibilities.

"I didn't think I'd have a chance to speak to you before you left," he murmured in his best imitation of Gordon's low, serious tones.

Daphne wrestled with a sense of unease, a sense of something not right, but his proximity was obliterating her usual perception. His golden head was bent with concern over her, the stiff folds of his cravat were just within reach of her fingertips should she raise her hand, and the clean scent of his shaving soap enveloped her. When his gloved hand caught hers and his other hand went to her waist, she did not even open her mouth to protest. The violin music seemed to swell in proportion to his nearness, and to her amazement, she floated off on waves of music.

They danced in silence, the dim lights of the sconces in the hall casting shadows across their faces as their feet glided along the wooden floor. Daphne forgot how to breathe as a strong hand guided her with easy grace around the obstacles a library presented, but she remembered how to waltz. She remembered how she loved waltzing, and she closed her eyes and let the music and the man carry her off to their own private heaven.

It was only then, with her eyes closed and the blue coat out of sight that she realized her error. A quiver ran through her, but she didn't stop dancing. Perhaps she was losing her mind. If so, she intended to enjoy every step of the way.

A blissful smile turned up the corner of her lips, devastating the man staring down into her face. He pulled her closer, felt the free sway of her body beneath his hands, and almost groaned at the surge of desire crippling him. How could he rage at her interference, curse at her stubbornness, and despise her feminine treachery, while his body cried out to take her, possess her, and never let her go?

When the music stopped, so did their feet, but they didn't separate. Daphne stared up in confusion at his square jaw and continued to cling to his hand. The hand at her back had become a permanent part of her, and she was suddenly, totally aware of the lean length of his body not inches from hers.

"Why?" she asked quietly.

"You wouldn't believe me if I told you." They could be talking about two entirely different topics, but the answer would still be the same. Did she realize who he was now? Or had Gordon succeeded in convincing her they were one and the same?

"Probably not, but you could at least give me the opportunity to try." Daphne backed away then, but he did not release his hold on her fingers.

"So you can turn me over to Captain Rollings? He has been at your side the better part of the evening, has he not?"

Only Gordon would have known that. Evan couldn't possibly have been the genial host in that salon. But this had to be Evan. She couldn't put her finger on the difference, but it was there. The confusion welled up and grew greater and she turned her head away in frustration.

"Do you enjoy tormenting women? Or is it only helpless women that you prefer to pick on?"

"Helpless? You're about as helpless as a she-wolf. If you had a care for my neck, you'd go back to London where you belong. When you grow impatient with the wheels of justice, will you oil them with your knowledge?"

This was Evan. She didn't know how he did it or why, but she could not mistake the harsh irony that was no part of his brother's nature. They were destined to ever be at odds. She wondered briefly at the relationship between these two, but there was little time for more. She shook free of his hand and turned to locate the library table again.

"Believe whatever you wish. It is no matter to me." Angrily, she turned her back to him. She had been sent here for a book. She would find the book and he could go to the devil.

He had danced her to the far end of the room, and the unfamiliar territory combined with the dusky light suddenly heightened her fears. In her haste to escape, she tripped over a knee-high stepladder, tried to catch herself on what turned out to be a spinning globe, and would have fallen had her nemesis not cursed and come out of the shadows to catch her.

"Why in hell don't you behave like a cripple so a person knows the difference?" Evan caught her by the waist and held her steady. The scent of her light perfume wafted around him, filling his senses and making him incapable of doing more. He remembered clearly her reference to an "old war wound"—indeed, he remembered clearly everything she had ever said—but he had never thought of her as imperfect. And still didn't, he realized, as he pulled closer.

Angry at herself, angry at him, Daphne tried to jerk away, but he wouldn't let her go that easily. "I'm not a cripple," she replied testily. "Do you wish me to sit in a corner and whine and demand that I be waited upon hand and foot?"

"Not any more than I expect Rhys to do the same. What in heaven's name persuaded you to find him employment?"

"I should have known he was a friend of yours." Finally shaking loose of his hold, Daphne reoriented herself. Finding the library table, she started in that direction, still shaken by the encounter. Odd, but it was no longer the dark she feared.

"More than a friend, but that is beside the point. He was a complete stranger of the most disreputable kind to you. Whatever possessed you even to speak to him? Do you do that kind of thing often?"

"What business is it of yours?" She swept her hand along the table, looking for the solidness of a book.

"I'm making it my business." Evan stepped forward and watched her quizzically. "What in the deuce are you looking for?"

Exasperated, Daphne straightened and glared at him. "Your language, sir, is abominable. If you cannot keep a civil tongue in your head, you may leave the room. And my business is not yours and never will be. Rhys Llewellyn asked for a job and I found him one. You could do the same for the rest of the men in the woods if you put your mind to it. It is one thing to take up the plight of the maimed with words and quite another to do so with actions. And if you will find me the volume of *Emma* that is supposed to be here, I will leave and you need not endure my opinions any longer."

Evan easily located the book and clasped it in his hand. "Are you planning on spending the remainder of the evening reading, Miss Templeton?" he asked smoothly.

"Of course not! I mean to spend the evening on the dance floor and end it with a jig. Aunt Agatha is waiting. May I have the book, please?"

This wasn't turning out at all as he had hoped. He had only meant to show her that he could play the gallant gentleman as well as Gordon. It was becoming increasingly obvious that he couldn't. All he had done was insult her and raise her ire. Perhaps Gordon was the better man when it came to women, but he'd be damned if he would surrender the fight yet.

"And you would have me find jobs for my men when I cannot set foot out of the woods without being hunted down like a fox? I did not choose this life, Miss Templeton, believe me. Not any more than you chose yours."

She didn't want to be reasonable. She wanted to remain angry at this provoking man who confused her so thoroughly whenever she was in his presence. It had never been necessary to do more than make polite small talk to any of the gentlemen of her acquaintance before. Why was it this one who led her down such circuitous pathways that what she thought was right became wrong with just a twisting of words?

"Then, someday, Mr. Griffin, perhaps you will explain to me just how you came to be a criminal. Until then . . ." Daphne walked the length of the table, knowing the door was just beyond that open space at the end.

A confusion of noise in the foyer caused her to hesitate. Had she been gone so long that the gathering was already breaking up? Aware that Evan lingered not too far behind, she hastened toward the door.

As she reached it, the sonorous tones of the butler announced to the company in the salon, "The Honorable Melanie Griffin."

At the heartrending groan behind her, Daphne turned a startled glance over her shoulder.

Slumped against the table, Evan gave her a bleak expression. "My sister."

NINE

"I'm so glad to have finally met you, Miss Templeton. I know all about you from Gordon's letter. I could not wait to meet such a paragon of virtue and courage."

Miss Melanie Griffin swung her lavender parasol over the tips of her lavender half-boots revealed by the highly stylish walking dress of sprigged muslin with three rows of flounces that stopped just at her ankles. Daphne had no need to judge this breathtaking ensemble to know her visitor was daringly lovely. The sudden silence of the two men at her side told her that much. Melanie's arrival in the company of Jane Dalrymple had effectively ended their wary and rather one-sided interview.

"I did not know Lord Griffin was given to exaggeration," Daphne replied dryly.

Jane Dalrymple giggled and continued the introduction. "Melanie, I don't believe you had a chance to meet Captain Rollings last night. He is here to save us from the dreadful Robin Hood." Jane hesitated as she turned to the second man standing in the drive beside Daphne. He had apparently brought a mount from Lord Griffin's stable for Daphne to use. She recognized the horse but not the man. His stance and mien were not that of the usual line of servant.

Daphne supplied the answer to Jane's questioning look. "Mr. Llewellyn was kind enough to note the mare Lord Griffin loaned me needed a shoe." She did not need to explain he was an ex-soldier currently working in his lordship's stable. The wooden leg and his horsy smell provided that information even to the uninitiated.

To Daphne's surprise, the lovely lady only made polite noises over the handsome captain but turned a melting smile on the groom. "Mr. Liewellyn! It is you! I thought it must be . . ."

Before the lady had a chance to say more, the unsavory groom gathered up the reins of the horse he was returning to the Templeton stable and started down the drive. "If you'll excuse me, ladies, gentleman," he tugged his forelock, "I'd best be getting on."

"But I have not yet . . ." The Honorable Melanie looked dismayed as the groom turned his back and limped down the drive. "Well, I never. I know I have met him somewhere. Is he one of your men, Captain?"

Rollings nearly choked before he could reply to that ingenuous question. "No, Miss Griffin, he is not. Much as I hate to leave three such charming ladies, I must beg my excuses. Duty calls, you know. Good-day, ladies." He bowed and took his mount with a graceful swing of his long legs.

The ladies watched him go before Jane broke the silence. "Isn't he just the most handsome man you ever saw?"

"I am currently not interested in men," Miss Griffin announced. "I am quite out of charity with the whole gender. Why, even your Robin Hood could not be bothered to stop my carriage, and I had a pistol all loaded and ready for him."

This time it was Daphne's turn to choke. Laughter welled up in her throat and kept bubbling outward despite her best efforts. She thought it could very well be hysteria. Imagine Evan Griffin throwing open the carriage door in his best Robin Hood manner to find his own sister pointing a deadly weapon at him! Oh, what a tangled web . . . !

"Miss Templeton, are you all right? Have I brought back terrible memories? Gordon was so certain that you came to no harm . . . . Please, let us take you back to the house."

Daphne waved off any offer of assistance but turned to lead the way back to the house. "I am quite fine. The thief does not normally stop carriages, only inebriated young men. Do not feel yourself slighted."

"Then why did he rob you? I so wanted to be as brave as you and show Gordon I am no longer a child."

Why her? That was an excellent question, one Daphne had

not resolved yet. She lifted her shoulders lightly. "It must have had something to do with Lansbury's crest on the door. Perhaps he had some grudge against Lord Lansbury. I did not think to inquire at the time." As they reached the front entrance, Daphne realized what had been bothering her since her first introduction to the lady, and she turned to inquire bluntly, "How is it that you and Lord Griffin do not wear mourning for your brother, Miss Griffin? Do not mistake me; I am not criticizing, only curious."

A shadow passed across the lady's face, but she replied honestly enough. "We had only gone into half mourning from our father's death when Evan was killed. Gordon convinced us that Evan would not want us to return to black on his behalf. As his twin, he knew best, so we all followed his advice, for Gordon's sake, if no other. I doubt that I saw Evan above twice since I left the schoolroom, but he and Gordon were very close. I remember Evan as a jolly fellow, always eager for a lark. I do not think heavy mourning would have impressed him."

"I'm certain you're right. Forgive me for prying. I am growing much too used to country ways, I fear. Will you be staying long? We really must arrange some entertainment for you, if so." Daphne led the way into the small parlor.

Melanie gave a deep sigh. "Gordon is very angry with me for appearing unannounced. He said it was a shatter-brained notion and he had half a mind to send me back to grandfather, post haste. Gordon has ever been a high stickler, so I assume it's only my shocking impropriety that has him in the boughs. I cannot imagine that I have interrupted anything improper on *his* part."

"That will not do at all," Jane exclaimed. "We shall have to speak to Lord Griffin and persuade him you are needed. I am certain he is glad of your company. He just feels obliged to act as a head of the household should."

As Lady Agatha joined them and the ladies all made plans for picnics and musicales and how they would persuade Lord Griffin to come around, Daphne remained relatively silent. She remembered all too clearly Evan's anguished groan at the appearance of his sister. She rather thought Gordon might have a more pressing reason than asserting his authority to send his sister home. There was no doubt that something was going on here, and apparently the danger was more than she had supposed. What would she have to do to persuade the brothers to let her lend a hand? And why on earth should she be so interested in becoming involved in what was, after all, not her business?

She could blame it on Gordon's kiss, but she had become much too involved even before that. She refused to think of Evan's ungentlemanly conduct, and she had no right to consider Gordon's attentions as anything more than a mild flirtation. Surely a London gentleman would have heard all the rumors about her mother and herself and would assiduously avoid her were he considering anything but a flirtation. So she couldn't take his attentions seriously.

Yet she shared the twins' concern over their sister's arrival. It was preposterous, of course, but she could not encourage what she knew would dismay the elder Griffins. She wasn't even certain if it was for Gordon's or Evan's sake that she was reluctant to press Miss Griffin to remain. It was confusing to the extreme.

That night, while Daphne debated the wisest course, she heard the sound of rapid hoofbeats on the road outside. Carrying a candle to the window, she wished she could see out, but the night was no more than a velvety darkness broken by an occasional gleam from window or lantern. The moon was in the wrong portion of the sky for her to even discern it.

But she could hear perfectly well over the nighttime silence. The hoofbeats thudded from the road onto thick turf, and now there seemed to be more than one set. Surely Evan wasn't chasing some poor victim across Aunt Agatha's property.

She caught herself, wondering why she would grace a common thief with the courtesy of a gentleman. That thought was interrupted by a violent explosion. Daphne jumped, startled, and tried once again to scan the night. A horse whinnied, and she thought she heard a man's curse. The heart-stopping noise sounded again, and this time she identified it clearly. A pistol!

This wouldn't do. This wouldn't do at all. Hastily, she sat down and tied on the slippers she had just discarded. Thank goodness she had not yet begun to undress. It would have been better if she had not given her maid the night off, but she could make do without her. She doubted if her aunt or the servants in the far side of the house had heard the noise, but perhaps someone was still up and about.

She slipped hurriedly down the stairs, wondering if she ought to rouse a groom or footman to accompany her since none seemed to be still awake. Not that she knew where she was going or what she was looking for, but she sensed something terrible was happening, and she had to find out what it was.

The house was dark. Everyone had retired long before her, when Aunt Agatha did, as was their custom. It didn't matter. She could find her way out without trouble. She had learned all the obstacles that might interfere with her progress and how to avoid them.

She slipped out the side door, which required only a turn of the key in the lock. Aunt Agatha's lax security could be found in every house in the shire. A true thief would have no trouble stealing a king's ransom in a few ambitious nights if he felt so inclined. That was one case in favor of the band in the woods. They couldn't be real thieves and ignore the wealth lying around to be had for the taking.

Outside, the night breeze tugged at her hair as Daphne hurried along the garden path she had learned by heart. She heard voices now, muffled and indistinct, but definitely more than one. She tugged her shawl more closely around the thin muslin of her gown and slowed her pace. She could do nothing against a band of men. What was happening out there?

She halted in the shadows of a tree and watched as a horse and rider emerged from the shrubbery to return to the road. Even in the darkness she could discern the glitter of steel and the blur of a red coat. Soldiers!

Heart in throat, Daphne watched as several more figures emerged on foot from behind the high hedgerows along the road. The man on horseback cursed at them, and gathering her courage, she crept closer. She had to know what had happened.

The men in the road wore uniforms, too, and she could hear one of them protesting, "We shot at him, just as you said to! Henry and me both shot, but he kept on going, flying that great black beast over a wall it woulda taken wings to fly. If you'd a' let us use the rifles . . ."

"We don't want him dead, you bloody fools!"

Daphne recognized that commanding voice at once. Captain Rollings. It didn't take much of a stretch of the imagination to know what had happened here tonight. The soldiers had set another trap, and Evan had ridden right into it. They had shot at an unarmed man!

"We winged him, I know we did. I heard him curse as that beast of his got away. Want us to start beating the woods after him?"

"And have his gang come out and make fools of us all? You don't know these parts as they do. We've lost our chance to take him this night. Let's head back."

Daphne trembled as the sound of voices trailed off down the road. Winged him? Did that mean what it sounded like? If he were wounded, would he head toward the Griffin estate and help? Or would he hide himself in the woods to prevent pursuit? Foolish question.

Agonizing inside, she picked her way back across the lawn. How could she possibly find him at night? The darkness pressed around her as it had that long-ago night, and it needed only the crack of thunder to bring her quivering to her knees. She might walk as far as the hedgerow dividing lawn from pasture and woods without harm, but beyond that, she would be at the mercy of the unknown.

Remembering the dance they had shared just the night before, Daphne felt tears prick at her eyes. Perhaps Evan Griffin was misguided and ill-humored and many other things, but he could be kind, too, and gentle. She wouldn't let him die in the woods. She had to get help for him, somehow.

Hurrying back inside, she picked up the candle she had left by the door and went in search of her aunt's medicine chest. She knew there were all kinds of salves and ointments in there, but she was too terrified of her own daring to stop and examine them. There were a few folded bandages, too, she remembered. Perhaps she ought to bring some old linen from the mending basket, just in case.

By the time she had filled a basket with all the supplies she could think of, the candle was ready to gutter out. She couldn't carry it outside, but perhaps a lantern . . . ? The soldiers had said they were going home. Would a lantern hurt? It would feel so much better out there if she could have some light. One day she might grow accustomed to these nighttime fears, but not just yet.

Deciding a lantern would be the most practical course, Daphne lit one she found in the kitchen, then set out for the woods. Her teeth chattered with fear, but she could not possibly return to her room and sleep and leave a man lying injured somewhere in those cold woods.

She tried desperately not to jar her weakened knee as she maneuvered gardens and pasture carefully. The shadowed outline of the trees ahead gave her direction and she concentrated on them and not the darkness around her. She could have no idea where to go once she got there, but she would think of something. If they were any kind of thieves at all, they would see her coming.

As it was, they did better than that. Before she was halfway across the field she met a shadow coming toward her. Not until he was practically in front of her could she discern the limp and know his identity. Breathing a sigh of relief, she waited for Rhys to catch up with her.

"I was coming for you, miss. It's not bad, but he needs looking after." Rhys glanced down at the basket on her arm, and then up to the remarkable woman holding it. She was no more than a slip of a girl, and the way she held her head, he knew she was terrified, but she had come blindly all this

way without being asked. An emotion he had not felt in a
very long time threatened to crack his composure, and he
hastily reached for the basket. "Let me take this. Can you
find your way back to the house safely?"

"You may carry the basket, but I'm coming with you. I'll
be the judge of how bad it is. He's a stubborn man, and I
daresay whatever your position is, it won't allow you to go
against his orders. I have no such qualms."

The limp betrayed her as she stumbled over a grassy
tussock. Rhys grimaced and hurried after her. He could have
argued with her. He could have outrun her and left her to
wander alone, but she had the right of it. Evan might not
listen to anyone, but he couldn't keep Miss Templeton from
acting as she saw fit. If a physician was required, she would
be the one best able to arrange it.

Silently, Rhys took the lantern and closed it, then placed
her hand on his arm for support over the rugged ground.
"Lights attract too much attention, Miss Templeton. It will
be safer this way."

They moved cautiously across the fallow field to the
shadows of the trees. Daphne no longer shivered now that
she knew what to expect. She didn't know why this Llewellyn
person came to be here at this hour of the night instead of
filling his post on the Griffin estate, but she wouldn't quibble
with fate. She was grateful for his company.

A guard rose out of the bushes to intercept them, but
recognizing Rhys, he stepped aside, and they went on,
entering a small clearing. A fire had been built inside the
entrance of a small cave where it couldn't easily be seen,
and a lone figure lay propped in front of the flames,
preventing more than a corona of light to escape. Daphne
bit back a gasp of dismay at thus seeing last night's gallant
gentleman once more reduced to a thief in the woods. She
would never read another Robin Hood tale again. The
romance did not erase the reality.

Evan glanced up and at the sight of his visitor, cursed and
tried to scramble to his feet. Rhys hurried forward to hold
him down.

"Deuce take it, man, I told you to sit still!"

The authoritative ring of the Welshman's voice caught Daphne by surprise, and she watched him with a new respect as he settled Evan back to the blankets. Cautiously, she approached bearing her basket.

"Are you out of your mind to bring her here? The place is probably crawling with soldiers. Get her out of here right now," Evan hissed, deliberately ignoring Daphne's presence.

"They've returned to town. It's much easier to drink a pint of ale and talk about the one who got away." Daphne moved into the circle of light and brushed Rhys aside as she lowered herself to the blanket to examine the hastily tied bandage on Evan's shoulder.

"Besides, she was already on the way out here when I found her. Should I have left her wandering about alone?"

"Damn it, yes!" Evan cursed as Daphne lifted the crude bandage. His gaze flickered over the pale oval of her face, the flash of her lovely eyes hidden behind long lashes as she pried the blood-caked rag from his shoulder. She was undoubtedly furious with him, but he read no disgust in her expression. With a groan, he surrendered and gestured for Rhys to bring the water heating over the fire to help her loosen the bandage.

"Why?" Evan demanded through clenched teeth as she pried at the last piece of thread, ripping it from the wound.

"So I could say I told you so," Daphne replied serenely. "Now all I have to do to tell you from your brother is punch your shoulder. The one who flinches will be you."

Rhys chuckled as he sifted through the basket of supplies. He held up one or two to the firelight and shook his head as he considered the odd assortment, wondering what they could do with sal volatile and rheumatics salve, but he held his tongue. The feverish light in Evan's eyes had very little to do with a rise in temperature as yet. It did him good to recognize his own mortality for a while.

"I didn't think you had much difficulty telling us apart in the first place," Evan muttered thickly as Daphne sponged the wound. The pain in his shoulder was as nothing to the pain in the rest of his body as her breasts brushed against his arm and her delightful scent filled his senses. At any other time had she dared to come this close he would have pulled her onto his lap and covered her with kisses. That behavior didn't seem particularly appropriate now. "Everyone else has confused us for years. We're experts at avoiding trouble because no one is ever willing to identify which of us was the culprit."

"I'm certain all they had to do was name you. Undoubtedly your parents could have taken it from there." Experienced at dealing with the injuries of her father's tenants for lack of anyone else to do so, Daphne knew enough to keep her patient talking to distract from the pain.

Evan winced as she probed the wound for damage, then grimaced at the knowing chuckle coming from the other side of the fire. "We're better than that. Gordon always insisted that he was the guilty party, and I always insisted he was innocent, until they never knew whom to believe. Perhaps their convictions were not so firm as yours," he added dryly.

"Perhaps they found it hard to believe that their sons would lie to them. I have no such misapprehension." Daphne accepted the jar of salve that Rhys handed to her. The bullet had evidently gone right through without damaging any bone, but the amount of blood he was losing was frightening. She worked hastily to stanch the flow. "You're both lying rogues and I shall wash my hands of you as soon as I figure out why you're playing the parts of utter idiots."

"Llewellyn, don't you have guard duty or a mare in foal or something?" Evan threw his friend's grinning features a look of irritation.

"You planning on taking the lady home yourself?" he inquired innocently.

"Insubordinate muddlehead," Evan muttered, throwing his head back against the wall and closing his eyes. Even not looking at her caused him pain. Her fingers were gentle against his skin, soothing wounds more raw than the one caused by a bullet. He clenched his teeth against the desire driving through him.

"Rhys, make certain I have missed nothing before I wrap

the bandage.'' Daphne spoke softly, thinking perhaps Evan had gone to sleep or slipped into unconsciousness.

Both men heard the faltering uncertainty in her voice and looked to each other in surprise. She may have spoken of cowardice upon occasion, but she had never evidenced it to their knowledge. Rhys sent her a puzzled glance and came over to inspect her work.

"It looks a fine job to me, lass. Let me hold the cloth while you wrap it.'' He pressed hard where she indicated, and Evan jerked at the pain.

They finished the work in silence, Daphne occasionally giving a glance to Evan's pale face. She could not read his expression, however, although this close, she could more clearly examine the angles and planes that had eluded her in the darkness. She ached to stroke the hollow of his cheek, but she kept her hands busy where they belonged.

When they were done, she glanced down at the torn and bloody shirt hanging from one elbow, concealing the masculine chest she so longed to lean upon. Her grimace caught Rhys's eye, and he hastened to assure her.

"I'll get him clean clothes in the morning. It's time I got you back to the house.''

Evan finally stirred himself to mutter, "And don't bring her back again. Daphne, get the hell back to London, now. And take Melanie with you.''

"When you see fit to explain why, I'll consider it,'' Daphne replied sweetly, rising from the blanket with the aid of Rhys's callused hand.

Evan glared at her, but Daphne refused to see his fury. Muttering another curse, he closed his eyes and let the pain in his shoulder mix with the pain of her departure into one swirling black maelstrom of guilt.

TEN

"**W**here on earth are you going at this hour of the morning?" Agatha looked up from the breakfast table with incredulity as her niece came into the room wearing an old brown pelisse and a sadly unfashionable bonnet.

"It's such a nice day, I thought I'd go for a bit of a walk." Daphne picked up a roll from the sideboard and contemplated the array of steaming hot dishes. The men in the woods would have nothing so delectable to eat, but she could not imagine how she would smuggle these out.

Since the day had looked gray and drizzly the last time Agatha had looked outside, she gave her niece a speculative stare. "You'd best have boots on," she admonished.

"Do you think Cook would mind terribly if I took some of these rolls and muffins? They smell frightfully delicious but I'm not hungry just yet. They'll taste good after I've walked a way."

Definitely suspicious now, Agatha tried to follow the convoluted byways of Daphne's mind. Undoubtedly there were poor families in the village who could use a good meal, but Daphne hadn't ordered the pony cart, and she doubted if her niece intended to walk all the way to the village in this mist. The possibility that she might actually eat all those things that were disappearing into the damask napkin was not even worth considering. Daphne ate little more than a bird at the best of times. This was most extraordinary behavior, but Agatha could not believe it was in any way dangerous.

She picked up her cup of tea and answered lightly, "Some of that fruit would be good for you, too. Why don't you make a basket and have a picnic of it?"

Daphne threw her aunt a surprised and grateful look. There wasn't any way she could read Agatha's thoughts, but her tone was that of understanding. Hurriedly, she did as told, gathering anything portable that she could find while keeping in mind that the servants would breakfast from this bounty, too. There looked to be plenty for all.

She wished she could bring something to guard against the damp, but there was little remedy for that. The house did not come provided with tents and oilcloths and any of the other things that men who live in the weather required. She ought to be angry with herself for bringing even the comfort of breakfast to men who chose to live by thievery. But she could not bring herself to acknowledge that Evan was actually a thief, and she was beginning to have her doubts about Mr. Llewellyn, too. Now that he was cleaned up and wearing proper clothes, he had almost an air of respectability to him.

She found a thin young man wrapped in rags waiting for her at the edge of the woods. He eyed the aromatic basket she carried hungrily but said not a word as he led her through the thicket of vines and rhododendrons to the concealment of the small cave on the riverbank. He disappeared quietly into the trees when Rhys hurried forward to take the basket from her hand.

"We'll eat like kings!" he announced happily as he examined the contents. "I haven't been able to get word to Lord Griffin yet, but you needn't risk doing this again. I don't doubt that he'll see Evan gets whatever he needs."

That answered a few of the questions in her mind, but not enough. "And the other men, will he provide for them?" she demanded.

"Of course, as best as he is able without arousing suspicion," Rhys soothed her.

As they approached the cave, Evan appeared to be asleep. His unshaven jaw was shadowed and pale in the gray light, and his golden brown hair fell in tousled clumps about his face, speaking of a restless night. He wore a clean shirt over the bulky bandage, and his frayed coat was thrown over his shoulders in protection against the damp mist. Daphne frowned at the battered coat, but remembering the rags the other men wore, she surmised the reason.

He opened his eyes as she sat on the blanket beside him, and for a brief moment, she felt the power of his gaze. Then he averted it to the wall above her head.

"There was no reason for you to come back. Rhys is well experienced in tending the injuries of war."

"There is only one way you will be rid of me, you know," she said conversationally as she peeled back his shirt to examine the bandage. "Have you eaten yet?"

"I'm not hungry."

Rhys came forward with a pot from the fire. "I've been making some meat broth, but he refuses to eat. He'll need it to get his strength back."

"Honestly, you're worse than a child." Daphne took the napkin covering the basket and tucked it in at Evan's neck. "If you don't eat, I'll take that basket of Cook's best rolls back with me and your men will have none of them. Do you wish to be responsible for a riot?"

Evan's glance returned to Daphne's fair face. How anyone could look so helpless and sound so much like a drill sergeant, he could not quite fathom. At the image of all that feminine beauty ordering a battalion of men to step in line, he grinned.

"If I'm ever called to duty again, I'm taking you with me," he murmured.

Daphne cast him a worried look and glanced up to Rhys. Was he fevered? She touched a cool hand to Evan's brow and thought it might be a little warm, but not enough for hallucinations. Grinning now, Rhys shrugged and walked away with the basket, leaving Daphne to deal with their recalcitrant patient alone.

"I'll not go," she announced defensively, just in case he was speaking in riddles. "Now open up and have a bite of broth."

"I can't bite broth," he replied irascibly. "Give me one of those rolls."

"Rhys took them all away. You can't have any until you eat your broth."

Evan glared at her, then appropriated the pot and defiantly sipped from its brim. Unperturbed, Daphne sat back and waited patiently for his temper to cool.

Managing more than enough of the foul brew, Evan set the pot aside and contemplated the stubborn female who had about as much regard for propriety as he did. The folds of the old pelisse disguised the slim curves he had held in his arms just a few nights ago, but the memory of them was still strong. Besides, she could be as bony as a rail and she would still fascinate him. He had never met a female who could be as blunt and direct as a man, and who didn't have the vapors or giggle when he displayed his errant humors. Apparently he had been looking in the wrong places for his match. He should have taken to holding up coaches long ago.

Remembering the sight of her in his brother's arms, Evan tried to shut out these thoughts. "I'm still alive, as you can see. There's no need for you to linger in this damp any longer. Your old war wound won't suffer it gladly," he said sardonically.

He was very likely right, but Daphne wasn't about to admit it. "And there's some need for you to stay here courting pneumonia? Would Gordon keep you from going home?"

Evan looked pained and leaned his head back against the cave wall. Drawing one knee up, he rested his uninjured arm over it and tried to sort out how much he could and couldn't reveal to this persistent female. Perhaps if he told her enough, she would go away and take Melanie with her.

"He's in enough danger without adding my presence. Can't you just take my word for it and get out of here before you are caught up in it too?"

"I don't doubt that you're in trouble up to your ears, but I cannot believe that courting pneumonia will solve it. I will need the whole story before I am convinced to leave you here." Daphne hid her shiver at her own temerity. The buckskin-clad knee just inches from her nose had much to do with that shiver. She had never been this close, this *intimate*, with any man. She could feel the warmth radiating from him, sensed the virile strength in the tension of that muscled leg, and wondered at her boldness in not removing herself at once. Instead, she wished to clasp those brown fingers in her own and feel their heat and strength and texture against her palm. She was quite simply losing her mind. This time, the thought did not startle or alarm her.

As if hearing her wishes, Evan lifted his long fingers to wrap a straying curl of her hair around them. His rough knuckles brushed against the velvet smoothness of her cheek, and he stared at her fascinated. What would it be like to feel those moist, full lips against his own? His body lurched in response, and he hastily diverted his thoughts.

"There is naught to tell that makes any sense." He stared at the wall but kept the silken strand of her hair wrapped in his hand. "My father was the heir to my grandfather's earldom. He had little interest in his inheritance, so Gordon took over his responsibilities at an early age, and I went off to make a profession of war. Besides my father and Gordon and myself, there were numerous other uncles and cousins who might inherit should we three give up the ghost, so no one was overly concerned with my dangerous choice of professions. Among ourselves, it was more or less expected that Gordon would marry and provide the next heir since the others were a rackety lot without a responsible bone in their bodies. Besides, Gordon has always had a way with the ladies, and it was to be expected that he would be married with children well before my father and grandfather stuck their spoons in the wall."

Daphne waited patiently through these family chronicles. The story was scarcely a new one. Born to wealth and aristocracy, most families bred few with the ambition or interest to perpetuate that status. It was much easier to fritter the money away than to earn it. Fortunately, every other generation of most families seemed to produce at least one heir serious enough to take care of the family fortunes. The others were generally content to live off his bounty. The Griffins didn't appear to be any different.

Not noticing her silence, Evan tried to find the right words for the rest of his tale. Idly, he pushed back Daphne's concealing bonnet so he could better see her face. Dew sparkled on her dark lashes and rose-tinted cheeks, and he rubbed his knuckles thoughtfully against her cheek again.

"My father died a year ago, when Wellington and Napoleon were decimating the Belgium countryside. I had no word of it until months later, when I lay seriously wounded in some desolate military hospital. I had responsibilities I couldn't desert, and the letter was so old that I thought there was no need to hurry. Gordon and Grandfather would be well in control of the situation. When the next letter finally found me, I was recovering and well enough to travel. It took time to sell out and arrange for what few of my men remained and to make the journey in midwinter."

Daphne wondered what the second letter said that had caused such haste when the first had not, but she daren't interrupt for fear he would suddenly close up on her again. Daringly, she rested her hand on the arm lying limply across his lap. She shouldn't have underestimated his strength despite his injury. He instantly turned his arm to grasp her hand.

"I didn't arrive until mid-February. I had notified no one of my arrival. It seemed the wisest course given the contents of Gordon's letter." He hesitated, watching Daphne's alert face with curiosity. "I really have no business telling you any of this. It's not a fair reflection on our family."

"I have met you and Gordon and Melanie, and I think I'm a fair judge of human nature. I'll not believe ill of you, and I'll not reveal your secrets without your permission."

He already knew the truth of that. He would not be lying here still were she one to tell all she knew. Resting easier, Evan resolved to tell her the whole miserable tale.

"Gordon's letter said there was some question as to whether my father's death was accidental. It had been assumed that he had taken a fall in a freak jumping accident, but later events called for further inquiries. The saddle had already been mended, but the groom who replaced the girth straps agreed there was some chance they might have been deliberately damaged. The saddle's slipping could have caused my father's fall."

Daphne's fingers curled tighter about Evan's as she stared at him in shock and disbelief. Things like that just didn't happen except in the worst sort of novels. The strap had undoubtedly been flawed, but what did any of this have to do with Evan's sleeping in the woods?

"What were the events that made Gordon go back and look at the saddle?" she asked cautiously, not wanting to voice her doubts just yet.

Evan sighed and tried to arrange his aching shoulder more comfortably against the wall. Daphne moved as if to help him, but he kept a firm hold of her hand. "He found is own saddle cut, a stray shot while hunting nearly took his life, the axle of his phaeton came loose—a number of suspicious accidents occurred. Gordon isn't given to flights of fancy, as you can imagine, but he was quite certain someone meant to kill him."

Daphne drew in a breath at the certainty in his tone. That wasn't really possible. People didn't do that in this day and age. This was positively medieval. "Why?" she finally asked. "Why would anyone suddenly decide to do away with your family? You said yourself there were none other interested in the estates but Gordon."

"They might not be interested in the responsibilities entailed by the estates, but in the money they represent. Haven't I said enough to show you there is danger here? Will you take Melanie and leave now? Dream up an excursion to Bath or to visit relatives in the north or anything but linger here. I have my hands full looking after Gordon. I cannot watch more of you."

Daphne was still working her way through the pieces of the puzzle. "When you came home they shot at you too? Is that why your horse went into the river?"

"Yes," Evan said curtly. "Only I daresay they thought I was Gordon. I was supposed to be dead on the Continent since no one had heard from me."

"So you couldn't go home or the murderer would have two of you to kill. That's gruesome. I cannot imagine it. Does your grandfather know of this?"

Impatiently, he replied, "My grandfather is not well. We'll not add to his worries. Obviously, whoever is behind this thinks Grandfather will not live long, and if he should die first, there might be a mad scramble for the inheritance. Gordon could rush out and marry, or I might have left a wife and child on the Continent, or some such flummery. Twisted minds might think like that. But if we're out of the way, then the title goes back to Grandfather's next direct descendant. I've told you more than enough, Daphne, it is time you promised to leave."

"Why should I be in any danger? I am not related to any of you. I can see that Melanie might be harmed in any incident that involved Gordon since the two of them will undoubtedly be much together, but I should think I would be able to help you without anyone suspecting otherwise."

Thoroughly exasperated, Evan tugged on her hand and brought her to sit closer, where she could not avoid his eyes. "Daphne, you cannot be so maggot-brained as that. If even I have seen you and Gordon together, surely you must realize that the entire area is aware of your attachment. This is the worst possible time for Gordon to finally settle on a suitable wife. It will make our killer frantic to be rid of both of you before there is still another heir to stand in his way."

Daphne stared at him in disbelief. "You are quite mad, Evan Griffin. There is nothing between us. How can there be? Any sensible person can see that. How can you conceive of such a fanciful notion?"

Evan's mouth twisted in a wry grimace as he watched her lovely face framed by a cap of silken brown curls. There didn't seem to be a duplicitous thought in her head, but females always knew these things. She couldn't be totally blind. "I saw him kiss you, Daphne. If he didn't declare himself then, he certainly should have. It is only this confounded masquerade that prevents him from doing so, I'm certain."

"That is absurd." Daphne tugged to free her hand and rise from his dangerous proximity. His grip was stronger than she expected. "It is just the mildest sort of flirtation that you have seen. I am certain Gordon is quite bored out here and he looks for a little amusement. I am old enough that he need not be worried that I'll take offense or that he will engage my affection. There is nothing at all between us. Anyone can see that it would be quite absurd for him to fix his interest on a female who rumor has it has not the wits or sense to see if her gown is buttoned correctly.''

That startling statement brought Evan's fascinated gaze in the direction of her bodice, but the pelisse adequately disguised any errors in fastening. Mischief combined with desire as his hand slid from Daphne's cheek to wrap around her waist. It was not fever that smoldered in his eyes as he drew her closer.

"Just a flirtation?'' he murmured deep in his throat as her wide-eyed gaze came closer. "Perhaps I have forgotten how to flirt. Refresh my memory.''

She could not tear away. It wasn't just that his hold was strong as he pulled her forward, but a fascination with the sight and sound and smell of him that she could not resist. Beneath the linen of his shirt, his chest was warm and hard where she braced herself against him. His cheeks smelled of whatever soap he had used for shaving that morning, and his hair held the fresh scent of rain as she leaned forward to touch her lips to his.

She could not protest that he forced her. She was a willing victim. She wanted the sensation of his lips on hers, craved the closeness of his kiss, needed the searing surrender of being taken in his arms. What she hadn't expected was this, the savage passion of a hungry man, the flood of desire and heat that swept between them so completely that she could only bend to his will as Evan crushed her against him and parted her lips.

Daphne's head swam with the discovery of his possession. She could not brace herself above him anymore but fell before his persuasive and passionate grip, curling against his chest and giving herself up to his hungry demands. A kiss should never be like this, some disconnected part of her brain warned, but she could not respond to the warning while he held her like this, while she could feel the pounding of his heart beneath her hands and the fire of his mouth on hers. Her hand slid to his neck, and she parted her lips willingly.

It was only when Evan used his injured arm to begin searching the enveloping folds of her pelisse that Daphne realized how far she had gone. With dazed shock, she pushed away, searching the familiar angles of his face for some clue as to his intentions. He let her go without protest, and she could read nothing into his silence.

"That is not how a gentleman treats a lady," she murmured, sitting up and trying to adjust her dignity.

"That is how a man treats a woman," he said without an ounce of regret as he watched her flushed face and nervous gestures. He had nothing to offer her. At that moment, he was a wanted criminal with soldiers seeking him. At best, he had no title and a small trust to support him now that he had resigned his military career. She belonged with Gordon, but she seemed to be singularly blind to her attractiveness. What was that comment about her wits? Perhaps now she would realize what a man's kiss meant. Pity Gordon was too damned polite to teach her.

Daphne backed out of reach of his dangerous arms. The fatalistic tone of Evan's voice warned that he could be expected to treat her like so again if she did not stay away. Yet how could she stay away? Her mouth burned where his had touched her, and her body seemed to tingle with the unexplored sensations he had taught her. She was in sad danger to linger in his company. Her reputation would be damaged for all time should word of her presence here get about. But she could not find it in her to leave.

"A very simple lesson, thank you," she replied acerbically. "I shall remember it in the future, but it does not change the present. I am no more likely to marry Viscount Griffin than his Robin Hood brother. I am destined to be a spinster, so leave me to enjoy my few pleasures while I can. And I can assure you, they are not to be found in London."

Evan ran his hand through his rumpled hair and glared at her. "You promised to leave when I told you our reasons."

"I did no such thing. I only said I would consider it. Besides, it seems to me you have left out the most important part. Whom do you suspect to be the guilty party and how do you intend to stop him?"

ELEVEN

"**D**aphne, had I full use of both hands, I would wring your neck." Evan reached for the pot of broth as the only available substitute for placing his hands on her delectable throat.

"I see his mood hasn't changed for the better." Rhys stomped cheerfully through the bushes like some modern-day Red Riding Hood, carrying Daphne's basket on his arm, now nearly empty of its contents. "You're supposed to sweeten his disposition, my lady, not sour it."

"One can sweeten lemonade, but not bad apples," she retorted. "I don't suppose you would care to explain how he means to help his brother by skulking in the woods and courting pneumonia?"

"Certainly. He doesn't believe his uncle will do the dirty deed himself but will hire someone. He rather thought to set himself up as evil respresentative for hire. Any other questions?"

Rhys had lost any trace of his uneducated accent and respectful behavior. Daphne stared at him in as much perplexity as dismay. The plan he recited sounded far-fetched to her, but she could not think of a better one. She turned to Evan to see if he would offer further explanation.

"Uncle? So you know who it is?"

"I didn't say that. Mackle-mouth did. Now it's time you left. Your aunt will be looking for you, and your suitors will be camped at your door."

His sarcasm fell on deaf ears. Now that she had almost reached the root of the plot, Daphne began to feel the excitement of the chase. No one had ever let her become involved in anything more complex than charades. She had always been left out of the planning and doing and had only been allowed to be listener to cries of triumph or throes of despair after the fact. Now she was almost as much a part of the plot as everyone else, and she refused to be cast aside like a helpless infant. Her brain worked feverishly to find her advantage.

She had already gone over the circle of her London acquaintance trying to place the name of Griffin to anyone she might know. It was not that common a name. She was quite certain she had never been introduced to either of the twins or Melanie, but she did remember her brother's mentioning an unusual acquaintance of his who had that name. She thought the man was considerably older than her brother, and since Michael was so much older than she, Daphne had dismissed the man from her mind. But if it were an uncle whom Evan sought . . . Something of the older Griffin's reputation came back to her, and she threw his name out just for a reaction.

"Is Robert Griffin one of your relatives?" she inquired innocently without rising as ordered.

Evan's face went blank, and Rhys whistled a single note behind her. Daphne felt satisfaction as she sensed the sudden tension around her.

"How do you know Robert?" Evan demanded harshly.

"He's an acquaintance of my brother's. They belong to the same club, I believe, though Michael isn't in London much anymore. I take it he is one of your relatives, then? Michael is a good deal older than I am, and this Robert is older than he. I'd judge him at about forty or so, old enough to be an uncle, I should think."

Evan ran his hand over his face. "I had forgotten how small a circle the *ton* is. Should I know your brother? I didn't even know you had one."

"He is not of the Corinthian set. We're of very modest means, after all, but he went to Oxford. I daresay you were at different levels, though. Michael is some years older than you."

"I am rapidly catching up with him, though." Evan stifled a moan and shifted his shoulder. He refused to think about this connection. His only goal right now was to get Daphne out of here. It was becoming obvious that that wouldn't be an easy task.

Rhys didn't have the same compunctions. He gazed on Daphne with a delighted smile and handed Evan a roll to keep him quiet. "So your brother knows Robert? How very interesting. We need to draw the cad out; prove his intentions, but he hasn't been on speaking terms with the rest of the family since the earl refused to pay any more of his debts. He couldn't show his face around here without rousing suspicion."

He drifted into thought which Evan rudely interrupted. "Whatever you're thinking, Llewellyn, don't. I'll not have Daphne involved any more than she is. Get her out of here, preferably to the other end of the country."

Rhys beamed. "And if I could do both?"

"You'd be a magician. What do you mean, 'both'?" Evan crumbled his roll and watched his friend with suspicion.

"Bring Robert out of the woodwork and get Daphne out of here. Wouldn't that work?"

"What would work?" Easing her aching knee, Daphne sat herself more comfortably on Evan's blanket and watched Rhys with doubt. She didn't want to be sent away, but if it would help resolve this mystery, she was willing to listen.

"Using you to draw Robert out and sending you away so you don't become involved when we expose him. Come on, Evan, you know this is better than sitting here waiting for something to happen." Rhys nudged Evan's leg with his wooden stump.

"I know no such thing. You've become the rogue you mock, Llewellyn, to even consider involving a lady in this," Evan growled, no longer looking at the slight female at his side. He wouldn't involve her. He couldn't.

"Well, then, we shall go to Gordon and see if he isn't more reasonable," Daphne said intractably. "I'm certain he will see the advantage in bringing you out of here as swiftly as possible."

She made as if to rise, but a hard hand reached out to grab

her arm and jerk her back. Evan glared at her. "Don't you think he has enough on his mind without adding this mad scheme to it?"

"You don't even know the scheme yet, Griffin. Don't go up in the boughs until you've heard it out. We can be all that is discreet and send Miss Templeton and Miss Griffin away and corner the fox without any interference, providing we have the assistance of Mr. Templeton. And since it would be a rather unwitting assistance, I shouldn't think that would be denied."

Even Evan became curious, and with a sigh of defeat, he signaled for Rhys to continue.

Rhys took that as a signal to make himself comfortable, also. Sliding down the cave wall, he sat cross-legged before them like some pagan story-teller. "Miss Templeton will write to her brother with private word of her betrothal to Lord Griffin. In the letter, she can explain there has been a bitter estrangement between the family and Robert, and she would like to bring peace to the family again. She can ask him to make the announcement of her marriage to Robert privately, before the public announcement, and see if he is willing to accept offers of amity."

Rhys ignored Evan's angry grumble and continued inventing his plan out loud. "Of course, by the time her brother receives the letter, Miss Templeton and Miss Griffin will have gone to Bath or somewhere. Miss Templeton, is your brother likely to act upon your request with any alacrity?"

"To see me married to a viscount? Do you have to ask?" Daphne answered wryly.

Rhys grinned. "Loving families are all alike. Will you do it?"

"How are you going to explain to her brother if Daphne doesn't marry Gordon?" Evan asked irritably.

"There is some doubt that she won't?" Rhys raised a sarcastic eyebrow. "We'll cross that bridge when we come to it. The main concern is to give Robert an excuse to appear here in person. He'll have to, if our theory is correct. He can't risk this marriage happening."

"But how will you stop him from hurting Gordon?" Daphne could follow the plan well enough to that point, but she couldn't see how a ragtag band of thieves in the woods could protect a viscount in his mansion.

"We know his ways, Miss Templeton. You are not to worry about that. It is just for you to agree with the rest of it. Is there somewhere you can go and take Miss Griffin while we straighten this out?"

Evan didn't even have to look at Daphne to know the signs of rebellion flashing in those glorious eyes. He caught her hand and squeezed it, causing her to turn that glare on him. "That's the only way I'll consent to this charade. Otherwise, I shall sit here and rot until Robert finds another scheme, and Gordon can turn gray with worry waiting to see where the next attack will come from."

"That's unfair," Daphne muttered bitterly. "It is little more than blackmail, Evan Griffin."

"You would do the same in my place," he replied unrepentantly. "Do you mind deceiving your brother just a little while, if deceit it is?"

"I do not want Gordon placed in a position where he feels obligated to marry should Michael and my father appear on his doorstep, which they are very likely to do. Perhaps I could just hint at the possibility of marriage in my letter, and indicate that reconciling the family would convince your grandfather of my suitability."

Rhys grinned, and Evan gave her an admiring look. "Very clever," Evan admitted. "But I expect Gordon won't appreciate the finesse. Never mind that. Will you do it? And will you take Melanie with you when you leave?"

Daphne sighed and sat back in resignation. "It seems a very poor thing to do under the circumstances, but I suppose I am not precisely the swashbuckling type. I have an aunt in Bath at this time of year. Who is to explain all of this to Melanie and Gordon?"

"Miss Griffin needn't know," Rhys hastily intervened. "I'll make it understood to his lordship so when you extend the invitation, he makes certain his sister agrees. How soon can you write your letters?"

They both waited on her anxiously. Oblivious to their stares, Daphne shrugged. "I shall do it tonight. I have always wondered what it might feel like to be a fiction writer."

They looked relieved, but Evan's voice revealed its concern as he reminded her, "No one must know of these plans. Robert is quite likely to have spies in every household."

Daphne looked startled at the thought. "Spies? How perfectly horrible. He cannot be in complete need of money if he can go to that much trouble."

"Little do you know the workings of the moneylenders, then. Before we trample your innocence any further, you had best leave to compose that letter. Then start packing your bag and saying your farewells. I want you out of here as soon as the letter is posted."

Daphne rose reluctantly, brushing her skirts and wishing for some means of delay. She felt more comfortable in these woods with these outlandish men than she ever had in the houses of society. And she had just agreed to leave them to some deadly danger she could not even envision.

"I cannot be so forward as that. Aunt Agatha would question such speed and think she has offended me in some way. And there would certainly be gossip over such impetuousness. Gordon will have to visit my aunt and ask if I will accompany Melanie to Bath. If he says she is not feeling well, that will give us excuse for some haste. If we say the journey will be only a brief one, it would require only the packing of a trunk or two. More than that, and the house will be in an uproar of washing and ironing and sorting and folding and it would be a week before we could get away."

With a despairing curse, Evan eased himself upright until he towered over her again. There was not an ounce of fear in her eyes as she gazed up to his undoubtedly disreputable visage. Had she been any other female, he would have terrified her into departing simply by his glare. He had caused field-hardened artillery men to shake in their boots when he turned his glare on them. Daphne Templeton merely stood there with moist lips partially open, tempting his kiss all over again.

His stifled groan had nothing to do with the pain in his shoulder, and Evan grabbed her hand as she reached to comfort him. "Go, at once. Buy a new wardrobe in Bath. Invent ailing relatives. Do anything, but get yourself out of here," he commanded harshly.

She couldn't read the anguish in his eyes, but she heard the anger in his voice. Shoulders stiffening, she nodded curtly. "Of course. Who am I to intrude where I am not wanted?"

As she marched away and a slight youth ran to guide her, Rhys sent his friend a speculative look. To his surprise, Evan's shoulders were shaking with what very much appeared to be mirth. Rhys felt anger rising at this disrespectful treatment of Daphne's obvious pain, and he clambered to his feet to confront his arrogant companion.

"How could you, you bastard? Just look at her! She's offered to place her life and reputation on the front line for you, and you . . . you impudent jackass, you laugh!"

Evan wrapped his arms protectively around his chest as the spasms of increased laughter sent shards of pain through his torn shoulder. He shook his head as he gasped, "Not intrude, she says!" He wiped a tear from his eye with the back of his hand and let the memory of her proud stance ease the anguish ripping through him. "Not intrude where she isn't wanted! Bigad, I have never met a more contrary woman in all my life."

Rhys shot him a skeptical look, then glanced back to where Daphne had disappeared into the trees. However she had done it, she had turned his cynical, battle-hardened officer into a laughing, crying human being again. Perhaps it was fairy dust. Mayhap if he ever got out of these woods again, he would re-read his Shakespeare. He remembered a scene in *Midsummer Night's Dream* . . .

Rhys shook his head. Evan might be a jackass, but he was no dunce. Things would start happening now.

* * *

The rain began in earnest before Daphne returned to the house. Her aunt and maid scolded and ordered her to bathe and change before she could even begin the arduous task of composing the letter. As she soaked in the warm water, she realized she really would have to show the letter to Gordon before she posted it. It was very well and good to plan these things, but the carrying out of such wild schemes entailed a good deal more detail. She couldn't embroil Gordon without knowing for certain that he approved.

Since speed was obviously of the essence, she hurriedly dried herself and dressed in the gown the maid held out for her. Then, left blessedly alone at last, she took up pen and paper and contemplated the words she could use to deceive her brother.

Michael would be in London by now. He had written he would be joining her there, but she had left before he could arrive. She hadn't wanted to hear any more sermons about her unfilial behavior. The difference in their ages had kept them from ever being close, but she was conscious of all his superior qualities. He had always been all that was respectful, proper, and dutiful, while she had always been rebellious, proud, and cynical to a fault. She didn't need her flaws thrown in sharp relief by his proximity.

But Michael's flawless character would undoubtedly lead him to rush to carry out her request, out of pity if nothing else. To find a husband for his invalid sister had been his intent when he had agreed to help Daphne escape to London. If he thought she had enticed some obscure country nobleman into marriage, he would dance to her tune, then rush to investigate her prospective bridegroom. She could imagine him thinking she had fallen for some rogue who would steal her money and leave her cold. Perhaps by praising Gordon's virtues she could stave off any such precipitous journey.

In any event, the laborious task of forcing her pen across paper limited her praises to her usual terse minimum. Besides, Gordon would have to be shown the letter, and she could not embarrass him with more. The request to talk to Robert she left to the very end, so Michael would remember it. It was difficult to convey her urgency, but just the fact that she had actually written should startle her brother into action.

By the time she had sanded the final version, the rain had momentarily returned to mist. With resolution, she sought out her aunt and requested the carriage, ostensibly to visit Melanie.

Melanie greeted her with open arms. The tedium of idling away a rainy day in the country loosed her already fluent tongue, and Daphne soon began to wonder if she would ever find the opportunity to speak to the viscount, let alone see him privately.

Gordon solved the dilemma for her. Coming from his office to discover Daphne's visit, he sent Melanie in search of his new volume of Scott, then hands in pockets, he turned to face the tense lady nervously clasping her reticule.

"I have just spoken with Rhys, Daphne. He tells me you know all. I cannot approve, but I thank you for coming to Evan's aid. He has never been one to sit still and wait for events to happen. I fear this masquerade of his is his most deadly escapade of all. I cannot wish you involved in it."

Daphne relaxed under his soothing tones. Evan always succeeded in making her angry and eager to throw things. Gordon was just the opposite. She smiled with relief and reassured him. "I cannot think I am involved enough. While he lies injured in the misery of this rain, I can do little. I am willing to do whatever it takes to restore him to his home. Did he tell you of the letter?"

Gordon came to sit beside her and take her hand. "Even the letter is asking much of you. I cannot feel it right to deceive your brother and compromise your reputation. If there were any hope . . . Could you ever think of me as . . ."

Hearing the sound of Melanie's laughter floating down the hall, Daphne hastily retrieved her hand and produced the letter. "It is only a very small deceit. Please look at it, if you will." She hesitated, biting her lower lip before adding, "Perhaps you will recognize the address. My mother . . ." She had to say it before Gordon could embarrass himself by making any sort of declaration. She did not know how much Gordon knew of her history, but she could not have him offering for her out of obligation. She tried to make herself clear, "Please, forgive me for deceiving you, but I . . ."

Gordon took her hand again and squeezed it, rising as he, too, heard the sound of his sister approaching. "I am well aware of your difficulty, Daphne, and it does not deter me in the least. Unfortunately, Melanie does. We will speak again soon."

He looked up and greeted his sister with a smile, with the letter now safely concealed in his coat pocket.

All the way home, Daphne played and replayed his words. "Aware of your difficulty?" could mean anything. "Could you ever think of me as . . ." What? Brother? Friend? Did she dare think: lover, husband? It was too preposterous. He couldn't mean that. She daren't believe it, or even think it. Not after all these years to prove her unsuitable. Not after a few weeks of acquaintance. It was only wishful thinking.

Sighing, she sat back against the squabs and watched the rain rolling down the pane of glass. Somewhere out there a man very similar to the one she had just left sat in a miserable cave with his shoulder swathed in bandages staring at this same rain.

Why was it Evan she thought of as Gordon's words of hope rang in her ears?

TWELVE

The rain poured steadily throughout the night, and Daphne began to glance worriedly to the road every time she passed a window the next morning. Aunt Agatha's front drive had turned to a muddy river. What could the lane at the bottom of the hill look like? And how high had the river risen during the night?

Perhaps the letter hadn't gone out in last night's post. Gordon might have decided against mailing it. Or the weather could have been so bad he hesitated sending anyone out in it. But remembering Rhys working in the stables, Daphne felt inclined to believe otherwise. Rhys would have gone looking for Gordon and the letter as soon as she had left.

So haste was of the utmost importance, but she could do nothing until Gordon arrived to ask Aunt Agatha for permission for her to accompany Melanie to Bath. And looking at those roads, she doubted even Gordon's expensive steed could wade through the muck.

The rain poured in torrents throughout the day, making it impossible for anyone to come or go. Daphne thought of Evan and his men shivering in the woods and prayed they had the good sense to retreat to someone's barn.

The knowledge that no one else could travel in the downpour reassured her. There would be plenty of time. Even if the mail coach made it to London in a day, which was very unlikely despite their speed, no one could come from the city while it rained so heavily.

Gordon arrived in a break of the storm the next day. Agatha exclaimed at his daring to brave the roads, but he modestly claimed that he had taken the fields quite safely.

There was no polite way he could send his hostess to another room as he had his sister, and he sent Daphne an

imploring look over her aunt's head. Overly conscious of
the proprieties under the circumstances, Daphne could think
of no means to ask for privacy. A walk in the gardens was
out of the question in this mud. Perhaps it was better this
way. She really must think of putting an end to Evan's
dangerous masquerade before even considering Gordon's
courtship, if courtship it were.

She made a gesture of futility and, resigned, Gordon spun
his tale of Melanie's desire to go to Bath. As Daphne had
known she would, Agatha left the decision up to her. The
arrangements were quickly made, with only the date of
departure left uncertain. The rains made travel too dangerous
in Agatha's opinion, and she insisted that they wait until the
roads were clear.

Hearing the muted torment behind Gordon's agreement
to this delay, Daphne surmised the letter had already gone
out. A bit of fear lodged in her middle and twisted, but she
refused to acknowledge it. It would take time for the letter
to reach London. Michael might have already left. Even if
he had not, it would take time for him to call on Robert
Griffin, time for Robert to act on it, time for anyone to travel
all the way to Devon. They would be well on their way by
then.

She walked with Gordon to the door, but a servant waited
with his hat and gloves and they still could not exchange
private words. Gordon squeezed her fingers as he bent over
her hand.

"Persuade her soon, Daphne. I cannot like this delay,"
he murmured in farewell.

"Have Melanie begin packing. Surely the rain cannot be
so bad elsewhere."

Gordon's smile was stiff as he gazed down on her slight,
brave figure. "I am going to write my grandfather. I daren't
take any more chances now that you are involved."

Daphne looked mildly alarmed. "If he is ill . . ."

Gordon brushed the objection aside. "I'll not tell all, only
just enough to see you safe. The terms I shall use will make
him quite happy."

Unable to say more within hearing of the footman, Gordon

bowed and went out, leaving Daphne to stare, wonderingly, after him. What could he possibly say of this hideous affair that would make the earl happy?

Captain Rollings lifted his mug of ale and sipped it as he stood in the tavern's front window and gloomily stared out at the mud-filled streets. The rain had let up enough to ease the steady river of water that had flowed earlier, but not enough to carry out his duties with any hope of success. He damned the weather and the stupidity of his troop and wondered how a highwayman spent his days in weather like this, particularly an injured highwayman.

His eyes narrowed thoughtfully as he considered how best to use the information he had purchased from the inn's stable boy. It didn't seem very reliable. He could not imagine a man like the Viscount Griffin being involved in the petty larceny of a highway robber, but there could be another story behind the tale. As much as he would like to believe it of the viscount, it was more likely the viscount's servants who were the guilty parties. The estate had been long neglected before this summer, he understood. Mayhap the servants meant to make up the sums the viscount's arrival had deprived them of from petty theft from the estate.

It was time to set his trap and put an end to it. The letter received from his superior officer showed his growing impatience with the delay. His failure at both his schemes would bring an end to life as he knew it, and he was not yet ready to give up all his hopes. Gazing up the street to the hedge concealing the squire's house from the village, Rollings drained his mug. It was early yet. Now that the rain had stopped, he could pay a brief afternoon call.

Just as he called for his bill, a mud-splattered barouche rolled grandly through the village street. Rollings stared at the gilded lanterns, the haughty, liveried servants, and the high-stepping horses, then fastened his gaze on the crest embossed on a once-gleaming ebony door and cursed. Beneath the filth of travel he could just discern the crest of the house of Griffin, the Earl of Shelce.

* * *

Daphne listened in dismay as Agatha read aloud the hasty invitation. Had Gordon taken leave of his senses? After three solid days of rain, the roads were only just now starting to dry. She had hoped the message would say the carriage would be at the door in the morning to take them to Bath. An invitation to dinner to meet the newly arrived earl was not at all what she had expected.

She had thought Gordon's grandfather an ill old man. What was he doing traveling in this kind of weather, if so? What had Gordon put in that letter to bring him out with such haste? She didn't want to know.

Her thoughts turned instantly to the man in the woods. The *men* in the woods, she quickly amended. She had not dared venture from the house again to see to their welfare. What would Evan think of this new development? She had a sinking feeling that he wouldn't be at all pleased by the news of the earl's arrival. That meant one more person to be endangered in the vicinity.

She would have to go. Perhaps she could determine the earl's reason for being here and convey the information to Evan so he wouldn't worry. The fact that Rhys was much better placed to do so completely escaped her. The need to see how Evan fared was greater than logic.

So she garbed herself carefully that evening in a lilac jaconet that ended in a small ruffled train. The slightly daring bodice had matching ruffles on the tiny sleeve but no other adornment. Daphne wondered if she should have chosen something more elaborate, but she disliked frills and cared nothing for delicate embroidery, so she limited her wardrobe to styles she could appreciate. She had no idea that the elegant lines and fabrics she chose could be appreciated even at a distance, making her entrance into any room a very effective one.

The effect came into play as Daphne entered the viscount's salon that evening slightly ahead of her aunt, who was still busily disposing of her various articles of travel. While servants gathered up cloaks and bonnets and veils and umbrellas behind her, Daphne drifted to the entrance and hesitated, trying to form a picture of the room and its inhabitants.

As she lingered there, her slender figure swaying like a lilac in a spring breeze, the eyes of several of the male inhabitants of the room were drawn to her. Daphne recognized Gordon first as he hurried toward her, and gratefully, she held out her hand to him, accepting his gentle guidance, keeping her knee stiff enough to bear her weight without limping. Perhaps Gordon had meant to say he knew of her infirmity—that was something Evan could have told him. Surely he could not know of her mother and still dance attendance on her as if she were an eligible *partie*.

"I was afraid you wouldn't come," he whispered as he led her toward the far end of the stately room where the earl held court. "I couldn't warn you. Please do not act surprised by anything my grandfather says. We will straighten this all out later. For now, your protection was most important."

This whispered warning served to terrify Daphne. Gordon wasn't inclined to impetuous acts and daring lies like Evan. What could he possibly have done to speak to her so? She glanced hesitantly up to his square jaw, wishing she could trust him. What if this were really Evan and not Gordon? A smile curved her lips as she realized she need only punch his shoulder for proof. Wouldn't that incite a little excitement for the evening?

The smile acted as buffer as she was introduced to the tall, distinguished, gray-haired gentleman sipping port by the mantel. He immediately set his glass aside to take her hand and look her over thoroughly. Daphne felt as if she were a horse at market, but she bore his scrutiny gracefully.

"So this is the one you would wed, eh?" The earl sent his heir a sharp look. The two were much of a height, and they understood each other very well. When Gordon didn't quite meet his eye but looked instead to Daphne by his side, the earl snorted and returned his gaze to her. "Templeton? Some relation to Lord Templeton of Northampton?"

"My grandfather, sir." Daphne's fingers continued to cling to Gordon's coat. Wed? What had he done? She tried not to stare as she gazed up to the earl. What could the man be thinking at news that his heir meant to marry a distant relation of a very minor title? Or did he recognize the name from the infamous tales of her mother?

"Ahhhh, yes, of course." The earl nodded his head and apparently traced her family tree through the Debrett's of his mind, but his face never revealed his thoughts. "Where is your father? Is he here now?"

"No, my lord, he is at home. I reside with his sister, my Aunt Agatha. Are you acquainted?" Daphne asked this nervously. It was one thing to suddenly discover you're about to be married without knowing of it, but to have the news announced to a family not previously forewarned brought staggering visions of hysterics and congratulations and a trap never to be escaped.

Gordon hastily intervened to reassure. "Not a word, sir. I have promised Daphne. I have told you, the roads have been such that I could not ride out to ask Mr. Templeton's permission. You have been very precipitate in coming here before I could arrange the formalities."

Instead of reproving his heir for this disrespectful rebuke, the earl barked with laughter and raised his head to watch Agatha approach. "My spoon's not in the well yet, you young pup. I'll not have any more of this havey-cavey nonsense out of you. I'll be at the bottom of it soon, no doubt." Without disturbing a note of his voice, he made an elegant leg as Agatha came up beside her niece. "Ahh, my good lady, we meet again."

Daphne felt as if she had just been run through a thresher. Distinguished earls of her grandfather's age or older weren't supposed to speak common cant and hint that their heirs weren't to be trusted, particularly when their heirs were someone as proper and staid as Gordon. Then to start a flirtation with a lady obviously twenty years his junior and well into her dotage, also—well, that was beyond the bounds of any behavior she knew.

With relief, she felt Gordon lead her away as her aunt and the earl engaged in the animated conversation about a garden party that had obviously taken place in the last century. This really could not be happening. She would wake up and find it all a dream soon. She had meant to retire to a quiet life in the country, bury herself in the wilderness of the moors. How was it that she now found herself temporarily affianced to a viscount and conversing in the same circles as earls? Not to mention hob-nobbing with thieves and plotting against murderers.

Gordon felt a twinge of sympathy at Daphne's dazed expression, but he had other guests and could not neglect them long. Covering the hand she kept trustingly on his arm, he said reassuringly, "It will be fine. My grandfather can be very discreet, if somewhat disconcerting. He only wished to meet you to be certain I am not about to do something remarkably out of line. I am certain he will be gone shortly. I have explained that you and Melanie have made plans to travel. The sooner all of you are gone, the better I will feel, if you will excuse my sentiments under the circumstances."

Daphne managed a smile, but she did not feel his same certainty. She very much suspected the earl knew his grandsons only too well. She doubted if this were the first mad escapade they had engaged in, but if someone didn't act soon, it could very well be their last.

Anxiously, before Gordon could escape to his duties, she asked, "Has Evan been notified? Is he well? With all this rain . . ."

Gordon patted her hand. "The innkeeper is a trusted friend. I insisted that he stay there so we could communicate with more ease. And his men are housed in various barns and sheds and are not likely to die of starvation. There is nothing you need worry yourself about but having a good time and getting off to Bath."

She really would like to scream at him, or perhaps beat him with a parasol as she had his brother. She didn't know which was more infuriating, Evan's arrogant courage or Gordon's unflappable assurance. Both assumed she was little more than fragile porcelain to be protected and wrapped in cotton wool. Perhaps she ought to seek out Rhys. He at least had the insolent attitude that she could be used for something.

But a lady did not cause public scenes, and she really did

not need to draw more attention to herself than she already had. Her smile did not reach her eyes as she dismissed the viscount and turned to Melanie for conversation. It was going to be a very long evening.

"She's what!"

"Daughter of Maria Templeton, sir," Gordon replied patiently after their guests had departed.

"*The* Maria Templeton? The one who drove her perfectly good horses off the cliff? Have you lost your mind as well? I thought the chit behaved as if a cat had leapt down her back, all jumps and starts. She's her mother all over again. One look at those eyes will tell you that."

Gordon held onto the shreds of his frazzled nerves. At the moment, he would rather be Evan and sleeping in the woods and dining off berries than dealing with his cantankerous and only too sharp grandparent. He poured himself a small brandy and offered the decanter to the earl.

"Daphne had reason to be nervous after what you put her through. You have not even given me time to obtain her father's consent and already you're setting her to your paces," Gordon grumbled, sick with irritation. "And there is nothing wrong with her eyes. They're lovely eyes. It is her leg that pains her, as I understand, a result of the accident, I believe."

The earl gave his grandson a scathing glance and drained his glass before continuing to stalk up and down the floor. "And you wish to marry this poor creature you have scarcely known a fortnight? I find that deuced suspicious. Her mother was quite mad, you know. Does madness run in the family? What can you be thinking of to introduce tainted blood to the line? Can you imagine a legacy of mad earls? It will not do, Gordon."

Gordon stiffened. "I have not been so rude as to inquire into the family's weaknesses. The mother's fault is not the daughter's. Daphne is far from being a poor creature. You cannot know the courage and compassion she has revealed to me. A few earls with a backbone like Daphne's would serve this family well."

Shelce grunted at this revelation. It sounded very much as if his grandson were truly smitten, for the very first time. It would pay to examine this issue a little more closely. "Very well. Then you will not mind if I stay a while to get to know her better. You have had the pick of all of London's finest, and you have chosen an unremarkable nobody who cannot stand still without jumping at every little sound. I wish to learn what it is that she possesses that the other ladies did not."

Gordon ground his teeth together and wished he had not agreed to any of this. He had never believed his grandfather would stir himself to come to Devon because he mentioned he was considering marrying. He was eight and twenty and quite capable of choosing a wife without anyone's help. He had thought the earl knew him well enough to accept that.

No, there was something else bothering his grandfather besides the impending betrothal. He watched the earl's irritable pacing of the room and resigned himself. Sooner or later it would all come out. He would just much rather it be later.

"Daphne and Melanie have made plans to travel to Bath, sir. Perhaps you ought to accompany them."

The earl sent his heir a shrewd look and finally accepted the decanter offered. The night had only just begun. His heir just didn't know it yet.

He refilled his glass and, smiling wickedly, asked, "And just where does Evan fit into these arrangements?"

THIRTEEN

Daphne sent the overcast skies a despairing look, then opened the formal note from Gordon. It had been addressed officially to herself and her aunt, so she could not expect it to say all she wished to hear, but even a stiff message was better than none.

When the note was read, her vexation did not ease. Delaying another day so the earl could rest before traveling with them did not sit kindly on her already frayed nerves. Undoubtedly the earl's luxurious barouche would be more comfortable, but the company of that irascible old man would not ease her mood. She just might blurt out the whole story to keep him from testing her like a prize mare, and then they would be in the basket for certain.

She wanted to talk to Evan. He would be as furious and irritable as she over this delay. But the note contained more of an order than an invitation for tea, and Daphne dared not ignore it. Perhaps if the rain held off, she would be able to make a quick trip into the village afterward. The clouds made evening seem to come earlier, but there would be sufficient light for some hours.

The earl presented a certain gruff charm over tea, but Daphne felt as if she were present under false pretenses and said little. Gordon's attentions were so pointed that even Melanie and Aunt Agatha noticed, making Daphne even more ill at ease.

She liked Gordon very well. He was everything that she had ever thought a gentleman should be: kind, thoughtful, undeterred by her flaws, intelligent, considerate, attentive . . . The list could go on into infinity without even adding attractive and wealthy. Why, then, wasn't her heart pounding with expectation whenever Gordon touched her hand or

looked upon her? She had wanted a flirtation to remember.
She had wanted to experience love even if unrequited. Why,
then, couldn't she take advantage of this once in a lifetime
opportunity to play the part that Gordon offered her?

She tried. She smiled into his eyes when he sat beside her
as he sipped his tea. She was quite certain he was a very
exciting and handsome man and that women had swooned
over him for years. She let him offer her a plate of cakes,
and when their fingers touched, she was quite positive she
felt a small shiver of something interesting. She walked with
him about the perimeter of the room as the others conversed
in the center, and their conversation covered dozens of
appealing topics. She really did enjoy Gordon's company
and his ability to make her feel like someone important, but
her thoughts kept straying disobediently to the injured man
at the inn and the visit she planned to make as soon as this
was over.

"Your thoughts are a million miles away," Gordon finally
whispered as they reached the far end of the long drawing
room where they would not be heard so easily. "Has the
delay made you as nervous as I? I thought nothing weakened
your courage."

He wasn't wearing blue today but a forest-green cutaway
over buff kerseymere pantaloons that fitted neatly to his long,
powerful legs. Even Daphne could see he was a fine figure
of a man, and her heart pounded a little stronger.

"I am worried about having both your sister and the earl
here. If Evan isn't indulging in flights of fancy, that could
be very dangerous. Do you think we will be able to leave
on the morrow?"

"I'm certain. It has all been arranged. Do you object too
strongly to traveling with grandfather?"

"No, of course not. It is only the delay I mislike. Did you
really have to give him the impression we are to marry? I
feel so deceitful like this."

Gordon's grasp tightened on her hand where it rested on
his arm. "Then agree in truth and there will be no deceit."

Daphne sent him a startled glance but they had once more
strolled within speaking distance of the others, and a question

from her aunt diverted the subject back to the general.

She was quite certain that Gordon knew of her lameness, if not her mother's crime, Daphne decided as they rode back to her aunt's afterward. How, then, could he possibly carry his flirtation so far as to actually sound as if he wished to marry her? His wife would be a countess someday. A lame countess didn't sound quite the thing. Surely he realized that. No wonder his grandfather was scrutinizing her so closely. She really hadn't thought Gordon meant any of this.

"You are terribly quiet, my dear." Agatha interrupted her reverie. "Are you worried that Gordon has been too precipitous in his addresses? He has, of course, but once a man of his age finally makes up his mind, he becomes quite impatient. I am not at all certain that going to Bath now is the wisest idea. Perhaps you ought to wait and give him time to press his suit."

Alarmed, Daphne shook her head and refused to meet her aunt's eye. "I do not know what has come over him. Perhaps if I go away a little while he will return to his senses and look among more suitable ladies. I am conscious of the honor he does me, but I cannot believe I am all that I must be to be a proper wife."

Agatha looked amused as she watched the emotions on her niece's lovely face. It was a pity the child could not see her own charms, but Gordon was scarcely blind to them. His gaze had seldom left Daphne all afternoon, and for good reason. Her niece was all that was fine in a woman: charming, demure, attractive, and intelligent. She would make an excellent countess. That slight streak of rebelliousness and stubbornness would add to her authority some day. They would make a lovely couple, although she expected Daphne might just give the staid viscount a real run for his money upon occasion.

"You do yourself no favor to speak like that," she admonished. "And you do Gordon a grave injustice. Are you certain it is not missishness that makes you think this way? A woman should be proud and honored to accept the suit of so fine a gentleman."

Missishness? Ordinarily, Daphne would have laughed at

the thought. She had always thought of herself as forthright and above the vaporish whims of ordinary females. But perhaps Aunt Agatha was right. She had never seriously received a gentleman's attentions before. It had been quite easy to laugh off the inanities of those few gentlemen who had politely kept her company. Gordon wasn't so easily dismissed.

That called to question all of her behavior. Had her own proposal in London frightened her into retiring to the country where she would never have to face such a predicament again? Did the prospect of marriage and all that it entailed so terrify her that she had resolved to be a spinster? Perhaps all her actions in London had been such as to deliberately frighten away suitors, and only when she thought herself not pursued did she find someone to see her as she really was.

Daphne didn't think she was frightened of marriage, but she really had not given it much thought. Girls grew up to be married. That was what she had assumed when she went to London. Now she knew differently, but she still had a secret longing to be loved and cherished. And she wasn't at all certain that a platonic friendship would suit.

Remembering the heat of Evan's kiss, Daphne blushed and looked out the window. Would Gordon kiss her like that if they were married?

Rather than sink in these disturbing thoughts, Daphne ordered out her pony cart as soon as she had changed her clothes. She needed some kind of exertion to divert her thoughts away from herself. The sky had been overcast all day without rain. It would very likely wait a little longer.

Going out without a maid was a little more difficult. Tillie had the sniffles and couldn't come out in the damp weather, but Marie looked disappointed not to be asked. It didn't matter. What she was about to do didn't need witnesses.

Agatha had retired to her room for a rest before dinner, so there was no one about to protest when Daphne donned a pelisse over her walking dress and called for the cart. The groom offered to accompany her, but she politely declined.

She felt a drop or two fall as she rattled over the bridge

to the village, but she was too close now to turn back. If it rained too hard, she could always stop a while with the Dalrymples until it was over. Jane would enjoy a good coze to discuss the earl's arrival.

The main problem was being inconspicuous. That wasn't a problem; it was an impossibility. The whole village would know she was there just from the sight of the pony cart in the street. Drastic measures were called for.

Before reaching the village proper, Daphne turned the pony down a hedge-lined lane. Evan had to be able to come and go from the inn somehow without being seen, and she rather imagined the river running parallel to the village street had much to do with it.

In triumph, she discovered a path along the riverbank. She daren't risk her pony and cart in this narrow terrain, but they would be safe enough tethered to a tree out of the way. If someone saw them later, they might think her maid had borrowed them for an errand or some illicit tryst. She tied the reins and set out to maneuver her way between hedge and river in the direction of the inn. Evan would no doubt ride his horse back and forth through here to the stables behind the inn. How would he enter the inn without being seen from there?

She would cross that path when she came to it. If nothing else, she would use the same ploy as earlier and pretend she was faint and in need of water. Female vagaries were always overlooked and forgiven.

As it was, she found the garden empty as before and entered it through the kitchen gate. If anyone saw her browsing through the flowers, they would think her eccentric and nothing more.

Before Daphne could devise a plan for entering the inn to search for Evan, she caught the flash of a red coat over the fence in the side street, and she stepped behind a large mulberry bush. The sound of steps did not go directly to the inn but seemed to amble down the alley toward the stables.

"What's our chances of catching a highwayman on a night like this?" a voice asked scornfully.

"Not much of a highwayman if you ask me. More like

a bloody Robin Hood. Did you see that widow weep when she found the bolt of cloth on her doorstep? Fair makes a fellow shiver to think how the rogue got it there without none of us seeing it.''

''Well, if the captain's right, we'll find how he does it tonight. But I still don't think he's fool enough to come near the only inn in town. We might as well find ourselves a dry spot and wait it out.''

The voices traveled on until Daphne couldn't hear them anymore. She was momentarily frozen to the spot, but her fear couldn't allow her to linger. Evan had to be warned. If only she knew more of their plans.

She hesitated, wondering if she ought to take a chance and find Captain Rollings first or just hurry to warn Evan. She feared the likelihood of going from the soldier to Evan safely was small. It would be better to do it the other way around and make some arrangement to send the information back to him.

With that plan in mind, Daphne waited until she sensed there was no one about, then cautiously crossed the garden to the side door of the inn. The sound of the captain's voice coming from the back room where she had once met Evan sent a ripple of fear coursing through her. She had hoped to find Evan there as before. That had been an idiotic notion. Now that it was dashed, she was at a loss.

Hugging her pelisse closer, Daphne slipped into the side hall and listened to the sounds around her, searching for any indication of Evan's presence. A public inn seemed a foolish hiding place for a known criminal, particularly one who was so identifiable. His resemblance to Gordon would cause marked suspicion in strangers. The villagers would know instantly that a hoax had been perpetrated.

The sound of heavy boots leaving the parlor sent Daphne's heart into a racing panic. Without thought, she dodged into the shadows of the back stairs. When she realized where she was, she caught her breath, looked upward for any sign of movement, then lightly hurried to the upper story.

The uneven floor boards made walking tricky. The lack of any source of light but a dirty window at either end of the narrow, low-ceilinged hall gave her pause, but she had come here for a purpose. She would not forget it now.

Skimming her fingers along the wall and watching for the darker rectangles of doorways, Daphne sought the room that might conceal an injured Robin Hood. Few strangers ventured through these parts. The rooms were seldom taken except by travelers caught by darkness or the weather, or an occasional drunken farmer unable to make it home after a long night of ale-swigging. The two open doors near the top of the stairs would not conceal what she sought. Daphne eased herself down the hall, ever alert for approaching voices or feet.

When she found the closed door to one of the front rooms, she hesitated. Her sense of the impropriety of what she was doing had fled long ago under her fear of the soldiers surrounding and filling this place. She had gone well beyond propriety the night the dratted man had appeared in her bedroom. She could only repay the favor in kind.

With that resolve of sardonic humor, Daphne tapped lightly at the worn wooden panel.

She heard a stirring inside, then a quiet voice that made her heart turn over in her chest.

"That you, Beckworth?"

She couldn't answer, not with soldiers just yards away in the hall below. Gently, Daphne turned the latch. It was locked.

Biting back a cry of frustration, she scratched lightly again, damning him for not opening the door at once. At any moment someone could choose to amble up either of those staircases, and she would be well and truly caught. How could she persuade him to turn the key?

She heard a mutter just the other side of the panel, and knew he was closer. "Open up, hurry," she whispered, praying he could hear.

On the other side of the panel, Evan stared at the cracked and peeling wood and wondered if his fever had returned. Had his boredom and wishful thinking created phantoms to whisper through the cracks of the door and haunt his lonely hours? He could almost imagine the fresh scent of apple blossoms wafting around him, and he rested his forehead against the old wood while a surge of longing swept over him. He remembered well the last time he had held a bundle of soft curves and feminine vulnerability in his arms, and the scent of apple blossoms had taunted him then. He was growing quite mad for lack of action, and he damned Rhys and Gordon for imprisoning him here.

The sound of boots on the stairs registered the danger of allowing his mind to wander, and he stepped back, but not before the unladylike hiss on the other side of the door caught his full attention.

Jerking open the door, Evan reached through and grabbed a handful of damp wool and jerked his visitor through the narrow opening, then closed and solidly bolted the door.

They stared at each other in fear and fascination. Evan sought the shadowed bruises beneath the lovely wide green eyes and cursed, then couldn't help allowing his gaze to travel over the trim figure displayed by the tight fastening of the fashionable spencer beneath the damp pelisse. He took the heavy garment from her shoulders and threw it aside. It was as conspicuous as a fur muff on a summer day. His lips twisted at her naive attempt at disguise.

"Is there a battalion of soldiers on your heels?" he inquired wryly.

Daphne's mouth was too dry to reply. She could see the white of Evan's bandages beneath the untied neckline of his open linen shirt, and for the first time, she acknowledged the manly chest beneath layers of gentlemanly clothing. His tightly tailored buckskin unmentionables were partially unbuttoned, and she jerked her gaze back to his face before she could look further.

A day's beard roughened Evan's shadowed cheeks, and his golden hair fell in tousled disarray across his forehead, but she was scarcely aware of these defects. She felt her eyes held by his, and her tongue froze in her mouth as his hand caught her shoulder.

"Speak, Daphne, or I shall die of heart failure here and now. What has driven you to this madness?"

The sudden crack of thunder and burst of heavy rain on

the tile roof overhead jarred her back to her senses, and the fear coursing through her roused her to action. This was Evan, the despot of the woods. She must warn him and get out of here.

"Captain Rollings has something planned for tonight. There are men below and stationed along the river. It seems to have something to do with the inn. I didn't know what to do."

"Had I been consulted, I would have recommended staying home." Evan's dry answer did not reflect the turmoil inside as he turned away and strode toward the rickety table that served as washstand and dresser. He poured a tumbler of water and returned to hand it to her. She looked paler than he had ever seen her. "Drink this, then tell me what the deuce you are doing out in weather like this, and without a maid."

Daphne sipped gratefully at the water, then glanced around at the room, gradually fading in the dying light of the storm. She could make out only the shape of a wide cot and the washstand, and the window on the far wall—dismal surroundings for the grandson of an earl, but a notch above the cave.

"I wanted to talk to you. Gordon told me you were here. And then I heard the soldiers talking . . ."

"And you hied yourself up here into an impossible situation. Did anyone ever tell you that you're a fool, madam?" Evan turned and strode away before her anxious face made a fool of him, too. He gripped the window frame with both hands and glared down at the darkened shrubbery below. The river was just beyond that line of trees. With a little imagination he could almost see the red coats through the leaves and the torrential rain.

Anger replaced anxiety as Daphne glared at his back. "Pardon me for being concerned. If you have the situation well in hand, I shall be happy to leave." She turned to unbolt the door, but his words halted her.

"It's pouring again. Where do you think you will go? Had you some notion of gaily flitting downstairs, twirling your parasol, and displaying yourself to a tavern full of randy soldiers and asking for a ride home?"

She had half a mind to fling the glass at him, but water

was not nearly as satisfying as ale. Instead, she refilled the glass and handed it to him. "Here, wash your filthy mouth. 'Tis a pity it cannot wash the dirt from your mind."

He swung around and glared at her, but she was halfway across the room now, and he could not keep his anger. She looked so fragile in this gloom, that it took all his strength to keep from reaching out to her. "That's the world the rest of us live in. Are you such a saint that you haven't noticed? What could have possessed you to come here when every precept of society warns against it?"

Daphne wilted beneath the harshness of his voice. He was right, of course. Their other encounters, while improper in the extreme, were also very private. This was something much different, and she had done it to herself.

Twisting the fingers of her gloves, she spoke to the floor. "Melanie and I are leaving with your grandfather for Bath in the morning. I wanted . . . I didn't know if Gordon . . ."

Voices broke out in argument on the front stairs, and Evan's head jerked up. With a despairing glance around he groaned, caught Daphne's shoulders, and pushed her toward the bed. "Take the jacket off, let your hair down, and get beneath the covers. Try to look as if you're asleep."

Not understanding what he meant to do but understanding his urgency from the vociferousness of the argument below, Daphne hesitated only a second over his orders. When it became obvious that Evan was releasing his breeches in preparation to removing them, she blanched and turned away. It scarcely made any difference if they were caught with or without clothing at this point. She was well and thoroughly ruined. Shakily, she reached to remove the pins holding her hair.

She heard Evan padding about the room behind her as she hurriedly unfastened the short jacket and threw it over the wash stand. She glanced at the narrow bed and down at her double layer of lovely skirts, and setting her lips, she hastily released the tiny buttons holding the eyelet overskirt in place.

She tried not to hear Evan's intake of breath as she let the hampering cloth fall to her ankles. She was still fully concealed beneath the thin muslin of her gown, but it had been designed to be worn beneath the concealing skirt and spencer. The bodice was low and the fabric, very frail. Telling herself he had seen more when she wore her night-rail, Daphne slid beneath the thin wool blanket of Evan's bed.

Evan had to force his gaze away from the shimmering waterfall of nut-brown tresses cascading down a slim, barely-clad figure sliding hastily beneath his covers. He had never tried to picture what she would look like in his bed. He was not a man given to flights of fancy. But the sight of her there stirred images no man could be blamed for having. He grabbed his brandy flask and sprinkled it liberally over his shirt. That was a trick he had learned well from his lady-love, though it had never fooled her. He did not think the intruders below were so perceptive.

The boots sounded alarmingly loud on the uncovered wooden planks of the hallway. Evan combed his hair into his face with his fingers, turned to see that Daphne was facing the window with only the wild tangle of her hair revealed, and held his breath as the pounding of fists rattled the bedroom door.

"Open up in the name of His Majesty!"

FOURTEEN

The rain pounded against the roof and thunder crackled overhead as Evan slowly slid the bolt open. He daren't turn for one more glance at the woman in his bed. If his plan failed, she was ruined for life, and he would be in no position to save her. Not even Gordon would be inclined to rescue her. He had to play his part well; her life as well as his depended on it.

The gloom of the storm clothed the room in darkness, and Evan breathed a sigh of relief as he realized the man outside carried no candle or lantern. For all practical purposes, it was early evening. Beckworth wouldn't have wasted good oil and tallow by setting out lights yet. Evan could scarcely discern the gleam of brass buttons as he peered warily around the door's edge. He crouched low to disguise his height, keeping his gaze fastened at the level of the soldier's chest.

"What's the meaning of this?" he demanded in the querulous tones of a Cornish squire aroused from sleep. He'd had a sergeant once from those parts. He'd learned to mimic him well.

"We have orders to search this inn for a wanted criminal. Who are you and where are you going?"

The soldier on the other side of the door tried to shove his boot through the crack, but Evan held the latch firmly while appearing to use it for drunken support. "I'm a merchant, sir, traveling with the wife. Can't a man have a decent night's sleep? Listen to that weather out there. Your criminal would have to be a madman to be about on a night like this."

"Let me in, you old fool, so I can search the place, and then you can have the comforts of your bed again."

The soldier shoved harder against the door, and Evan

allowed it to give just enough for the man to get a glimpse of the feminine form in the bed. He chuckled as the soldier stumbled and gasped. "Ain't she a rare one? Just wed, we are. The brandy's put her right off to sleep, and I'm like to hear about it in the morn, but not now, sir. So if'n you'll excuse us . . ." He stepped in front of the soldier's view.

The man muttered a curse, gave Evan's stooped and shirt-clad figure a disbelieving look, and clattered down the hallway again. Evan gently closed the door, straightened to slide the bolt home, and leaned against the wood with a sigh of relief. "Well, wife, you had best make room for me in there. It's going to be a long night."

Daphne sat up hurriedly, pulling the covers to her chin and staring into the gloom at the white ghost of Evan's shirt. "Long night? I cannot stay here any longer. I'll have to sneak out and go to the Dalrymples', tell them I was caught in the storm."

Evan advanced on the bed with a mirthless smile. "And what, pray tell, will you tell the soldier no doubt stationed at the end of the hall? That you've decided to run from your brandy-soaked bridal bed?"

"Surely, they haven't . . ." She stared in disbelief as Evan deliberately sat down on the mattress beside her and reached for his discarded trousers. His shirt came down to his stockings, and she couldn't stop her gaze from straying lower. In the semidarkness she could see little of the long, muscular legs disappearing into the buckskin, but just the knowledge of his near-nakedness caused her to blush profusely.

Evan watched her with growing amusement. This episode had its farcical side. If only dear brother Gordon could be here now . . . That wasn't a thought he wished to contemplate. "Did you hear him go down the stairs?" he demanded, forcing her to recognize their plight.

She hadn't. Daphne stared at him in dismay. "Perhaps he'll fall asleep?"

"When? Midnight? You wish to sneak past him then and pound on the Dalrymples' door?" Evan stood and pulled his trousers up, calmly tucking his shirttails in while she watched. He didn't know how much she could see, but it was too late for modesty for either of them now. He was just beginning to realize the full extent of damage this night had wrought.

Daphne pulled the pillow behind her and sank back into it. Her hair spilled over the short sleeves and drawstring neckline of her gown, and she impatiently caught the thick mass and pulled it to one side, absently braiding it with her fingers.

Evan stayed her hand, leaning over to release the silken mass and spread it across her gown again. "I like to look at it. If I were your husband, what would you say to me now?"

Daphne stared at her irritating and forceful companion, and opened her mouth to give him a scathing reply. Something in his touch and the tone of his voice caused her to close it again. Mischievously, she replied in the same spirit as his question, "You smell of strong spirits, sir. I wish you would bathe."

He laughed low in his throat and sat down beside her, folding his hands behind his head as a pillow against the wall's hardness. "What do you think our soldiers would say should I call for Beckworth to bring me a bath?"

"You needn't worry about the soldiers so much as what I would say," Daphne replied acerbically. "Be the tub shallow or deep, I would find some means to drown you in it."

"That's not fair, Miss Templeton. You speak as if this is all my fault. I did not invite you here, if you'll remember."

His genial tone did not ease her flush of guilt and confusion. She was quite old enough to know the extent of her rashness and the consequences, but she refused to think of it until she was certain there was no escape. What she had more difficulty ignoring was the man's large body seated so intimately beside her, in such a compromising place. She feared she knew what he was thinking, and she hastened to stamp out such notions.

"Your rash and criminal actions invited this outcome," she admonished him in as severe a tone as she could summon.

"Had you not set yourself in such a position as to be wounded and hunted down like an animal, I would not have been compelled to act as I did. I only hope this convinces you and Gordon to put an end to this charade and go to the authorities with your complaint."

She was good. She was very, very good. She could not have done better had she dumped a pail of cold water over his head. Evan gritted his teeth and stared at the far wall. "One does not go to the authorities with accusations against family. I take it you have met my grandfather?"

He did not need to say more than that. How could the twins accuse the earl's only surviving child of such heinous treachery? Particularly without proof. They had reached some kind of verbal stalemate. Daphne wrinkled her nose and gave a sigh.

"I was really not meant to be a viscount's wife at all. And heaven forbid, never a countess. Your grandfather is quite awesome in his authority. What was your grandmother like?"

Evan bent his diminutive companion a startled look. "Is that why the earl condescended to leave his noble tower? Has Gordon asked you to be his wife?"

Daphne threaded her fingers together and wished his gaze were not quite so intense. She was having difficulty enough adjusting to being alone with him. She refused to think of the miserable piece of furniture they were sitting on as a bed, preferring to pretend it was a parlor sofa where they conversed. But she couldn't pretend away his proximity, particularly when he stared at her like that.

"No, not in so many words, but I fear his sense of honor will require it. He had some notion of protecting me by announcing his intentions to your grandfather. I fear your masquerade has made Gordon very nervous. He did not mean for the earl to come down and inspect me, but I believe I have failed inspection."

Such bluntness from a female was a novelty to Evan, but a riot of emotions in his breast kept him from fully admiring her honesty, or her extraordinary cynicism, whichever it might be. He wanted to throw Gordon a facer, curse his interfering relations, and offer this tender morsel his eternal protection, all of which would be absolute faradiddle under the circumstances. Evan gritted his teeth against the words that threatened to come out.

"This night with me will certainly have you court-martialed should it ever be known. I'll make it right with Gordon, and he'll ignore the old man's decrees. Gordon's got a good head on his shoulders and doesn't blow with the wind. If he's made his mind up, he'll not change it."

He pronounced these words with a certain satisfaction. He knew his twin. Gordon would take Evan's word for what happened. Evan could offer Daphne this happiness in exchange for her mad attempts to save his worthless life. Of course, after the wedding, he might blow his brains out, but that was all part of a dim future. First, they had to get out of this predicament and run his Uncle Robert out of the country.

Evan's words had a dampening effect on Daphne's spirits, although she couldn't say why. It was good to know Gordon wouldn't think badly of her, but she couldn't help thinking it of herself.

"I'll not cause a rift between them. Can you imagine what the *ton* would think of me as countess? Me, the daughter of Mad Maria? No, I'm quite content to remain as I am, providing you make very good explanations to my aunt so she'll allow me to stay. Should I take a look at your shoulder? You seem to be favoring it more than earlier." Daphne turned inquiringly to him.

If she touched him, he would have her flat against the bed with her skirts about her waist in a trice. Evan didn't know what she rambled about and didn't care. It took all his concentration to keep his hands off her. He dropped his hands and swung his feet over the edge of the bed, clutching his fingers into fists as waves of desire smote him with the explosive force of breakers against a cliff. Lord, give him strength, for it wasn't his neighbor's wife that he coveted, but his brother's.

"It still aches when I'm weary. Why don't you get some sleep? I think I'll keep an eye on the river awhile."

"Sleep?" Daphne stared at Evan's broad shoulders with

incredulity. "I am trapped in a room with a notorious thief, surrounded by soldiers, my reputation is ruined, and you wish me to sleep? You may as well ask me to sing songs."

Evan grinned at the window as he rested his arm along the frame and stared out. "That should be amusing, too. Do you think we would keep the inn's inhabitants entertained if we lapsed into drunken song for the remainder of the night? Where would we start? Ballad or ditty?"

"Well, as a bridal couple, I should think it ought to be something jolly, but I am more inclined toward something doleful. Should we wail loud enough, mayhap they will all go home."

"I rather favor 'Johnny, I hardly knew ye,' but they may accuse us of being Jacobite traitors or some such. I suppose that eliminates 'Loch Lomond,' too." Evan tried to imagine the reaction of the man down the hall if these laments hit his ears, but the soft laughter behind him said it all. He tried not to watch her image in the darkened glass of the window.

"If I were able to sing, I would try those just out of curiosity. We would at least go laughing to the gallows. But since I cannot sing, you will need to tell me tales. How did you and Rhys meet? I think there's a story between the two of you."

Evan gave up and turned around. He was a gentleman and she was his brother's affianced wife. It was his duty to protect her. He would do his duty or die trying. Duty was something he understood. These other emotions now smothering him were foreign to his nature.

He sat at the end of the bed and leaned back on his elbows. "I don't think it's a story that can be told without Llewellyn's permission. I'll tell you a story about Gordon if you'll tell me one about you."

That was better. The taut energy that had been emanating from Evan seemed to relax to a cautious stance, and he was almost managing a smile. Daphne pulled her legs up under her and encouraged him to continue.

They talked the better part of the night as thunder rumbled and rain beat against the roof, drowning out all noises but their voices soft against the darkness. They talked of London and the things Daphne would have liked to have done and the ones that Evan missed and discovered they were both the same. Evan spoke uncertainly of a future he might never see, and Daphne encouraged him, knowing she had no future beyond these moors.

Laughing in the darkness, they made up a future in parliament for him as a candidate from Gordon's pocket borough. He would provide funds for needy soldiers and their families, and Daphne insisted that he provide equal funds to train all those who could not find employment due to their physical disabilities. Evan laughed and asked if he should provide equal training for those with mental disabilities and inquired whether she would join the program then and learn to be a sheepherder.

Her sudden tears at this suggestion brought Evan apologetically to her side. "What is it I have said? I meant only to tease."

His concern brought another rush of tears, but Daphne took a deep breath and determinedly wiped them away. It was more than evident that Evan did not know all the tales about her, so no doubt Gordon had never heard them either. It seemed quite preposterous when she was certain all of London had nothing better to talk about, but perhaps she was overemphasizing her importance. And then, Evan had been on the Continent these last years. He hadn't been near London to hear the tales.

"You hit too closely to home, sir," she finally replied. "There ought to be some help for people with mental disabilities, but sheepherding and Bedlam are not what I have in mind."

Puzzled, Evan touched her chin and turned her to face him. "I will agree to that, but there is no reason for my facetiousness to cause your tears. There is something you have kept from me. Isn't it time I have the whole?"

Daphne sighed and looked away. Her little charade of normalcy had to end sometime. Much better now, before Gordon could say or do anything foolish. It would be easi-

to tell Evan and let him pass on the story. Then she wouldn't have to meet Gordon's eyes when this was over. "You have not heard of Mad Maria?"

At his shake of the head, Daphne clasped her hands on her lap and gazing straight ahead, continued as if repeating a bedtime story. "My mother was a loving, charming woman, but even when I was a child, I can remember how emotional she would become if I came to her with a bloody knee or if we laughed too long over a silly game. She would cry or laugh until she was ill and my father would have to come and send her to bed with her medicine. There would be days she would never come out of her room, but there would be weeks of sunshine and laughter, too. She was my mother and I just thought that was how mothers acted."

Hearing the painful catch in her voice, Evan tried to halt this speech, but Daphne held a finger to his lips and hurried on.

"No, I want to tell you the truth, before someone tells you the rumors. My mother was a beautiful person, and no one can take that from me. I am not at all like her, but there are times when I wish I could be. When she was well, she enjoyed every minute of life with a fullness I may never possess. Unfortunately, when she was not, she visited some hell where no one could follow.

"The physicians supplied her with medicines to calm her when she became uncontrollable, but there was an incident when she took too much, and my father had to lock the medicine away where she could not find it. He tried sending her to her family in London, thinking she would be happier in the social world where she had grown up, but she always came home after a few months.

"That last time she came home, she wasn't well at all. Nothing returned her spirits. I think it hurt my father badly, and he stayed away from home much of the time. Anyway, I was the only one home except for the servants the night she took out the chaise. Even our stableboy was gone. It had been drizzling all day and I knew the fog would rise in the valleys, but there was no one there to warn her or stop her but me. And it had begun to thunder and lightning. It wasn't a safe night to drive. There wasn't time to saddle a horse to follow her, so I took father's gelding, the one he kept a bridle on all the time. I fastened the reins and found a fence I could stand on and rode it without a saddle.''

Daphne ignored Evan's intake of breath. She had been young and impetuous, but she dared say she would do it again. Now that she had begun the story, there was no point in stopping it to examine the full extent of her youthful stupidity.

''The chaise was going too fast down the fell, and I had difficulty catching up with it. It all happened too quickly. I saw her horse run in one direction, and the carriage went the other, off the road and toward the tarn. I must have screamed, or perhaps it was the lightning striking just ahead. My horse reared. And then I knew nothing else until I woke in bed in excruciating pain.''

Evan started to gather her into his arms, but Daphne placed a hand against his chest and held him off as she spoke against his shoulder.

''I was in horrible pain and didn't understand the import of what I was saying when I tried to explain what happened. But my father did. And the physician did. And before long, the whole village had heard some version of the tale. They knew my mother had to have deliberately unhitched the horse for the accident to have happened as I said. Of course, someone checked the harness, as they never would have done had I not told what happened. My mother's carefuly planned accident became known as the suicide it was. She had been known as 'Mad Maria' before for her lively manners and eccentric emotions, but now the whole world knew she was mad in truth.''

Evan stroked the thick silk of Daphne's hair and let her continue. He knew of nothing he could say to comfort old wounds.

''My accident kept me invalided for almost the length of our mourning. The physicians said I would never walk again, but I knew I would follow my mother to the grave if I were bedridden for life. So as soon as my leg was healed enough, I began moving it, a little at a time, more each day. I would get up at night when no one was watching and practice walking again, holding onto the furniture. When I could stand on my own, I walked out of my room in daylight, and they finally had to consent to let me downstairs for a while each day. It is a tedious story, but suffice it to say, when it came time for my come-out, I went to London, against my father's wishes.''

She wasn't done yet. Daphne lifted herself from the tempting comfort of Evan's arms and stared at the faded mirror across the room. "I am afraid of so many things. After the accident, I was terrified of horses. And carriages. Rain. Darkness. Thunder. Lightning. Anything could return the nightmare of that night. People began to whisper I was as crazed as my mother. I was determined to prove them wrong.

"My mother's family tried hard to be kind. Before I arrived, they prepared everyone to be all that was amiable for their poor, invalid relative. The tale of my mother's death made the rounds again. Everyone watched and listened, waiting for me to give evidence that I was all that they expected, while being sympathetic. I'm afraid I was rather rude to some, and lost my temper with others, and the rumors didn't go away as I had hoped. Whatever I might or might not be never really mattered. The gossip was so much better.''

The cynicism had returned to her voice as Daphne pulled away and sat with arms folded across raised knees. She didn't look back at Evan as she concluded, "So, you see, I am rather sensitive about jests as to my state of mind. I am also a coward, and somewhat lame when it rains, and none too certain on my feet when it does not. A far from perfect specimen in anyone's book.''

"Coward,'' Evan snorted scornfully from behind her. "You are the least cowardly female I have ever had the misfortune to come across. Name me one woman who would have taken that ramshackle cart out at night, in the rain, and driven it to the river. I cannot think of even one who would dare that much, no less all the rest. Coward, you are not. Fool, quite possibly.''

Daphne turned on him with rage, but Evan caught her small fist before it could beat his sore shoulder. "Pax, little heathen. This is neither the time nor the place to judge ourselves. Let us save that for others to do when we escape this little scrape. I have a feeling recriminations aplenty will fly then. Sit back, and I will tell you of my unfortunate father, of if you prefer, I'll create lies of my hectic social life in London. What story would you like to hear?"

The tears and the tension leached out of her with these rough words, and Daphne had to smile wryly at the half-dressed man in the bed. He was not the polished viscount at all, but a rogue and a warrior with no polite words of comfort to offer. But he offered what he had with a sincerity that made her feel at home in this preposterous situation. She hadn't felt at home anywhere since her mother died. Sighing a little in relief, she went back to Evan's comforting shoulder and scraped a finger daringly over his bristly cheek.

"Robin Hood. Tell me the story of Robin Hood."

"And Lady Marion," he added.

Their easy companionship in the dark made the night comfortable. As their stories lapsed into fewer and fewer words, and Daphne struggled to keep her eyes open, Evan found it easier to pull her closer until her head rested comfortably in the curve between his shoulder and chest. By dawn, she was sound asleep and curled against his side and Evan held her securely wrapped in his arms, his cheek resting against her soft cloud of hair. It was as close to heaven as he would ever come, he reasoned, but he took no advantage from it.

He watched a rosy dawn break through the grimy window, and glanced down at the long sable lashes spread across fair cheeks in sleep. The dawn spilled a fresh hue across Daphne's skin, and her moist lips parted in sleep stirred longings he tried to set aside. She was warm and softly curved in his arms, and he ached with more than just physical longing. He had never spent a night like this in his life, and he could easily imagine a lifetime of such nights and more.

Evan wondered what it would be like to have the right to

kiss those lips every night. That led him to wonder all manner of wondrous things, and before he was quite aware of what he was doing, he bent to cover her mouth with his.

He only meant a gentle kiss, but Daphne's lips seemed to wake beneath his, gradually dawning to the delights of this tender touch, and their mouths began to blend with a will of their own. Evan gathered her closer, feeling the soft curve of her breast beneath his hand as he lifted her to him, but she made no protest. Her arms slid willingly around his neck, and he was lost in the tender delights of her charms.

The sound of voices rising in the hall below did not disturb them immediately. Too engrossed in the discovery of what lips and hands can do, they were beyond considering the outside world. Daphne shivered with previously undiscovered need as Evan's hand slid from her waist to reverently touch uncharted curves, and her lips parted in a startled "oh," allowing him full access to further exploration. Her body quivered with taut expectation beneath his unhurried caresses, and she scarcely heeded the noises indicating the inn was awake and bustling.

Only the sound of a familiar voice rising in cheery greeting belowstairs penetrated their haven. As Gordon's voice battered at their senses, they drew apart and stared at each other in dazed incomprehension.

This wasn't like it was supposed to be. Evan caught his fingers in the curling silk of Daphne's hair and gazed down in disbelief at the fathomless depths of her wide eyes. He winced at the sight of her reddened cheeks where his beard had chafed her, but her kiss-swollen lips beckoned him to further mischief. He had not touched the drawstring of her gown, but one sleeve had slid aside and his wandering hand had pulled the fragile material to expose the creamy curve of her skin beneath. She was thoroughly compromised, and he could see the knowledge of that fact rising in those glorious eyes.

He gently straightened the bodice of her gown and set her back on the mattress, grateful he'd had the sense to don his trousers before climbing into bed with her.

More to himself than to her, he said, "At times like these,

I wonder how much it is you understand, and actually find myself praying that it is very little. I'm not certain that I know myself this morning.''

Daphne knew the feeling, and because she did, she raised her hand to stroke Evan's bristly cheek. "I know enough, my gallant Robin, to know we are both a sight. That does not bode at all well for your explanations to Gordon.''

"No.'' Curtly, Evan rose and checked the water in the pitcher. "There's enough here that you might freshen yourself. I don't know what Gordon plans, but he knows where this room is. I have no doubt that he'll be here shortly.''

Daphne reluctantly rose from the rumpled bed. She did not at all feel herself, but she wasn't certain who she might be either. She just felt as if she were a stranger to herself as she rose from this man's bed and crossed the room to wash away the evidence of what they had been doing.

She didn't dare scrutinize their behavior too closely. It had seemed perfectly right at the time, but now, with the sun shining across the room and Gordon's voice speaking cheerfully below, it suddenly seemed rather sordid. She sent Evan's profile a quick glance as he stood by the window, but as usual, she could read nothing of his expression. Only his stiff stance told her he felt much the same as she.

She scrubbed at her face and used Evan's comb to pull some of the tangles from her hair. To search for her pins would be futile, so she hastily made a loose braid and tied it with a ribbon. She had donned her spencer and overskirt and was fastening the tiny buttons when Evan finally swung around to face her again.

"I cannot offer you the wealth and title that Gordon can, but I can offer you what little protection my name affords. Do not worry on that account. I just wish I were in a better position to protect you from the embarrassment that will follow.''

"You are scarcely to blame. We would be better concerned with how to keep you from the gallows. I cannot believe this is a safe hiding place any longer.''

The rapid knock at the door prevented further reply.

Stealing himself, Evan crossed the room and threw the bolt, placing himself between the visitor and any sight of the room as he opened the door a crack.

"Let me in, you devil, before I call Rollings up here myself." Gordon's normally affable voice, even though spoken in a harsh whisper, came all too clearly into the room. There was nothing of affability in it now.

Daphne stifled a moan of dismay and stepped forward to stand firmly beside Evan.

FIFTEEN

Evan opened the door sufficiently to allow his twin to enter, then bolted it behind him. Gordon stared at the two of them with their rumpled clothes and guilty expressions, and the anger fled his face, replaced with a quiet despair.

"Rollings's story of finding only a couple of drunken newlyweds in the rooms upstairs rather had me concerned, but this isn't what I had imagined. You'll have to give me a minute to sort this one out. I hadn't expected to have to get two of you out of here. The soldiers below aren't in the best of humors for having lost a night of sleep to the cold and wet with nothing to show for it."

Evan did not move from Daphne's side, but neither did he touch her to lend support. Stoically, he faced his brother's condemnation. "It is not as you think. We'll make explanations later, but first we must smuggle Daphne out. It will not be so easy in the daylight."

Daphne met Gordon's questioning look without flinching. She had done this to herself, and oddly, now that the first shock of discovery was over, she felt no shame. She felt sorrow for any hurt she might have caused, and perhaps later she would regret what she had done, but she did not now. "I came through the garden and up the back stairs. My cart is down the alley from the river. I daresay it will have been seen."

Gordon nodded, but Evan was the one who spoke. "You'll have to smuggle her maid back here, pretend it was the maid who had the cart and abandoned it in the storm. If we maneuver it right, you can make it look as if you brought Daphne here to look for her maid."

The two men exchanged glances. In boyhood, they had

played many a trick on their elders by disguising their identity
and seemingly being in two places at once. There had been
incidents with various willing maids and the like, but none
quite like this. Never before had they attempted to deceive
soldiers or hide ladies.

"Daphne, will your maid help? Your aunt is frantic, but
I can think of no other alternative."

"Tillie fancies herself too high in the instep, but Marie
is good for a lark. She's rather silly and giggles too much,
but she'll do whatever you ask." Daphne didn't dare say
more. She wanted to send abject apologies to her aunt, offer
never to darken her door again, propose that a carriage be
sent to take her directly to Bath in disgrace, but she sensed
neither of the twins was ready for that, for all she knew that
was what it would come to. She would let them plan their
strategies and feel as if they protected her. But she knew her
plans of living her life out here had come to an end.

"Fine. I'll go below and mention that I have just
discovered the identity of the 'drunken couple' and say I have
gone to inform you of the sad news." Gordon sent his brother
a sharp look. "While I'm gone, manage to shave, if you will.
And trim his hair up, Daphne. I'll not have him posing as
me looking like that."

He left without further explanation, leaving Daphne more
bewildered than relieved. She turned to the stiff man beside
her. "What does he mean to do? I'll not have Marie's
reputation besmirched because of me."

Evan shrugged and strode toward the washstand. "This
is the way we've always worked. Gordon is good at details.
I'm only good for ideas. You'll have to trust him."

It was Gordon's safety that had put Evan into this position,
Daphne realized. She was just beginning to understand the
strength of the bond between the two men. They would do
anything for each other. But somehow she was beginning
to come between them. She didn't want it to be like that,
and she stared at Evan's turned back with helplessness. He
had grown cold and prickly when Gordon entered the room,
and Gordon had become aloof and unreachable. That wasn't
natural for either man. She couldn't allow this to happen.

Out of respect for her presence, Evan kept his shirt on as
he lathered his face. She perched nervously on the window
ledge, but it wasn't the greenery outside that held her
attention. The broad play of Evan's shoulders as he leaned
to look into the wavy mirror did strange things to her pulse.
When he lifted his chin to work the straight edge underneath,
her toes fairly curled in her boots.

Daphne stared down at her leather halfboots and emitted
a giggle that sent Evan's head swinging in her direction. At
his quizzical stare, she held out her leather-clad toe. "Do
you think Gordon will understand we did nothing if we tell
him I kept my boots on?"

Evan watched the sun dance off her hair and in her eyes
and gave a ragged sigh, releasing all the minutes of tense
guilt and self-condemnation that his brother's presence had
engendered. Miss Daphne Templeton was a world unto herself, and he had to grin in appreciation. The rest of the world
might very well count her mad, but whatever drummer she
marched to, he would like to follow. "He'll only understand
if I offer to die with my boots on, and he's allowed to wield
the weapon. We're well in the briars right now. It will take
some fast talking to bring him down out of the boughs."

Daphne loved it when she could hear the grin in his voice
like that. She rather thought Evan used to laugh more than
he did now. Perhaps war had taken the fun out of his life,
but he needn't be as solemn as Gordon anymore. She felt
satisfaction in having relieved some of his tension. "He will
fly up into the boughs even higher should I begin talking like
that, or Melanie. Your language is quite abominable, you
realize."

Evan grew sober at the mention of his sister, and he
returned to his task. "Right now my only concern is to get
you and Melanie and Grandfather out of here. I don't know
what Gordon is about to allow you to linger."

"I should think it would be more than difficult to order
the earl to do anything he didn't wish to do," Daphne replied
with a trace of acerbity. She didn't wish to be sent away any
longer. Her place was here, whether he liked it or not. Of
course, if Evan didn't want her here, she would have to leave,

but she wasn't prepared to consider that eventuality. "But he was to go with us to Bath this morning. I fear I may have overset Gordon's plans."

"If you're packed, there should be no reason for you not to leave this afternoon. I'll make things right with Gordon while you're gone, and one of us will come for you when it's all over."

Daphne sent his back a quizzical look. Did he truly think this incident could be wiped clean, that Gordon and her aunt would pretend it had never happened? She could not be allowed to accompany Melanie after this. A fallen woman scarcely made a suitable chaperone for a young girl. Evan had made the obligatory offer, but obviously, his heart wasn't in it. The brief hope that had flickered within her died quickly. It was very well and good to imagine two men fighting over her, but experience said that they fought to see which one was stuck with her. It was a good thing she had a level head on her shoulders. Imagination was a dangerous thing.

"I rather think you'll find some objection to that," she replied, "but do not worry. I am quite accustomed to traveling alone and have any number of relatives on whom to call. If my aunt writes them of my disgrace, it will make things a trifle difficult, but I have my own income and need not rely on anyone. I'm certain your grandfather will agree to take Melanie away once you explain to him that there is some danger in keeping her here. Make up a story if you cannot tell the true one. Dangerous highwaymen and drunken soldiers always put fear in the hearts of protective parents."

Evan set his razor aside, wiped his face clean, and stared at Daphne in bemusement. She seemed to have dismissed his offer entirely. She was quite right, he supposed. For all their talk, he had no future, and she no doubt had set her heart on Gordon. Daphne had too much character to settle for a man she did not love or could not care for. Thinking Gordon would abandon her now, she had decided to leave the area entirely. He would have to make things right with Gordon. Of all people, Evan knew how much Daphne needed the home she had found here.

"Do not dwell on it. First, we must get you out. Can you use my knife to trim my hair?"

The task seemed an impossible one, but the chance to touch Evan's thick, golden-brown locks gave Daphne incentive to try. While Gordon raced to smuggle her maid back to the inn, Daphne carefully cut the lightly curling ends of Evan's hair. She did not pride herself into thinking she had accomplished a stylish Brutus cut, but it did not curl about his collar when she finished. If Gordon brought a hat, the top would be well concealed.

The soldiers in the tavern below grinned and nudged each other when the Viscount Griffin arrived escorting a slightly sodden pony cart driven by a lady in silken bonnet and voluminous pelisse. Evidently the lady had reclaimed her cart, for her horse was tied on behind, and the incongruous sight of a thoroughbred trailing a cart pulled by a misbred pony tickled their fancies.

Captain Rollings strolled out to greet the pair, but the lady hurried for the stairs clutching her pelisse closely around her, before he could offer a good day. Griffin stopped to give him a word before swiftly following. Rollings contemplated offering to escort the fallen maid out of town rather than let Miss Templeton suffer the embarrassment, but Miss Templeton had struck him as a rather obstinate-minded young lady. If she had taken a notion to chastise the maid herself, or save her from her wanton ways, he wanted no part of it.

When the aristocratic pair came down again, trailing the brightly smiling maid behind them, Rollings lifted a questioning eyebrow. This time, Miss Templeton saw him. Fastening the silken pelisse, she stopped before him while the top-hatted viscount escorted the maid to the waiting cart.

"Good day, Captain. I hope you are well. Have you seen Miss Dalrymple lately? I have been meaning to stop in and say hello, but the rains have been dreadful."

"Miss Dalrymple has been bemoaning that fact. Do you mind my curiosity in asking why you have come to fetch a maid who obviously shows no remorse for running off?"

Daphne shrugged. "Aunt Agatha is very fond of her and believes she has learned her lesson. I trust you and your men will not speak of this to anyone. The fellow has promised to marry her, so I can only do what is best for her under the circumstances.''

The old rogue his man had described last night scarcely sounded the best kind of husband, but the maid seemed satisfied. Miss Templeton probably had the right of it. It was one way of ridding herself of a troublesome wench. The captain made a polite bow. ''Many would not be so kind. Your generosity is to be applauded.''

Daphne smiled and offered her hand in farewell, then tripped lightly into the overcast day when her escort waited anxiously on his stallion and her maid sat, giggling, in the cart. The soldiers returned to their seats as the trio rode off, leaving the village street empty.

Some while later, a soldier making use of the necessary behind the inn noticed a gentleman striding through the kitchen garden toward the stables. The man wore the same beaver hat and elegantly fitted navy frock coat as the viscount had earlier, and the soldier scratched his head in puzzlement.

Returning to the tavern, he mentioned the viscount's appearance and inquired the reason for his return. Captain Rollings heard the inquiry and slowly came to his feet, a troubled expression on his wide brow. With a curt word, he sent a man upstairs to check on the prospective ''bridegroom,'' then he hurriedly turned his own feet in the direction of the stables.

The viscount was leading a suspiciously familiar bay mare out of the shelter when the good captain intercepted his path. Griffin halted at the man's approach, patting the mare affectionately as he waited.

''You seem in a hurry, Rollings. Is there something I can do for you?'' The viscount's good-natured drawl seemed unhurried and relaxed as the officer stopped in front of him.

''Is that not Miss Templeton's mare you have there?'' Perplexed, Rollings watched the viscount's expression carefully. The young nobleman seemed truly unaware that he was doing anything unusual in returning to the inn so shortly after he had left it in the company of two women.

''Mine, actually. I gave Miss Templeton the use of her

when she arrived. Lady Agatha's stables are rather on the dull side. Did you have some interest in her?'' Gordon played the game with good cheer, reading the captain's suspicions easily from years of experience in such looks. He was only grateful that Evan had had time to disappear down the river path on foot after boldly returning the mare to the stable in the guise of viscount. He should be well on his way back to the lane and the waiting stallion by now.

The captain had the grace to look slightly embarrassed. ''No, it seemed odd you just returned after leaving with Miss Templeton. Was there some trouble?''

''As a matter of fact, yes. The mare seems to have loosened a shoe. Miss Templeton insisted that I return to have it looked at. Actually, I rather think she meant to give her maid a good scold before returning to Lady Agatha's and thought the shoe good excuse to be rid of me. Old Abe says the mare is fine.''

Something was not quite right here, but Rollings couldn't put his finger on it. There was nothing he could do, however, and he let the viscount go on. Not until his man came down to report the ''bridegroom'' had disappeared did Rollings curse and swear and stare at the empty road. He didn't know how they had done it, but he knew he'd been had.

Some miles away, a tense trio drew within sight of the tree-lined drive to the Griffin estate. Rather, a tense duo, for Marie thought the adventure a great lark and laughed and chattered the whole way. Daphne sent her a look of irritation, but her grip on the reins relaxed slightly as they halted on the ridge overlooking the estate. Cautiously, she watched Evan's proud back garbed in the same navy as his brother as he halted to overlook the home he was finally able to return to openly after so many years away.

''Will you go in? Or must you continue this silly charade a little longer?'' Unable to bear the silence, Daphne voiced the most important question on her mind.

Steeling himself for the inevitable confrontation, Evan edged his horse down the road. ''I'll not leave you to face the consequences alone. Gordon said he took Lady Agatha to meet with Grandfather. We'll go there.''

Daphne felt a shiver of apprehension at the implacability in his voice. She was beginning to understand that Evan abided by a very rigid sense of duty that allowed him to overlook any number of relative trivialities, such as the law and people's feelings. She supposed a man could have worse flaws, but this one could be very uncomfortable to live with. She sent him a surreptitious look, but all she could see was the breadth of his back as he approached his home. She found it difficult to believe this was the same man who had held her and kissed her not more than a few hours ago.

The servant who opened the door stared at the man doffing his hat and assisting the lady from the cart. Everyone in the kitchen knew the viscount had gone in search of the missing lady, and here he was returned all right and proper with the lady and her maid unharmed. But it wasn't the same man who had left here earlier this morning. Lord Griffin never wore his hair in such an abominable manner, and his complexion was of a gentlemanly fairness, not this weathered color of a gypsy. Lines of suffering pulled at the corners of this man's mouth, but lines of laughter etched his eyes. It did not seem possible. It could not be. The servant stared as the lady took the gentleman's arm and traversed the steps. A never-to-be-forgotten wink of the gentleman's eye sent the servant's spirits soaring, and a grin broke out on his solemn countenance.

"Master Evan! It is you! May God preserve us and welcome home, sir!"

The smile forming on the gentleman's lips transformed his face to the youthful merriment of years ago. Daphne clung to Evan's arm in astonishment as the staid butler beamed and spouted more words than she had heard from him in a month. She couldn't help noticing Evan's lighter step as he entered his boyhood home and gazed around.

"Nothing's changed, Emery. I suppose there are still kittens in the coal scuttle and tarts in the pantry?"

"They're old enough to scamper about the kitchen, sir. It's time they go to the barns. And Cook just took them out of the oven. Shall I bring you some in the drawing room?"

Dazed, Daphne wondered if the tarts were going to the barn or the kittens to the drawing room, but Evan seemed to understand. He chuckled and nodded and clasped his fingers warmly over her arm.

"You had best show us to the earl and Lady Agatha, Emery. Then bring the tarts. We've neither of us broke our fast, and it's deuced difficult to be scolded on an empty stomach."

The servant grew solemn, aware from years of such confrontations that the young master was in the briars again. The explanation of his appearance months after his funeral would somehow filter down to the staff sooner or later. Properly trained, Emery turned and led the way to the formal salon where the earl paced and Lady Agatha worked sedately at her embroidery.

Both older people glanced up as the young couple entered. Lady Agatha gave a cry of relief and rose to embrace her niece before stopping and staring, puzzled, at Daphne's escort. The earl scowled, took a step forward, then glancing closer at Evan's face, gave a curse that reddened Daphne's ears.

Evan forced a smile to his lips as he released Daphne to her aunt and made a polite bow. "It is always good to be welcomed home, sir, although you could have saved your exuberance until the ladies were out of hearing."

"I ought to box your impertinent ears," the earl growled, taking another step forward as if to carry out his threat.

"Shelce!" Agatha interposed with a warning, clasping Daphne's arm and preventing her niece from rushing back to the young man's side.

To the surprise of both women, the men held out their hands and shook warmly, Evan wincing at the older man's rigorous tug on his injured arm.

"Damned pup, I'll wring your neck this time." The earl still spoke harshly, but there was a hint of some softer emotion behind his words. "Where's that other young rascal? I warrant I'll do more than ring a peal over his ears. It's inexcusable for my heir to behave like this at his age. The

pair of you deserve a caning, always did. I'll have my
explanations now, boy, and they had better be good ones
or you'll be out on your ear in a trice.''

Evan sent a glance to Daphne and her aunt, then shook
his head. ''We had best wait until Gordon returns. It might
be best if I saw the ladies home, first.''

Lady Agatha straightened to her full height. ''If that is you,
Evan Griffin, I'll not be shunted off like some ailing caper-
wit. I've watched your mischief from afar for years, but now
you've involved my niece, I'll know the meaning of this
one.''

Before the argument could continue, a slight figure in
sprigged muslin careened into the room, hesitating only
briefly before flinging herself into Evan's arms.

''Damn you for a lying rogue, Evan Griffin! You ruined
my come-out for naught and I shall kill you for this! To
imagine the servants must tell me of your arrival!''

Evan's dark features puckered with laughter as he gathered
his suddenly grown-up little sister into his arms to prevent
her flailing fists from causing grave injury. ''Whoa, twirp!
Do I deserve no last words before you lay me out?''

That laughing question cut too close to the core and resulted
in a sudden wail as Melanie fell, sobbing, against his
shoulder. Evan paled slightly and threw Daphne a pleading
look. She did not need further explanation to know his plea.

Releasing herself from her aunt's hold, Daphne gently took
Melanie by the arm and disentangled her from her brother's
embrace. ''Go see what is keeping the tea from being served.
Evan is still weak and in need of nourishment,'' she
whispered as she led the younger girl away.

Melanie's sobs dwindled to a sniffle, and hugging Daphne,
she did as told. When Daphne turned back to the room, both
men were staring at her as if amazed by the miracle she had
wrought. Unaware of their stares, she gratefully lowered
herself into the nearest chair to ease the weight from her
aching limb. Adventures might be wildly exciting, but they
were a trifle hard on a person.

''I have never seen a watering pot turned off faster,'' Evan
marveled. Without realizing, he moved next to Daphne's

chair, catching himself only when he lifted his hand to touch her hair. Knowing the mistake such a possessive gesture would be, he hurriedly rested his hand on the chair back and leaned against it for support. This interview would be more trying than he had imagined.

"You're injured!" Agatha exclaimed. "You poor boy, sit down! Wherever could those servants be? Daphne, did you send Miss Griffin to find them? Perhaps, Shelce, you should offer him a little brandy?"

By the time the tea tray arrived, Agatha had whipped her troops in line. Evan sat in a chair beside Daphne, and the earl presided over a decanter of brandy. Melanie was ordered to serve as soon as she returned, and a rather stilted tea party was in progress when Gordon finally burst through the drawing room doors.

SIXTEEN

The normally sedate viscount appeared slightly rattled as he came upon the seemingly harmonious tea party. Ready for battle himself, he found it difficult to rearrange his rampaging emotions. Sending his errant brother a glaring look, he refused Melanie's offer of a cup but accepted the brandy from his grandfather.

The earl watched in amazement as his heir swallowed the strong liquor without flinching. "It is morning yet, as I recollect. Are you in the habit of imbibing heavily before noon?"

Gordon grimaced and set the glass aside. "Only when my twin arises from the dead. I wish to speak to the two of you when you have finished your repast. I'll be waiting in my study. I don't believe I make pleasant company at the moment."

As Gordon started to leave, Melanie gave a shocked cry and glanced from brother to brother with a worried frown. Daphne struggled for some way to ease the situation, but not at all certain that she understood the argument, she felt helpless. She wanted to rise and go to Gordon and somehow reassure him, but he must certainly think her a fallen woman now. She was not certain she could bear his scorn.

Instead, she set her cup aside and offered, "I think it best if I return to my aunt's and finish packing. Melanie, perhaps you ought to go upstairs and do the same."

Having no idea that her friend had been caught out all night and wishing only to hear how Evan had returned from the dead, Melanie appeared prepared to protest. Rising at the same time as Daphne, Evan confirmed her suggestions.

"There are urgent matters Grandfather and Gordon and

I must discuss, brat. You'll be duly informed of my misdeeds later, I promise. Now be gone with you.''

Daphne felt his hand briefly brush hers with a quick squeeze, but she disliked leaving him here to fight the battle alone. She looked to Aunt Agatha for support, but the old lady seemed to be enjoying herself hugely, without any notion of removing herself from the family squabble. Unable to order her elder around, Daphne took herself to the door, with Melanie trailing behind.

No one raised any objection to their leaving, and once outside the drawing room, Daphne gave a small sigh of defeat as the door closed behind her. Melanie glared at her accusingly.

''You knew Evan was alive! Why didn't you tell me?''

Daphne shook her head, feeling a small ache forming between her eyes. ''It was not my place to do so. Evan and Gordon had their reasons for keeping it a secret. I'm certain they'll explain all when the time is right.''

Melanie looked doubtful as voices rose in the room behind them. ''They are very angry. They'll think I'm too young to understand. But I'm not too young. I'm old enough to be wed, aren't I?''

Daphne managed a tired smile. ''Men never think we're old enough. We have to find other ways around them. I'm sorry that our trip to Bath has been postponed, but I believe the earl will be ready to go soon. Perhaps he will explain things if you ask.''

She knew she wouldn't be there when they went. It would be back to her father's house for her. Perhaps an invalid's lot was fitting punishment for allowing herself to think she could manage her own life. She had grown so bold in the idea that she had all but thrown herself into a man's arms to prove she was as much a woman as any. Perhaps her wits were to let after all.

Sending for Marie and parting from Melanie, Daphne set out for her pony cart. She couldn't wait any longer in the hall, listening to the argument over her fate. She had no intention of marrying Evan out of obligation, but they weren't in any humor to hear that yet. They could argue and explain and work things out until everyone was calm again. When they were ready to come to her, she would have her say.

Holding tightly to that thought, Daphne barely waited for Marie to settle in her seat before urging the pony into a small canter. If nothing else, she had brought an end to the neighborhood Robin Hood. The news of Evan's return would be all over the shire before nightfall.

Before she was scarcely out of the drive and on the road, a familiar figure stepped into her path. Marie gave a squeal of fright, but Daphne calmly brought the cart to a halt and gave the one-legged ruffian a chance to catch up.

"I heard some talk in the village, and Evan wasn't in his room. I just wanted to make certain everyone was all right." Rhys had tipped his disreputable hat before he spoke, but he made no other indication of servility as he boldly accosted his better.

Daphne did not find his attitude in the least odd any longer. She spoke with him as an equal and a friend. "He's explaining things to the earl right now. I think Captain Rollings has come too close for comfort. You'd best warn the others."

Rhys nodded, then cast her shadowed eyes a concerned look. "And you, Miss Templeton? Is there aught I can do for you?"

At this rare expression of sympathy from the cynical thief, Daphne had to smile. "Can you wave magic wands and make us perfect? If not, there really is nothing else you can do for me."

Rhys shook his head. "You are already more perfect than any other lady of my acquaintance, and I think you know that. If I can ever be of service to you, please call on me."

She did not find his gallant bow any more odd than his refined speech. Daphne thanked him and sent her pony on down the road. Rhys Llewellyn was an exceptional man. 'Twas a pity he could not find a place among the landed gentry where he so obviously belonged, but he had no right to throw himself away on thieves, either. Still, she had more problems than she could deal with on her own as it was. She didn't need to borrow more.

As she turned the pony cart up the drive to Aunt Agatha's home, a coach and four rolled wildly down the hill in her direction, and she was forced to take the grass to avoid it. A shouted curse and a cry from the driver as he slowed his horses followed, and Daphne watched in amazement as the equipage swayed to a halt just beyond her. There was something vaguely familiar about that curse.

A sensible female would have taken to her heels and fled for safety from the madman on the coach, but Daphne waited in curiosity as the door flew open and a slim, compact figure leapt out, followed by a slower, sturdier one. Rather than running to them in greeting, Daphne continued to sit and stare in dazed recognition. This really could not be happening to her. No day could be as bad as this one. Surely whoever was in charge of punishment had meted out more than enough justice for one day.

"What in the name of all that is holy are you doing in that cart, daughter?" The sturdier man shoved forward to confront his frozen child.

"Father?" Questioningly, Daphne stared into the face of the man she had seen every day of her life until she turned nineteen. She had seen him briefly on holidays since then, but the distance between London and Gloucester was too great to cover frequently. She had not quite realized that distance was cut in half by her move to Devon. "What are you doing here?"

"What am I doing here?" he exploded. "Can I not come to see the man my daughter intends to marry, even though she doesn't have the respect to tell her own father? There is something havey-cavey about all this, and now your aunt's addlepated servants tell me you've been gone all night and half the neighborhood's out searching for you, and you come riding up like the Queen of May, if you please. And you want to know what *I'm* doing here?"

"Father, please." The younger man put a steadying hand on his father's shoulder. His parent's voluble tirades were well known but not conducive to explanations. Michael turned an expressive look to his sister. "Perhaps we ought

to allow Daphne to return to the house and refresh herself
before we bombard her with questions.''

"I would be grateful for that," Daphne managed to
murmur politely, if not actually gratefully. She was much
too tired to think of explanations quite yet.

"Then get in the carriage with me and let your brother
drive that dangerous contraption. I knew my sister was all
about in her wits, but what she could be about by allowing
you to—"

Daphne picked up her reins and adamantly refused to
budge. "Leave off, Papa. I am in less danger here than you
are if that's William driving the coach. I'll not be bullied
and set upon like a child."

Leaving her father ranting and raving and Michael to
comfort him, Daphne urged the pony into motion. If Gordon
was surprised at his grandfather's overweening concern over
their supposed marriage, she was doubly so by her father's
appearance. She really had not expected Michael to break
the news without her permission. She had insisted on privacy.
How could he abuse her trust so?

While the carriage was lumberingly coming about, Daphne
sent the pony into a sharp clip and reached the house first.
She intended to wash and don fresh clothes before this
interview. It would be lovely to have a few hours sleep, also,
but she could see that wouldn't be on the agenda any time
soon. The ache behind her eyes grew a little fiercer.

She could hear her father's roar from her room as she
hastily undressed with the help of a disapproving Tillie. She
washed more quickly than she had intended as she imagined
the confrontation should Evan come riding up to make his
obligatory offer. She shuddered at the prospect. It was one
thing to reject the man who had compromised her when she
was the only one affected. It was quite another under the
stern eyes of father and brother.

By the time Daphne was done, had she a black gown to
wear she would have worn it, so low had her spirits sunk.
Instead, she found a particularly drab brown and pinned her
hair in a coronet of braids rather than allow even a hint of

curl to escape. She had set out to be a spinster and so she would be. Her father would have to see that somehow.

Wondering how on earth she would explain away her letter and Gordon's fictitious suit, Daphne trailed down the stairway to her aunt's front drawing room. There didn't seem to be any feasible way of sending her family off before Evan arrived. Even should he take the time to get some rest first, they would still be here when he came. And she knew he would come. His sense of duty would not allow him to act otherwise.

Michael was staring out the front window at the rolling moor while her father sat edgily in Aunt Agatha's favorite horsehair chair. He rose instantly at Daphne's appearance, giving her dowdy attire a scathing look.

"I sent you to London to dress like that? Where's that yellow thing you had on? If you're to wed a viscount, you ought to dress the part."

"Papa, I'm not to wed a viscount." Daphne sent her brother's back a murderous look.

Michael turned in time to intercept it and gave an apologetic shrug. "Father was visiting when your letter arrived. A letter from you is such an auspicious occasion that I could not keep it from him without causing undue concern."

Daphne sighed and sank down in the nearest chair. Never in her life had she ever done anything the least little bit improper until she met Evan Griffin. And her one attempt at doing anything just the tiniest bit out of the way had not only been caught out, but blown into a fiasco far out of proportion to the error. Never again would she try to be something she was not.

"I don't suppose you took the time to find Robert Griffin before you came galloping out here?" she asked with resignation.

"Of course I did. He was at the club the night the letter arrived. He seemed amenable to the suggestion, but we made no definite plans. I thought it wisest to talk to you first."

Daphne allowed the horror of this knowledge to slowly seep through her. Robert Griffin, the twins' dangerous uncle, now thought she and Gordon were to be married. Despite the heavy rain, Michael had had time to arrive from London. That meant Robert had had an equal amount of time to arrive. And the entire Griffin family was neatly ensconced in their home, all in one place. Could anyone be so devilish as to . . . ? Surely not. She stared wildly at her brother.

"What kind of man is he?" she demanded.

Michael looked vaguely startled. "I scarce know him, Daph. He's considerable older than I and belongs to a fast set that I have never aspired to. He did not cut me for my daring to intrude in his affairs. He even seemed vaguely amused. Why do you ask?"

Daphne rose and nervously clasped and unclasped her hands as she paced the faded carpet. She ignored the vague ache in her leg as her thoughts tumbled about. Surely the twins knew the urgency of the situation, but they did not know that Michael had carried out his task with such alacrity. They might not even know the roads to London were open now. Caught up in their argument, they might not even consider it until it was too late. And if Evan came riding over here alone . . .

It did not bear considering. As her brother and father watched her in amazement, she straightened her shoulders and started for the door. "We must notify the Griffins at once. If your horses are weary, I'll send for Aunt Agatha's."

"Daphne Elaine! You come back here at once, do you hear me?"

Her father's roar scarce made an impression as she went in search of someone to bring a carriage around. Perhaps she ought just to send a message. To unleash her father on the already disturbed Griffin household was not an act of kindness. But she acted on an intuition that she could not explain, even to herself.

Her father and Michael followed her into the hall, but Daphne was already calling for her bonnet and gloves, and the carriage that had just arrived with her family was now pulling up to the door once more.

Michael caught his sister's elbow as she tied her bonnet strings. "What's this all about, Daph?"

"It's not for me to explain. Why don't you and father rest and have some tea or something? I will be right back." She could only try. It really did not matter if she failed to dissuade them.

"Rest!" her father roared behind them. "Do you think me some senile invalid that I need rest while my daughter gallivants about the neighborhood without so much as a chaperone?"

"Aunt Agatha is there. I'm certain she makes quite an adequate chaperone." Daphne took the umbrella the servant handed her and started for the door.

"We're coming with you!" Lord Thomas Templeton hurried after his impetuous daughter and, shrugging his shoulders, his son followed in his footsteps.

Daphne did not try to speak as she stared, white-faced, out the carriage window as it traveled the lane she had just traversed. Perhaps she was just overwrought and seeing goblins in the shadows, but she could not help but search the hedgerows as they passed by. Mayhap it would be better if Captain Rollings stationed his men around the Griffin estate, only she could think of no way of persuading him to do so.

None of this seemed quite real. Yet she could not imagine a man like Evan living the desperate life of a criminal in the woods without reason, nor Gordon allowing him to do so if he had not thought it safest. She had to trust the twins and warn them.

"Daphne, you will scare us half to death if you do not tell us what is wrong," Michael said, intruding cautiously upon her reflections. His father's stiff-lipped silence did not bode well, and he sent the older version of himself an anxious look.

"There is naught wrong," Daphne replied absently. "I am quite fine, if rather annoyed."

"Annoyed, she says. Ha!" Lord Thomas snorted *sotto voce*.

Daphne ignored him. "I pray you will not cause a scene. The Griffins have suffered several hardships in past months, and tempers are not of the best. If you should make mention of my private confidence, I shall never speak to either of you again.''

"Havey-cavey, that's what it is," his lordship continued muttering.

"It does not sound quite the thing, Daph," Michael objected. "Why should the viscount keep his suit a secret? Father is right. He has not conducted himself at all with honor."

"Oh, do be quiet, Michael," Daphne finally snapped, turning to face her stiff-laced brother. None of her family was of any great stature, but Michael was a well-looking man with an air of pride and self-assurance. That he was also so high in the instep that he couldn't see the ground had always been the barrier between them, but she knew he meant well. "I never said Gordon had proposed. I am certain when and if he wishes to do so that he will be all that is proper. But not now."

She said it with such finality that they traveled the rest of the distance in silence.

Evan was just mounting his horse as the carriage rumbled up the drive. He halted his stride as he caught sight of Daphne's pale face in the window and handed the reins back to the stableboy as the reckless driver rocked the ancient equipage to a halt. He glanced at the surly, slouch-hatted coachman in surprise but hurried forward to assist Daphne as the door flew open.

To his further surprise, a slender man with broad shoulders and chestnut hair descended first. A feeling much like that of the one before battle gripped Evan's stomach, but he came to a stiff halt beside the carriage door and engaged in a bout of eye-to-eye combat with the stranger as Daphne started to step out.

Both men held out their hands, but Daphne could only see Evan. She reached for him gratefully, taking solace from the strength of his clasp as he helped her to the ground. He did not release her immediately as she turned to wait for the third passenger to descend, and they waited in silence as Lord

Thomas clung to the carriage door, cursed the coachman, and descended with an angry thump, glaring at Evan all the while.

"I suppose you're the bumptious wretch who means to ruin my daughter," were the first words he spoke.

Daphne hid a resigned smile at Evan's jerk of shock. She pressed his fingers reassuringly and made the introductions.

"Papa was with Michael when he received my letter," she explained hurriedly. "They've already spoken with your uncle."

Evan's jaw locked in a tight knot at this news, but he managed a grim bow of greeting. "Your haste is to be commended, my lord. Do come in. I'm certain my grandfather will be pleased to meet you."

Evan longed to pull Daphne aside and question her privately, but the time for that was past. Her father's arrival actually made things easier. He could ask for her hand and arrange to have her spirited to Bath all in one day. The only difficulty might be that Lord Thomas had come expecting his daughter's betrothal to a wealthy viscount, not a near-to penniless ex-soldier.

"Grandfather?" the irascible old man grumped. "What the deuce do I want with your grandfather? It's you I've come to see. There's something havey-cavey here and I mean to get to the bottom of it. Where's that sister of mine? Fine idea she has of acting the chaperone while her niece is all about the countryside endangering life and limb in that ramshackle vehicle."

Amusement began to dance about Evan's lips as he listened to the older man's complaints and watched the exasperation on Daphne's mobile features. If only he could take her in his arms and tell her everything would be all right . . . But he had not yet earned the right for that. He contented himself with keeping her hand on his arm as he directed the Templetons toward the drawing room, where his brother and the earl waited.

SEVENTEEN

Gordon swung around in surprise as his brother re-entered the room after so recently leaving it. His eyes widened at the sight of a primly unhappy Daphne on Evan's arm, trailed by two men whose family resemblance marked their names even before introductions were made. As he realized their purpose here, his resolve firmed, and he swiftly came forward to greet both men.

The Templeton men stared in some dismay and bewilderment as a duplicate of the man they had just accosted came forward to take their hands and stand beside Daphne. She stood between these twin giants, her hands resting familiarly on both their arms much as if she were perched between the arms of a comforting chair. Despite the concealment of her bonnet and pelisse, she appeared quite natural and proud there, not at all the diffident invalid they thought her. And the looks the twins gave her delicate beauty were not that of pity or sympathy. Lord Thomas harrumphed loudly, and Michael stepped aside to greet his aunt.

"Which one of you is the viscount?" Daphne's father demanded.

"What's it to you?" The earl strolled from his corner, brandishing his walking stick as if it were a riding crop.

The sturdy Lord Thomas swung around fearlessly. "She's my daughter and I've a right to know!"

Gordon stepped into the breach, clasping Daphne's hand firmly with his and tugging her gently toward their elders, away from Evan. She had no choice but to follow without making a scene, and he seized the advantage. "I'm Gordon Griffin, sir. Your arrival is a timely one. I have just been discussing with my grandfather my desire to marry your daughter."

Daphne felt her knees give way, and she clutched Gordon's arm desperately for support. She sent his serious mien an aghast look, but he never turned to notice it. Why was he doing this? She had enjoyed their flirtation, toyed with the idea of being a viscountess, but she had known it was only a fancy. Did she really think that one silly letter had placed him in this position?

Lord Thomas harrumphed again and gave the young viscount a considering look. He was a handsome devil, but then so was the man behind him, glowering like an evil genie. He hadn't missed his daughter's expression, either. A woman didn't look at the man she wanted to marry as if she had been poleaxed when he asked for her hand. His nose for the suspicious twitched mightily.

"Is that so? And have you discussed it with my daughter?"

Gordon's lips tightened. "I have tried, but it was not seemly to ask too much when I was not in a position to ask your permission first. We have known each other but a short while. I thought it wisest to give Daphne time to consider the idea."

The other young man seemed prepared to explode, Lord Thomas noted with satisfaction. He turned to acknowledge the earl standing silently beside him. "You know aught of this? The girl's my daughter and one of a kind, but as much as I love her, I can't fancy you're happy with the idea of your heir marrying into a country family like ours."

The earl's mouth opened and clamped closed. He looked from one twin to the other and shook his head. Evan had just overridden all his brother's objections a moment ago to insist that he was obliged to offer his name to the girl. But Gordon's suit had first brought him here and his heir seemed most vehement now. This was one fracas where he wouldn't intervene, as much as he was tempted to.

"My grandsons are old enough to know their minds," Shelce announced, praying fervently that was so. He looked to Agatha for confirmation, and she nodded smilingly.

Taking up her needlework, Agatha leaned comfortably back into her chair. "I'm happy to hear you believe your brother's story about last night, Gordon. I knew Daphne could do nothing improper. And Evan is a gentleman, after all. He would never harm a lady, particularly his brother's intended."

She could not more successfully have exploded the waters had she shot a cannonball into their midst. Lord Thomas turned a wrathful gaze on the darker twin, and Michael stepped forward as if to demand immediate satisfaction. Thinking he had neatly rescued the situation without Daphne's impropriety being revealed, Gordon appeared resigned. Only Evan stoically showed nothing of his thoughts as attention swung to him.

His gaze met and held Daphne's as he spoke. "I would never do anything intentionally to harm Miss Templeton. I should hope that I would only act in her best interests. Daphne, perhaps you and your aunt would join Melanie to prepare for your journey to Bath. I think it time that Gordon be apprised of the news you have brought."

For once, Daphne felt only relief at thus being dismissed, and she gave Evan a grateful, if somewhat weary smile. He looked as tired as she, and she felt a small measure of alarm at the thought. What if Robert were somewhere outside now, looking to cause harm? Evan was the only one with any training to deal with such a situation. He had to get some rest.

"I can leave with my father. Do you think Captain Rollings might escort Lord Shelce and Melanie as far as the toll road? You must get some rest and have someone tend your shoulder."

"Wait just one moment, young lady!" Lord Thomas roared. "You'll not be going anywhere until I get the meaning of this. What have you and this damned upstart got to say to anything? I'll hear this whole tale before I ove myself an inch further!"

Evan sent his twin a speaking look, and gauging the urgency of the situation, Gordon acted. "Explanations will come, but with all due respect you must bear with us a moment. Daphne has made a very good point. If you will excuse me, I shall be back directly."

Daphne breathed easier as he left, no doubt to summon Captain Rollings. This foolish argument over her betrothal had delayed their departure to inordinate lengths. It might even be dangerous to leave now. Surely there was safety in numbers. Her gaze returned briefly to Evan, but he had turned his back to stare out the windows overlooking the park. Recognizing the wisdom of that, Daphne went to take a seat beside her aunt. She didn't know why Agatha had done what she did, but she supposed her misbehavior had to come out sometime.

While Gordon was gone, Evan began a very expurgated version of the events leading up to last night for the benefit of Lord Thomas and Michael. It was evident that his grandfather had already heard it. There would have been no other way of explaining how she had come to be in Evan's room all night. Daphne wished she could read the earl's expression, but it was as closed as Evan's. Michael's honest visage expressed surprise and alarm as the story unfolded. Her father's face she did not need to read however. He was quite capable of making his thoughts heard even as Evan spoke. His mutters and curses filled every pause in the story.

Gordon returned to the room just as Lord Thomas rose to his feet with a shaking fist and a loud curse in reference to Evan's origins, and a demand for immediate reparations to his daughter's honor. With Gordon returned to the line of fire, he set his artillery on the viscount, too, until all the room filled with the shouts of men demanding to be heard.

Michael tried to press his father to silence. The earl vehemently protested the insult to his grandsons. And the twins rose to the defense of each other and the protection of Daphne. The cacophony was tremendous and pointless, for none heard a word of the other.

Agatha sat smiling into her embroidery. Daphne gave her an amazed look and started to rise to lend her pleas to Michael's, but her aunt held her arm.

"Let them bluster and let it out of their systems. Then we'll have some sense. Have you decided which of them you prefer? I should think you would have your choice when the fur stops flying."

Daphne shook her head. Choice? She had come here a month ago prepared to be a spinster. She was not at all certain that she was prepared to give up that decision in favor of men who thought her incapable of directing her own life. Her gaze fell thoughtfully on the darker twin, who had retreated to watching the window again. It was evident he had already resigned her to his brother without a protest. She didn't see much choice in that.

"I don't give a devil for your reasons!" Lord Thomas shouted above Gordon's reasoning protest. "My daughter's been compromised and I mean to see her wed. Dashed if I care which of you does it, but it will be pistols at dawn if one of you don't step forward. My Daphne's a good girl. I'll not see her ruined by your frippery notions. Murderin' bounders and highwaymen! The devil take the lot of you. I ain't certain there's a one of you deserves her."

Evan smiled at that, though only his reflection in the window noted it. The blustery old man might just be right. He and Gordon had played a fool's game from the first, and Daphne had been the innocent victim. She made a lovely victim, he had to admit, with her delicate beauty and wounded eyes and defiant spirit that had turned both him and his brother head over heels. He turned and placed his back to the draperies so he could better observe her reaction to the scene swirling around them.

She seemed quite confused and bewildered by all the shouting. There were shadows under her eyes from the late hours they had kept with their foolish talk of nonexistent futures. He noted again how frail she was, the thin skin pulled tight over cheekbones of the most delicate grace. Her fine, longfingered hands clasped and unclasped in her lap, forbidden the outlet of needlework that her aunt used. She needed the comfort and security of a home where she could be protected and treated gently as she deserved. And he could not offer it. He had meant to try, but Gordon was making it all too obvious that he was the better choice. Even now, he was pacifying their growling elders, bringing order out of chaos, and restoring peace to Daphne's drawn features. Evan's only inclination had been to spirit Daphne off to Gretna and put an end to the argument once and for all. He could see already that that was not a satisfactory solution.

"My heir is right." The earl spoke into a sudden lull in the roar. "The choice should be Miss Templeton's since both my grandsons have shown their desire for this marriage. I cannot but think there ought to be more time before making such a momentous decision, but if you insist upon it, Templeton, I'll not stand in the way."

Daphne felt the sudden silence and realized she had become the center of attention. She had not been seriously attending to the conversation, having already made up her own mind. To be set abruptly in the midst of it left her even more bewildered.

Gordon resolved her confusion by coming to kneel beside her chair. His coat of blue superfine fit superbly over strong shoulders and fell gracefully over narrow hips. The white linen at his throat was still immaculate despite the day's activities. A gold watch fob was the only adornment on his discreetly striped buff vest. He was every inch the nobleman from the crown of his golden head to the tips of his polished Hessians. And he lifted Daphne's hand with great respect and gentleness as he spoke.

"I realize we have been arguing your fate with all the selfishness of our natures, but it's time that you make your desires known, my love. I've tried to tell you of how I feel. I think you are not unaware of it. Could you possibly find it in your heart to forgive my slowness in speaking my mind and accept my suit?"

Gordon was all that a lady could want in a husband. He was kind, generous, intelligent, respectful—she had run over the list in her mind a dozen times. And now he was opening himself to public rejection for her sake, to give her a choice. She did not know if he did it out of sympathy or honor or a misplaced sense of gratitude, but none of these were enough to base a marriage on. Yet she could not bring herself to reject him in front of all these people. She owed him that much for his consideration.

Daphne clasped his hand between hers and tried to express with her touch what she could not say with words. "I am more than honored, my lord. I am overwhelmed. But I do not think this is the time or the place to decide. You must see to the care of your family first. You, of all people, know that any harm that has come to me has been of my own doing. I would not have your suit from fear of the consequences I must face. I am quite content to face them on my own."

Evan felt a wave of both pain and relief wash over him as the room broke out in a babble of angry voices once again. But this time, he was able to avert it. Giving the window another quick glance, he stepped forward and with a voice that carried on the field of battle, he announced, "I believe Captain Rollings has arrived. Shall I turn myself in now or wait until he is introduced to the company?"

The almost ascetic features of the older man were reflected in the carriage window as he stared pensively out on the rolling moor. His blond hair had grown somewhat thin and receded with age, but his slender height and aristocratic features showed none of the ravages of time. His thin lips were pressed together as if in anger, but his companion disregarded the expression.

"After all these years, why are you doing this now? You said yourself you made a bundle on that last roll. Why grovel at their call when you don't need to?"

The older man returned his attention to his son. Hugh was a well-looking lad of four and twenty, the dark locks he had inherited from his mother framing a face not quite handsome, but certainly striking. There had been very little wealth with which to spoil him, and certainly little in the way of attention or affection from either of his parents, but he had grown up passably enough despite this neglect. There might be hope for him yet.

Patiently, Robert explained, "Since I am in need of nothing, I am arriving at their request, not mine. I do not know what it is that they want, but I will not be the one groveling."

"Well, it seems deuced odd that they acknowledge your existence after a score or more years. If it were not for mother's insistence, I would not have joined you. We've lived without them all our lives. I, for one, have no need of them now."

Hugh's father suddenly looked weary, but his hands continued resting easily on his elegant walking stick. "Family and connections can be important. Your brother has already discovered that, to his grief. I'll do what I can to make it easier for you. You should not have to continue paying for my mistakes."

The young man grimaced irritably but did not belabor the point. "I don't see why my cousin Gordon did not make the request himself. It's deuced shabby of him to go through his fiancée's brother."

"My nephews were still in leading strings when last I saw them. I cannot know their minds. It could very well be a madcap notion of his fiancée's. Women have strange fancies. You have only to consider your mother to know the truth of that."

"Do not bring my mother into this. She has done the best she could, under the circumstances."

Robert Griffin sighed. "Neither of us has ever done the best we could, but it is too late now to correct that. At least give me credit for having married her. I have yet to see her reasoning in refusing the name it cost me so much to give."

Hugh knew they had touched upon the one sensitive issue that still rankled after years of separation. His parents had kept different households since his birth, for excellent reasons on both their parts. The idea of two such self-centered, arrogant, irresponsible people living together was far beyond his limited ability to imagine, but he had spent the better part of his life speculating on the question between them now.

Carefully, he voiced his opinion on the matter. "I do believe she was trying to protect you, sir. All the *ton* thinks her your former mistress. There is no credit in being leg-shackled to a common actress."

Robert sent his younger son a skeptical look, then leaned back in his seat to consider the scenery once again. The damned fool woman in a fit of temper or passionate loyalty might have thought to protect him once, but it was at a high cost to his sons now. The time had come to rectify the mistake.

Trying not to hope, he cursed the miserable wilderness around them and gave no thought to the next few hours.

EIGHTEEN

Captain Rollings let his gaze roam over the respectable occupants of the elegant drawing room. Scattered about on satin settees and velvet upholstery, illuminated by crystal lamps, protected from the dreary weather by silk-lined walls and brocade draperies, they possessed all the trappings of the wealth and indolence he craved. He could not believe half their tale, and his gaze strayed back to the one man who remained standing.

Damn Evan Griffin for making a bloody fool of him. An officer who bought his commission was no trained soldier. Captain Evan Griffin must have nine lives to have survived the war. Rollings swung his gaze to the pampered heir sprawling in the chair beside his fiancée, watching his every move. They were lying to him, he felt certain, but what was at the root of their lies he could not comprehend.

The wily old earl the captain disregarded entirely. He was too old to be of consequence, and his conniving days were past. The women he disregarded, too. The younger two were good to look upon, but his tastes ran to the lively miss back in town, not the elite atmosphere of these fragile creatures. Women had no thoughts of their own, so he would find no truth there.

He briefly considered Lord Thomas and his son but could not quite place them in the way of things. The older man appeared ready to burst a blood vessel, and the younger posed little threat. He was obviously no Corinthian, and of little influence.

That left the twins. It was always the twins. Even now, seeing them together, he found it hard to believe they were so much alike. They had tricked him, but he was not exactly certain as to how yet. It didn't matter. Time was growing short, and they had left him only this one opportunity. It wouldn't be the same as nabbing the highwayman, but with the two of them alive, there was little else he could do. He heartily regretted the murderous rage that had set these events in motion, but it was too late to turn back now.

Rollings nodded reluctantly, his gaze returning to the viscount and his fiancée on the settee. Miss Templeton didn't appear too happy about being sent away. He had been of the opinion that all females preferred the fashionable districts of Bath to the isolation of Devon, but that was none of his concern. She was harmless enough, as was Miss Griffin. The task should be quite simple.

"If the matter is as urgent as you say, my men and I will be ready within the hour, my lord." Rollings made a formal bow to the earl.

"Good, good." The old man rose to dismiss the young officer. "The gels will be waiting. I'll have the carriage brought 'round."

Rollings stepped quickly from the room, leaving a vacuum of silence behind. No one seemed pleased with the decisions made here today, but now that they were made, none dared risk further argument. Daphne glanced at Evan, but he seemed a million miles away. She could only be content that he had been persuaded from making a confession of guilt. The captain had obviously believed very little of his story of his return from the dead, but that was of no consequence for the nonce. What mattered was putting an end to the danger to Gordon. She wasn't at all certain they had found a satisfactory conclusion to that problem. And it was obvious the twins weren't happy about the earl's decision to remain with them, thereby increasing the number of targets. But she had no influence in their argument. She could only agree to accompany Melanie to safety and hope for the best.

They decided for the sake of convenience and comfort it would be best to take only Daphne's maid with them in Gordon's landau. The rest of their baggage and Melanie's maid could follow later. While Melanie went upstairs to complete her packing, Daphne thought to take her aunt's vehicle to gather up her belongings and Tillie's, but the twins became adamant that she not travel anywhere without an escort. Since no one could agree on who that escort would be, it became obvious that she would have to wait for Captain Rollings to return with his men. She had very little left to do. It would just be a matter of carrying down her trunk and listening to Tillie's hysterics for not being given better notice. That was better than watching Gordon and Evan glaring at each other over so small a detail.

She listened in resignation as her father and Michael argued over whether they ought to follow in their carriage or stay to await Robert Griffin's arrival, in whatever form it took. To Daphne, the unknown uncle seemed more a character from a fanciful novel than a real person, and Daphne was finding it harder and harder to believe in him. After all, she had been here over a month and there had been no incidents that she knew of. Perhaps the twins were guilty of overactive imaginations. Accidents happened all the time. Their father's death and Evan's fall could easily have been accidents. That was much easier to believe than that one's family might try to kill one.

But in the end, Daphne acquiesced quietly to being bundled into a carriage with Melanie and her trunk. She needed time to think, and it would be much easier without the pressure of the men pushing her this way and that. Maybe when this was all over they would forget her indiscretion and let her live her own life, but she wasn't at all certain that she even wanted that anymore. Evan's caresses had awakened a longing inside her that she could no longer pretend didn't exist. If she closed her eyes, she could feel him next to her now, and her imagination easily sketched in what might have happened had Gordon not arrived to stop them. She didn't know the details of physical intimacy, but she could feel them inside herself, and she wasn't certain she could live without them forever.

But those were scarcely suitable thoughts for a fashionable young lady on her way to Bath. Daphne discreetly kissed her father and brother's cheeks in farewell, ignored Evan as he ignored her, accepted Gordon's assist into the carriage, and wrapped her fingers primly in her lap as Captain Rollings inspected the carriage harness and supervised the loading. He had two of his men with him, apparently the only two capable of riding or fortunate enough to own horses.

Daphne tried to remember the conversation she had overheard once on the differences between infantry and cavalry, but she could only remember the young ladies of her acquaintance exclaiming over the dashing uniforms of the Hussars. Evan had been a Hussar, she knew, but she had never seen him in uniform. She didn't think Captain Rolling's uniform was that of a cavalry man, and she remembered Evan's saying the soldiers who hunted him didn't have horses. Perhaps Gordon had offered part of his stable for the soldier's use. Captain Rollings had evidently brought his own horse, for she remembered his chase of the highwayman. Perhaps officers were allowed horses.

These ruminations carried Daphne through the final farewells. If she thought only neutral thoughts, she could get through this without a tear. She really didn't think she would ever come back, but that was one of those things she had to try not to think about. She lifted her lace mitten in a last wave from the window as the carriage jolted into motion.

She tried to memorize their faces as they stood there on the stone steps, watching the carriage drive off. Evan stood aloof, his arms crossed forbiddingly across his wide chest, a black frown between his eyebrows. Gordon stood beside the earl, lending his arm in support. Whatever his expression, it was not so easily visible as Evan's frown. Michael stood with hands in pockets beside his father, who held a large handkerchief to his nose. Daphne smiled at that. Perhaps her father wasn't quite so bad as she once had painted him. They might deal well with each other now that he realized she was no longer a child and had no intention of becoming an invalid for his sake.

As the carriage rolled down the drive and into the lane, she looked for the bold uniform of Captain Rollings, but he obviously rode on ahead. She had heard the others ordered to ride behind, and she did not envy them their position behind the mud-spattering wheels of the vehicle. Perhaps they would ride far behind.

Melanie looked solemn as she stared at the seat before them, and her voice was less than its usual exuberant tone when she spoke. "Will you tell me what is happening? I am so tired of being treated as a baby."

It really ought to be one of the family doing the explaining, but the earl had refused to accompany them as originally planned. And Melanie really had a right to know some of the story. How much, was the problem. Daphne turned her attention to this problem and away from her own, and haltingly set out on explanations of events she wasn't at all certain she understood or believed herself.

The carriage pulled to the side to allow another vehicle to pass by in the narrow lane. Both Daphne and Melanie glanced up in surprise for few others in the area possessed carriages and those few seldom had need to come this way. The vehicle looked little more than a hired hackney with the curtains drawn, and they could only speculate on the occupants. Daphne felt a qualm of fear but steadied it by telling herself that a dangerous murderer was unlikely to drive up to the gate in broad daylight in a hired coach.

The carriage traveled faster now, as if the small delay had put them behind schedule. Daphne winced as a wheel hit a rut washed out by the rain, throwing her against the window. She had gradually overcome her fear of carriages, but not of speed, and she clenched her fingers nervously. Such haste was not only unnecessary, but dangerous. Drawing a deep breath to summon her courage, she beat her umbrella against the driver's door for attention. This was as bad as riding with her father's Wild Willie. The two old men were devoted to each other, and they were quite likely to die together if her father didn't pension the coachman off.

The carriage only slid into another muddy rut and lurched and drove on, the driver heedless of her angry rap. Daphne pursed her lips, planning the stiff scold she would deliver once they reached Aunt Agatha's. She might as well take William on as to continue at this pace.

When they rolled right past the drive to Aunt Agatha's, Daphne flew into a rage. This was the outside of enough! Melanie stared in wonder as her mild companion beat furiously at the driver's door, then tried to unfasten the window so she might give vent to her fury. The carriage jostled and rocked so, she was only thrown back into her seat for her efforts.

Melanie attempted to reassure. "Captain Rollings will see the error shortly and come back for us. He must have ridden on ahead and the driver did not see where he went."

Daphne shook her head. "Gordon's driver knows the way as well as I do. And he does not treat his equipage with such contempt. There is something wrong here, but I cannot know what."

Melanie's eyes grew wider. However vaguely informed by Daphne's expurgated explanations, she understood enough to know they could be in danger. She pushed back the curtains and tried to find the reassuring sight of the uniformed soldiers. "Do you think something happened back there when we pulled over? I heard nothing untoward, but I was listening to your tale and not to what was happening outside."

Daphne frowned. "But the soldiers are armed. They could not be replaced without our hearing their struggle. Perhaps we are imagining things. Did you notice the driver when we left? Perhaps he is not Gordon's usual driver but one of the soldiers in disguise." Or Wild Willie, she thought to herself. It would be just like her father to assign his favorite servant to the task of seeing her to safety. Safety, indeed! She caught the carriage strap as the wheel hit a rock and sent them bouncing off the leather roof.

Melanie shook her head. "I cannot say for certain, but I would have noticed had he worn other than Gordon's livery." She pressed her face against the glass, straining for some sign of their guards.

Earlier, Daphne had wondered how this day could be any worse. Now she knew. It was becoming quite obvious this was not any normal ride. Whether they were racing away from something or toward something, she could not detect, but the chances of their getting anywhere in one piece seemed increasingly small. This was no solid wooden mail coach meant for a team of six and high speeds, and this rutted lane was no improved turnpike. The fragile wheels of the carriage

and the delicate legs of Gordon's high-stepping horses could
not keep this reckless pace for long. Daphne grimly clenched
her teeth and hands and prayed rapidly.

Melanie gave an eager cry and grabbed Daphne's hand
as she bounced excitedly in her seat. " 'Tis Rhys! Oh, see,
Daphne, he's riding over the moor. He must have been a
Hussar like Evan! I've never seen anyone take the hedgerow
like that. Has he come to rescue us?''

Her companion's excited comments sounded more as if
this were some splendid game in which the best man always
won. Daphne wouldn't rate Rhys as the best man in any
game, but she would take her chances with him before this
mad driver. "We'll have to help him. He can't stop the
carriage all by himself.''

Daphne threw herself into the seat behind the driver and
fumbled for the latch to the driver's door. Melanie grew
suddenly solemn as Daphne's words took new meaning.

"Surely he won't try to stop the carriage alone. The
soldiers . . .'' She couldn't express the horror of that thought.

Daphne jerked open the door, caught a glimpse of scarlet
and not Gordon's discreet gray and black livery, before a
sudden bounce slammed the door shut again. The shock left
her breathless, and her mind spun in useless circles. Was
Rhys the one they ran from? Could he have been sent to
deliver them to the murderers? Or had Captain Rollings gone
berserk? Perhaps he didn't recognize the rider approaching.
But why would Rhys be so recklessly racing after them if
there weren't trouble? And where was Evan?

That thought struck even greater fear in her heart. Evan
trusted Rhys. If Rhys had turned traitor, what would he have
done to Evan? And the others? It was becoming more than
obvious that if they were in trouble, it shouldn't just be Rhys
out there chasing across the moor. All the Griffins and her
father and brother should be galloping down the road.

The sound of gunfire startled Daphne from her thoughts.
Melanie gave a terrified scream and glued herself to the
window where the passing landscape had become a blur of
motion. Daphne reached to struggle with the door to the
driver's box again. She didn't know what she would

accomplish by doing so, but she could not sit helplessly and go to her destruction.

Looking out, she could see no sign of the driver's livery, and she did her best to school her rising panic. She could not tell for certain, but from the slope of the land in front of them and the blur of trees, she very much suspected they were heading toward the river. Taking that narrow bridge at this pace was foolhardy to an extreme, and Daphne glanced anxiously at the soldier wielding the reins. Was this his idea of protecting them?

Evan swallowed his fear and rage as the carriage careened down the lane toward him. The driver would shortly be in firing range of his pistol, but he dared not use it while the horses were for all practical purposes out of control. The rain-swollen river lay directly ahead, the wooden bridge appearing little more than a toothpick against the debris of the flood. The man was mad to aim at that, mad or supremely confident of his driving abilities.

Gambling on the latter, Evan gave the signal his men had been waiting for. With yells and curses, the motley band of ragged ex-soldiers began heaving the heavy branch-laden top of a fallen tree across the muddy lane.

It was a gamble that could cost him the lives of those nearest and dearest to him, but it was no worse than allowing them to cross that bridge and the swollen river. Here, he would be in control. Down there, the bastard on the driver's box would have the advantage.

Evan held his pistol steady as Rhys wildly rode between the carriage and its outriders. Gordon came up from behind them, neatly throwing the two soldiers into a quandary. Uncertain who was the enemy, they threw up their hands in surrender, but Evan breathed no sigh of relief. His gaze focused intently on the man with the reins in his hands, and his breath almost left his lungs as he recognized the pale face appearing in the driver's door.

He wanted to scream at her to get down, to take the floor and lie flat, but he was helpless at this distance. He could only watch in horror as the scarlet-coated driver realized what was happening and began to haul at the reins. The carriage could overturn at any minute, and Evan would be the one responsible for sending two innocent females to their fate. Anguish squeezed at his heart for being given two such impossible choices, but his hand never wavered from the pistol.

NINETEEN

The carriage's sudden jerk forward flung Daphne back
to the seat. The light vehicle began to sway dangerously.
Acting on instinct or feeling the wild fear of Evan's unspoken
cry, Daphne grabbed Melanie's arm and pushed her to the
floor. Too frightened to protest, Melanie curled in a ball
between the two seats, her light pelisse engulfing her from
head to toe. Daphne squeezed down beside her, half on top,
forming a protective cushion against whatever might come.

She closed her eyes as the horses screamed a protest against
the sudden restraint. She felt the wheels sliding uncontrollably
on the muddy road and knew a crash was imminent. It was
akin to reliving that horrible night so many years ago, only
from the inside looking out this time. All they could do was
pray.

The carriage tilted precariously as it hit a rut, then righted
itself under an expert hand. In the next minute, a wheel spun
off into the ditch, the carriage lurched, shuddered, and slowly
fell onto its side.

Melanie screamed as they were left hanging feet first over
the ditch, the door to freedom above their heads. Any sudden
movement might tilt the carriage further, and they would be
sliding down the embankment. Wild curses and pistol shots
reverberated through the air above them, and both women
crouched in panic on the panel that had become their floor.

The door over their heads flew open, and Daphne gave
a gasp of relief as she recognized the glittering braid of
Captain Rollings in the opening. Before she could offer a
word of gratitude, a long, black pistol was aimed at her head,
and a menacing growl replaced the polite tones she had
learned to expect from the soldier.

"Climb up out of there and don't say a word unless I tell you."

He might as well have told them to part the Red Sea for all they could oblige. Daphne glanced down at her feet where the window showed the dangerous embankment sloping to the river, then glanced up at the opening where Rollings evidently clung to the underside of the carriage. The horses were raising furious screams, but they didn't seem cries of pain. She strained to hear other sounds, but fear limited her abilities. She greatly suspected they could die whether they remained here or not.

The only advantage she could find in the situation was if their movements could throw the carriage into a long slide down the embankment, they would also undoubtedly dislodge the fiend in the doorway.

Daphne glared up at him. "Do you think we are some kind of monkeys to perform acrobatics? The carriage needs to be brought back to the road before we slide into the river."

The captain's curse was quickly cut short by a shout from outside. Crouched on the panel, Daphne hugged Melanie's shivering shoulders and gave praise to the heavens above. Evan's voice. He was here.

Rollings turned so violently that the carriage shook. "Stand off, Griffin, or you and your brother will not see your ladies again."

Evan halted his horse in the road and glared at this man he had known as enemy in his highwayman disguise, but had never considered a danger to his family until now. "Don't be absurd, Rollings. Where do you think you will go from here? The trick is up. Throw away the weapon and no one will be harmed."

"I think not." Rollings clung stiffly to the carriage containing his hostages. "All I want is a share of the fortune. You may argue all you like, but the ladies stay with me until my demands are met. They are likely to grow quite uncomfortable shortly, and if the rain begins again, they could be in some danger. I suggest you consult your top-lofty brother and proceed to find a satisfactory sum posthaste. Since it seems I will now have to leave the country to enjoy it, it had best be a sum large enough to persuade me to let these very attractive ladies go."

Evan could feel the first dribble of rain begin again, and despair took root in his bones and began to grow. He didn't dare look to the men crawling from the woods and along the embankment. Rollings had to know he didn't act alone, but there was no reason to let him know where the others were. If only there were time before the rain began in earnest . . .

"Gordon!" Evan shouted in the direction of the line of trees behind him. The sound of a horse cantering in his direction was sufficient to let him know that his twin was not far away. Together, they could tackle the officer on the carriage, except his pistol was not aimed at his antagonists, but at the innocent women inside.

"This gentleman seems to think we possess a fortune in which he wishes to share. How much do you have on you?"

Gordon shrugged his broad shoulders against the damp superfine of his tailored coat as he rode up. "I didn't come prepared for travel. Will my watch and fob suit?"

Rollings's pale face grew dark with anger. "Do not play the fools with me. It is only your damned almighty luck that I'm not the next heir to your title, and I can arrange it still. But I can live without names and titles if wealthy enough. I suggest you hurry back to our holy grandfather and find out how much gold you can uncover if you wish to see the ladies alive again."

Less than an hour ago, Evan had learned of the existence of his Uncle Robert's two sons and the fact that they lived under the name of their actress mother—Rollings. It had taken only a few additional words to realize they had sent Daphne and Melanie out in the dubious care of an embittered, melancholy young man. It had scarcely taken his uncle's warning that the Shelce coach was moving at remarkable speed to send Evan flying after it; he had already been halfway across the room in the direction of the door.

Now Evan held his gaze on his newly found cousin as Rhys surreptitiously slid beneath the carriage with a stout limb in his hand. A few more of those and the carriage would be steadier, if not upright. He prayed the cousin he knew now as Gregory Rollings wouldn't notice the difference until it was too late.

The stealth of the ex-soldiers as they slid logs and debris down the ditch to balance the carriage made Evan proud of their training. They were good men, all, despite the fact that they had come home with parts of them left behind on the battlefield. Somehow, he would see them well rewarded. In the meantime, he must keep Rollings distracted from their presence. Why had it never occurred to him that his uncle might have sons?

"Would you have us sign over the deed to the estate? Or drive the contents of the stables down here? How do you propose that we raise funds while our sister and Miss Templeton dangle over a riverbank? It could take days. Be reasonable and come down from there. Your father is back at the house with the earl. Come talk with them and let us get the ladies out of that wreck."

"You think I want to hang? Do you think for a moment that my father cares if I do or not? Had he cared, he would have seen to it that we had the same wealth and respect and name as the pampered favorites. But all he cares about is his own selfish pursuits. He would not even fight for me when they asked me to resign my commission. I've earned this rank. I've made my way despite him. And I'll not let my life be thrown away because of him. I'll not follow in his footsteps and live on the edge of poverty when there is all the Griffin wealth to be had for the asking. Go back to the earl and demand my rights!"

From below, Daphne heard this outraged speech and felt her spirits sink lower. They had reached an impasse of a certainty. From the anguish in Rollings's voice it was apparent that the loss of his commission had been the final blow to his precarious hold on respectability. Without even the life of a soldier to uphold him, he had no future at all. Daphne hoped Evan realized the dangerous despair behind this admission.

She glanced down to the window where they had already discovered the quiet activity below them. Rhys was struggling valiantly with a large timber, and to Daphne's surprise, even her brother was crawling through the mud to prop the carriage in place. If they could only stabilize it, the windows could be removed and they could crawl out the bottom. How long would it take to balance a carriage?

As if sensing the activity, Rollings swung around and pointed the gun at the interior again. Daphne swiftly lifted her arm to balance against the seat, blotting out the view of the window with her pelisse. With any luck, at this angle, Melanie would hide the other window.

Rollings glared down at the two fragile women quietly crouching against the carriage side, their light summer silk pelisses glowing in the dusky light, their prim bonnets still perched fashionably upon their curls despite the upheaval. He had no grudge against women. This had not been his choice of revenge, but they were leaving him with little enough to live for.

"Quit rocking the carriage or you'll be in the river before I am," he warned them firmly.

"We cannot sit or stand like this," Daphne protested. "Can no one right the carriage? Or at least help us out? I do not know your argument, but it cannot be gentlemanly to allow us to languish like this. Miss Griffin has been recently ill, and the damp may irreparably harm her. Can you find no other means to have this discussion?"

Daphne cried her lament for as long as she was able, hoping to give the men beneath the time they needed. Rollings's frown warned she had pushed far enough.

"This isn't a picnic, Miss Templeton, and I am not the local Robin Hood. Perhaps you should speak to your lovers out here and persuade them of your desperate plight. They do not yet seem convinced."

The insult flew right by her head. Daphne heard something else in his voice, and she tested it carefully. "If you found that Robin Hood, would they allow you to keep your commission?"

That tactic startled Rollings, and he stared move carefully into her upturned face. "I had some hopes of that, but it is too late now. Unless you wish to climb up here and speak with my cousins, you would do best to sit there quietly.''

"I would like to climb up, but I cannot move without disturbing the carriage. Evan can help you find the thief. He has been on his trail all along. That would be a much more honorable solution to the problem, would it not? And then Miss Dalrymple would have reason to be proud of you. She is inordinately fond of you, you must know.''

Rollings desperately wished to believe her for he knew he was in a more than precarious situation, but the hard experience of his youth warned that the honorable way never won him riches. His reply was bitter. "Once the squire learns I am no more than an unnamed son of a common actress, he'll no longer welcome my suit. It makes no matter that by law I have my father's name when he does not admit it to anyone.''

"Don't be daft, Gregory,'' a new voice intruded with bored languor. "Your mother thought her stage name more suitable than mine. If your argument is with me, come down from there and leave the ladies out of it.''

Rollings swung around to confront the tall, handsomely tailored gentleman who was his father stepping out of the hackney they had passed earlier. An older version of his father joined him, the earl's dark gaze avidly sweeping over the scarlet-suited soldier without heed to the twins in the road beyond him.

Before Rollings could answer, Evan's anger boiled over. "Your argument is an old one, sir. The villain will face me for his deeds this day and in the past. I have lost a father due to his vile actions. I would have lost my own life and that of my brother had he had his way. And now he threatens my sister and my fiancée. I will see him hang first.''

Being labeled Evan's fiancée did not give Daphne the thrill it ought for her attention was solely on the anguished man clinging to the pistol pointed at her head. She could not see who had arrived, but she had heard the carriage and could hear something of the newcomer's words. Could this be the infamous Uncle Robert they had feared?

The captain's furious outburst at Evan's words halted further inquiry. "Your father! What in hell had I to do with your father? Are you that desperate to see me hang? Thanks to my own loving father, I was stationed at White Hall when he died, instead of on the Continent where I belonged. He can use his influence when he chooses."

Even the bored gentleman raised a golden eyebrow as he regarded his mounted nephew. "What bee have you in your bonnet? Your father broke his neck in a drunken riding accident. Have you come all the way home from the wars to accuse us of murder?"

The hint of amusement in his voice brought furious color to both men in the saddles, and they turned their attention fully to the man they had originally labeled villain.

"It was no accident, sir," Gordon replied with dignity. "The straps of my saddle were cut in a similar incident. I was fortunate enough to survive. My father was not."

The newcomer looked startled, then grim. He turned to the earl beside him. "You told me nothing of this."

The earl snorted. "I knew nothing of it myself, and I certainly wouldn't have told you if I had. You haven't concerned yourself with your family in years. Now look at the results of it standing there on the carriage like some blasted tobyman. Get down from there, boy, and let us discuss this like gentlemen."

Daphne gave a sigh of exasperation at this irascible command. Did the earl truly think a desperate man would bow to being treated like a child? What did they mean by standing there arguing while she and Melanie were in imminent danger of sliding down the hillside? It was time someone put an end to this impasse, and if no one else did, she would.

Kneeling gingerly, feeling the carriage rocking only lightly with the movement, Daphne ran her fingers over the window frame, searching for the mechanism that removed the window when the top was down. From below, Rhys reached up to guide her search, and between them, they unlatched the leather hood and gently urged the window from its frame. A rush of cool air swept Daphne's face, and she took a deep breath. She had not known how stifled she had been in there until now.

. Melanie grasped her arm and glanced nervously upward to where the head and shoulders of Captain Rollings stood framed in the doorway, but his attention was fully on the irate argument outside. Daphne shook her head and carefully sat down on the edge of the open window frame. She hoped the men below had the decency to avert their eyes from her ankles as they dangled out the opening.

To her surprise, two strong hands reached in to lift her out, and she was suddenly crouching beside her brother as the carriage teetered overhead. She gave a gasp at the rocking motion caused by her departure, but Rhys and several of his men were already grasping the vehicle to hold it steady while Melanie edged toward the opening.

Daphne crouched low and moved out of the way as Michael reached to lift Melanie down. The loss of this last weight sent the precariously balanced vehicle into another groan and shudder, and a shout from above warned all was not well. Rhys grabbed her arm and Michael grabbed Melanie's, and everyone scampered for the relative safety of the muddy hillside.

Evan noted the first lurch of the carriage with nervous expectation, praying Rhys and his men knew what they were about. When the second lurch jarred Rollings's hold on the undercarriage, Evan was ready. Kicking his heels into his mount, he raced forward, raised his riding crop, and swung it viciously at his cousin's upraised gun hand. The move called for a careful maneuver and perfect timing to hit the target and bring the horse out of the carriage's wheels without harm. Evan felt a jolt of satisfaction as the crop connected and Rollings screamed. The gun exploded behind him as he jerked his horse to the left, but Evan ignored the mass confusion he left behind. With a cry, he raced toward the hillside and the muddy figures emerging from beneath the carriage.

TWENTY

Daphne dashed into Evan's arms as he dismounted and held them out. Her cheek scraped against the smooth weave of his coat, and she breathed deeply of the scents of starched linen and horse sweat and bay rum, reveling in these sensations she had feared never to experience again. Hard arms clenched her fiercely, briefly, and she had time to feel the swift beat of his heart before they were torn asunder.

"Unhand my sister," Michael intoned tersely, his pale but muddy face a picture of fury at the sight of the reckless adventurer crushing Daphne against him.

Evan obediently released her, knowing he had no right to stake his claim. He had just needed the reassurance that she was unharmed, he told himself, and his gaze strayed guiltily to his sister.

Melanie was staring adoringly into Rhys's grim but awestruck visage. Were he not in such pain, Evan would have to chuckle at the Welshman's expression. Instead, he turned his attention back to the chaos he had left on the road, ignoring the emptiness at his side when Daphne reluctantly took her brother's arm to find safety on level land.

Gordon had successfully relieved Captain Rollings of any other weapons and brought him down from the carriage to face a jury of his peers—his family. The boredom had been wiped from Robert Griffin's face as he came to stand before his eldest son, but the arrival of an erratically driven ancient barouche ended any opening for hostility or peace.

Daphne gripped her brother's arm and sighed in exasperation as her father's coachman nearly ran over the earl, sideswiped the hackney, and came to a halt in the ditch. The various scars on the vehicle's wooden sides told tales of more than one such landing, and Daphne waited impatiently for the tirade of mutual curses to end as her father leapt out and berated the impudent Willie. To her surprise, a second figure jumped from the overturned barouche and stood expectantly surveying the scene of chaos.

Finding the figure in scarlet, his eyes lit and he strode forward shouting, "Gregory!" The resemblance between the two was such that they could almost be mistaken for twins.

Before Daphne could reconcile all these events in her spinning head, Gordon was at her side, appropriating her other arm and returning Michael's glare with equanimity. "I think the ladies should be escorted home immediately. The hackney is still upright and Llewellyn can maneuver it around while the others are righting my carriage, if that is all right with you?"

Before Michael could murmur an assent, Daphne jerked her hands from the arms of both men. "You might ask if it is all right with me. It isn't. Nothing has been settled yet, and it appears very much as if Evan is about to come to fisticuffs with both your cousins at once. I know upon occasion I misunderstand people's intentions, but I don't think I am so bad as to mistake that particular stance. Perhaps all three of them ought to be bound and gagged for safety's sake."

That startling announcement brought her companion's gaze swinging back to the road, and with a curse, Gordon hastily leapt to his brother's side.

As the cousins dived into the fracas and the muddy lane became a sprawling free-for-all of flailing arms and legs, the older men watched with resignation and a touch of sorrow.

"Gregory didn't do it, you know," Robert spoke idly, poking his cane into the mud of the road. "He was at White Hall, just as he said, raising hell and demanding his transfer to Brussels. I'm not saying he wouldn't have tried it if he had thought of it, but I rather believe George's death coupled with the end of the war is what started him resenting his cousins."

The earl wearily attempted to maintain his noble carriage as he watched his heir plant a facer squarely in the center of the captain's nose. He winced at the crunch, and sighed. "I have had time to think on what Gordon said. It is very possible that George's death was an accident. There was never any evidence that his saddle was damaged. George had been blue-deviled for a long time, and that jump was a bad one even when he had all his faculties about him. I'll accept that it was an accident, but there is no such explanation of the incidents toward the twins afterward. Evan could have been killed when his horse went off the bridge. You can see the river from here. If Gregory shot at a man on that bridge, he intended murder."

Robert's aristocratically narrow face deepened into gray lines of anxiety as his eyes sought his sons in the melee. They were younger than the twins, but not by enough to make a physical difference. He flinched perceptibly as the younger went sprawling backward under Evan's forceful blow. "The shooting incident must have happened shortly after word that Gregory was to resign his commission. With the war over, they had no need of the excess of officers. He was devastated and petitioned for relief, but he received no promises. I think it festered inside him. We have never been close, so I can't speak in certainties, but today's episode reveals much of his state of mind. If I had only known . . ."

Both men grew silent over this sad commentary on the lost years between them. The argument over Robert's marriage to an actress had been violent and irrevocable, but at this distance, it could also be seen as the folly of youth and not worth a score of years from their lives. The brawl before them now was as much a result of their separation as it was of the marriage. It could easily have been averted.

"Never mind that. What should we do now?"

Robert looked startled as his father consulted his advice for what surely must have been the first time in his life. His lips quirked oddly in the corners as the earl refused to meet his eye but continued staring at the brawl in the road. It was as much of a truce as he would ever be offered, and he accepted it. Age had a way of mellowing even the most virulent of emotions.

Robert's glance went to the scruffy scoundrels on the

hillside and the two horrified women being held back by two husky young men. He had been the villain for so long, he wasn't certain anyone would consider his change of heart now, but he had to begin somewhere.

"I'd suggest recruiting those young brutes to pull apart the melee. They're already filthy. There is no sense in our emulating them.".

The earl's lips turned upward wryly at his son's bored drawl. He had forgotten Robert's tendency to distance himself from any form of disagreement. How he had ended up with that fractious harridan of a wife was beyond the earl's ability to comprehend, but Robert's coolness in the midst of fury was always welcome. He nodded his head in agreement and signaled the wooden-legged groom currently preventing Melanie from running to join her brothers. If Rhys Llewellyn were a groom, he'd eat his whole damned carriage. But that was another story.

Rhys reluctantly surrendered Melanie's arm to Michael's care and bounded down the hillside. At the earl's command, he put his fingers between his teeth and gave a whistle that caused the horses to whinny and jump in their traces. The ragtag band of ex-soldiers swarmed down the hill to the lane.

Daphne breathed a sigh of relief as Rhys ordered the men into a circle around the combatants and sent them into the brawl. She actually leaned on Michael's arm for a moment when Rhys caught the back of Evan's coat and Evan came up swinging. Rhys went down, but another man was there to jump on Evan's back, and in a few brief moments, it was over.

She wanted to run to them, but seeing Gordon emerge from the fight, she wasn't certain it would be appropriate. She wasn't even certain how she knew which twin was which since all she could recognize of them were torn coats and mud. But she knew. Her gaze lingered a moment longer while the earl and his son marched forward to give their verdicts, and then she squeezed Michael's arm and looked up to him.

"Let us go now," she urged softly.

Michael looked to the two women on his arm, down at

his father berating the coachman's attempts to right the barouche, and nodded. "Miss Templeton, would you care to accompany us to my aunt's? I can't think this is the healthiest place to linger at the moment."

Melanie looked questioningly to Daphne, and at her friend's resolute gaze, reluctantly agreed. The women gave a last backward glance to the shouting argument and mud-covered figures in the road, then silently returned to the only upright carriage remaining.

Agatha had apparently been returned home by one of the viscount's vehicles and was waiting in anxiety when the weary trio showed up on her doorstep. She immediately sent the servants into a frenzy of activity fetching hot water and tubs and clean clothing and relieving all concerned of any thought but of making themselves respectable.

Not that she would ever be respectable again, Daphne thought wryly as she resisted her aunt's suggestion that she retire to bed. The bed looked exceptionally inviting, and she thought she must ache in every bone in her body, but she could go nowhere until she knew what had happened. Sooner or later, Evan would come for her. She had to be ready when he did.

She wasn't ready for the whole lot of them, however. Daphne stared in disbelief and sank down into the nearest chair when a few hours later two carriages and two mounted horsemen rode up the drive. The twins together would be sufficient to wreck what remained of her sanity. Did she truly have to endure the earl and her father, too?

She ought to give thanks that Robert Griffin and his sons did not join the parade. She supposed someone would explain sometime why Captain Rollings wasn't called Griffin, but she really did not need to know right now. She clenched her hands in her lap and waited for the butler to show them in. When she heard Melanie tripping eagerly down the stairs followed by the sturdy tread of her brother, Daphne gave a silent moan of dismay and considered fleeing out the back door like the coward she was.

"For the last time, I tell you, this is most impolite! A

delicate lady like Daphne must be given time to recover before you descend on her like locusts.''

The insistent tones carried from the foyer, and for once, Daphne almost agreed with Gordon's verdict, but she had no intention of letting him know. She might be exhausted. Her knee might ache worse than after the accident. Her emotions might be thrumming in terrifying beats through her center. But she intended to be as regal and composed as her aunt. She would give no one the opportunity to see her weakness.

The men burst into the room still arguing, growing quiet only when they found Daphne patiently waiting for them. Freshly washed and groomed but sporting the vivid reminders of their fray, the twins bowed correctly and stepped aside to allow their elders to take seats. Melanie rushed in to hug them both and burst into tears, which she hastily dried upon Michael's appearance. Daphne merely signaled the servant to fetch a tray.

''We regret the intrusion, Miss Templeton,'' the earl began quite formally, almost giving the appearance of embarrassment as he glanced at his grandsons.

''But I want this settled once and for all, daughter,'' Lord Thomas finished the sentence for him. ''I never saw such a ramshackle lot in all my life. Actresses and highwaymen and murderin' thieves! It's a frippery lot for all their toplofty ways. My advice is that you come home with me. See what happens when there is no one to look after you.'' He sent a murderous look toward the twins.

Tears sparkled in Daphne's eyes at these words, but she was given no time to reply. Gordon stepped forward and made a formal bow before her.

''I realize you have not been given sufficient time to consider my suit, but events have made it necessary that some decision be made. If you will agree to be my wife, I will give you all the time that is necessary to grow accustomed to the idea.''

Leaning against the mantel, Evan watched this display with cynical disinterest. It was patently obvious that his brother had thrown his cap over the windmill to behave in such a manner. It was equally obvious that Gordon was the better choice for a delicate lady. At the moment, he felt considerable sympathy for his Uncle Robert. A younger brother had little to offer a lady of station. If he did not wish to sell himself, he was better off looking among the petticoat line for companionship. But Evan's expression of disinterest dissolved with Daphne's reply.

She did not look at the man slouching against the mantel. Overriding Melanie's cry of joy, she met Gordon's gaze with equanimity. "I am no wife for you, Gordon, for all I know the honor you do me. I cannot know how much you know of me or my history, but suffice it to say that we would not suit. Your wife will be a countess someday, prepared to meet society on the highest levels. I would not let my past and temperament ruin your happiness."

Before she could add any more such faradiddle, Evan interrupted with a vile curse. Striding forward, he glared at Daphne and his brother. "I never heard such drivel in my life, Miss Templeton. If you don't want to marry him, just tell him so. What your mother did or did not do has no bearing on anything."

Daphne returned his glare. "And who asked your opinion, Mr. Griffin? It seems to me you have been wrong more than once in these last weeks. Leave me to make my own decisions, if you please."

Lord Thomas stepped in with a nervous plea. "Daphne, do not become overset. Perhaps I have rushed things precipitously . . ."

Evan spoke as if there had been no interruption. "Your own decisions! It was your own hare-brained scheme that landed us in the suds last night. Anyone who would ride out like that hasn't the wit to decide what to put on in the morning. The only fault with your past is that you're an impudent hoyden with more temper than sense. You need a keeper, my dear. If Gordon isn't strong enough, then it shall have to be me."

"Now wait one minute—" Gordon protested, but Daphne gave him no time for reply.

"I wouldn't have you if you were the last man on earth,

Evan Griffin! You think I need a keeper? You are the madman who lived in the woods for no good reason at all. And they question *my* sanity!''

Several voices rang out in protest at this, but the couple looking daggers at each other had no heed for any interference. The earl and Lord Thomas exchanged glances, and interpreting that exchange, Michael offered his arm to Melanie, who accepted it with a worried look to her brothers over her shoulder as he escorted her toward the door.

''There is nothing wrong with your sanity, Miss Templeton. It is your wits that are lacking. Gordon is a damned viscount, for pity's sake! And don't give me that clanker about not being suitable as a countess. There are more harebrained countesses out there than I can count.'' When Daphne opened her mouth to interrupt, Evan rode roughshod over her words. ''And I don't want to hear about your damned leg or your mother again. If you love him, then marry him and be done with it! Noble martyrs give me a pain.''

''Martyrs! Of all the insensitive, idiotic . . . Were I a man, I would call you out, Evan Griffin! If you think for one minute that I don't know my own mind . . . Never! Never in my whole life have I been so insulted.'' Daphne rose with shaking rage and shook a fist in the face of the broad-shouldered man leaning over her.

Gordon's shoulders visibly slumped as Agatha gently touched his arm and nodded toward the exit. He appeared ready to protest, but the old lady held an admonishing finger to her lips. Ahead of them, Melanie and Michael had already disappeared from the room. The two older gentlemen shook their heads as the argument escalated into a shouting match that could be heard by the servants in the attic. It was more than evident, however, that no one would be able to come between these two. With a slight smile as the ''delicate'' lady rammed her fist into his grandson's broad shoulder, producing a distinctive moan and wince, the earl took Lord Thomas's arm and steered him toward the door. The north country lord turned and gave his ''invalid'' daughter one last questioning look, then reluctantly followed. Even he could see that Daphne had made her choice. His last look showed the younger twin retaliating by lifting Daphne from her feet, but Lord Thomas didn't think fisticuffs were the young man's intention.

TWENTY-ONE

"They say her mother was quite mad, you know," the elderly lady with her hair in a turban whispered to the stout woman on her right as the bridal couple weaved their way through the crowd.

"His uncle is here!" The stout lady replied with rapture at the *on-dit* she would have to relate later. "They say he is married to a common actress. That's his son over there, the one with the black eye. They say there was some sort of trouble—"

"And look at the groom!" A third lady interrupted in hushed tones. "He looks as if he's just been in a fight. Such a fractious family!"

"He *has* just been in a fight," the turbaned lady sniffed. "He and his cousin were threatening each other to a duel, but unfortunately, no one would provide them weapons. I believe the bride poured cold water over them to break them up. See, his jacket is still dripping. Mad as her mother, I daresay."

"Just in love, I'd say," Lady Agatha sniffed, coming up in time to hear this last. "Lord Shelce means to put Evan up for parliament, so you shall have plenty of opportunity to observe their madness. It's about time the stodgy government heard some youthful voices."

"Well, if fighting in the streets is the manner in which the young man makes his point, I daresay we will hear much of him." The lady in the turban nodded stiffly to her acquaintance before whispering aside to her companion, "Madness runs in the family, you know. Parliament, indeed!"

At that moment, the subject under discussion was carefully manipulating his bride through the crowd toward the door. She sent him a nervous look as she recognized Evan's direction, but his hold remained firm as he guided her through the shoals of gossiping relations and into the freedom of the hall.

"We cannot leave so early," Daphne protested, throwing a last look to the crowd before facing the emptiness of the stairway ahead.

"We cannot leave soon enough for me." Without a word of warning, Evan swung her up in his very wet arms and made his way toward the upper floor.

Daphne shrieked as the damp seeped through the fragile silk of her gown. "Put me down, Evan Griffin! You are ruining my gown."

"Fair enough," he replied with equanimity. "You have ruined my best coat. We shall have to shop in London for new clothes."

He had looked so absurdly handsome standing there at the altar garbed all in brown and gold; Daphne's heart pounded just at the remembrance, and she clung a little tighter to Evan's broad shoulders. "I want to go to Italy first," she murmured against his wilting cravat.

"We have to go through London to get to Italy. And if I am going to be the breadwinner of this family, I must present my credentials to the proper people before we go. Grandfather's given me introductions to the ministers most influential in the interests of our ex-soldiers. Do you think you can behave yourself long enough for me to make a place for myself in their cabinets?"

That was a considerably appropriate question since now that they had reached the privacy of a spacious bed chamber, Daphne was busily decimating the knot of his linen. "Oh, I shall be all that is proper. You, I fear, are the one who will make a cake of the entire process. Imagine inviting Rhys to be your best man instead of your brother! They will have naught else to talk about for weeks. And you never have told me his story."

Grinning, Evan eagerly abetted his bride's attempts to remove him from his sodden clothes. "Rhys will tell his tale in all due time, my love. And I think the biddies might think of one or two other things to cluck about. The bride's pouring a pitcher of water over the groom is not a wedding custom that I can remember, but no doubt everyone else will for a long time to come.''

"You were the one who gave in to the urge for fisticuffs,'' Daphne said stiffly, starting to pull away from the eagerness of Evan's fingers as they strayed from his shirt to her bodice.

"Young Hugh needed to be set to rights somehow. I wasn't the one who sent his bloodthirsty brother to India. Grandfather did. If he wouldn't listen to reason, he would have to listen to the point of a sword.''

"A sword? You would have fought with swords? How very quaint. And here I thought it was my honor you were defending.'' Daphne gave a happy sigh as her fingers at last found the warmth of Evan's hard chest through the linen of his shirt.

"Everybody knows that was already lost,'' Evan whispered maliciously as he began to work on the row of tiny seed pearl buttons down her bodice front. "Which reminds me, I owe your brother Michael a good thrashing when I see him next for reporting that little incident to the earl. He knew I had every intention of marrying you. It wasn't as if we were doing anything we hadn't done before.''

Daphne laughed against her husband's coat, then quivered a little as his hand eased into the openings of her bodice. "He didn't know that you made a habit of visiting ladies in their chambers in the middle of the night. I fear Michael has grown quite stodgy with age. He was most thoroughly shocked to find you there.''

"He would have been even more thoroughly shocked had he waited a few minutes longer. You have been driving me out of my mind since the first night I met you. I love you beyond all reason, Daphne Elaine. It is about time I had some satisfaction.''

"I thought we were going to London,'' Daphne protested faintly as Evan's hand successfully breeched the second barrier of her clothing.

"And so we will,'' he murmured indistinctly as he took

advantage of the now open neckline of her gown to press his ardent kisses there. "When I have taught you how the proper wife of a government official behaves."

Daphne's hands crept over the warm skin of Evan's shoulders to the strength of his neck as his embrace tightened. "I've changed my mind. I wish to be the wife of a country squire," she whispered maddeningly against his jaw as he carried his kisses closer to her lips.

"And you shall be that, also, my willful wife." As Evan's hand finally took control of the firm flesh beneath Daphne's beaded bodice, he silenced her cries with his mouth. As the kiss deepened and promised a passionate future, Evan tore himself away long enough to gaze down into his bride's rapturous eyes. "Gordon and Grandfather have given this to be our home when we are not in London. Do you think you can lead the life of Devon's splendid isolation?"

"Only if you are by my side every night. I am afraid of the dark, you know," Daphne whispered with a wicked glint in her eyes.

"Oh, no doubt you are quaking in your shoes at the thought of the night to come. Let me put an end to your fears right now, Mrs. Griffin. I know the best way of curing night terrors. . . ."

And murmuring idiotic reassurances mixed with all the words of love there hadn't been time enough to say, Evan carried his bride to the turned-down bed and began to divest her of any hindrance to his cure, while Daphne did her wifely best to prevent his catching cold from the damp humors of his own clothing.

And the only fears evidenced anywhere were of the guests below when they discovered the bridal couple had disappeared. The ladies shivered quite giddily at the thought of the kind of children such an outrageous couple could produce, and the men lifted their glasses and their gazes to the ceiling in toast to the same idea.

THE GENUINE
ARTICLE

To Katherine Bernardi,
whose devious mind will put her name
into print any day now.

One

"Have you ever thought of marrying, Reginald?" The speaker sat sprawled across a bench in the Cock and Crow on the London road.

"Whyever should I?" His companion seemed completely taken aback by the question, as if it were one that he'd thought would never come under consideration, somewhat akin to asking whether a Turkish emperor wore corsets. He set down his mug and gazed across the table at his friend with serious concern. "Your mother after you again?"

The young man ignored the question. "A man ought to get married sometime, you know."

Reginald snorted. Some men snort and look piggish. Reginald was not one of those men. Expensively if not elegantly turned out in doeskin pantaloons, linen cravat, and double-breasted green riding coat, he managed only to look haughty when emitting this inelegant noise. His dark hair was rakishly disheveled, not by design but by the force of the increasing wind they had stopped to avoid.

He crossed one Hessian-booted leg over the other as he scanned the occupants of the tavern. His attitude was such as to show that he did not expect a sensible reply to his challenge: "Give me one good reason why I should marry."

The young man squirmed unhappily and pulled at his high, starched collar. The starch, which fashion's arbiter Brummell insisted made a gentleman, left red weals on Darley's neck, and he gazed enviously at Reginald's unstarched but pristinely white linen. Reginald had told Brummell he'd rather wear hemp than starch, and rather than being ostracized for his boldness, he was considered a top gallant. Darley was quite certain that if he had said such a thing, he would be scorned by all.

"Why, a man should marry to have children, I suppose."

Reginald quirked an eyebrow in Darley's direction. "Whatever for? I suppose if I were inclined to a nursery, Madelyn would agree for a small sum. It's not as if I need an heir, after all. That's Charley's duty."

Darley glumly sipped his ale. "A wife would see to your house and that sort of thing, keep things neat and orderly and keep the cooks from quitting, I suppose."

Reginald was growing amused. "I have servants to keep things neat and orderly, and Jasper is most functional when it comes to keeping the servants in line."

The younger man ripped at his cravat until it loosened, then moved his neck gingerly inside his collar. "Well, there's entertaining, then. A man needs a wife at his side when he entertains. A good hostess can be very helpful."

Reginald waved at a waitress to bring more ale. She had been keeping an interested eye on both of them since they walked in, so the service was excellent. He waited until she had departed with a saucy wink before answering Darley's last nonsensity. "Whyever would I entertain at home? There's nothing of any interest there, and no one to talk to. A man only needs a good club for entertaining. He's more likely to be entertained with good wine and good sense at his club in the company of other men than with listening to the simpering ineptitudes that typify polite conversation in the company of women."

Darley gave it up. "And of course, you always have Madelyn if you need a woman in your bed. I only wish I were in your position."

Reginald gave him a look of sympathy. "Being your father's only son is a sad thing, but you're not earl yet. Tell your mama you are looking for the perfect countess and will settle for no less."

Darley didn't look appeased. "That's easy for you to say. Your mama has been gone these many years. You don't know what it's like to be harped at by the woman night and day. I have come to think that if I can find a gentle, quiet maid, I would be much better off under her care than at home."

"Maybe so, but it has been my experience that the tenderest of maids can turn into dragons once harnessed by marriage. I would be wary, if I were you, Darley, or you could find yourself in worse suds than with your mama." Reginald drained his glass and reached for his hat. "It looks as if the sun's back out. I'll be on my way then. Promised Charley I'd put in an appearance for the heir's birthday. I'm so grateful for his existence that I'll go to any lengths to please him. Don't go getting yourself leg-shackled before I return."

Darley merely looked more miserable as his gaze went longingly to the door. Upstairs, his mother and sister were adorning a private parlor. It had been mere chance that he'd found sympathetic company in the tap room. He lifted a mug in farewell and watched Reginald march out, a hale and hearty fellow with no cares in the world.

Maybe he would be as bold as Reginald if he had the other man's height. At five-eight, Darley was merely average. Had he not been an earl's son, he would go unnoticed by the larger portion of the females of his acquaintance. He was not so well set-up as Reginald—the padding in his coat was necessary. His dark coloring did not meet the popular taste, and he was quite certain his long thin nose had been compared to a quill point by more than one clever miss.

Of course, Reginald could not be called handsome in the traditional sense, either, but women seemed to flock to him anyway. It had to be his height and the breadth of his shoulders. Women liked to feel helpless and protected, and men of Reginald's size always made them feel that way, Darley supposed. He gazed gloomily down at his knee-high boots. Perhaps he could have the heels extended.

"I could wish that we had our new clothes now, Marian. Did you see how elegant that lady in the carriage looked? Such beautiful fur she had on her collar! And the feather! It drooped at just the right angle. Do you think I will ever reach such heights of sophistication?"

Since Jessica had stopped growing at age fourteen, she

wasn't likely to reach any heights at all, but Marian consci-
entiously refrained from mentioning that fact. She was already learning her new role well, she decided in a moment
of self-congratulation. The old Marian would have said
what she felt without thinking.

"There is no use in spoiling a good gown until we are
somewhere to be seen. You know there is no money for
more. And you know you are always spilling something on
your bodice or dragging your hem in the mud. Poor Lily
cannot get all those stains out, especially with the silks."

Jessica looked resignedly out the window at the rapidly
falling twilight. They had stopped early for fear of the thun-
derclouds lining the horizon. That meant they would not arrive in London for another day. "I know you have said we
will arrive early to give us more chance to choose, but do
you really think we will take, Marian? Whatever shall we
do if we do not?"

Marian didn't have to look in the mirror to know she
would not take. Her dark hair, eyes, and complexion were
not at all the thing. Worse than that, she had the tongue of
an adder and a mind quicker than that of most men. If men
despised anything more than a woman smarter than they,
she didn't know what it was. But Jessica had no such problems.

"You will take, Jessie, there is no doubt of it. You will
look just like the fashion plates, all golden slenderness and
dimpling smiles, and your nature is as sweet as any gentleman can desire. You will have swarms of beaux. You need
only choose a rich one."

Jessica clapped her hands anxiously as she turned back
toward the room. "But I am not clever like you, and not
only do I not have any dowry, I do not have any family
connections."

Admittedly, that was the fly in the ointment, but Marian
did not say so. "Nonsense," she disagreed heartily. "Our
mother has the very best connections, else how would she
have married my father? If she can capture a marquess, you
surely deserve an earl."

"Yes, but her father was the younger son of an earl. My

father was merely a country squire. It is not at all the same thing, you know."

And a poor country squire at that. Poor and not very bright when it came to business, Marian added to herself a trifle waspishly. That wasn't in keeping with her new style of behavior, but surely she was entitled to think what she might for a little while longer. Her stepfather had been a kind and generous man. There, she had thought something pleasant to balance out her unkindness. Poor James Oglethorp had just been so mightily impressed at landing the beautiful widow of a marquess that he had lavished everything he owned on her. The fact that the widow had been left with only a small trust fund for herself and her daughter had meant little until the crops had turned bad two years in a row. Marian quite sincerely believed that her stepfather had died of a broken heart when he no longer had a cent left to lavish.

So here they were, the next best thing to penniless, and their mother was no longer young enough nor wealthy enough to attract the best of suitors. It was left to Marian and Jessica to save them all from penury. Marian was quite determined to do it by herself. Jessica was too tender-hearted to take any wealthy man who came along, but Marian was no such thing. She had already gleaned enough information from her gossips in London to know which gentlemen to set her hat for. She had only to focus her attention on those few gentlemen until one of them came up to the mark. She was clever. She could determine what he liked in a woman and be that, just long enough for him to fall for the act. He would be wedded faster than he could get the words out.

She had already decided that was about the only way to do it. Her wayward tongue would otherwise give the game away sooner or later. She would be sweet and demure and empty-headed until the band was on her finger and her husband's pockets were at her disposal. Then she would set about educating him.

Still, there was Jessica to reassure. Patting her sleeve gently, Marian disposed of her sister's arguments. "There have been Oglethorps in government since there was a gov-

ernment to be had. You will make a fine politician's wife, I
am certain. You need only look around and find the one
you wish and smile at him for him to come tumbling to
your feet. We shall both be married by June, just you wait
and see. Now let me go find Lily and see what detains our
dinner."

Since the chambers were so small, Lady Grace and Lily
had taken a separate room from Jessica and Marian. Not
wishing to disturb her mother if Lily were already downstairs, Marian made her way down the narrow hall. Her
mother had not been well since the death of her second husband. Marian was quite certain it was the pressing worry of
their non-existent finances that had her in the dismals. Once
they restored the family's security, Lady Grace would be
fine. Until then, she was best left undisturbed.

The front room of the inn was fairly deserted at this hour.
Most of the patrons had settled in for the evening meal, either in the tap room or in private parlors. Apparently the
last coach had already gone through, so there were no new
arrivals expected. Marian glanced down at the worn wool
of her brown traveling gown and decided no one would
look twice at her if she went toward the kitchens. She
wasn't dressed much differently from Lily.

Before she could act on that decision, the front door
swept open with a rush of wind and rain.

"Miss! Don't leave yet. Be so good as to tell me if there
is room left in the inn. I don't fancy traveling farther in
this."

Wide-eyed at being addressed in such a manner, Marian
turned to gape at the jackass who brayed so loudly. He wore
the caped driving coat of a coachman and seemed to have
lost his hat. His linen was loose and unstarched, and his
boots were coated in mud. He was of an unseemly height,
and the haughty arrogance of his handsome features was reflected in his manners. No doubt he thought himself God's
gift to women. She'd seen louts like that before. They
smiled at poor naive country girls, charmed them out of
their virtue, and then when they were in the family way, either left them or lived off them until the next one came
along. Marian had little use for men, and less for scoundrels.

"'Tis a pity then. Mayhap you'll enjoy the stable instead." She turned and started for the kitchen once more, but a large gloved hand caught her shoulder and swung her around. She glared at him in astonishment.

"Whatever have I done to you to deserve such treatment?" He released her shoulder and began to peel off his soaked gloves.

"You exist. That should be sufficient reason." Without excusing herself, Marian turned on her heels and once more sought refuge in the rear of the inn.

"I trust you don't need this employment," he called after her, "for I mean to tell your employer of your behavior."

Fury colored Marian's cheeks that he could think her no more than a common servant. Her gown might not be of the best quality, but surely he could see she was no ordinary maid. Without stopping to think, she swung around to face him again. "I thought you a braying jackass when first you walked in here. I must congratulate myself on my perceptiveness. Please do talk to the landlord. I will be happy to speak to him personally and tell him I heartily recommend the stable for you. That's where we always keep the animals at home."

Reginald's eyebrows shot up toward his hairline as the young woman stalked out of sight in the direction of the kitchen. He had undoubtedly made a foolishly hasty judgment, but the young lovely had retaliated with an unexpected and totally unladylike vehemence. Still, he couldn't help grinning just a little at her retort. Perhaps if she had been less lovely he would have found it less humorous. But delivered from rosy lips surrounded by a creamy complexion and enhanced by a wealth of very dark hair, the setdown achieved a certain savoriness he could appreciate.

Perhaps she was some lady's maid. If so, she was probably as unattainable as the lady herself.

Shrugging off the incident, Reginald rang the bell for the innkeeper. He seldom had the opportunity to exchange insults and witticisms with the fairer sex. He didn't see any particularly good reason to begin now, or he would chase her down into the kitchen and see if she took as well as she gave.

Two

Marian caught Jessica's wistful look in the mirror as she fastened the heavy braided gold chain around her neck and tested the effect of the exquisitely mounted ruby against her tawny skin. She turned and straightened her sister's seed pearls gently.

"You know I would give it to you if it would serve any purpose, but not only would it not suit your coloring, you are only seventeen. A young unmarried lady must not wear jewels. I cannot possibly pass myself off as less than my twenty-two years, so I must take advantage of what few assets I have." She turned around and frowned at the ornate jewel. "I only wish I could sell it so we might live a little more easily."

Jessica shook her head and sent a cascade of golden curls flying. "No, it is all you have of your father's inheritance. It must be very old and valuable. We could not sell it. Mother would be distraught."

Marian sighed in resignation. She was much too practical to be sentimental about family heirlooms, but she was also wise enough to know her sister was right. Mother would be more than distraught were the piece to be sold, although to Marian's mind, one piece of gaudy jewelry was the same as another. She was certain a lesser piece would be just as effective as ornamentation, and the difference could go a long way toward buying the silks and muslins needed for their foray into society.

"Well, we are not in dire straits as yet. Lily's handiwork will keep us outfitted a little while longer. If only our heights and coloring were a little closer, we could exchange clothes and then have twice the wardrobe." Marian sighed at the waste as she pulled on her elbow-length gloves.

Jessica glanced down at her gown of pale tulle over a delicate ice-blue silk, then over at Marian's more daring gown of rich gold accented with wine-colored trimmings. She smiled slightly. "I don't think so, Marian. Even were you blonde, you would not wear this."

That was probably so. Jessica often hit closer to the truth of things than Marian wished to acknowledge. She frowned at her reflection and played her fan as her mother had taught her. Her frown deepened. "I will never be sweet enough or silly enough to capture Lord Darley's interest. Perhaps I should set my cap for Mr. Henry. He is said to be quite wealthy and an older man may be less inclined to wish for a younger woman for wife."

Jessica started for the door. "Don't be silly. Mr. Henry must be at least forty, and he's practically wall-eyed. Lord Darley is a very handsome young man, and he seems quite pleased with your attentions. I only wish I were bold enough to attract a man as you can. I do not dare even look them in the eye."

Marian could tell her she would do well when she was older and more sure of herself, but Jessica wouldn't want to hear that. She wanted to believe she would be able to help the family fortune by marrying soon and well. Marian was just as determined that her sister should wait until she was in a better position to choose a husband suited to her gentle nature. To that end, she must capture a suitor quickly. Then Jessica would be free to relax and enjoy her season as a young girl should.

Lord Darley was the ideal candidate. A wealthy viscount rumored to be in search of a wife, he had fallen readily for Marian's bold smile, then believed the shyness in her hastily lowered lashes. She had listened intently to every word from his mouth, adroitly given him her fullest attention without offending the company around them, and never uttered one cross or ill-chosen word in his presence. She had easily determined he was slightly shy around women, but he seemed good-natured enough to make a suitable husband. She might wish for a man who was taller than she and a little more forceful in character, but that was not to the point. He was a man who would gladly lend a hand to his bride's family and not complain when Marian began to show signs of intelligence after the vows were said. She could not find one flaw to her plan.

"Is Mama ready? We shall be fashionably late but in plenty of time to find partners for the supper dance. Then if she is not feeling well and we must leave early, we will not have wasted the better part of the evening." Marian efficiently tugged on her gloves as she started for the door.

"Lily was fixing her hair when I left. I think Mama is feeling better now that she has found some old friends with whom she might chat while we dance. I think she was worried no one would recognize her after so many years away."

Again, Jessica's observation was exceedingly astute, Marian realized as she hurried down the stairs. Her steps were quick for a purpose. They had only the one male servant to serve as footman and butler and guardian of the house in general, and they were all half afraid of him. Hired London servants were so much haughtier than the simple country folk back home. It would not do to keep him waiting by the door longer than was deemed necessary.

They had hired a carriage along with the house for the season. The house was not in a fashionable neighborhood and the carriage was quite plain and ordinary, but there had been no sense in going too far in debt to pretend they were what they were not. Their lack of dowries had been the main reason for Marian's decision to use subterfuge in her own presentation. They must be judged on their looks and characters and breeding alone. Knowing full well she was deficient in all categories but one, she felt justified in blurring the image a little.

Allowing Lady Grace to nap late had delayed their arrival until after the usual stream of carriages at the door. The three women entered the elegantly appointed salon after the reception line had dispersed, and the footman's announcement of their arrival went virtually unnoticed. Marian had no complaint about that. They would have gone unnoticed had they arrived at the height of introductions. A Lady Grace and a Miss Jessica Oglethorp were of little consequence in a glittering assemblage such as this. It was only their mother's connections through her family and first marriage that allowed them entry at all. Even Marian's courtesy title held little meaning since her father's title had passed on to a distant cousin. She would never be a countess or a marchioness, only a Lady Marian—until she married. She glanced around unhurriedly for Lord Darley. His wife would be a viscountess and some day, a countess.

He came hurrying forward as if he had been waiting for them. Marian felt sincere gratitude for his eagerness. She might even learn to love a man with such a generous character. She just felt sorry she had to deceive him to distract him from her own true nature. She was quite certain he and his mama would not approve of a woman who read Coleridge and Hannah More and thought the majority of the aristocracy little better than useless wind chimes.

"Lady Marian!" he cried happily, taking her hand. As an afterthought, he added a polite bow to her family, "Lady Grace, Miss Jessica, it is good to see you." When they nodded shyly and moved discreetly away, he turned his attention back to the object of his interest. "You look in fine fettle this evening, my lady." He colored slightly as he realized the slang was not particularly applicable to a lady.

Marian hastened to reassure him with a shy swirl of her fan as she hid behind it. "You put me to the blush, sir. The ball is quite lovely this evening, is it not?" Simpering idiocy did not come easily, but she was satisfied she had done it properly when he looked more at ease.

"Indeed it is. Will you honor me with a dance or two? I hope I have caught you in time to inquire."

She offered her card. "As you can see, I have just arrived. You may have your choice, although I believe Mr. Henry requested that I save him a cotillion."

He dashed his name across the supper dance and looked up at her daringly. "Might I have the final waltz also, or is that saved for someone special?"

Marian wished she could blush at will, but she could not. She merely hid behind her fan again to pretend she was blushing. "I would be honored, but you must not hold me to account if my mother grows tired and we must leave early."

Growing more sure of himself with every passing simper, he said, "Then you must hold an earlier waltz open and send word to me if she begins to tire. And if she does not, we will sit out the dance together."

"You are too kind, Lord Darley. You cannot know how much I appreciate your thoughtfulness." Marian laid her hand on his arm as he offered to lead her over to her mother.

"You may show your gratitude by agreeing to go for a drive with me in the park tomorrow. I have just bought a prime set of grays and am eager to see them sprung. I would be honored to have you by my side when I introduce them."

Marian batted her lashes in eager surprise. "Why, that would be lovely, sir! Tell me about your horses. Did you buy them at Tattersall's?"

Since horses were the one topic he could converse upon with great animation and intelligence, Darley launched into a colorful description of his new acquisitions. Such animation from the usually quiet viscount drew attention around the room, but the young couple appeared oblivious to the whispering.

Mr. Henry arrived to claim his cotillion, and several other young gentlemen took the opportunity to claim her remaining dances. Marian glanced anxiously at Jessica, who was doing her best to disappear into the woodwork, and with a pleading look from beneath her lashes, she sent Lord Darley in that direction. With a pleased smile and a polite bow, he went to do his duty by her sister.

Relieved to know that Jessica wouldn't be left holding up the potted palms, feeling gratitude for the young viscount's generous understanding, Marian allowed herself to be escorted onto the dance floor. With a man like Lord Darley for husband, she might even lose some of the sharp edges to her tongue, for who could complain in the presence of a man who sought to please at just the bat of an eyelash?

Her sense of well-being and satisfaction lasted well

through the next few sets, until she happened to glance up and catch the entrance of a tall, dark-haired man dressed in casual elegance. She started nervously and looked away, for though she could not place him immediately, she was certain that she had seen the man before, and equally certain that it had not been under pleasant circumstances.

She had been more than charming to all the young men she had met these last weeks, even the ones with no wealth and no brains. Marian attributed her feeling of unease to nerves. Things had been going too smoothly. She was leaping at shadows. There was no reason she could think of that this particular man might have a poor opinion of her.

She watched him surreptitiously when she could. In a room full of stiffly correct swallow-tailed coats, starched linen, and elaborate cravats, he seemed at ease with his coat unbuttoned and his cravat in a single fold and his collar all-too-obviously unstarched. His height and grace of manner made him appear as elegant as any man around him; that in itself was intimidating. Marian had to work hard to achieve any semblance of elegance herself, and she did so by copying the standards of those she most admired. This man obviously set his own standards.

She would not be cowed by a man who was patently out of her class. He must be a duke or a marquess or some such, far too elegant for even this crowd. She did not know why he had come, but he would most certainly leave soon and she would not ever see him again. She smiled winningly as Darley came to claim his supper dance.

Marian did not see the immediate frown upon the elegant man's face as he watched Darley lead her into the set.

Reginald turned to the tall woman beside him. "That is the young woman about whom you spoke? There is something familiar about her, but I do not think we've been introduced."

Lady Agatha Darley smiled with satisfaction. "She only arrived after you had left to visit your family. She is the daughter of the late Marquess of Effingham. I believe her mother's lines are through the Earl of Avon. Eminently suitable, don't you think? Perhaps a little older than I could

have wished for Geoffrey, but I understand her stepfather
kept the family in straitened circumstances. Now that he is
gone, the mother has come to town to marry her daughters
off. Not for everyone, I think, but Geoffrey has no need to
marry for money. That is in his favor. She seems quite a
charming, pleasant young woman."

Reginald frowned and narrowed his eyes as he watched
the young couple circle through the dance. The pair were
nearly of a height, and he could see the foolish grin on Darley's face as he looked into his partner's eyes. As the
woman's face came more into view, he took a sharp breath.
There couldn't be two of them alike in this world. Flashing
dark eyes and heavy chestnut hair were not that common in
these parts, nor was the dark complexion. Even the richness
of her gown could not disguise the sharp-tongued servant
he had encountered at the inn.

Charming and pleasant were certainly things that she was
not. In how many other ways could she have deceived the
good-natured Darleys?

Three

Darley courteously summoned one of his friends to escort Jessica into supper with them so that she wasn't forced to sit with her mother and her cronies. Jessica managed a shy look of delight before turning her attention to the young man in painfully high collar who was to be her escort. The young man blushed red when she turned beguiling blue eyes to him, before assuming an air of cool aplomb as he seated her and asked what delicacies she preferred from the table. Marian noted their antics with amusement from the corner of her eye while ostensibly keeping her entire attention on Darley's rhapsodies over some other man's stable. She was quite inclined to despise this Reginald Montague on sight simply from the extensiveness of said stable.

Perhaps she could educate Darley somewhat in the arts. He obviously had a superb memory if he could recite bloodlines clear back to whatever that confounded racehorse's name was. Perhaps he could learn the classical artists and she could interest him in collecting. That might give them some common ground to converse on. It would be even better if she could persuade him to read, but she had learned at an early age that gentlemen weren't inclined toward the literary arts.

Planning Darley's improvements, Marian wasn't aware of the approach of the elegant gentleman she had noted earlier in the evening. Caught up in her conquest, she had managed to forget all about him. His arrival at their table after Darley's entreating wave dashed all possibility that she would ever be so gifted as to forget him entirely. The gray-green eyes glaring down at her from his towering height slowly turned to just an icy gray as Darley made the introductions.

Reginald Montague.

The braying ass from the inn.

Darley's closest, dearest friend.

Disaster. Marian tried not to close her eyes and resort to prayer as she smiled innocently into those furious eyes. She was mentally counting her markers, racking losses against gains to see how she stood and if she had a chance of winning this hand. The odds looked about even, depending on how much of a gentleman Montague might be. If he told Darley of their encounter, all was lost. If he held his tongue and just disapproved of her, she might counter this disapproval of a male friend with the feminine wiles of a potential countess. She knew Darley's mother approved of her. That would load the odds in her favor.

She had to make him hold his tongue. She had spent three weeks setting her cap on Darley. She didn't have a great deal of time left to lose. There were second and third runners in the contest because she was a practical woman, but none of the others were as appealing as Darley. She wouldn't let this disagreeable Corinthian stand in her way.

"Lady Marian." Montague acknowledged the introduction with the barest of nods and none of the effusive greetings to which Marian had become accustomed. She wasn't a great beauty, but she was a new face, and the gentlemen seemed to react with pleasure to anything or anyone different from the usual. It wore off quickly, she knew, but generally most of them managed to be pleasant through the introductions. This man hadn't even the common decency to smile through that.

"Mr. Montague." She managed a syrupy voice and a light smile. "Lord Darley has been telling me about your stable. You are indeed a fortunate man as well as possessing a skilled eye for horses if all he tells me is true." A compliment like that on top of a subject about which most men were usually mad, generally put them at ease. She sat back and waited to see how he would react.

He merely gave a curt nod and turned to Darley. "Will I see you at the club later?"

The man was impossibly rude. Marian wasn't much accustomed to rudeness. She wondered if she kicked his shin under the table would he even notice. With a rump as stiff as his, he probably had no feelings below the waist.

She almost giggled at the thought. Some of her laughter must have escaped, because he quickly turned a wary eye in her direction. Marian pretended not to notice as she turned her attention to Jessica's young gallant, complimenting him on his elegant attire. He turned red but set out upon a learned discourse on the topic of available tailors.

Once Montague had departed, she gratefully returned her attention to the viscount. At least Lord Darley conversed intelligently without stuttering and stammering. Poor Jessica. Marian really was going to have to look into a proper suitor for her sister just as soon as she had Darley firmly attached, which wouldn't be ever if Montague had any say in the matter.

Marian listened with dread as Darley sang the man's praises. What hope was there for a mere woman against a man who knew the best tailors, stocked the finest wines, owned the fastest horses, and in general was the male epitome of perfection? It was quite apparent whose word would be believed first should it come to a confrontation.

Drat her dreadful tongue. She had held it carefully for three entire weeks. Would that she had held it one day earlier. She could see disaster looming with every pearl of praise falling from Darley's lips. She had to bite down hard to keep from asking why—if Montague were so superior—Darley did not just marry him. Obviously, they were well suited.

Finally, Marian could not take any more of it without offering something in her own defense. Biting her bottom lip and lowering her eyes to the table, she affected a small sigh. Into the brief lull of talk that ensued, she murmured, "I could never aspire to the heights of such a paragon of perfection. You must find me very poor company indeed in comparison. I do not think I could learn half so much as a man like that must already know."

Darley looked horrified. He reached for her hand and patted it. "Don't be such a goose. Of course you cannot. You are a woman. But if Reginald is a paragon of perfection, then it is only of his gender, for you are the epitome of all that I hold dear in the fairer sex."

Had she been herself Marian would have ripped his tongue out while informing him that a female—any female—was five times more preferable to a puffed-up ass who knew nothing but horses and tailors. But she gave him a gratified smile, took his hand, and allowed him to escort her from the supper room. She was quite certain her tongue would bear scars before the season ended.

To Marian's relief, there was no further evidence of the disagreeable Mr. Montague's presence after supper. And her mother was rested enough to stay for the final waltz, so she spent a whole interval talking with Darley as well as claiming the last dance. Gossip was already swirling. She smiled into his eyes, melted into his arms, and willed him to see her as his viscountess. She was quite certain she would be very good at the position.

Reginald Montague sat sipping brandy, glaring at the noisy gaming tables around him while he waited for Darley to tear himself away from the ball and his latest folly. The viscount was too good a man to ever see the scheming qualities of another soul, and he was too diffident around women to see beyond their pretty paint and manners. The last two mercenary witches who had tried to dig their claws into him had been routed easily by Lady Agatha. This time, the little fraud had managed to fool even that daunting lady. How many others had she deceived? Was he the only one aware of the lady's true nature?

If lady she were at all. Remembering her manner of dress and the fact that she had been all alone in an inn of a less-than-respectable nature, he had to doubt even that quality in the woman. The pretty young thing she had called sister seemed innocent enough, but then, looks were not the best cover to judge by. Even this spurious Lady Marian passed easily as a lady of quality in her fashionable gown, but her bold looks and saucy mouth betrayed her. The show she was putting on for Darley's benefit was very well done, so well done that Reginald thought she might be an actress. Perhaps he could investigate her true background. That would be the wisest course to take: confront Darley with cold facts instead of subjective opinions.

Having decided that, Reginald waited with less impatience for his friend's appearance. He hadn't been looking forward to informing Darley of his inamorata's despicable behavior. Now he could keep his personal opinion out of it. He would set Bow Street on the matter tomorrow. It shouldn't be difficult to determine lies from truth if she wasn't Effingham's daughter. He might even present the facts to Lady Agatha first and let her lead the way. Darley more or less always bowed to that lady's opinions.

By the time Darley arrived, Reginald was complacent with brandy and good intentions. When his friend took the seat across from him and demanded, "What did you think?" he managed a good-natured smile.

"I thought about the beefsteak I had for dinner, which horse I prefer in the spring meet, whether to attend Lady Jersey's fete or the boxing match, and any number of fascinating topics."

Darley scowled and sipped the port the waiter brought to him. "I mean Lady Marian. What did you think of Lady Marian? I know you did not stay long, but surely you could see she was an absolute diamond."

More like coal, Reginald ruminated, but to say so would only get his friend's back up. He answered honestly, "She is quite attractive." For a brunette, he amended to himself. Fashion didn't favor brunettes. He, himself, was inclined to be less concerned with coloring than character, but he was more peculiar, as well as particular, than society in general.

"Isn't she? I'm glad you agree. I was afraid after you turned your back on her this evening that you had taken her into dislike already. But she was much too good-natured to comment on your rudeness."

Remembering what he almost certainly thought was a snicker from the young lady in question, Reginald also had the courtesy not to comment. He rather suspected the lady might be a mischief-maker in addition to all her other faults. While Bow Street worked on her background, he might do some investigating of his own. It was possible the lady could be diverted from her course with the proper inducements.

"I had not realized she was anyone of importance," Reginald replied carelessly. "I shall take better note next time."

"If I must marry, she is all that I could wish," Darley said eagerly. "I could talk to her for hours. You know how my tongue gets all tied up around women, but she is not like that at all. She even shares my interest in horses and has made some very interesting suggestions. We get along famously. And she does not have an encroaching family who would be forever dangling on my coattails. All she has is a mother and sister who are very shy and circumspect. No daunting fathers or rakehell brothers to be fished out of the River Tick."

Reginald groaned inwardly as he rose from the table. This was much worse than he had suspected. He should never have stayed so long in Somerset. If Darley weren't his closest friend, he would wash his hands of him now. But Darley was the only one of his companions who had gone through school with him and understood his position and accepted it. Darley's friendship was very valuable to him. He wouldn't see it destroyed by a scheming, conniving female.

"What about the current marquess? Will he not have some say in the matter of a cousin's marriage, if that is what you are contemplating?"

Darley drained his glass and accompanied his friend as he left the club. "As I understand it, Effingham is an old curmudgeon who never comes out of the woodwork. Lady Marian and her family never say anything against him, but it is apparent he has never taken any interest in their welfare. They appear to be living on very limited means. If they will let me, I intend to correct that situation."

They strolled down the gaslit street in the direction of the park near which Reginald had only recently purchased a small lodging. Even at this hour the streets were active. Gentlemen strolled to and from their clubs. Carriages rattled by filled with elegantly dressed fashionables going from one entertainment to another. Street urchins lurked on every corner, eager to hold a horse's head for a penny or sweep the street of droppings so their betters might cross without endangering their polished boots. A watchman snoozed in his box, unaware of the young bloods drunkenly eyeing his weight and wagering on who could tip him first.

Reginald and Darley ignored the night life around them. Wandering from the gaslit street into the darker environs of the park, they continued their desultory conversation.

"You have all the time in the world, Geoff. Do not waltz hastily into something so permanent as marriage. You remember that mare you had to have because her bloodlines were so aristocratic and her price was so low? She turned out to be a nasty, mean-tempered sort and never bred true. Had you made a few inquiries, you would have saved yourself some trouble."

Filled with the generosity of spirit that comes with happiness, Darley laughed at the comparison. "I shall interview the lady's servants to see if she is biddable, but I don't believe I can inquire into her abilities to breed."

Reginald allowed himself a smile of amusement at the thought. At least Darley was not too far gone as to have lost his sense of humor. "I had not thought that before, but there's the advantage to marrying a widow. If breeding is what you seek, you would do better to marry a woman who has proven her ability by producing a son or two already."

Darley snorted with laughter, then without changing his pace or his tone of voice, he said softly, "Don't look now, but we are being followed."

Reginald carelessly swung his walking stick. "I know. Not very good at the game, is he?"

"Young, I'd say. Perhaps he's not been about long. P'raps we ought to break him of bad habits before they start."

"My thoughts exactly. Let me offer you a sip from my flask when we stop under this next tree."

With apparent drunken carelessness, they halted their progress in the thick darkness of shrubbery and trees at the far edge of the park. The quiet residential street corner not far from this spot offered little in the way of observers. Reginald slipped a flash from his pocket and handed it to Darley.

The slight figure following them was better at his business than they had anticipated. He wheeled out of the darkness, bumped lightly against Darley, mumbled a drunken apology, and had begun to stagger off again when Reginald reached out and grabbed him by the coat collar.

Jerking the thief up to his toes, Reginald said patiently, "The purse, sir. I believe you have misappropriated the gentleman's purse."

Dangling by his coat collar, the young man kicked his feet in an anxious attempt to reach the pavement. He managed a drunken whimper. "In my cups, sirs. 'Pologize."

It was too dark to discern much about him other than that he was slightly made, wore the remnants of a gentleman's clothing, and smelled badly. Since there were any number of people in the fashionable world who disdained bathing, the odor was nothing new. The fact that he spoke without the uneducated dialect of the slums did indicate an oddity, however.

Reginald deprived himself of the pleasure of shaking the young rascal until he dropped the purse. Instead, he ordered, "Darley, search him."

The young man struggled again. There was the vague sound of something brushing against the bushes, then he held his hands up in protest. His educated speech slipped slightly to the vernacular. "I didn't do anything, guv'nor. I'm just a poor man down on his luck. Search me, if you like. I been drinking, and I know that's wrong, but I've not done anything else."

Sighing, Reginald lowered the culprit to his feet but kept a firm hold on his collar. "Search the bushes, Darley. We should have just called the watch and allowed them to handle the rogue."

Darley cursed as the bushes tore at his elegant cuffs, but he finally located the small purse that had shortly before been in his coat pocket. He lofted it in his hand to show Reginald he'd found it, then returned it to his pocket. "Shall we wake the Charlie back there?"

The thief quivered. "I didn't do anything! I been lookin' for employment, I have. I haven't got anything to pay the nippers at Newgate. They'll throw me to the hounds. If they steal my clothes, I'll not be able to find employment anyways."

If he didn't have coins to pay the jailers at Newgate, he would undoubtedly lose his fine jacket and more. Reginald hesitated. He had no desire to allow a pickpocket back on the streets, but he didn't wish to see a young lad destroyed over a few coins Darley could easily afford. He hesitated long enough for the thief to look hopeful.

"I'm a good valet, I am. My father worked for the late Marquess of Effingham, and he taught me all he knew. The new one ain't got no use for valets or much else. I thought I'd make my way in London, but I can't get references from a dead man, and nobody'll look at me elsewise."

Reginald exchanged glances with Darley. They didn't have to speak. They both knew Darley had an old and trusted valet, a family retainer, but Reginald had never hired a man before. They had even discussed the possibility of his hiring someone besides the ubiquitous Jasper, who was more secretary and butler than valet. It seemed the time had come.

"If I let loose of your collar and you run, I'm calling the watch. If you don't run, I'll consider your petition for employment in the morning. I don't hire pickpockets in the general run of things, but I am feeling generous tonight. We'll see if I feel the same in the morning."

He loosed the culprit's collar.

The man looked around nervously, rocked on the balls of his feet, then evidently deciding he had nothing to lose if he stayed instead of running, he remained where he was. "Name's Michael O'Toole, guv'nor. I'll have your clothes looking a treat 'afore morning if you take me in."

Reginald scowled. "I'm more likely to lock you in a broom closet than I am to allow you access to my wardrobe. Come on, let's go. I've had enough of this evening."

The three of them traveled down the street in the direction of the silent houses ahead. The young thief's head nearly turned in circles as he took in the massive limestone buildings, ornate entrances, and spotless steps of his new surroundings. Breathing a sigh of deep pleasure, he awaited his fate.

Four

"We have invitations to Devonshire House." Lady Grace Oglethorp held them in her hand as if they were the Holy Grail, using the same note of wonder one would use at such an occurrence. "The young Duke cannot know me. How is this possible?"

It did seem distinctly odd, but Marian said nothing untoward as she took the invitations from her mother's hands. There were three of them, all very distinctly engraved in each name. There could be no mistake. "Perhaps he has a secretary who has acquired the guest lists of all recent entertainments, and he is sending invitations to everyone on those lists. Dukes are peculiar people. Perhaps they don't care if they know their guests."

Grace's eyes were alight with hope. "He is not yet married. Perhaps he has decided to choose a wife and is inviting all eligible parties."

Marian rather doubted that. She frowned, but she could think of no other likely reason for this unexpected good fortune. She did not generally believe in Cinderella stories.

Jessica stared in awe at the heavy vellum. "What does one wear to a ducal ball?" she inquired hesitantly.

A terrible silence fell at this question. One did not wear gowns made over from ten years before. One did not wear gowns made by one's lady's maid, however cleverly stitched. One went to a modiste and ordered the most exquisitely made gowns suitable to one's fortune and figure for a ducal ball. Their fortunes, however, could afford them a lace stocking apiece.

"I will find some way," Marian announced decisively. She was the family keeper of finances. She knew the value of tallow and wax and dealt out the candles accordingly. She had bargained Squire Oglethorp's remaining horses into this trip to London. She would have to be the one to find the funds for ball gowns.

"Not the ruby," Jessica whispered as her sister started toward the study.

Not the ruby. It was becoming a symbol of last resort. She needed to bring Lord Darley up to snuff before the ruby must be hocked.

She had no dreams of acquiring a duke for husband. Every ambitious mama in London had their caps set for the dashing Duke of Devonshire. The competition was far too stiff and out of Marian's means. But to be invited to a ducal ball gave a certain cachet that would see them in good stead in the future. She might only aspire to a viscount, but Jessica was lovely enough to look where she might, even if she was only an Oglethorp. Her appearance at Devonshire House would make that apparent to all the *ton*.

Retreating to the study, Marian opened the trunk that had been transported there at her request from their house in Wiltshire. Since Marian had always possessed a literary bent, no one had questioned her need for a trunkful of books despite the extra trouble it caused in transportation. Neither her mother or Jessica understood that this trunk held the remains of their fortune. Squire Oglethorp had inherited an extremely valuable library from a more literary ancestor.

She hated parting with any of them. Her fingers caressed the leather volumes of an earlier century. She had read all but the Greek and Latin ones. Her education had never been broad enough to include languages, living or dead. She would more readily part with those she could not read, but she suspected they were not nearly so valuable as some of the others. Her fingers found the ancient volumes at the bottom of the trunk.

She knew there was a good market in Medieval illuminated manuscripts. She had already sold several. It broke her heart to give up these last, because they were the most magnificent of all. The jewel tones of the illustrations cried out for admiration. The lettering lovingly penned in perfect script spoke of years of hallowed work. To part with such love and respect in exchange for the coins for ball dresses seemed sacrilege, but she must consider the living before the dead. Her mother and Jessica needed to go to the ball. They had no care at all for these old tomes packed away in a trunk. Marian would be the only one to suffer when the books were gone.

She had already made inquiries against the day this would be necessary. She had the names and directions of several respectable dealers in books and antiquities. All she must do was force herself to decide which of her lambs to sacrifice, and she could be on her way.

She chose several rare volumes from the fifteenth and sixteenth centuries for which she had already been given quotes. She knew they would not be enough for three gowns from a modiste. Sadly, she chose the smaller manuscript, the one in old English, with the carefully drawn flowers and herbs in the borders. Not only were the drawings exquisite, but the descriptions and uses of the various plants were of immense interest once she learned to read the highly ornate writing and odd language. She could imagine some monk making careful observations over a lifetime and having it faithfully recorded by some younger assistant eager to learn all he had to tell. The book cried out of history and love and patience. But it was worth far more than all the other modern volumes in her care.

She could not be so selfish as to keep this treasure when it might provide a future for her family. Wrapping it carefully in cloth, she included it in the satchel she would take to the booksellers'. She would obtain various appraisals until she knew which seller was the most knowledgeable and honest. It would be nice if she could find one who would appreciate the books as much as she did, but she had little hope of that. Men tended to be rather mercenary when it came to antiquities.

Calling for the carriage and her maid, Marian donned a bonnet and spencer and prepared herself for the expedition. Lord Darley had other appointments today, so she could not expect him to call or come by and ask her to go driving with him again. She would not be missed when her mother and Jessica went to make their calls. She could have the whole day to herself if she desired. She just wished the day could be spent on more uplifting activities.

By the time she had traversed the streets of London and haggled with three booksellers, she wished she could be anywhere else in the world but here. These men were avaricious monsters. They had no respect, no sensitivity, no concept of the preciousness of the volumes she had to sell. They gave her unfashionable gown a sniff, glanced through the leather volumes to check their condition, riffled the manuscript pages with raised eyebrows, and quoted figures as low as the ones she had obtained in Wiltshire. She had thought surely they would bring more in the enlightened population of the city.

The quotes were so universally similar that she had the horrible notion that there was some small imp running from stall to stall warning all the sellers that she was coming. The fact that these same vendors had been recommended by the vendors in Wiltshire added to her suspicions. It did not seem quite possible that they could all know each other and price all books the same, but it appeared that way.

Struck with the notion, Marian set her jaw and stopped the driver at the next sign of a dealer in books and antiquities. This one was not on her list, but it was in a very respectable section. She had seen a lady in fashionable muslin just leaving carrying a neatly wrapped package, and there were several elegant people admiring a display of jewelry in the window. She was quite certain this seller had the respect of the *ton*. She would see what he had to say about her books.

Lily exclaimed in weariness at having to stop at still another musty store, and Marian took pity on her. Lily was more family than servant. She worked for terrible wages and with a quiet steadfastness that endeared her to one and all. She stayed up late to help her ladies undress and rose early to mend and sew and press their gowns. She deserved a little rest now.

"I will be just a minute, Lily. Why don't you wait here

and admire the ladies' hats while I run in and see if the store owner is in?"

"I couldn't, miss. You oughtn't to be about without me. 'Tis not proper."

Marian climbed down from the carriage with the help of their driver. She turned to prevent Lily from following her. "I just saw a friend of mine enter. Surely that will be company enough?" It was a lie, but she wasn't above telling lies to make people happy. She had worked through the old debate about whether the means or the end were more important and came to the conclusion that it depended on the means and the end. In this case, the means were negligible and the end was by far more beneficial than a lie was hurtful.

Lily sat back and smiled happily, and Marian hurriedly carried the heavy satchel through the respectable portals of Aristotle's Antiquities Emporium.

She ought to have a footman, she realized, as she stepped onto a floor covered in thick Turkish carpet. Crystal glittering in glass cases made her think of the expensive reception areas of the grand houses she had been in these last weeks. Magnificent oil paintings adorning the walls reminded her of the museums she had visited at every chance. One did not attend these places without maids or footmen, clothed in one's oldest gowns, carrying battered satchels. This place was obviously not the vendors' stalls she had been frequenting.

She was terrified of being stared at and criticized, and started to turn and make her escape before anyone could possibly recognize her. Perhaps she could come back wearing one of her better gowns, and she could borrow a footman somewhere to help her carry the satchel. That would gain her a good deal more respect before she made her inquiries. Perhaps a place like this did not even deal with people like her. Perhaps they only dealt with kings and queens. Stomach tightening in anxiety, she started out, when a familiar voice taunted her from the interior.

"Lady Marian, I believe?"

She contemplated pretending she did not hear. Perhaps he would think he was mistaken. But men like that never made mistakes, she thought, grimacing; Only women like her did. He was Darley's best friend. She would have to try not to repeat her earlier mistake of rudeness. Besides, she sensed him coming up behind her. Pasting on her most pleasant smile, she turned to greet him.

"Good morning, Mr. Montague," she said softly, without any elaboration such as "Are you slumming today?" or "Have you had your morning drink of blood yet?" She kept her equilibrium by thinking these things only to herself while the elegant man in expensively tailored bottle-green coat and tight-fitting fawn breeches looked her up and down.

"Come slumming, have we?" he asked, noting her satchel.

Marian nearly choked as her own words came back to her without their ever having been uttered. The man had the tongue of an adder. She smiled sweetly, and was rewarded by his instant look of suspicion. "If I were, I was undoubtedly misled. You must excuse me, sir; I've left my carriage waiting." She liked the sound of that immensely. It made her sound like a royal princess.

A portly man with silver buttons on his vest and a monocle dangling from a silver chain came up to stand beside Montague. He quickly inspected the company and, without a word of warning, bent to open the satchel Marian had set on the carpet.

Marian made a startled cry, but the man's soft whistle of respect stayed her hand from slapping him away. Montague's fingers on her arm further held her.

"Jacobs knows the business inside and out. If you are a collector or purveyor of antiquities, he is the man to see."

The man called Jacobs reverently removed the Medieval manuscript from the satchel. Setting it carefully down on a glass counter, he donned a pair of soft white gloves before picking the manuscript up again. His expression was one of great awe and fascination as he delicately turned the pages.

"Surely you do not mean to sell this, miss," he murmured, his gaze never swerving from the pages.

Marian was aware of the sharp look from the gentleman at her side. She was not easily embarrassed, but the situation had her struggling for some semblance of dignity. All the *ton* undoubtedly knew the Oglethorps were not in funds. She would not be revealing family secrets by assuring him she must sell the manuscript. Her embarrassment came from the fact that it was this book that she was selling. She would rather it were the family jewels any day. Any lover of books would despise her for what she was doing.

"I must," she whispered, wishing Montague to the devil. It was much easier to be angrier at him for her humiliation than at the genial man who so respected her precious manuscripts.

Jacobs let the monocle fall from his eye as he glanced up at her. His sharp gaze took in her dowdy attire, the battered satchel, and the expression on her face. Without a word to her, he gestured to someone in the back. "Bring the lady some tea and a chair. Tell her driver to come around in half an hour."

Montague asked her sarcastically, "You do have a carriage, don't you, Lady Marian? I wouldn't want the poor boy to waste his time looking for it."

She bit her lip and prayed hard. Her nerves were on edge; her emotions were all-too-clearly on the brink of exploding. She really and truly needed to tell this braying jackass what she thought of him. She merely gave him a thoughtful look and accepted the gilded chair the boy brought for her.

Montague took out another chair and sat down without invitation, leaning over to rifle through the rest of the contents of her bag.

"Just precisely what do you think you are doing, Mr. Montague?" she asked tartly. It was impossible to be completely quiet with this arrogant monster.

"Seeing how much your soul is worth, Lady Marian," he replied idly, examining the dramatic hand-colored illustrations of her copy of *Odyssey*.

"It is not any of your business, Mr. Montague." She resisted the urge to jerk the book from his hands. She would behave as a proper lady; she would, even if it killed her.

Jacobs was still engrossed in the manuscript, much to the

detriment of other customers. The boy who brought the tea hurried to wait on a young gentleman looking for something in carved ivory. Neither looked to the trio poring over old books in the corner.

"I make it my business, Lady Marian. I am a collector of old books. These are extraordinarily rare and valuable. Have you some proof of ownership?"

Marian knew what it was to see red. Through a haze of fury she glared at the gentleman who so insulted her. It was quite possible that he was a handsome man. He had a strong chin with a cleft, and thick, dark, remarkably mobile eyebrows. She wasn't aware of ever having seen him smile, but his mouth had a handsome tilt to it. She wanted to bash him in the middle of his aristocratically patrician nose. She wouldn't be satisfied until the red she saw was his blood.

Clenching her gloved fingers, she turned to Mr. Jacobs. "I am sorry, sir, I have evidently come to the wrong place. If you will please return my manuscript, I will be leaving now."

Jacobs's small mouth fell open and he sent a beseeching gaze to the arrogant gentleman. He looked near to tears. Marian wished she had only to deal with him. Perhaps she could come back and find him alone later. She held out her hand demandingly.

Montague set her teacup in it. "You will be doing no such thing. You will break Jacobs's heart. Besides, I will wager every other vendor you've seen has offered you only half the sum these are worth."

Marian sent him a scathing glance. "Not one of them accused me of thievery, either. I would thank you to return the volumes to the bag, sir."

Montague retained his hold on the *Odyssey*. "I only wished some documentation to go with them. Volumes as rare as these will sell at a better price when their history is documented."

She clenched her hands around the teacup and tried not to look at him. She had always wished she could read the book he was holding now. The illustrations had held her captivated. She tried to remember the duke and the ball and her anxious family. "They belonged to my stepfather, sir. It would be a trifle difficult for him to come back from the grave to cite their history. Not that he would know it, anyway," she added a trifle bitterly. She might not be able to express all her anger and humiliation and sadness, but a dead man wouldn't care about sarcasm.

Montague's expressive eyebrows raised a trifle. "He was not a collector?"

"He didn't even know what he possessed, or he might have sold them with the paintings." There wasn't much use pretending anything else. She needed this honesty to balance the pressure of being polite to a man she despised and feared.

"But you knew?" He scarcely bothered to keep the incredulity from his voice.

If only she could smack him. Or throw the teacup at him. Or simply tell the ass what she thought of him. She would feel so much better. Marian tightened her lips and clenched her teeth. She couldn't speak through clenched teeth. She gave him what she hoped was a speaking glare.

Amusement flared briefly in his gray-green eyes, as if he understood her predicament. Then an expression of cool disdain dropped in place, and he was back to normal. "Of course, if you were a collector, you would know the value of the good squire's library. And if you were aware that antiquities have become very valuable of late, you need only make inquiries to ascertain their worth. If you were a true lover of books, you would not even think of parting with them."

There was the proverbial straw. With a great effort of restraint, Marian set the cup down, jerked the book from his hand, and stood up. "My opinion of you has not changed one iota, Mr. Montague. You are still a braying ass."

She returned the book to the satchel and reached for the manuscript.

Jacobs scrambled up and clutched it longingly to his chest, refusing to let it go.

Five

The situation was quite impossible. Marian was much too practical to be a watering pot, but she felt dangerously near to tears now. She could not leave without the manuscript. She could not stay in the company of the infuriating Mr. Montague. Tears might actually be the only solution, but she refused to allow the monster to drive her to them.

"Please, Mr. Jacobs, I must leave." She rose from her chair, holding out her gloved hand with what she hoped was a gesture of authority. She rather thought it looked more like a plea.

"Don't be ridiculous." Montague did not retrieve the *Odyssey* from the satchel, but stood up when the lady did. "I will give you forty pounds for it. I am certain that is more than anyone has offered you for all the books combined. The manuscript belongs in a museum, somewhere that it can receive the proper care and appreciation and can be shared by all."

Jacobs looked equally horrified by this suggestion. A man of obviously few words but eloquent expressions, he continued clutching the book and began to back away. Had the situation not been so rife with other emotions, Marian might have laughed.

Forty pounds. It was more than twice what she had been offered. Forty pounds could provide three gowns and all the accouterments and still leave funds for emergencies. She could not possibly turn down such an offer. Yet she could not possibly accept it from Montague.

When it seemed she still hesitated, Jacobs finally managed to squeak, "Fifty pounds, miss. I will give you fifty pounds."

Slightly startled, Marian glanced to her nemesis. She had thought the two were somehow together on this transaction, that Jacobs was an appraiser and Mr. Montague a rich collector. Mr. Montague's frown put an end to that theory.

When he made no further offer, Marian gave a hesitant nod. "Thank you, Mr. Jacobs, you are a true gentleman."

Positively glowing with relief, caressing the cherished manuscript, Jacobs hurried to the rear of the establishment to obtain the necessary funds.

Montague looked down his impressive nose at her. "He is not a gentleman, you know. He is just a wealthy Cit."

My, how she despised the man! Marian gave him a frosty look and disdained to answer.

He seemed determined to draw some comment from her. "You would have done better to hock your jewelry, you know. There are more people inclined to buy jewels than books."

He seemed intent on rubbing her nose in it. She saw no reason why she should not rub his as well. Back stiff as a poker, staring at the doorway where Mr. Jacobs had disappeared, she replied coldly, "Jewels? You mistake me for someone else, I am sure. Had I jewels to sell, I would surely have done so by now." Let him know that she had reached her last straw before she lowered herself to selling books.

"I see you are a liar as well as a mercenary, sharp-tongued little actress," Montague responded pleasantly. "The ruby and diamonds you were wearing the other night would bring a small fortune in a modern setting."

Another female would have had the vapors by now. Marian could see where that would be an extremely convenient ploy for avoiding such unpleasant situations. There was obviously little purpose in arguing with the gentleman, if gentleman he truly was. She didn't see how he could be, given his behavior. So a fit of the vapors would quite satisfactorily put an end to his obnoxiousness. She just wasn't inclined to falling into a heap on the floor. She was more than certain that Montague wouldn't bother to catch her.

Just thinking about Montague catching her gave her the vapors. He was exceptionally tall, and she didn't think the breadth of his chest beneath that coat had the benefit of padding. She tried not to think of just what lay beneath the gentleman's clothing. Obviously, her wits had gone to let at his insults.

"It is none of your business, but that necklace is my mother's, the only gift she retains from my father. Had I found some way of selling it without breaking my mother's heart, I should have done so long since. It is much more convenient to have a horse and carriage than to wear a stone around one's neck."

Montague raised his eyebrows. He had taunted her in all manner of ways, but she had not responded at all as he had expected. He had not produced ladylike tears, dramatic faints, or vitriolic insults. All in all, he had proved nothing about this enigmatic little harpy except that she was in desperate need of funds—and that she had the character of a stone Medusa when she wanted.

He almost had to accede to some respect for her intelligence and strength of character. He had tried to pretend he didn't see her despair at parting with the manuscript, but in light of her reaction to his suggestion of selling her jewels, he could see where her priorities lay. He knew very well what it was like to have to part with something precious, and like her, he had a distaste for wasteful ornamentation. He, too, would prefer to keep the treasure of words than the glitter of gold. But he'd be damned if he'd let her know that. It was more than obvious that this woman was not the sweet helpmeet Darley wished for wife. A woman made of steel and stone would walk all over the young viscount.

When Jacobs returned with the pouch, Montague made a show of counting out the sum for Marian's benefit. She held herself aloof from the transaction, but he noticed her eyes followed every movement. Had he attempted to pocket a single shilling, she might have leapt upon him like a tigress defending her young. He was well aware that her kind of hunger came from going without for too long.

When he was finished counting, Montague slipped the pouch into his coat pocket, picked up her satchel, and held out his arm to the young lady. "I think it best that I escort you home, Lady Marian. It would not do at all for a lady like yourself to be carrying such sums through London streets. Your carriage should be waiting by now."

Reginald could see the fury leap to her eyes, followed by suspicion. He wondered idly if she would snarl and pull a knife from that frothy little reticule or if she would remember her place and act as she ought. She did neither.

Apparently deciding he wasn't worthy of the treatment she gave Darley, she merely turned her back on him and walked out, expecting him to follow like a hired flunky.

That irritated him more than he cared to admit. It was much too early in the game for the little witch to be getting under his skin. If he was not careful, she would be married to Darley and he would have to endure this treatment for the rest of his life or write off the only true friend he had.

As he climbed into the carriage after her, Reginald had to admit that the contest was becoming personal. It was no longer a matter of saving Darley from himself, but of self-preservation. He eyed the perfectly respectable lady's maid beside her and counted another round lost. He had thought to catch her out alone again.

Idly, as if continuing a conversation, he mentioned, "It has become common practice to copy expensive jewelry. Thieves in London are rampant, and it is much more practical to keep the real jewels in a vault."

Lady Marian merely settled her skirts around her and looked through him as if he were not there. Her maid gave him a look askance, but being a good servant, she did not question his presence aloud. Knowing the importance of staying on the good side of a lady's servants, Reginald gave her a smile and would have tipped his hat had he been wearing one. Mostly, hats annoyed him, and he had a tendency to forget them at all times. The maid still looked a little wary.

He knew better than to condescend to make explanations to servants, but he had also learned at an early age how to make his way around any obstacle. Keeping his expression pleasant, he addressed the maid rather than Lady Marian. "Your mistress is a bit peeved with me at the moment. Would you tell her I am most heartily sorry if I have offended?"

Flustered at being addressed by an elegant gentleman for the first time in her life, Lily fluttered her hands, looked to Marian's stony expression, and glanced fearfully back to the gentleman. "I don't think she accepts the apology, my lord," she whispered.

"Mister. Just plain Mr. Montague. I suppose that explains the lady's reticence. She does not accept apologies from those of lesser rank."

He was rewarded by a furious glare from the lady in question. He had never seen eyes that flashed quite so delightfully. It was no wonder Darley was head over heels. If Reginald had not already seen her flash her true colors, he might consider giving his friend a run for the money. Not that marriage would be his objective. Smiling still, he sought another perspective from which to reach her.

"Would you explain to the lady that I am quite circumspect? I do not go about boasting of my collection and I would not presume to do so in the case of another collector. The lady's secrets are quite safe with me."

The lady's shoulders seemed to relax slightly from their stiff stance as she turned to look out the carriage window. Her maid clenched and unclenched her fingers nervously, uncertain how to address this situation. Having been relegated permanently to hired flunky, Montague resolved to put the maid at ease if he could not do so for the mistress.

"Will the ladies be attending Devonshire's ball?" he asked cordially, as if conversing with servants was an everyday occurrence. Considering his new valet, it might become so.

The maid's face brightened. "Aye, they will. They are to have gowns made by a modiste for the occasion."

Reginald raised his eyebrows. "I did not know gowns could be made by anyone else."

Marian made an inelegant snort but continued to stare out the window. The maid looked nervous at having spoken out of turn. When she remained silent a little too long, Marian glanced back into the carriage. Reginald noted her expression of resignation rather than irritation at her maid's unwise words. It threw him momentarily off-balance.

"Most of the world constructs their own gowns, Mr. Montague. A few might hire a seamstress. Only the very rich and very fortunate can afford a modiste." As if that were lesson enough for the day, she turned back to the window.

"I cannot believe you are trying to tell me you and your family are trying to take London in homemade gowns." His gaze dropped to the drab bit of brown cotton she was wearing now. He could believe that was homemade. And so was the one she had worn at the inn. But he had seen her in evening wear as fine as any he had ever seen anywhere. What hoax was she up to now?

Marian gave him a scathing look and when her maid did not dare offer explanation, she replied, "I do not much care what you believe. You and your ilk no doubt go about running up enormous debts at tailors and trust in luck or families to pay them. We prefer to live honestly. Lily is a very fine seamstress. With her talents and our helping hands, we do very well, thank you."

The carriage was pulling to a halt in a less-than-fashionable but respectable residential side street some distance from the mansions of Mayfair. Reginald scarcely took note of his surroundings as he sought some means of resolving this situation peaceably. He found it hard to believe any word out of the woman's mouth, but then, he found it hard to believe that any impostor could sound so brutally honest. If he were to get to the bottom of her trickery, he would have to be more in her company. He could not do that unless he smoothed the feathers he had ruffled. Unfortunately, it was much more fun to ruffle them than smooth them.

"Then let me congratulate you on your fortune in finding such a paragon. I trust you pay her accordingly. Talent should be rewarded." He climbed down from the carriage as the door opened, pulling the heavy satchel after him, leaving the lady to stare after him in open-mouthed dismay.

She was forced to take his hand to descend. When she stood before him, she glanced deliberately at the pocket containing her money. Reginald toyed with the idea of making her ask for it, but even he could not sink that low. He removed the purse and handed it to her.

"If you truly wish to keep the rest of your library, remember what I have said about the jewelry," he reminded her in low tones as her maid waited a respectable distance away.

"I fail to see your interest in my jewelry, sir. In actuality, I fail to understand anything about you. My driver will return you to your destination." Carefully clutching the purse, she turned away.

Reginald watched her go with a hint of admiration. She had the proud manner of a duchess when her temper was riled. She had just successfully dismissed him as if he were a footman rather than the son of an earl. Of course, she no doubt thought him closer to a footman than an earl. He had a suspicion Lady Marian and her family had not exactly acquired a coat of town bronze yet.

He gave the driver the address of his residence rather than returning to the shop. Wouldn't it have delighted the lady to discover that he was owner of the shop and not a patron? She would have spread it all about the *ton* and forced him into permanent retreat. But he had dealt with much more sophisticated members of society without any of them ever having guessed that he was more than an eccentric collector of antiquities. He didn't think Lady Marian had any inkling that he wished to acquire her manuscript for resale, not for his own collection. He was quite annoyed with Jacobs for acquiring it as if he were bidding against him. It would be difficult to make a profit on fifty pounds. As much as the piece belonged in a museum, museums did not have that kind of money.

Maybe he ought to inform Darley that his beloved had an intellectual bent that included collecting rare medieval manuscripts. Darley had the funds to buy back the blasted piece and give it to her as a betrothal gift. Of course, once Darley realized the lady had real brains, he would turn into a rabbit and run. The viscount had been under his mother's thumb too long to want to spend the rest of his life with a wife of the same ilk.

Reginald toyed with various possibilities as the carriage rolled sedately through the streets. He had already hired a man from Bow Street to investigate the lady's background, but he was beginning to believe she was the genuine article. Even a very good actress could not produce that air of hauteur with which he had been dismissed. It was bred into the bones, he believed. An actress would overdo it, making some gesture or grimace to emphasize her displeasure. Lady Marian had merely turned her back and said everything by saying nothing.

He ventured to say that she was really a lady, but a particularly bad-tempered one. She must be practicing restraint while on the hunt for a husband. He had managed to crack that restraint a time or two today, but she had only once given vent to her real feelings. It would be amusing to see how long she lasted if provoked in front of Darley.

As Reginald stepped down from the carriage and tipped the driver, he turned his thoughts with satisfaction in that direction. Perhaps he could accomplish his goals before Bow Street accomplished theirs. He need merely be in company with the lovely Lady Marian and Darley to the extent that he ultimately wore down her patience.

How better to do it than to court the shy Miss Jessica?

Six

"O'Toole, give back the watch!" Reginald looked in the mirror as he fiddled with his cravat and yelled at his wayward valet. His new hireling was not adept with cravats, but his hands were exceedingly deft in other ways.

The valet innocently polished the gold watch with a handkerchief before handing it back to his employer. "It was just in the need of a spot of polish, my lord. A fellow needs to keep his hand in, if you know what I mean."

"I don't have a title, you needn't 'lord' me, and you had better keep those blasted hands to yourself from now on if you don't want to end up in Newgate. Thieving is a reprehensible habit for a valet."

O'Toole gallantly brushed an invisible dust mote from his employer's expensively tailored shoulders. The black swallow-tailed coat possessed not a wrinkle as it stretched over broad shoulders and narrowed to a taut waist. He was rather in sympathy with his employer on the matter of starched collars, but it was impossible to acquire the correct degree of elegance in the cravat otherwise. Instead, Mr. Montague had to aspire to strikingly done rather than elegant. Spotless linen, a fashionably embroidered white waistcoat done in gold threads, and a hint of color in the gold watch fob added to the impression. Except for the cravat, his master was a credit to his valet.

"'Tis not thievin' if I give it back," he replied insouciantly.

Reginald snorted, and picking up his walking stick and

hat, started for the door. "You need not wait up. I am quite capable of undressing myself. Just leave the maids alone. I cannot keep Jasper from sacking you if you can't keep your bloody hands to yourself."

From behind a shock of thick auburn hair and a nose full of freckles, O'Toole grinned easily. "The lasses can't leave a fella alone. You want I should spend the evenin' readin'?"

Thoroughly exasperated with his insolent servant, Reginald slammed the door on him and started down the stairs. Why in the name of all that was sane he had taken on the petty thief, he could not fathom. If he had any wits left at all, he would throw O'Toole out on his ear in the morning.

But the man knew his trade. He had polished every boot and shoe in the closet, saw that all Reginald's linen was bleached to a pristine white, and made certain every coat he owned was pressed and in good repair. And he had done it all at a minimum of expense. A man like O'Toole could be worth his weight in gold just in tailor and laundry bills. Reginald was not making such profits that he could afford not to take expenses into account.

He was well aware of this as he climbed into the carriage that he could only recently afford. It cost a great deal of money to keep up one's reputation as a wealthy aristocrat, which he needed to do to keep his business profitable. He had to be accepted into the best of homes and rub shoulders with the best society so that he could direct them to his establishment at every opportunity. Because everyone considered him a collector of excellent taste, they took his recommendations when they wished to make a purchase or a sale. It allowed him to skim the cream from the top and keep the best antiquities emporium in London. So far, no one had ever made the connection between the younger son of the Earl of Mellon and Aristotle's Emporium, and that was the way he meant it to stay.

But the carriage and the town house and the showy string of horses at Newmarket had been hard won. His family had wished for him to marry an heiress, had even picked one out whom they considered eminently suitable, but Reginald had refused the honor. He had nothing in particular against women, except that most of them seemed to be empty-headed and frivolous. Mostly, he valued his independence. He did not wish to report to a wife every day, or to be accountable to her for every penny he spent. He thought better of himself than that. He thought far too highly of himself, in his father's opinion. The earl had cut off Reginald's allowance after the argument over the heiress.

That had forced him to recognize his predicament soon enough. If he wished to be independent, he had to be independent of his family, also. He could not accept his father's money without accepting the strings attached. So he had taken what remained of his quarterly allowance, the funds he had invested in the market, and his gambling winnings, and set out to make his own way in London.

After all these years, he was finally on the way to being comfortable. He had run up excessive debts those first few years in his attempt to continue living as he had, but those debts were now paid. He had learned the difference between frugality and miserliness. It was not being tight-fisted to keep only one horse and carriage in town, but sensible, particularly at the high cost of upkeep in London. With the money saved, he could afford to buy manuscripts like the one presented by Lady Marian. Larger profits could be made on larger purchases, and the amounts grew from there, turning a penny saved into a fortune earned. He rather enjoyed the game.

But he could not afford to let society know he was a shopkeeper. Only Darley knew, and that was because Reginald had had to borrow the funds from him to buy his first inventory. Darley had been repaid with interest since and kept the secret very well. For a friend like that, Reginald would move mountains. He would also do his utmost to save that friend from a disastrous marriage.

Arriving at the rout where he had been assured he would find Lady Marian and her family, Reginald gave up his hat and stick to a servant, greeted his gratified hostess, and began the hunt.

This was not a *haut ton* affair. The assemblage was small and less than glittering, but everyone present was extremely respectable. Reginald mentally stifled a yawn as he found his prey. He had long ago lost interest in the malicious gossip, the required flirting, and the lavish entertainments for which the bulk of society existed. But it was necessary to attend these occasions to keep his ear to the ground for valuable acquisitions and to drum up new customers. That was the challenge that kept him going. Unfortunately, an entertainment such as this did not have the kind of recklessly wealthy guest that made his expensive inventory so profitable.

Reginald was here merely for Darley's sake. He smiled gallantly as the shy Jessica noticed his approach first. He was a cynical two and thirty, and she was a naive seventeen, but ambitious mamas did not object to age differences. He had no real intention of fixing the chit's interest though. He didn't think she was capable of fixing any interest at all at this age. He merely needed to dance attendance on her occasionally so he had some excuse to be close enough to rile her sister's temper in Darley's presence. The task shouldn't take as long as it would to light a candle, much less become romantically attached.

He bowed politely over Lady Grace's hand, nodded briefly to a suspicious Lady Marian, and paused in front of the lovely Jessica. "Miss Oglethorp, might I say you look ravishing this evening? Have you been introduced to my cousin, Lady Mary? She is right over there." He turned to her anxious mama. "Might I borrow your daughter for just a bit? Mary has been quite eager to meet her. I believe they are of an age."

Lady Grace gave her permission without a qualm. Everyone knew Reginald Montague. Although he was merely an "honorable," he was considered quite a catch. He came from a wealthy family and dressed with the arrogance of wealth, so it was assumed he was well to grass. There wasn't a hint of anything untoward to his reputation. He had been introduced by Lord Darley, who was the epitome of everything respectable himself. How could she possibly refuse Jessica this opportunity?

Knowing full well what was going through her mother's mind, Marian fumed. She knew the cad a shade better than her mother. She suspected the devious devil had something up his sleeve, for a man like that had little interest in a green girl like Jessica. Marian looked up with relief as Darley returned to her side with a cup of punch.

"Your friend Mr. Montague has graciously offered to introduce Jessica to his cousin," she mentioned with a small smile and a look of concern. "I do so hope she remembers her manners. She is very young yet."

Darley looked in the direction of her gaze with some surprise. This was not the kind of affair Montague generally attended, and his friend seldom bothered even speaking to his relatives. To go out of his way to make an introduction was a curiosity indeed.

"Let us go keep an eye on her if that is what you wish," he suggested, offering his arm. Not being entirely a fool, Darley knew his friend's sterling character was thoroughly corroded by cynicism, and he felt a certain sense of responsibility for the shy Jessica, since he had made the introduction.

Marian accepted his arm and they were soon part of the circle to which Montague had introduced Jessica. Marian's shy sister was listening with eyes alight at the quick badinage exchanged by these young people who had known each other all their lives, but Jessica was scarce offering a word herself.

Reginald easily made room for them beside him, giving Lady Marian a slight nod of acknowledgment. "You have joined us just in time to extol the merits of the Season's leading beauties and to lay your wager on which one will win Devonshire. I am sure Lady Marian has an opinion on the subject."

"Since I do not know the gentleman, I cannot judge what he prefers in a female, sir. Besides, I am not objective. I believe my sister is all that is perfection in a lady."

Jessica turned red as all gazes turned to her. She had no witty words to say in reply, and Darley gallantly jumped in to assist her. "Miss Oglethorp is indeed a rare orchid in a hothouse full of beautiful flowers. Like many rare flowers, it would take a wise man to recognize her worth."

Someone else laughed. "That leaves out Devonshire,

then. Unless she is an expensive and gilded wall hanging, he will not notice that she exists."

"He cannot look at all eligible females as wall hangings," Montague protested. "He must choose among them some time. Perhaps we could present Lady Marian in a gilded halo and cloth of gold. What odds could we take then?"

Marian flashed him a look of irritation but responded sweetly, "The odds would be very good that I would trip and fall under the burden of a halo, I'm certain. I have no aspirations to be a duchess."

Darley sent her an appreciative glance, and Montague hid a grimace. Round one, score one to naught. He turned to his young cousin. "Mary, you have been introduced to the gentleman. Do you think he would prefer a bookish female to a beautiful one?"

The young lady gave a trill of laughter. "Wherever did you mean to find a bookish female, Reginald? Do not look in my direction. I cannot remember seeing the inside of a book since I left the schoolroom."

Jessica spoke hesitantly. "Marian reads. She is all the time in the library."

A young gentleman eager to impress her with his wit leapt into the debate, "But what does she actually do there? The dark corners of libraries offer more interesting delights than books."

This conversation was growing entirely too risque for an innocent like Jessica. Marian sent Darley a glance, but Montague was the one to respond first.

"Harrington, there ought to be enough light in your pate from the holes in it that you never need a candle. Miss Oglethorp, would you care to accompany me to the buffet?"

Marian and Darley followed, leaving the more sophisticated young people to laugh and gossip behind their backs. Marian sent her escort a veiled look. How had Lord Darley taken the news of her literary bent? He was frowning slightly, but she could not tell if it had to do with her or with the foolish remark of the young gentleman. She was terrified of saying anything that would make him think less of her. Drat Montague for introducing the subject of books. She desperately needed to bring Darley up to scratch soon.

As they reached the table, Montague turned and offered Marian a plate. "A bluestocking, Lady Marian? I never would have guessed it."

He was deliberately provoking her. She could see it in the laughing challenge of his eyes. He wanted her to slap him or do something equally outrageous. Marian knew her temper and her sharp tongue were her worst weaknesses, and this man was aiming directly at them. She wasn't certain why he was doing this, but she didn't intend to play into his hands.

"I daresay there are a great number of things that you will never guess, Mr. Montague. It takes an open mind to see all possibilities." She serenely took the plate offered and began to fill it with dainties from the table.

Darley chuckled and reached to help Jessica slice a piece of cake. "The lady is much too quick to bite at your bait, old boy. Leave off and let us enjoy the evening."

If he continued to pick at her, he would only make a fool of himself, Reginald realized. Darley was so smitten that he could not see what was right before his face. The lady had all but admitted to being a bluestocking. Her quick wit and quicker tongue should have made him wary. But his friend simply couldn't see beyond a pleasant voice and a bosom too round for fashion. Admittedly, he was having some trouble looking beyond that enticing display himself. The lady's maid/modiste had an eye for emphasizing the positive without disregarding propriety.

"I apologize for any offense you might have taken in my cousin's company, Miss Oglethorp," Reginald offered as a sop to his conscience, "Mary's friends tend to be a bit fast. I had forgotten that."

Jessica gave him a blank look before hastily returning her gaze to her plate. "I thought they seemed very nice, but I do not understand what they said about dark corners. It is very difficult to read in dark rooms. Marian always lights a lamp."

In another moment, Darley would be rolling on the floor with laughter, Reginald thought with disgust. Courting Jessica was going to make an ass out of him, proving Lady Marian's roundly stated opinion. He would do better to court the lady herself.

Even as he thought this, something inside him began to hum with anticipation. Reginald glanced toward the lady as she bit into a piece of marzipan and licked delicately at her lips. She wasn't beautiful, but she exuded the sensuality of an experienced courtesan. He could see why Darley was smitten.

It would give him a great deal more pleasure to seduce the Lady Marian than to smile pleasantly at the lovely Jessica.

Then Darley would be forced to recognize the fickleness of his lady-love.

Seven

"Mr. Montague seems to be quite a pleasant young man," Lady Grace said absently as she made a neat slice through the seal of the next letter on the stack beside her. "I don't know what you hold against him, Marian."

Marian sipped at her morning tea and frowned at the hideous hunting picture on the wall opposite. "He is not at all what he seems, Mama. I cannot fathom why he showed such particular attention to Jessica the other night. And the flowers are completely out of character."

"The flowers were addressed to all of us, dear. You mustn't put much store in it. And what can you possibly know of the gentleman's character? You have barely spoken with him." She set one invitation aside in the acceptance pile, discarded several pieces of mail, and started on the next.

Marian couldn't admit that she had more than spoken to the man. It would serve nothing to tell her mother that they had exchanged insults on several occasions, for that would not reflect any better on her than on him. And she preferred not to discuss her means of obtaining funds. Her mother was inclined to be hysterical, and she would worry fiercely if she knew the kinds of places Marian had been visiting in order to sell the books. So she couldn't mention meeting the man at an antiquities emporium.

She crumbled her toast instead. "I suppose I must be pleasant to him for Darley's sake, but I cannot find it easy to like the man." She also couldn't say she didn't like the way he made her feel when he looked at her. That didn't seem at all the thing to be discussing over the breakfast table. But she remembered very well how Montague's assessing gaze had rested on her, and how it had made her skin tingle and her stomach feel quivery. Despite his reputation, the man was no doubt a rake. No other gentleman looked at her like that.

Her mother's puzzled exclamation from the end of the table made Marian turn her thoughts back to the present. "What is it? Surely we have not been invited to another ducal ball? Those gowns we have ordered will cost the earth as it is."

"Do you think we can cancel the order?" Lady Grace asked in a low voice, staring at the letter.

Growing alarmed, Marian put down her toast. "What is it? Do we need to return home? Has something happened to the house?"

Her mother handed over the paper with a frown of puzzlement. "I'm not at all certain, dear. What can this mean? I'm quite certain the squire said his man was all that was honest. Surely he would not be asking for such sums without reason. Perhaps he means they are debts that come due when the harvest comes in?"

Marian scanned the letter once with dread, then began again to be certain she understood correctly. Squire Oglethorp had always handled the family business dealings. He had a steward to manage the farm. After he had died, the steward and the family solicitor had dealt with the bulk of the family finances, leaving Marian only to manage the day-to-day business of surviving on the meager allowance given them. She could see that had been a mistake. She should have made more inquiries about the family's state of affairs.

"It says the taxes have not been paid and there is interest coming due on the mortgage," she murmured, more to herself than as explanation to her mother.

"We cannot possibly pay such a sum until the harvest comes in, can we? Why do they send this to us? It is their business to handle the farm, is it not?"

"They say there are no funds for paying the debts. They

have spent all on seeds and labor. We must borrow the money to pay the rest. If there is a good harvest, we can pay the loan then."

Lady Grace looked at her blankly. "How does one go about borrowing money? Isn't that what we have the solicitor to do?"

Marian folded the letter slowly. "He has found no one willing to extend such a loan. He thinks we might have better luck among our friends here in London."

Lady Grace picked up her teacup and stared at it in bewilderment. "We are to ask our friends for loans? That does not seem at all proper."

Crushing the letter in her hand, Marian pushed away from the table. "Do not worry about it just yet. Perhaps we can cancel the gowns, as you suggested. I will look into it."

Her mother looked relieved. "And I am certain Lord Darley is at the asking point. He will help us understand what to do once you are betrothed. We must wait until then."

Marian hurried out of the room and toward the study, her favorite hiding place since the town house did not possess a library. Canceling the ball gowns would accomplish little. Their cost was negligible compared to the sum quoted in the letter. She still had a goodly amount of the fifty pounds left after judicious negotiating over materials with the modiste, but even that sum wouldn't come close to touching the amount of taxes and interest due. Why hadn't someone informed them of the debt before? Perhaps if they had not come to London they could have scraped together enough to satisfy their creditors.

But the amounts would only come due again next year, and if the harvest failed again, they would be out of a home. They had to come to London to find husbands who could support them. Somehow, she must stall for time until she was safely wed. She had to bring Darley up to scratch soon.

Had she been a man, she could have gone down to her club and found a drinking buddy who would gladly extend a loan for a few months. Women did not have that alternative. She could not very well ask Darley for a loan. Perhaps when they were betrothed she could act helpless and ask his advice, but not before then. It might be weeks or months before Darley summoned the nerve to ask for her hand. This letter seemed to indicate that they didn't have that long.

Marian sat down in the massive chair behind the desk and stared helplessly at her trunk of books. She was certain Mr. Jacobs would be delighted to buy every one of them. If he gave her twice what she had been quoted previously, she might manage most of the sum needed, but she rather thought Mr. Montague was responsible for the earlier extravagant sum. Mr. Jacobs would surely not be so foolish a second time, without the wealthy gentleman looking on.

Thinking of Mr. Montague stirred the germ of another thought, one she wished she could shove aside. He had said the necklace was very valuable, and that there were ways of making copies, that many people did it. Would it be so very awful if her mother possessed only a copy of her precious necklace? It would still look the same, and she would still have the memory of her husband giving it to her. At the same time, they would have the money to save their home.

She didn't know if she could make herself do it. She got up and paced the room, from the glass-encased bookcase of musty tomes to the heavily draped window overlooking the mews. If she should ever be wealthy enough to have a study of her own, she would have it built with windows everywhere and draperies on nary a one. That was a fine thought, she realized, when she was about to lose the one study she owned.

Her mother had no desire to marry again, yet she needed a home of her own. With the proper care, the farm could produce again. It had made Squire Oglethorp wealthy once. It just hadn't made him wealthy enough for extravagance. By living carefully, her mother could be comfortable in a short time—if she still had the farm to live on. It would provide her an income for the rest of her life. Selling it would leave her subject to the whims of any husbands her daughters might acquire. That did not seem at all a satisfactory solution given the nature of men and the vicissitudes of life.

Perhaps it would be possible to just pawn the necklace

for a little while. She had heard of such things. It would be like borrowing money with the necklace as collateral. If it brought enough to pay off the debt and have a copy made, no one would know what she had done. Then when the harvest came in, she could retrieve the original.

That thought brightened the situation considerably. Had the stone been entirely hers, she would have had no qualms about selling it outright in order to ensure her mother's future. She held no sympathy for a father who had left her a mere pittance and a single heirloom to survive on. She was not in the least sentimental about the wretched rock. But her mother was.

She would have to ask Mr. Montague how to go about pawning the necklace and getting a copy made. She hated the thought of speaking to him at all, but he was already aware of their desperate need of funds. He had apparently said nothing to Lord Darley, and for that she had to be grateful. She simply could not lower herself in the viscount's eyes by admitting their financial desperation. She must seem sweet and unconcerned about such things until she had Darley's ring on her finger. She would have to work at making that sooner rather than later. In the meantime, she needed to deal with the obnoxious Mr. Montague.

She wasn't at all certain how to go about it, however. She couldn't very well send a note around to his house explaining the problem, and she couldn't count on finding him at the emporium. She must somehow wait until they met again and find a way to get him alone.

The thought of being alone with Reginald Montague was enough to give her the shivers. He was a tall man of considerable strength, she wagered. She had read enough stories of what happened to foolish young women who trusted themselves alone with such men. She would have to rely on the fact that he despised her. Surely men did not molest women whom they despised?

Fortune smiled on her for a change the very next day. While her mother and Jessica were out making calls, Marian chose to stay at home and read. She knew Darley had been called out of town this morning on some estate business, so she grabbed this opportunity to be alone. She found

the social whirl of London quite fatiguing after a lifetime of
rural serenity. Her sanity survived on these moments of
solitude.

When their manservant announced a gentleman caller,
she almost had him say she was not at home. But glancing
at the card presented, she took back that hasty thought.
Montague.

He had never presented himself here before. She could
not imagine why he was doing so now other than out of
friendship to Darley. If she were to have him brought up,
she ought to have Lily with her. She shouldn't entertain
him alone.

But she needed to speak with him alone. She couldn't
very well ask him about pawning the ruby in front of Lily.
Fortune had been kind enough to grant her this opportunity.
She had to have the courage to grasp it.

"Very well, Simmons, have him brought up, then bring
us some tea. I am certain Mama will be home shortly and
will wish to see him." She hoped that placated the stiff and
proper London servant's disapproval.

Montague looked surprised when he entered to find only
Marian present. He hid his momentary consternation well
when he accepted the seat offered.

"This is a pleasure, Lady Marian. I did not expect to find
you alone. Darley told me he was being called out of town
and asked that I look in on all of you upon occasion. Are
you already mourning his absence?"

He was twitting her, she was certain. She held her tongue
as a maid carried in the tea tray. When the girl was gone,
she attempted a pleasant expression. "You are refining
upon nothing, sir. Lord Darley is free to come and go as he
pleases, as am I. It would be presumptuous of me to mourn
his absence under those circumstances."

He nodded approvingly as he sipped his tea. "You do not
count your eggs before they are hatched, I see. A wise
woman, indeed. Do you set your sights on the duke then?"

Marian's lips tightened and she set her cup carefully on
the table. "If you have come to be insulting, sir, I would
thank you to leave now."

Montague held his hand up in a gesture of peace. "I

thought only to speak with you honestly as we have done previously. If you wish the usual drivel, so be it. Is not the weather very fine for this time of year? Would you care to go driving this afternoon?"

Marian scowled and handed him a plate of scones. "I cannot fathom what Darley sees in you, sir, but as we are on the subject of honesty, I will admit that there is a reason I allowed you up here unattended."

His expressive eyebrows raised. "I had wondered," he murmured. "I had not thought it was because you wished to seduce me."

She flung a pillow at him. He cleverly managed to divert the pillow while keeping a precarious hold on his teacup, thereby preventing a disastrous spill on his stockinette breeches. "That could have been uncomfortable," he murmured, carefully setting the china back on the tray. "Do you often indulge in these fits of pique? Is Darley aware of it?"

"You deliberately bring out the worst in me, Mr. Montague. If you tell Lord Darley about this visit, I shall have to inform him of your insult. I thought we were to call a truce."

"Why is it that ladies must turn jests into insults? Is it because they possess no sense of humor?"

"It is because their sense of humor does not rely on the vulgar, sir. I find nothing humorous in being accused of seduction, even if I had any knowledge of such things, which I don't. Your assumption that I do is insulting."

"The fact that you speak of such things with anger instead of fainting dead away tells me you know a great deal more than most ladies about these subjects. Let us cut the pretense, Lady Marian. You are no young innocent to wear white and pale at the mention of a man's inexpressibles. You are well-read and have a brain behind that pretty face. We will get on vastly better if you admit to it instead of playing the part of sweetness and light as you do with Darley."

So that was it. Entwining her fingers in vexation, Marian sent him a venomous glare. "I try very hard to be what is expected of me, sir. You do me no favors by encouraging me otherwise. But for the moment, let us set aside our differences. I need your help."

Montague looked interested at that. He even dared to retrieve his teacup. "Please go on, my lady. I am at your service."

She had a good reply to make to that, but she held her tongue. She needed his help, not his anger. "My mother received a rather distressing letter from her solicitor today. It seems we are in need of borrowing a rather serious sum to keep our home. It can be paid back immediately upon the harvest, but apparently the man has been unable to find a lender." She spoke succinctly, if with considerable distaste at revealing such matters to a relative stranger. She hastened to continue speaking before he could interrupt. "I might conceivably obtain much of it by selling the remains of the library, but you once mentioned the worth of my necklace. Is it possible to in some way use it as collateral for a small loan?" She breathed easier once she had the words out.

Montague considered the question carefully, swirling the tea in his cup. "You would wish to make a copy of it so your mother does not find out?"

Biting her lip, Marian nodded.

"And you do not wish to sell it outright?"

She shook her head. "I feel enough of a thief to consider even this. I know the stone is to come to me, but it is all my mother has."

"It suits your coloring more than hers," he said thoughtfully. "Your father must have been dark."

"I believe so. I was very young when he died. His portrait stayed with the estate, so I have not seen it since we left." She continued to watch him anxiously.

He took another sip of tea and watched her over the edge of the cup. "The current marquess cannot be called upon for help? Perhaps he would be interested in acquiring the jewel if it is an heirloom."

He wasn't going to help. Trying to hide her despair, Marian glanced at the mantel clock. Perhaps her mother and sister would be home soon to put an end to this distressing conversation. "I do not know the gentleman. He was in the

Americas when my father died, and as I said, I was very young. The solicitors arranged for our removal, I believe. From something the squire once said, I don't believe the estate was much in funds at the time. Apparently much of the unentailed land had been sold off for generations. I do not know the details. I just know I could not ask a total stranger for help."

Montague understood pride. He had too much of it himself. He nodded absently, then returned the cup to the table. "You cannot expect to obtain as great a sum by pawning it as by selling it outright. May I ask how much you need?"

The sum she quoted wasn't unreasonable, but it would take every penny of cash he could scrape together.

Montague sighed and stood up. "Go get the necklace. I think it is time we went for a drive."

Eight

"Where are we going?" Marian murmured as Mr. Montague wheeled his fashionable curricle toward the park. She had already noted with a great amount of nervousness that he had no groom in the seat behind.

"We shall show ourselves in the park as is expected, then make a slight detour to a jeweler. I shall have you back in your parlor in good time."

Marian clasped her hands in her lap and tried to look pleased. The ruby necklace in her reticule made that more than difficult. "It will take time to make a copy, will it not? How will I explain the absence of the necklace while it is being done?"

"Tell your mother that I am a great expert on jewelry and that I recommended it be cleaned to keep its beauty." Montague steered the horses into the park and joined the steady procession already there.

Marian was grateful that she was wearing one of her new London gowns as they met the stares of the *ton* in the park. The light jonquil yellow of her gown almost matched the tiny rosebuds and ribbons of her bonnet. She did not look completely dowdy, but she was aware of being nowhere near as fashionable as the other young lovelies in plumes and vivid carriage dresses. She told herself she did not care, but she disliked being judged and found wanting.

"How much will this copy cost?" She tried to keep her mind on business and not the picture they were presenting to the crowds. Mr. Montague looked very fine in his curly-brimmed beaver, driving his matched bays. His height made him seem exceptionally distinguished, but mostly it made her nervous. She was much more comfortable with Lord Darley beside her.

"The price of a few gowns, I daresay. Are you certain you would not prefer selling outright? Perhaps if you consulted your mother—"

Marian stiffened her shoulders. "We will make do with what gowns we have. I count them a fair price for my mother's peace of mind."

He sent her a long look before returning his attention to the fashionable crowd around them. He raised his whip in greeting to several young bloods and made nods to a number of dowagers taking the air. "You make it difficult to tell when you are giving me Spanish coin, my lady," he murmured while keeping an affable smile fixed to his countenance.

"Since it is utterly of no consequence to you, sir, it should not matter." She responded with the same insincere smile as she waved at an acquaintance.

"I stand corrected. There is Lady Jersey, smile pretty. I had not realized it has become fashionable to expose so much flesh in the afternoons. Do women not feel the chill?"

Marian nearly swallowed her tongue at this outrageous remark, said with the same smile and gallant greeting he had been using since they entered the park. She had some difficulty managing a pleasant expression while in the process of swallowing her tongue, and she nearly choked before Lady Jersey's carriage moved on in the other direction.

"You are a dreadful man," she remonstrated once she'd recovered.

"There is a phrase I remember from my misspent youth: 'It takes one to know one,' I believe is how it went." He serenely guided the horses out of the park and into the busy street.

"No matter what you think of me, you cannot call me a man," she reminded him. "And I fail to see in what way I am dreadful. It was not I who made that remark about Lady Jersey."

"But you were thinking it," he pointed out unreasonably. "Besides, 'dreadful' covers quite a few sins, lying and deceiving being among them, I am certain."

"If consenting to help me gives you liberty to insult me at will, I shall withdraw my request, Mr. Montague. You may return me home now."

"We are almost there, and it is your own behavior that gives me reason to insult you. Darley is my best friend. I will not see him shackled to a harpy."

Marian was given no time to form a reply. He curbed the carriage and swung down in one fluid motion, flipping a coin to a street urchin to grab his horses' heads before reaching to assist her out of the carriage. Now that the battle lines were drawn, she wasn't at all certain what she ought to say. Somehow, she had created a formidable enemy. She did not know what to do to combat his opinion of her.

So she said nothing, and allowed him to escort her into the jeweler's. While she examined the glittering displays, he spoke to the jeweler about insurance and values and the need to preserve family heirlooms. The jeweler seemed most sympathetic, and when he quoted his appraisal of the gem's worth, she nearly sank through the floor. She had been carrying that much wealth around her neck?

Montague made the arrangements for the copy to be made, received a receipt for the necklace, and returned to Marian's side. He glanced at the case of brooches she had been admiring.

"The ivory is very fine," he said, taking her elbow, "but I suppose it is the diamond that has caught your eye."

Marian started stiffly toward the door. "Had you asked me, I would have told you that the ivory would look very well with my new willow-green morning gown. I do not think diamonds would suit it at all." She swept out the door and toward the carriage.

He kept a strong hold on her elbow and steered her down the street. "I think we have time for an ice, don't you? We ought to have some pleasure from this day."

Marian turned her head to stare up at him in surprise. "I cannot imagine why," she said honestly. "We both dislike each other heartily. Why should we draw out the punishment?"

His lips curled in amusement as he glanced down at her. "Does that sharp tongue of yours not give you pain occasionally? I should think you would have cut your mouth to pieces if naught else."

She bit her tongue and stared straight ahead, saying nothing.

"All right, this time I was wrong. You were being honest, but you injured my high opinion of myself. It had never occurred to me that my company might be a punishment." He held open the door to Gunter's and helped her in.

"It is only reasonable to assume that since you find my company so unpleasant, that the feeling would be returned." Marian took the seat offered, nodded to a few acquaintances, and proceeded to play with her gloves rather than face the unsmiling man taking the seat across from her.

He gave their order before answering. When he returned his attention to her, he halted her fidgeting by the simple expedient of covering her hand with his. "When did I ever say that I find your company unpleasant? Challenging, perhaps. Amusing, occasionally. Certainly enlightening at all times. But I cannot remember one occasion of unpleasantness."

Immediately suspicious of this polite behavior, Marian jerked her hand away and glared at him. "You did not find it unpleasant being called an ass? You constantly complain of my sharp tongue; do you find pleasure in the pain of it? If so, you are a most unusual man."

Montague smiled, transforming his normally staid expression to one of charm. "I am that, I admit. Even Darley will tell you so. Can we not cry *'pax'* and be friends?"

"I cannot see how." Marian returned to worrying at her gloves. "You have all but stated your desire to keep Lord Darley from my 'clutches,' as I assume you perceive them."

The waiter placed the ices on the table and discreetly departed. Marian picked idly at hers. She would have delighted in the luxury at any other time. Now, her mind was elsewhere.

"You do not love him," Montague pointed out, heartily enjoying his confection. "All you see in him is his wealth."

Marian favored him with a look of annoyance. "It is not. Admittedly, I cannot marry where there is not wealth, for my family's sake, but there are plenty of eligible bachelors with plump pockets. It may be my duty to marry well, but I will have to live with my choice for the rest of my life. Lord Darley suits me very well, and if I suit him, I cannot see your objection. Marriages are made on a great deal less than that all the time. I have not deceived him in any way as to the portion I can expect."

Montague cleaned his dish during this tirade. When she was done, he answered calmly, "No, you have deceived him as to your true nature. Darley needs a quiet, biddable wife, one who will not run roughshod over him as his mother does, one who will make his life pleasant and not a living hell. I am aware, where he is not, that you are not what he thinks."

Marian folded her napkin and stood up. "That is your opinion. We will never agree on this matter. I wish to go home."

Her cold tone forbade any other alternative. Montague escorted her from the confectioner's and down the street to his waiting carriage.

As he climbed in beside her, he said, thoughtfully, "I realize I am not titled, but am I considered wealthy enough to deserve a place on your list of eligible bachelors?"

She stared at him in horror. "You and Jessica would not suit, I assure you. If I marry well, she may wait and marry where her heart lies. Do not try to confuse her into thinking it is her duty to marry elsewhere."

He gave her a thoughtful look. "You are a most unusual woman. Most would have assumed I meant to pursue them."

She settled back against the squabs. "You have already discovered I am not stupid. I would have to be extremely silly to be that vain."

A secret smile curled his lips again. "I can see you are

going to lead me a merry chase, my lady. Let us get you back to the house before your mother calls the watch."

"O'Toole, you do have your uses. The lady will be able to see herself in those." Reginald glanced down at the polished gleam of the knee-high boots his valet was returning to the rack.

"The lady is in the habit of admiring herself in boots?" the insolent valet inquired as he came up behind his master to brush off the coat waiting to be donned.

"Actually, the lady I had in mind is more likely to bite off my nose than admire my toes, but her young sister has an affinity for admiring floors. Perhaps my boots will keep her amused while I woo the elder."

The valet looked mildly interested as he helped his employer into the tightly tailored coat. "If you are going to continue escorting ladies through the park, you ought to have a groom. Did I mention that I often served as the marquess's driver?"

Reginald raised a disbelieving eyebrow. "Why am I inclined to doubt that?" he asked the ceiling as he adjusted his cravat.

"Well, if he were not dead, he could confirm it," O'Toole assured him. "And any nodcock can act the part of groom. All I need do is stand at the back of the carriage and look handsome. For a few extra coins, I am willing to sacrifice myself in your service."

There was some truth in that. If Reginald could be certain that the wretch wouldn't decide his horses were worth more than honest employment, he could leave his valuable animals in the care of someone experienced instead of relying on street urchins. And he might have less difficulty persuading Lady Marian from the safety of her home if she felt they would be properly chaperoned. His two-seated carriage wouldn't hold her lady's maid or sister, unless they wished to sit in the groom's seat. He hummed thoughtfully as he fastened his coat buttons.

"I suppose I would have to wear one of those devilish box coats in forest green or something equally dismal," the valet continued gloomily. "That would be cheaper than turning me out in a monkey suit of red and gold or something equally outlandish. I might even have something suitable in my own wardrobe if you will trust my discretion. I could be ready when the carriage is brought around."

"Your presumptuousness is scarcely outweighed by your arrogance, you young idiot. Have I said I need a groom?"

"You did not say that you did not," he replied reasonably. "And if I go out with you of an evening, you will know that I am not flirting with the maid."

"Or stealing from the wine cellar. Jasper keeps an inventory, you know. I think you owe me a few evenings' service to pay for that bottle of burgundy that has disappeared."

O'Toole did not look overly concerned with the accusation as he put away the gentleman's shaving gear. "I can offer my services on trial, as it were, for a few nights, until you see how well it will work out."

A thief, a groom, and a valet, all in one, Reginald thought to himself as he picked up his hat and stick. He was certainly getting his money's worth. "Then go find your bottle-green coat or whatever, and let us be on our way." He was going to regret this, he had a feeling, but he would never know for certain until he tried.

Actually, the idea of using O'Toole as his groom was an excellent one, if the man could be relied on. Reginald did not keep a stable in London. He stored his horses and carriage in a rental stall. He had to hire someone to look after them whenever he attended an entertainment not within walking distance. It was a pestilent nuisance, but he hadn't the funds to maintain a town house like his father's with a mews in back. Having someone within the household to handle the chore of ordering the carriage brought around and keeping the horses in hand would be convenient. He should have thought of it sooner.

Of course, O'Toole probably wasn't the ideal person, but he was available and willing, and Reginald did have several stops to make tonight. If it didn't work out, the thief could go back to amusing the maid in the evening.

He didn't go so far as to allow the wretch to drive, however. Reginald took up the reins himself as his valet adopted a suitably correct position in the back. The lad could emulate a duke if he tried, with his posturing and posing. He smiled at that. Perhaps he could introduce O'Toole to Lady Marian as a wealthy substitute to Darley. He wasn't making much headway with the lady on his own.

He wheeled up in front of the Earl of Tunningham's town house and sent O'Toole up to announce his arrival. Darley would appreciate the jest when he saw the messenger.

When the viscount came down to join him, he scarcely seemed aware of O'Toole's presence. He had been gone several days at his father's request on some estate matter, but it looked like the weight of the world had found him while he was gone. Reginald gave his friend a concerned look as he picked up the reins.

"You look like the blue dismals have wrapped around you, old boy. Anything I can do?"

Darley slouched in the seat to prevent wrinkling his trousers. "You've already been more than helpful, I hear. I understand you've been escorting Lady Marian in my absence?"

Reginald raised his eyebrows but kept his attention on his horses. "At your request, you'll remember. She's something of a handful. Did you know yesterday she wished to see Elgin's marbles, but because we had exchanged words the day before, she refused to get in the carriage with me? I had to leave the carriage and follow her and her sister through the streets to make certain they didn't get into any trouble."

"That doesn't sound like Marian." Darley crossed his arms over his chest. "If you don't like her, why did you drive her to the park and take her to Gunter's and escort her to Hatchards?"

Reginald scowled. "Because a certain friend of mine asked that I look after her, and I knew of no other way to do it. She's seldom available for a discreet morning call. The woman is all about traipsing across town every minute of the day."

"You could have suggested she wait until I was there to escort her."

Reginald finally sent him an incredulous look. "Wait? Does she know the meaning of the word? I found her at Hatchards without her maid because the multitalented Lily had a gown to repair. I missed an appointment at Jackson's because she desired to see the Tower and intended to go with her sister if I couldn't escort her. The woman is a perpetual motion machine. You try suggesting she wait until you have time for her."

Satisfied, Darley drew a deep sigh of relief. "I apologize. I'm not much with the ladies and you are. It's demeaning to know I can be jealous of my best friend. If I weren't so hen-hearted, I'd go to her mama immediately and press my suit so I wouldn't have to put myself through this. What if she sets her cap for Devonshire?"

Reginald kept his voice nonchalant to hide his alarm. "She's too sensible by far to set her cap so high. A few weeks isn't enough time to be certain of your affections. Let the lady enjoy her freedom a while longer, while you enjoy yours. A lifetime is too long to pay if you decide wrong."

"I haven't thought of Marian wishing to enjoy her freedom a while longer. I suppose you're right. She's been cooped up in the country all these years. She has a right to spread her wings a little before I clip them. Do you think she'll have me, though? I'm not much to look at, and the ladies put a lot of store in that."

"They put a lot of store in wealth and titles too. She'll have you, no doubt, rest assured on that." Reginald's tone was wry.

Darley sent him a swift look. "What if her affections fall elsewhere? All the wealth and titles will serve nothing then."

Affections had nothing to do with anything when you were up the River Tick, but Reginald refrained from saying that. He managed to merely reply, "You must set your sight to capturing her affections, then, hadn't you?"

Behind them, the spurious groom listened with great interest.

Nine

Reginald watched grimly as Darley headed straight across the room in the direction of Lady Marian. While listening to his hostess prattle about the highly successful squeeze of the crowd and the need to open a few windows in such unusually wicked heat, he managed to see Marian give Darley a slow, sweet smile that made even his own toes tingle. Damn, but she was good at what she was doing.

Excusing himself from his hostess and making his way toward the refreshment table, he watched as Marian made graceful gestures with hands that occasionally lighted on Darley's arm. He saw Darley laugh at some witticism that had her hiding behind her fan. She was no doubt batting her eyelashes for all they were worth, Reginald concluded dismally as he helped himself to the punch. No wonder Darley was smitten.

That complicated matters severely. He had no desire to lose Darley's friendship in a competition over a woman, particularly not a lying, deceitful woman like Lady Marian. If his friend's affections were truly attached, he would have to surrender the game and hope for the best. But he was rather certain Darley's interest was more in the lady's seemingly biddable nature and easy accessibility. He would not give up quite yet, not until he had made some attempt to show Darley the lady's true colors.

How he was going to do that without making a total clunch of himself was up for debate. The Bow Street Runner had come back with sufficient evidence that the lady was who she said she was. The ambitious detective had even attempted to interview the current Marquess of Effingham, only to be told he was away from home. The few servants the Runner had managed to interview had all been new and of little help, but Lady Marian's whereabouts had seemed to be common knowledge, and it had coincided with the truth. There was no evidence that the lady flirting with Darley now was anyone other than the daughter of the late Marquess of Effingham.

So Reginald was going to have to rely on his own abilities to unmask the lady's character. It would be no easy task. She had shown no particular interest in his suit these last days, and for good reason, he supposed. He had no title and as a younger son, his wealth was suspect. The lady wasn't so impractical as to fall for a pretty face. And she had already warned him away from her little sister. He could not fathom how he was going to play out this charade.

Feeling as if he were made of stone, Reginald made his way across the crowded room in the direction of the happy pair.

With a graceful flourish of long, skillful fingers, a silver coin appeared behind the groom's grubby ear. Lamplight glittered off the coin as the fingers bounced it lightly up and down, flashing silver against a gloved palm, until suddenly, it disappeared in mid-air.

"How'd you do that?" Suspicious, the old man in wrinkled livery glared at the smooth cotton of the now-empty glove.

"As I said, magic." Propped against the carriage, O'Toole crossed his bottle-green–clad arms over his chest.

"'Tis a trick. Show me how to do it." The old man shifted his glare to the younger man's grinning composure.

"It's not a trick. It's magic. One has to be born with the magic touch."

The old man scowled. "If 'twere magic, you'd be living like a king instead o' grubbin' stables."

O'Toole shook his head. "Magic cannot be used for

one's own profit. Greed destroys the power. Magic can only be used for the benefit of others."

The old groom glared at him stubbornly. "Then make me rich."

O'Toole laughed. "Your greed isn't any better than mine. Besides, making you rich wouldn't necessarily be for your benefit." He glanced toward the tall mansion glittering inside and out with lamps and candles and the sparkle of jewels. "Look at them in there. They got more than we can dream of, but do you think they're all happy?"

"Ought to be," the old man grumped, easing his aching bones onto a mounting block. "But they ain't all plump in the pocket. Some's not worth a bean more than we are. They just put on a good show."

"There's that, I suppose." The silver coin flipped in the air over O'Toole's hand again as he uncrossed his arms. "There's some that would leave the likes of us unpaid for years rather than give up their pleasures."

"Not my ladies," the other man answered loyally. "They do their own mending and the like so as to make sure we get paid every quarter day."

"Out to find rich husbands, are they?" The coin twirled in mid-air, disappeared, and reappeared as a penny.

Trying not to be impressed by this flashy display, the old man adjusted his baggy breeches. "Way of the world, it is. The young miss is a bit of a shy 'un, but my lady has already found 'erself a viscount. Belowstairs is waitin' a 'appy announcement any day now. The young gentleman is said to be generous with his pockets. We'll all be well to grass soon enough."

"Well, I'm sure congratulations are in order. Does the young lady seem happy with her choice? Not stuck with an old codger, is she?"

The groom shrugged. "'Appy enough, I'd say. 'E's not a well set-up sort, but 'e's young. There's nothin' to complain of."

"That's good. The young lady my master's been seein' has a devil of a tongue. She ripped up at him royally the other day."

The groom chuckled. "My lady 'as a bit o' temper too.

She's taken a friend of the viscount's into dislike. 'Eard 'er out on the street once a'tellin' 'im what she thought of 'im. And Simmons said as 'ow she threw a pillow at 'im the other day, near to knocked the tea from his 'and and into 'is lap. Mighty uncomfortable that would 'ave been, I wager."

The penny became two silver coins, then three, spinning and swirling in the lamplight between O'Toole's gloved hands. He was grinning happily as he watched the coins. "I daresay it would. Reminds me of the marquess I used to work for. Devil of a temper that man had. Wife was a quiet, pretty woman, didn't quite know how to handle it when he went off on one of his rages. Never took them out on her, though. He'd ride his horse 'til it came back lathered, apologize to the lads he'd combed over good, then go back to work with a smile as if all was well with the world again."

The old man couldn't help staring with widened eyes at the coins flickering silver in and out of the shadows. "That's the way of my lady, all right. Do summit wrong, and she'll scold until she peels the hide off your back, but do it right, and she gives you coins she ain't got to spare." He cackled softly to himself. "Teaches the young 'uns right quick to jump when they ought, it do."

"Lady like that needs a strong man for husband, I would think. The young viscount come back at her when she wields her tongue?" The coins disappeared in the wink of an eye. O'Toole leaned over to remove one from the old man's coat pocket.

"She ain't 'ad cause to wield 'er tongue at 'im far as I 'eard. They get along like peaches and cream." The groom began to surreptitiously search his other pockets.

"Odd." A second coin appeared behind a horse's ear. "The marquess used to yell at his daughter when she did something wrong, but then he loved her until she laughed after. When she got a bit older, she yelled right back. Sassy little chit. But anyone could see they adored each other. Seems like a lady with a temper ought to be that passionate about the one she is to marry."

The groom shrugged and stood up as several footmen ran down the steps to search out requested carriages. "Ain't fittin' for a young lady to yell at a suitor, now, is it?"

As one of the footmen approached them, O'Toole disappeared his spinning coins. "Keep up the illusion until the vows are said, eh? Makes sense, that."

He ambled off to his master's carriage at a gesture from a footman. The old groom scratched his head and watched him go. The red-headed young man made an odd sort of groom with his fancy speech and all, but he was a good enough fellow.

Carefully, just in case, he searched his pockets one more time. The silver coin in his breeches pocket glittered just the way he remembered when he held it in the lamplight. Just for good measure, he bit it soundly. Real, not illusion.

"Mama, I do not know how to bring him up to scratch." Marian ignored her image in the mirror and turned to her mother, who was attempting to straighten the bow at her back.

"If only James were here, he would speak to him. This cannot go on much longer without an announcement being made. Perhaps I ought to say something to the gentleman." This last came out with such doubt as to make the likelihood next to none.

Marian bit her bottom lip and turned around to examine the seed-pearl necklace at her throat. Mr. Montague had said the fake necklace would be ready in plenty of time for the ball. She tried not to think of her mother's gentle admonition. She was devoting a great deal of time to Darley, at the expense of her few other suitors. If Darley never proposed, her reputation could be tarnished and she would never find another husband. It didn't bear thinking about.

"I know it is all Mr. Montague's fault," she said out loud, then wished she'd bit her tongue. Hurriedly, she added, "I know Lady Agatha approves of me. Perhaps you could speak quietly of your concerns with her this evening, and she will make Lord Darley see his duty."

"She is rather a formidable lady." The doubt was not as strong but still evident in Lady Grace's voice as she stepped back to admire her handiwork.

Marian thought the lady quite congenial, but then, she was not prone to her mother's diffidence. She had been told time and again that had she been a boy, she would be the spitting image of her father, and that evidently included her character, too. The late marquess had been a neck-or-nothing type of man. She wished she could have known him better. It seemed a tragic fate that so vital a man could have been carried off by such a trivial complaint as an abscessed tooth that went neglected too long.

But with no father to press Lord Darley for his intentions, she was left to dangle at the viscount's will. She would be angry with him, if she did not know Mr. Montague was undoubtedly behind her friend's dilatoriness. She had two options: She could make Lord Darley see that his diffidence was hurting her, or she could rake Montague over the coals. Neither alternative seemed practical, but the latter would be exceedingly satisfying.

She could hear Lily answering the door belowstairs, and she hurried to tie her bonnet ribbons. Darley had been unable to attend the lecture with her today, but he had offered Montague in his place. Perhaps this was the opportunity she needed. Somehow, she would have to persuade the man that she was not the monster of deceit that he claimed.

As she ran down the stairs, she saw Lily speaking to a red-haired man at the door. He was wearing what ought to be a groom's jacket, she supposed, but it appeared to be rather fashionably tailored for all that. He was young and not overly tall, and his gaze was a trifle too insolent as he glanced up at her arrival. She almost imagined laughter in his eyes as he appraised her.

He hastily made a subservient bow and extended his hand with a note in it. "Mr. Montague regrets that he is unable to keep his appointment, but he places his carriage at your disposal, my lady."

Marian gave the note a hasty glance. She had no reason to recognize Montague's writing, but the hasty scrawl possessed his character. Irritated, she glared at the note as if its writer could feel her anger through the paper.

"At my disposal?" Marian gazed consideringly from the note to the young groom, who shifted uneasily at her expression. "Then I shall take my maid."

Lily hurried to fetch her bonnet. The groom appeared in-

creasingly nervous at being left standing in the foyer, but
he held his hat and managed to twitch only once or twice
while waiting. Marian still regarded him with suspicion, but
she had no experience at driving a carriage. She needed his
help.

When Lily was up in the groom's seat and the groom
was wielding the ribbons, Marian settled back against the
cushions with a sigh of satisfaction. "Now, take me to Mr.
Montague."

The groom looked startled and allowed the reins to fall
lax. The horses shook their heads in impatience. "He says I
was to take you to the lecture, my lady."

"He says he places the carriage at my disposal. I have a
word or two I wish to say to Mr. Montague. Now where is
he? Gossiping at Boodle's? Admiring horses at
Tattersall's? Perhaps he is swindling some poor unsuspect-
ing collector out of his books?"

The young groom sent the horses into a slow walk. He
gave the lady beside him a sideways glance. "Greek curiosities, my lady. He is to see a man about some Greek curiosities."

"How lowering to be cast aside for Greek curiosities.
Very well, then I shall have to see these curiosities, too."

The groom ducked his head and muttered something that
might have been, "Yes, my lady." He clucked the horses to
a faster pace.

It took only a few minutes to recognize they were heading in the direction of the proposed lecture and not of the
shops where such things as Greek curiosities might be
found. Marian gave the red-headed groom a sharp look.
"Where are we going?"

"Where Mr. Montague said to take you," the groom
replied with a hint of stubbornness.

She should have known Montague's servants would be
as disagreeable as he was. The horses had picked up their
pace and were now trotting neatly down Grosvenor. "Stop
the carriage," she ordered.

He sent her a surprised look. "At which residence, my
lady?"

"It does not matter. Just stop. I wish to get out."

The stubborn tone returned to his voice. "I cannot do that, my lady. A lady cannot walk unescorted through these streets. My master would have my position if I allowed that."

"Your master will never know if you just do as I say. I have no intention of going any further with you. Either you stop the carriage or I scream."

Behind him, Lily leaned forward nervously and whispered, "She will do just that. Please, do not cross her any more."

The freckles on the groom's nose wrinkled into annoyance as he glanced at the irate lady. "Give me time to come about. I will take you home."

Marian clutched her parasol and glared ahead, conscious that the young man beside her was larger and stronger than she was. She had never before had a servant argue with her. She wished she could box his ears.

"I do not wish to go home, sir. I wish to speak to Mr. Montague."

The groom brought the carriage around and headed it back the way they had come. Jaw set, he replied, "And just as your father wished his bad tooth would go away, you will not get your wishes, my lady."

He set the carriage to a fast pace, leaving Marian to stare at him in stunned silence.

Ten

The fellow was, above all, insolent. You did say the carriage was to be at my disposal, did you not?" Still enraged and a trifle fearful of the encounter, Marian swirled about the drawing room, her skirts fluttering around her as she paced. She had excused the groom's knowledge of the circumstance of her father's death as common gossip. She couldn't excuse his behavior.

Reginald tried to hide his amusement. "I did not say it was to be used to track me down so you might ring a peal over me. O'Toole is a bit of a character, though, I'll admit. It would not surprise me to discover that he is not at all what he is said to be. But I cannot complain of his work, and I applaud his actions of yesterday. He did exactly right. You could not be left to walk home by yourself."

Marian clenched her fists and swirled around to glare at her grinning nemesis. "Did you come just to gloat? Or had you some other reason to be here?"

"I have had word that your necklace will be ready on the morrow. I wish to be certain that you are still desirous of pawning it. I can handle the transaction in confidentiality and bring you the sum as soon as it is concluded, if that is your wish."

Marian stared at the elegant gentleman lounging in the gilded chair. She had sent Lily off to fetch tea. They had only a few minutes for this discussion. She wished she could think faster. He was all that a gentleman should be, from the cropped curls at his brow to the polished toes of his Hessians. The only exception to his character was the laughter in his eyes and the tone of cynicism in his voice. She really ought to smack him for both.

He knew her dilemma. She did not wish to lower herself to dealing with those types who would loan money on a lady's jewelry, yet she could not trust him to return with the entire sum. Her necklace might be lost forever if she did. She had heard the terrible worth of the necklace and knew she could never obtain such a sum as a loan, but she did not know precisely how much she could expect. It would be simpler to sell it outright and live on the proceeds.

Marian did not have time to voice her decision. The door swung wide and her mother entered, waving a heavily sealed letter. "It's from him!" Her voice was breaking with excitement and trepidation.

"From whom?" Marian tried folding her hands calmly together as her mother entered, entirely ignoring the gentleman rising from the chair behind her. Lady Grace was not generally excitable. Marian sent Mr. Montague an uneasy look, but there was no simple way he could disappear.

"From the marquess! He has asked us to attend him at the manor. The note is from his secretary. It seems the marquess is something of an invalid. I cannot believe it! After all these years, why would he write to us now?"

Marian noted their visitor's frown. Knowing Montague was a great deal more informed about the *ton* than they, she took the letter from her mother's hands and scanned it carefully. Without comment, she handed it to Mr. Montague.

He raised one expressive eyebrow at the contents, then returned it to her. "It's been my understanding that the marquess had not been in England until recently. It is possible that he merely wishes to make your acquaintance."

Lady Grace nervously twined her fingers. "It has been nearly twenty years. He could have sent some acknowledgement sooner than this. I don't believe I shall go. I do not wish to go back there."

Marian clenched the heavy vellum and tried not to scream a protest. She had only been three when her father died and her world turned inside-out. She had very little memory of the manor house to which she had been born. She would dearly like to see it again, to find out if it jogged any memories of her father. But if the visit would be painful for her mother, she could not object.

Reginald gave her white-faced expression a thoughtful look before turning to Lady Grace. "The gentleman does not ask only for your company. He merely says he will send a carriage for your convenience. Perhaps you could return his note suggesting that you would prefer to bring your own escort? I am certain Lord Darley would be happy to accompany you, as would I. It might make . . . " he hesitated, in search of a proper word. Finding none, he continued vaguely, " . . . things a trifle easier for all concerned. After all, the marquess is the nominal head of the family."

Stunned at this realization, Lady Grace looked at the letter as if it were a snake that might bite. She met Marian's eyes, and the knowledge gradually sank in. If Lord Darley were to make an offer, it would most properly have to be made to the marquess first.

Shaking her head, Lady Grace took the paper. "If you do not mind," she murmured absently, "I would thank you for your escort. If you would excuse me?" She departed without making any notice that she was leaving her daughter alone with the gentleman.

Marian took a deep breath and walked to the window. "You know more about the marquess?"

"Very little." In truth, Reginald had made it a point to find out all he could, but his success had been limited. The marquess hid himself very well. "Mostly gossip. They say he is a recluse. None claim to have met him, leastways. The rumors only started a few months ago, so I suppose there is some truth to the gossip that he has only recently come to England. Does your mother not know anything at all?"

"All I know is what I have heard or overheard over the years. The manor has no dower house. Most of the lands were not entailed and were sold off over generations. The house and the park were entailed, however, and the solicitors said we must leave as there weren't funds for upkeep. We had a small trust left by my father and lived off it a while. There were rumors that the new marquess was an American and they had to send there for him, but that is all I know. What remains of the estate is in Hertfordshire, and we moved to Wiltshire when Mama married the squire. We heard very little there."

Reginald made an impolite noise. "If the estate was in sad shape, there would have been no particular reason for the man to return, particularly if he was wealthy. Americans hold very little store by titles, I understand."

"That's true." Marian turned away from the window to face him. "I suppose now he is ill, possibly dying, and thinks to clear up matters he has neglected. Should I be gratified that he has chosen now to interfere in our lives?"

"Perhaps he is childless and means to make you heir to all his wealth," Reginald responded maliciously. "Do you wish to wait before pawning your necklace?"

Marian's eyes widened as she remembered their earlier conversation. "The necklace! It's a family heirloom. Do you think he means to ask for it back?"

"You mean it is not yours to sell?" Reginald gave her a shocked look.

"It is." Marian set her chin stubbornly. "My father gave it to my mother. It was not on the inventory of entailments or my mother would never have taken it with her. It is ours to do with as we wish."

"Then perhaps you will wish to wait to sell it until after you discover if he means to make you any monetary gifts. Dying men sometimes like to salve their consciences."

She heard the cynicism in his voice and chose to ignore it. "He is more likely meaning to make my life miserable in some manner or another, but you are right. I cannot pawn the necklace until I know what this is about. Perhaps he might even lend us the money of his own accord. I would sleep much easier if I knew the necklace was where it belonged."

Reginald lifted his hand as if he were about to touch her, but Lily came hurrying in with the tea tray then, and his arm fell back to his side. Making his excuses, he collected his hat and left.

Oddly enough, Marian felt strangely bereft with his departure.

Reginald jiggled the two boxes in his coat pockets uneasily. He had retrieved the necklace and the copy just after leaving the shop for the day. He knew Darley had the lady occupied for the evening. There would be no good opportunity for returning the jewels to her now. He wished he had a safe in which to deposit them. He'd never had enough valuables for anyone to steal to acquire one.

The elongated boxes were difficult to hide, and he had a thief for a valet. Questioning his sanity, Reginald withdrew the plain box in which rested the copy. As he entered his chamber, he threw it on his dressing table in plain sight. He could not conceivably keep both boxes hidden from his nosy valet, but he might distract him with one long enough to get the other to the lady on the morrow. She would want to take the original with her on her visit to the marquess.

The real necklace in its velvet container he secreted among the belongings already packed in his valise. Upon hearing that his master was invited to visit the manor house of the new Marquess of Effingham, O'Toole had been beside himself with delight. He had begun packing immediately. Reginald wasn't certain whether to be relieved by his valet's behavior, or suspicious. Either the man was happy to be returning to his home, or had no reason to fear returning because he'd never been there. Reginald hadn't quite decided which.

The object of his thoughts came in bearing a stack of laundered shirts, grinning happily as he caught sight of his employer. "You are home. What entertaining jaunt will we take this evening? The Opera? Or will you wish to visit your ladybird before going on an extended journey?"

"O'Toole, you are insolent to an extreme. Just see that I have sufficient clean linen for the morrow and I will take care of myself for this evening." Reginald pulled off his wilting cravat and began to shrug out of his coat.

O'Toole pretended offense. "Everything is all prepared. It is only a matter of knowing where to load it. Surely the curricle will not be sufficient for the journey? Shall I hire a phaeton?"

"I will be traveling with Darley in his landau. There will doubtless be more than adequate room for everything you have managed to pack in every valise and portmanteau in the house. Do not concern yourself."

"You have not told me how long you plan to stay. I have no choice but to be ready for any event," the valet replied huffily, as he helped his employer pull out of the coat. "Your lady will expect you to look your very best."

"She is not my lady, confound it." With his arms freed of the tight coat, Reginald began on his shirt buttons. "She is Darley's lady. I only accompany them out of friendship."

"Lady Marian is much too spirited for a gentleman like Lord Darley," O'Toole replied disapprovingly. "She needs a gentleman with the strength of character of yourself."

Reginald flung the shirt across the room. "I do not intend to marry, O'Toole, and I am certainly not wealthy enough to meet the lady's standards. Now leave off, or you're sacked."

O'Toole hummed happily to himself as he assisted his employer in his ablutions and in preparing for the evening's excursions. Matters were far from perfect, but they were proceeding obligingly. He doubted that he would be rewarded for his outstanding diplomacy, but playing strategist was much more amusing than standing in the pouring rain moving walnut shells and peas around for the entertainment of spectators. Perhaps he should have made a career out of politics.

As soon as Montague left for the evening, O'Toole settled himself at the dressing table where the jewel box had been resting temptingly all evening. He was already familiar with all the jewels in the Montague household, and this box wasn't among them. He snapped open the lid and whistled thoughtfully.

The ruby winked in the lamplight. The diamond setting sparkled. The gold glittered almost as if genuine. O'Toole ran the ornate chain between his fingers. It wouldn't fool an expert, but it would fool just about anybody else. He didn't have to think twice to know where the original came from. The necklace was unforgettable to anyone with any familiarity with jewelry at all. He had admired it more than once on portraits of the late marchionesses of Effingham.

Still whistling quietly, O'Toole replaced the necklace, stood up, and gazed consideringly around the room. Where there was a copy, there was bound to be an original. It might not be here, but he could think of no other reason for his wily employer to leave the fake sitting out.

He started with the partially packed valise.

The Eighth Marquess of Effingham, Earl of Arinmede, Viscount Lawrence, stared at the single candle lighting his neatly ordered and exceedingly dust-laden desk. The heavy, moldering draperies on the windows behind him adequately insulated against night sounds, but they wafted gently every so often in the breeze from the broken windowpanes. The candle flickered against the darkness whenever they did so.

Volumes of books lined the study wall across from the desk. The candlelight occasionally caught a flicker of gold on a binding here and there, but the marquess wasn't overtly aware of it. There was another room just down the immense hall with more volumes than this, a veritable library larger than any he had seen in America other than in cities like New York. He was still rather in awe of the generations of history and knowledge patiently stored within these walls. But it wasn't the past that concerned him at the moment.

Crumpling a hastily scribbled note and flinging it at the faded Turkish carpet covering the floor, he muttered a "Damn Michael to hell and back." Reaching for a brandy decanter, he poured a sizable amount of liquid into a snifter.

He couldn't see the mirror on the side wall that reflected his image as he bent into the candlelight to pick up his glass. The image wouldn't have looked out of place in the portrait gallery above. It reflected a tall, broad-shouldered man with black hair too long at the nape for style, a dark, sun-weathered complexion, and a sharp, aristocratic nose with a slight hump in the middle. Piercing eyes beneath heavy brows added to his brooding appearance. When he turned, the candlelight did not quite catch the fine white scars shattering one side of his face.

The marquess sipped the brandy and damned his own curiosity along with the absent Michael. It had only seemed natural to look up the relatives he had never known once he had finally made his way here. He glanced derisively upward at the ornate ceiling and faded gilded molding above the bookcases that represented "here."

He had only been a boy when he came into the title, and he had not learned of it until the death of his mother. It had taken him years after that to scrape together the funds to arrive in England in some semblance of style. He'd had visions of a rambling stone mansion with servants and tenants and all the things he had remembered hearing about when he had been a child. He should have known an estate that couldn't afford to finance an heir's trip to England wouldn't be worth arriving to claim.

And now Michael was giving him this folderol about the penniless dowager and her daughter as if he were capable of resolving any problems of his unknown relatives. In actuality, he had hoped to locate a rich earl or two on the family tree to hit up for loans on the sentimental basis of saving the family homestead or whatever. A penniless widow wasn't precisely what he had in mind.

He groaned and sank back in the chair. It exuded dust with every movement, but it was one of the few pieces that hadn't been covered by those infernal ghostly linens that were scattered everywhere in the house. He wondered how far it would get him to sell off the moldering furniture. Back to the states, at least.

He ought to wring Michael's neck for this. They had spent the better part of their lives surviving on their wits alone. Why didn't Michael know to leave things as they were? What was he supposed to do, wave his magic wand and open the manor for a house party? Michael was the one with the magic wand. Let him wave it.

That thought relieved the marquess's disgruntled mood. Grinning irreverently at a worn tapestry blowing slightly in the breeze, he lifted his snifter in toast to his own good sense. Let Arinmede Manor welcome guests one final time.

Eleven

When the travelers set out the next morning, Darley's landau carried two valets and an assortment of baggage. The gentlemen chose to ride alongside the carriages, where they could occasionally lean over and converse with the ladies through the windows of the marquess's coach.

The coach was of the old-fashioned kind, with badly sprung wheels and four unmatched hired horses. The driver was taciturn and undemonstrative, occasionally tippling from a flask in his coat pocket as the day wore on. Both Reginald and Darley kept cautious eyes on him.

But Reginald was also distracted by the wealth he was carrying on this journey. He did not like taking the necklace with him, but he'd had no time to find a safer place to deposit it. He would have preferred to return it to the ladies, but the opportunity had not yet arisen. He hoped this evening he could find a moment alone with Lady Marian, when the necklace could be returned.

He hadn't breathed easy on the prior night until he had returned to his chamber and checked to find the duplicate where he had left it and the original safely tucked in his valise. O'Toole had said nary a word about it, which was suspicious in itself, but he had left the ornament alone. Uncomfortable allowing the necklace out of his sight, Reginald had taken the original out of its box and tucked it in his purse before setting out this morning. As a precaution, he carried a pistol in his saddle.

The early morning journey had started out under blue

skies. A spring breeze tossed the heads of jonquils in flower gardens along the way as they entered the country. Bird song filled tree branches covered with new green leaves. The fresh air had made the ladies smile until even the shy Jessica was laughing over some jest of Darley's. Reginald thought perhaps he ought to get out to the country more often.

His gaze strayed to Lady Marian's thinly drawn face framed in the window as she gazed pensively over the fields. She was wearing her yellow bonnet again, and a ribbon curled enticingly against her cheek. She brushed it away impatiently, only to have it fall back again an instant later. She didn't seem to notice.

He tried to follow her gaze, but Darley was on the other side of the carriage, and she was seated with her back to the horses, staring behind them. He didn't think she was seeing the lovely spring day at all, but rather some dark cloud she imagined on the horizon.

Reginald discreetly allowed his mount to nibble at a patch of grass along the roadside while glancing back the way they had come. To his surprise, there *were* clouds on the horizon. If they did not stir the carriages to a faster pace, they would no doubt be caught in a rainstorm.

The blamed woman should have said something. Irritated, Reginald spurred his horse to take up with Darley's. Pointing out the clouds, he got his friend's agreement that a faster pace was needed, and he ordered the driver to spring the horses. The taciturn coachman just gave him a disgruntled look and reached for his flask.

Cursing, Reginald ordered the driver to halt. The driver didn't obey that order any better. All he had succeeded in doing so far was attracting the interest of the ladies. Lady Grace and Jessica seemed oblivious to the consequences of this little spectacle, but Marian had begun to frown in concern. No doubt she meant to reach through the trap door, grab the driver by the coattails, and box his ears if he did not respond to her liking.

He ought to let her do it, but he had been raised to be a gentleman. With a word to Darley, Reginald rode his mount as close to the coach as he dared, reached over and found a handhold on the side, caught his foot on the driver's box, and hauled himself out of the saddle and into the driver's seat. Darley caught his horse and rode back to the trailing landau to tie the horse on behind.

The surly coachman raised his whip as if to strike, but Reginald hadn't spent years sparring with Gentleman Jackson for nothing. Short of laying the bastard flat, he caught the man's arm, pried the whip loose, and grabbed the reins that were falling lax in the struggle. With a muffled curse, the man gave up and curled in the corner of the box with his flask for sustenance.

"Bravo," a soft voice whispered behind him.

Reginald hadn't been aware that the trap door had been opened until then. He cast a quick squint to the face framed there before returning his attention to the horses. He hadn't expected any other than the dark curls and dancing eyes of Lady Marian, and he wasn't disappointed. The lady was a rare handful, and that was God's honest truth.

"How do your mother and sister fare?" Reginald asked quietly over his shoulder as he found the horses' paces and urged them on.

"They think you very odd but have decided you must belong to the Four-in-Hand Club they have heard about. Apparently the club members are capable of odd stunts." Her voice was soft so as not to be overheard by the ladies chattering with Darley through the window.

Reginald made an inelegant noise. "I have better to do than wear hideous waistcoats and waste my time destroying good horses. I trust they will not be too disappointed in my lack of dash."

"I am certain they will be quite delighted if you get us there before that storm breaks. My sister is afraid of storms."

So that was the reason for the pensive look. Well, he should have known better than to expect her to be idly daydreaming of true love. Reginald cracked the whip over the horses' heads. "Close the trap, my lady. These nags aren't much, but I mean to spring them."

The coach pitched forward with a jerk and settled into a rocking rumble as the horses took up their new pace. Marian turned back to her mother to discover her looking mildly alarmed. She should have known they were trading Jessica's fear of storms for her mother's fear of speed. Between the two of them, they had enough timidity for three ladies. Marian felt quite justified in surrendering any frailty in herself.

"Mr. Montague wishes to arrive before it rains," she said in pacifying tones.

Lady Grace nodded hesitantly and, clasping her hands in her lap, refused to look out the window again.

The clouds were directly overhead and the wind had grown to a gale by the time they reached the crumbling gates of Arinmede Manor. If there had once been an actual gate, it was gone now. Only the loosened stones of the posts remained. Gravel slid from the decaying mortar as the coach rattled past.

The drive was lined with ancient evergreens that swayed threateningly in the wind. Marian gazed anxiously out the window for some glimpse of the house, but it was obscured by the trees. Lightning crashed overhead, and Jessica gave a shrill scream and moved closer to her mother.

"Is this how it looked when we lived here?" Marian asked, eager for any information about the life she had never known.

"The trees were young then. Your grandfather had them planted. He had seen the like somewhere in his travels. They weren't nearly as formidable then."

"Are we close? Did you used to be able to see the house from here?"

Lady Grace wrapped her arm around her younger daughter as thunder rocked the air around them and the coach lurched hurriedly in and out of ruts. "The park is extensive, but you should see it soon enough."

The trees appeared ready to whip from the ground in the wind and the first drops of rain began to fall as they rolled from the secluded drive into the curving entrance of the manor. Marian tried to drink it all in as the coach turned and the house loomed before them, but there was too much to see at once.

The manor itself loomed upward in a solid wall of gray

stone. The windows were large and evenly spaced, indicating a house built early in the last century, but both glass and stone were mostly covered in wandering ivy. Brambles that might once have been roses scratched at the bottom rows, and the noise was slightly eerie when heard through the silences between booms of thunder.

The small party waited briefly for some sign of footmen or grooms to come to their aid, but the rapid patter of rain sent Reginald and Darley to ordering their valets into action.

Without waiting for admittance, O'Toole dashed up the steps burdened with several valises, shoved open the massive carved doors, and led the way. Astounded by this impropriety but reluctant to remain in the rain, the ladies hurried to follow.

Marian glanced upward at the grand entrance hall. A skylight several stories above glistened with stained glass and she could imagine the dancing patterns it would send across the marble floor on a sunny day. Vague recollections of lying on the floor and letting the light dance over her simmered somewhere in the back of her mind, and she could almost hear the deep laugh of her father as he found her. Perhaps it was just her overactive imagination.

The walls were of a heavy dark wainscoting, without any of the grace and ornamentation of an Adams interior. There was a certain dignity in their lack of ornamentation that carried through in the formal paintings of Greek gods that provided their only decoration. Marian suspected the long hallway stretching out beyond the foyer led to masculine studies and offices and billiard rooms. Her attention was drawn upward to the graceful curve of the mahogany stair rail.

That was the direction in which O'Toole led them. With still no sign of a servant in sight, the little party could only mill aimlessly in the foyer, watching the rain come down in buckets as the last piece of baggage was carried in. The coaches drove off around the bend to the stables, and still no one came to greet them. Taking the initiative, Reginald grabbed a valise and followed his valet up the stairs.

Lord Darley attempted to prevent Marian from carrying

any of her own luggage, but it seemed the height of silliness to leave everything sitting belowstairs when it was becoming more than obvious that the manor was seriously understaffed. She managed their jewelry and cosmetic cases while Lily carried hatboxes. Even Lady Grace and Jessica picked up an item or two to carry with them as they ascended the magnificent stairs.

Glimpses of the rooms to either side of the hall when they reached the top told the tale of abandonment. Holland covers still hung over the furniture. Spiders scurried into corners and cobwebs dangled from doorways. Desperately, Marian groped for some familiarity in the scene, but there was nothing.

Lady Grace led the way from here, directing the gentlemen to their wing, leading her daughters to the ladies' wing. Lily and the valets scurried between them, arranging boxes and trunks in some semblance of order as the ladies chose two separate chambers and the gentlemen found their own.

Marian found Mr. Montague in the hall when she went in search of one of her boxes, and he allowed her to go through the assortment he carried until she had identified those that belonged to her. He set the stack on an inlaid ebony table covered in dust and rearranged his burden, while thunder roared overhead and the pounding of rain on tile hit the roof.

"Your marquess is more eccentric than I imagined," Reginald muttered as he dusted off his coat sleeve. "There are probably two fortunes in Ming Dynasty china in the sitting room connected to my chamber, but there doesn't seem to be a single servant to see to the fires to keep out the damp. I shudder to imagine how much has been damaged just by neglect."

Marian kept her voice to a whisper as if the walls might have ears. "Have you seen the library? It is utterly immense. I'm afraid to go in it. What if the roof has leaked? The thought of all those volumes ruined makes me shudder."

Montague grinned. "Plan to snatch a few, do you? The

old goat will probably not miss them. Shall we rendezvous there when we are unpacked and see what we can find?"

She gave him a sharp look, uncertain as to how much was said in jest, when Darley came up the stairs with the remains of their baggage.

"I say, this is the strangest house party I have yet to see. Do you think we're the only ones here? I have an odd feeling that we ought to turn around and go back." He had doffed his hat and his lanky dark hair bore the signs of wet weather, falling into his eyes until he impatiently shoved it back. His anxious gaze instantly went to Marian.

Realizing how their whispered conversation might be misconstrued, Reginald stepped out of the shadows and away from the mischievous Lady Marian. The skylight over the foyer provided some illumination for this end of the hall. "O'Toole has gone down to the kitchens to see if he can arouse someone. If nothing else, maybe he can find some candles and fuel. We're likely to get quite damp and dark before long."

Marian picked up her boxes and started toward her end of the hall. "Damp and dark are unpleasant enough, but I am starving. Unless he scares up a cook, I mean to go down and see if the larder is as empty as the rest of this house."

"You must allow me to accompany you when you do, my lady. There could be rogues secreted in these rooms and none would know until they were stumbled upon. If it were not for the weather, I would be in favor of returning to London." Darley set down his own valise and hurried to take Marian's burden.

She gave him an impatient glance but allowed the courtesy. "Mother would be most disappointed. She is taking a sentimental journey through the bed chambers at present, and she means to show me my father's portrait when I am done here. After all, she was once lady of the house. It seems natural that she act the part of hostess again."

Darley glanced at the niches along the halls filled with busts of Greek gods on marble pedestals and shook his head. "It is in serious need of redecoration. These styles went out with the first George, I should think. Perhaps the new marquess wishes to ask your mother's help in renovating this monstrosity."

"Do not let us dream, my lord, we will only be disappointed. Come, if we hurry, we may catch up with her tour."

Reginald watched them go with Marian's words ringing in his ears. Do not let us dream. He gazed up at the particularly ugly portrait of some earlier marquess garbed in the court dress of the sixteenth century. Lousy bastards, all, he decided, to steal a young girl's dreams.

It was a damned good thing he was a practical man. Otherwise, he might be tempted to find the last sorry bastard who had stolen the lady's dreams and beat some sense into him.

The sorry bastard of Montague's thoughts was leaning against a wall, listening to the scurry of footsteps up and down his dust-covered stairway. With a minimum of effort he could listen to their conversations, but the snatches he had heard were enough to make him uncomfortable. Eavesdropping had never been one of his vices.

But his damned curiosity had him watching for the ladies as they explored along the west wing. The building was still in sound repair so far as he had been able to determine. There shouldn't be any danger in their explorations. He just wished to have some glimpse of his only living relations outside his addle-pated brother.

The hidden corridor he occupied hadn't been built for viewing. When he had first discovered it, he had thought some perverted ancestor had enjoyed watching the inhabitants of the various bedrooms off this floor. But he had been unable to locate viewing holes. He had since come to the conclusion that the hidden corridor was there so the master of the house could visit his mistress undetected. It led directly from the master chamber to a prettily decorated room at the far end of what he now knew as the ladies' wing.

He waited outside the door to that room now. It was hidden behind a wardrobe, and he had left the wardrobe door ajar. If they stood in just the right place, he would be able to see them.

He heard their voices. Already he was beginning to separate the sounds and identify them. The placid, assured tones of an older woman was undoubtedly the Lady Grace, his late cousin's wife. The timid, whispery voice of a young girl apparently belonged to Jessica, Lady Grace's daughter by her second marriage. The third voice . . .

The owner of the third voice was standing just where he hoped, at the foot of the portrait that was her father. The eighth Marquess of Effingham leaned back against the wall, arms crossed, and studied his young cousin.

She was just as Michael said. Lawrence blood ran true. Dark curls framed a slim face of no great beauty, but the velvet darkness of her eyes and the rosy flush of her cheeks and the soft exclamation of her lips as she looked up at the portrait painted her in all the character of her ancestors.

The marquess fingered his scarred cheek, a cheek that had once been the same sun-warmed hue as hers. His gaze went to the portrait of the man with those same features. His own father had looked much like that, although he scarcely remembered the man. His memory came from the miniature in the watch that he had inherited from his mother. The resemblance was strong, although his father had apparently tended toward corpulence in his old age. The marquess didn't like thinking of that, because then he would remember how much younger his mother was, and he began to make excuses for her.

Well, now they were here. What in hell was he going to do about it?

To find Michael and thrash him within an inch of his life seemed the only alternative open at the moment.

Twelve

Reginald sat staring morosely at his mud-spattered boots as the air rang with laughter around him. It seemed the ladies of Effingham and Oglethorp were as familiar with kitchens as they were drawing rooms. They were having a grand adventure exploring larders and pantries and wine cellars, sending the maid and valet scattering in search of fuel for the ancient stove and the lanterns hanging from the beams overhead. His own valet had gone missing at the first hint of any work that might besmirch his immaculate cuffs.

Reginald fingered the necklace in his pocket to reassure himself. He had already hidden the copy from his valise in a secret drawer he had located in the desk in his sitting room. Let O'Toole spend his hours searching for that.

His trouble wasn't related to the necklace, however. Reginald grimaced as Darley asked if he had minced the carrots fine enough. The resulting laughter answered the question without need of further explanation. Reginald's trouble was that he was almost beginning to believe that Lady Marian might be the wife for his friend after all.

He didn't know why that should bother him. He should be relieved. Instead of sitting here admiring his boots and tending the fire, he should be on his way back to London to fetch a preacher and a license. Darley's wealth would set the ladies up in comfort and they need no longer worry about a pestilent marquess who hadn't the grace to put in an appearance in his moldering castle.

Perhaps he ought to make one more attempt to make

Darley see the lady's true colors. He couldn't let his friend go into marriage thinking his lady all sweetness and light when she could also be tart as a cold lemonade on a hot summer's day, and swift and sharp as a surgeon's scalpel. Reginald wasn't certain Darley would be as appreciative of these character traits as he ought, but he was smitten enough to accept them if he must. He just needed to have his eyes wide open before he proposed this marriage.

The thought of the scene that must be enacted made him surly. Reginald poked at the fire and announced it ready, then started for the door with the immediate goal of hiding in the library.

"Mr. Montague! You cannot desert us now, unless you are going to fetch that annoying valet of yours. Someone needs to slice the bacon, and these knives seem quite dull." Lady Marian indicated the assortment of cutlery hanging near the cutting board.

Reginald scowled. He wished to say he knew nothing of kitchens or knives, but in reality he did. He would have starved long since if he had not worked out a few of the intricacies of his landlady's kitchen in the days of his misspent youth. He crossed the floor, grabbed a knife, and went in search of the whetstone.

"I do believe Mr. Montague is sulking," Marian said brightly to the room in general. "P'raps we ought to let him sit upstairs and enjoy the must and damp while we wait upon him."

Darley grinned at his friend's rigid back. The scene earlier when he had discovered the lady in earnest and intimate conversation with Montague had left him feeling uncertain, but Marian's teasing tones now reassured him. Ladies did not generally insult gentlemen whose attentions they wished to attract.

"I thought I saw a throne in one room. We could sit Reginald there and fetch a few hounds to lay at his feet. But I think we need game with bones he can gnaw and fling to the dogs. I believe his valet can successfully play the part of fool for his master's entertainment." Darley brandished his knife so his carrots could be inspected again.

Lady Grace swiftly gathered the vegetables and added

them to the pot, ignoring the badinage between the young people. She hummed happily to herself as she stirred the contents of one pot and kept an eye on Jessica, who was managing the egg dish.

"If I am to be crowned lord of this castle, I'll demand better peons than the lot of you, I should say. Insolence will get you horsewhipped." Reginald finished sharpening the knife and slammed the hunk of bacon on the cutting board for slicing.

O'Toole miraculously appeared through the back entrance with two plucked chickens, and the entire company turned to stare. The storm was still rattling the rafters, but the valet didn't appear in the least bit damp. He looked questioningly to his employer.

Reginald gave him a surly glare. "Excellent. We shall have eggs for dinner and fowl for breakfast. You're a trifle late, lad."

Lady Grace gave the young man a gracious smile and relieved him of the hens. "I shall simmer these tonight and we can have them for lunch tomorrow."

Darley looked uneasy. "I think we should leave in the morning. It does not appear as if our host is at home."

"He sent his coach for us," Marian reminded him. "P'raps we ought to instigate a search of the house after we eat. He may be lying ill in a chamber we have not yet discovered."

"Oh!" Jessica let her spoon clatter against the pan. "If he is ill, we should go look for him right now. The poor man could be dying as we speak."

"Unless the 'poor' man is given to doing his own cooking, he is undoubtedly caught by the storm in the village with his servant. He is probably tucked up at the inn keeping his frail old bones warm and dry while cackling at the thought of our arrival."

The hint of sarcasm in Marian's voice drew Darley's questioning look, but then a sound that seemed to echo from the walls made them all jump.

"That sounded like a moan," Jessica whispered, her face growing pale with fright and anxiety as she scanned the dark shadows in the far corners of the kitchen.

"I'd say it sounded more like some dimwitted ghost laughing," Reginald said dourly, then regretted the remark when the timid Oglethorp ladies both went white. Marian, on the other hand, appeared intrigued.

"I could not tell the direction," she said softly, listening for a repetition.

"It was, no doubt, squirrels in the walls. We had them once in our hunting box. The wretched things made all kinds of racket until we chased them out. I'll take a look after we eat." Darley offered the women a reassuring smile.

Lady Grace and Jessica went happily back to their cooking, but Reginald noted Marian gave her suitor a look of irritation. Squirrels did not moan or laugh. Or perhaps it was a groan or chuckle. Whatever it was, it was more human than squirrel, unless one believed in ghosts. Remembering their jests about the missing marquess, Reginald had his own theories on the matter.

He waited until after their impromptu supper—which was quite good considering he had been hungry enough to eat boiled haddock if need be. Then while Darley was lighting the way to the drawing room, Reginald slipped back downstairs to explore.

Minutes later he heard the sound of light footsteps, and he stepped behind a door to hide his candlelight. The thunder had moved away, but he could still hear the rapid patter of rain on the windows. The roads would, in all probability, be impassable on the morrow. He ought to save his explorations for morning.

"Mr. Montague, I know you are in there. Do not try to scare me or I'm likely to set the place on fire with this infernal candle."

At the sound of Marian's voice, Reginald stepped from his hiding place. "I should have known better than to think you'd sit quivering in the drawing room with the others. Do you have no fear of what happens to young ladies who wander about strange places all alone?"

In the candlelight, her upturned oval face seemed smooth and serene. The dark hair pulled back from her brow and dangling in curls about her ears was no more than a shadow in the darkness. Reginald had the insane urge to bend and kiss those parted lips. He wasn't at all certain that wouldn't be the best thing to do for all of them.

"This was my home, sir. Why should I fear it?" she asked before he could move to take action on his thoughts.

Reginald moved to a safer distance, searching for a lamp on the desk. "It hasn't been your home for nearly twenty years, as best as I can determine. Anything can happen in that length of time."

The lamp, when he found it, was freshly filled. Reginald frowned at that, but the sudden flare of light as he lit it removed some of the temptation of darkness. He turned and found her still clinging to her candle. So she wasn't entirely impervious to the perils of darkness.

He reached in his pocket and produced the purse that had bothered him all day. "Here is your necklace. I would rather that you held on to it until you decide what to do about it."

Marian didn't take the offered purse. She looked at it sadly, then turned to examine the book shelves behind her. "I don't think there is any decision to make. It is rather obvious that the marquess is not going to be able to help us save our home. He must be in danger of losing his own from the looks of it. The necklace will have to be pawned."

Reginald frowned at so casually being left in charge of a piece of jewelry worth almost more than he was. He opened the purse to inspect the piece and reassure himself once more of its existence.

The lamp light caught on the brilliant red stone and glittered on the setting of—

Reginald gasped and turned the necklace to the light again. A setting of crystal?

He tried to remain calm. After all, the necklace had been in his possession all day. He had dealt with gems for years and was well aware of when he held the genuine thing. It had been genuine diamonds and rubies he had pocketed this morning. It could not change by magic during the course of a day.

He turned the gem to a better angle. Glass. The ruby was glass.

The strangled sound he made must have been heard

across the room. Marian swung around to face him with curiosity.

"Are you all right? You look a little pale. Perhaps you ought to sit down. I'm certain there must be brandy or something around here. I thought I saw a decanter earlier." She held up her candle in search of the decanter she distinctly remembered seeing on a table when she had explored in here before dinner. It was gone. She blinked in confusion, but Mr. Montague was shaking his head and staring at the necklace with such a terrible look on his face that she forgot her search and hurried to stand beside him. "What is it? What is wrong?"

As if unable to speak, he held out the necklace for her inspection. She saw nothing wrong with it. She fondled the intricate chain, but it felt real to her. She glanced up to his face for explanation. Usually, his cool gray eyes were aloof, and pride made his expression seem stiff and unyielding. Now, there was a terrible panic revealing his true humanity beneath the handsome mask.

"This is the copy," he managed to grind out between clenched teeth. "It is not possible. I put the genuine article in my pocket before we left this morning."

Cold seeped around her heart as Marian gazed at the glittering jewel. "It looks real to me. I don't find this a very funny jest, Mr. Montague."

"It's not in the least funny, I assure you. Come, I left the copy upstairs. If this is the genuine thing, then the copy will still be where I left it."

As the sound of their feet echoed away into the distance, the figure behind the tapestry sighed and fingered the weighty necklace in his pocket. If Michael was right about the worth of this jewel, it would be sufficient to fund the purchase of enough lands to set this estate properly functioning again. He just hadn't realized he was going to cost the ladies their home by stealing it.

Carrying the brandy decanter, the eighth marquess stepped out of his hiding place and settled into his desk chair. He took a healthy swig of the potent liquor and sighed again. Not bad for an old man with frail bones, he chuckled to himself as the brandy burned a trail to his stomach. That damned young cousin of his was too clever by half, and she had a sharp tongue to boot. His empty insides growled in complaint. His guests had finished off the entire delicious meal they had cooked right before his very eyes. He wondered if ghosts could be credited for eating chicken legs.

Carrying the decanter and staggering only slightly, he went in search of the kitchen and the chicken that had been stewed for the morrow. He didn't know how long his unwelcome guests would stay, but he would enjoy their cooking while they were here.

As Mr. Montague turned down the hall to the gentlemen's wing, Marian wanted to protest that she couldn't follow him, but she wasn't about to let that necklace out of her sight, either. She didn't know what kind of trick he meant to pull, but she was determined to catch him at it. She couldn't believe a gentleman like Mr. Montague could be so dishonest as to steal their only source of income, but she wasn't inclined to trust anybody for very long.

Unheeding of the lady's qualms, Reginald turned into the chamber at his left and went directly to the spindly-legged secretary near the fireplace. Setting the lamp down on the open surface of the desk, he felt around at the back of one of the drawers until he sprung the catch. Within seconds he was withdrawing a plain box that should contain the copy.

Marian came up beside him and watched with bated breath as he snapped open the box. The box of white satin was empty.

With a soft cry, she swung away and stared out the rain-spattered window. Reginald followed her with grim sympathy, touching a hand to her shoulder, not knowing how else to comfort her.

"I will find it, Marian. I have a suspect, and I shall have it out of him if I must beat him to a pulp to do so. I am only sorry that I have given you cause to worry."

She didn't even notice that he had addressed her familiarly. She only knew she wanted to lean back into the comfort of his arms and weep. She was tired of being the strong one. She wanted someone else to help share her burdens, someone to make things just a little easier for a change. For some odd reason, she had relied on Mr. Montague to be that someone. She should have known it was a mistake to rely on anyone but herself.

She stiffened and pulled away. "I wish to be there when you question him. Who is it? That insolent valet of yours?"

The woman was too damned quick for her own good. Reginald retreated a few feet, removing his hand. "I can understand your concern, but a woman would give him hope of some sympathy. He knows he will receive none from me. Go back to your mother while I track the wretch down."

She would go back to her mother all right, but it wouldn't be to quietly sit before the fire. Straightening her back, she marched out of the room without looking behind her. Reginald had an eerie premonition of what would come next if he didn't act quickly.

Throwing open the door to the antechamber his valet had taken for his own, he yelled, "O'Toole, get yourself in here now or I'm coming after you with a whip!"

The room was terrifyingly empty.

Thirteen

The search for the missing man and jewel in the dark in a strange house on a rainy night had little chance of being successful. The small party eventually returned to the dying fire of the drawing room with nothing to show for their efforts.

Marian felt guilty for telling her mother anything at all. She could simply have produced the fake and allowed her to think all was well. But her first thought had been to find the thief before he could escape, and that had necessitated explaining the necklace's disappearance. Now, they had nothing, neither thief nor necklace, and her mother appeared thoroughly shaken by the experience.

She could still miraculously "discover" the copy, she supposed. That would relieve her mother's mind if not her own. But she could not do it tonight. Everyone was weary to the bone, and no one would believe the discovery directly after such an extensive search. It would have to wait until morning.

Lord Darley hovered sympathetically near her as if he would speak to her alone, but Marian didn't have the heart for his words right now. She had been disappointed too thoroughly this day to give anyone the opportunity to hurt her more. She couldn't bear to be proposed to out of sympathy, and she didn't wish to have him offer her a replacement for her jewel or other such nonsense right now. She might feel differently in the morning when her better sense had time to catch up with her, but right now she was too lost to the dismals to care.

She didn't even have it in her to blame Mr. Montague. He appeared to be as miserable as she over the loss. Unless he was a great actor, he had suffered a terrible blow to his integrity and was not likely to recover until he had redeemed himself. She had seen him furiously striking the walls as if they would speak. No one else knew that he had been the one carrying the necklace, but the knowledge lay unspoken between them like a guilty secret.

She didn't want to have guilty secrets with Mr. Montague. He made her feel quite guilty enough every time he looked at her when she was with Lord Darley. The loss of the necklace made it imperative that the viscount come up to scratch soon, but she couldn't think of how she would do that right now without it looking like pity. She would worry about it in the morning.

Jessica was extremely quiet as they readied themselves for bed. Lily always tended to their mother, so they aided each other now in the unbuttoning and unfastening of their gowns. The room was chilly and damp but not cold, and they made no effort to start a fire. Marian slipped between the covers without questioning her sister, but Jessica wasn't ready to sleep yet.

"Was the necklace worth a very great deal, Marian? Will that poor man be transported when Mr. Montague finds him? Mr. Montague seemed to be in a terrible temper. I would not want to be that poor valet."

"His pride has been hurt, that is all. I daresay I should like to whip the odious man if he is found, but I shan't imagine he will be. Go to sleep; there is nothing more we can do about it."

Jessica snuggled deeper into the pillows, but she continued to toss restlessly. "Mr. Montague is a trifle frightening, is he not? I'm rather afraid of him. Could we go home in the morning?"

"The only one who need be afraid of Mr. Montague is Mr. O'Toole. We'll talk about going home in the morning."

"Lord Darley is such a nice man. I don't understand why he has a friend like Mr. Montague."

Marian didn't bother to answer this nonsense. She was

out of charity with the entire male gender right now. She didn't wish to speak about them.

As the company gradually drifted off to sleep or continued to stare miserably at the ceiling depending on their state of mind, the drunken ghost below settled on the library couch and began to snore.

"I tell you, the wretch was here last night. He wouldn't soil his precious coat by going out in the pouring rain." Dawn was just breaking over the muddy horizon as Reginald swung his leg over his mount and settled into his saddle.

Darley stood in the stable yard, shaking his head. "You cannot know which way he went. None of the horses are missing. He seems to have vanished into thin air. At least break your fast and let us discuss a sensible course."

"There is no sensible course but murdering the thief. I mean to find the magistrate and set a hue and cry if nothing else. He'll not get off easily."

Darley watched his friend ride off before returning to the house through a side entrance that led in from the stable. He didn't think the ladies were up and about yet. A little exploration might be called for, under the circumstances. If the valet was still here, he might find some clue that would track him.

Darley carefully scanned the gentlemen's smoking and billiards room and saw nothing out of place. The lord's study was a dark little room toward the back of the house, and he pulled the draperies back to allow in the morning sun. An antechamber was stacked with generations of estate records, the dust virtually undisturbed for twenty years, if not more. In the study itself he found a table much like the one in his father's study. A silver tray held a collection of crystal glasses and a stopper that still smelled vaguely of brandy. Darley's eyebrows rose as he sniffed the glass and looked around for the bottle that it belonged in. His father's tray always held an ornate decanter. This one also had, sometime in the very near past.

He found no sign of the decanter that the stopper belonged in, but he could see where the dust on the desk had recently been disturbed. A trail of what could only be a woman's footsteps marred the dust near the bookcase. One of the ladies must have been in here when they searched last night.

He could not remember any of the ladies coming downstairs to search, but Darley pushed that thought aside as he continued his examination. The tapestry hanging from one paneled wall seemed to drift slightly in the morning air. He glanced to the broken window beneath the drapery he had pushed back, but no air came through there.

Darley had never prided himself on his intelligence. He had always been a mediocre student with more interest in horses than books. But he did possess a modicum of common sense, and common sense told him that heavy tapestries did not normally move without some very good reason. Dragging a chair over to the wall, he stood on it and reached for the wooden rod holding the tapestry up.

"Lord Darley! Whatever are you doing?"

The soft voice nearly startled him into falling from his perch. He glanced down to see the surprised expression on young Miss Oglethorp's face. It occurred to him that if it had been her sister standing there, the expression would have been much more suspicious. He didn't know what made him think of that. He let the rod and tapestry fall to the floor with a dust-exuding thump.

Jessica stepped hastily backward, waving her hand before her face to rid her nose of the particles.

"'Pologize for that, Miss Oglethorp, but the thing weighs a bloody ton. Excuse me. Didn't mean to say that. Slip of the tongue. Hadn't you ought to be with your mother?" Darley climbed down from his chair and nervously dusted his hands on his trousers.

Jessica gave him an innocently questioning glance. "I thought to look for the necklace before anyone got up. Marian scarcely slept all night, and I thought I heard her crying once. Do you think the thief hid behind there?" She nodded to the newly uncovered paneling.

"I thought there might be something behind the wall, leastways. There's a bl—a bad draft coming through. Look, I think there is a crack along here." He ran his hand down

the wall, searching it with his fingers. "One of our houses
has a place like this where one of the ancestors kept his
valuables. There's usually a little dent . . . " He gave a
grunt of satisfaction as the wall swung outward.

Jessica gave a little scream of excitement. "Oh, my, you
are so clever! Is he in there?"

Feeling just a little proud of himself, Darley explored the
recess behind the wall. It wasn't particularly deep, large
enough for a man perhaps. And as he suspected, there was
a vault in the wall. But the vault was open and empty. He
stepped back in disappointment.

"He could have hidden here, I suppose, but there is nothing here now. I wonder how many other hiding places there
might be?"

Jessica didn't look in the least downhearted by his failure. Looking at him with gleaming eyes that made him feel
ten feet tall, she responded eagerly, "Mother will know! Let
us go see if she is up yet."

"I'm afraid he might escape while we are gone. Let me
stand at the bottom of the staircase while you run up, just to
make certain you are safe. Then I will stand guard in the
hall and listen for any suspicious noises."

Neither of them seemed aware that their shyness had disappeared in the excitement of the chase. Jessica obediently
ran up the stairs as fast as she could while Darley looked
on. When he was certain that she was well on her way to
her mother's room, he wandered around the octagon of the
entrance foyer, admiring the faint glimmers of color from
the skylight while listening for any oddities in sounds.

On the couch in the library, the eighth marquess
squeezed his aching eyes closed and pinched his nose to
halt the throbbing. If he were not mistaken, his unwanted
guests were about to descend upon him en masse unless he
acted soon. He had no grand desire to explain himself, particularly when his head felt like an overripe melon. He
wasn't certain he could explain himself even if his head
was in working order, which it very definitely was not right
now. And he had no desire to find himself transported or
hung from a gibbet for stealing what rightfully belonged to
him.

Stifling a moan as he eased himself upright, the marquess sought a position of safety. If he did not miss his guess, the clank of boots on the marble entrance floor indicated one of the gentlemen patrolled there. He cast a reluctant gaze around the solid library. If there was an escape route here, he had not yet found it.

With a sigh—he was beginning to think he knew why ghosts sighed and moaned—the marquess eased himself from the couch and crossed to the tall window. At least he'd had the sense to pass out on the ground floor. Figuring the dogs would be on his heels in minutes, he shoved upward on the casement and felt it give, but not without a great deal of noise.

By the time Darley raced down the hall and discovered which room had the open window, the phantom intruder was gone.

Cursing vehemently, the viscount threw his boots over the low sill and followed the path of footsteps in the muddy turf. Behind him, he heard Jessica's shouts, followed unmistakably by those of the Lady Marian. His heart quailed at failing that redoubtable lady, and he added speed to his flight.

Inside, Marian quickly located Darley's route. She stuck her head out the window just in time to see him disappear around the house in the direction of the kitchen garden. Not seeing any reason why she should wet her good shoes, she picked up her skirt and raced down the hall in the direction of the kitchen.

She popped out the back door in time to realize there indeed had been hounds in the stables. Darley had evidently released them and they were howling across the distant hillside in search of their prey. The viscount himself was saddling his horse with every intention of following.

He turned to see her standing there as he mounted, and she waved as he rode off. It didn't seem very practical to attempt saddling a carriage horse even if a saddle happened to be lying about. She would have to content herself with waiting for Darley's efforts.

Surely a thief on foot could not long escape a pack of hounds and a man on horseback.

"Did you see him? Is the thief out there?" Behind her, Jessica excitedly wrung her hands. "Isn't Lord Darley just the bravest person you've ever known?"

Marian would wait and pass judgment on that later. What she wanted to know was the precise location of Mr. Montague while all this was going on. It seemed highly suspicious that the noise hadn't aroused him.

But she was left to wonder as her mother and Lily wandered down, followed by Darley's valet. There were fires to be stirred and water to be heated and breakfast to be made. Chasing thieves had become men's work, apparently.

By the time a breakfast of sorts had been put together, Darley was back with two hares and a quail, but no thief. He slung the game sheepishly on a pantry table, set the shotgun against the wall, and cleansed his hands in the basin Jessica brought for him.

"What happened?" she asked eagerly. "Did he dash over a cliff?"

Marian raised her eyebrows slightly at her sister's sudden boldness, but Lord Darley was answering Jessica and not looking in her direction, so she held her tongue.

"The hounds were just out for a romp. They weren't on anybody's trail. I don't know where the thief got to." His disappointment was so evident that no one could chastise him, not even Marian.

"That means he could still be on the grounds," Marian answered thoughtfully. It wouldn't do to worry her mother, but she wished to get her hands on O'Toole and personally wring his neck. She set down her pitcher and casually glanced at the door that Darley had just entered.

"Step one foot further in that direction, Lady Marian, and I will personally haul you back to London so fast your head will spin."

The voice roared from the doorway behind her, and she spun around to glare at Montague. "How dare you speak to me that way!"

Having achieved next to no sleep and spent the past hour attempting to locate some semblance of a magistrate only to be told he was away, Reginald wasn't in any humor for argument. He slapped his hat and riding crop down on a cabinet and glared back. "He's my bloody valet and if anybody goes after him, it will be me. You're a damned sight better off not witnessing his capture."

He strode through the kitchen and out the door, leaving his audience open-mouthed behind him.

Lady Grace was the first to recover her aplomb. Reaching for a heavy frying pan, she said, "He must be a bit peckish without having had breakfast. Jessica, do you think you could find the ingredients for those little muffins we used to make?"

Flushing, not knowing how to excuse his friend's behavior toward her, Darley gave Marian a tight smile and hastily followed in Montague's path. When he was gone, she threw a pewter sugar bowl at the door. She was tired of holding her tongue. One of these days she was going to let them all have it, bound and gift-wrapped.

Fourteen

The men returned some time later, muddy, hungry, covered with straw, and irritated beyond speaking.

Lily hurried to pour their tea while Darley's valet relieved them of their filthy coats. Lady Grace attempted to send her daughters out of the room while the gentlemen were in their shirtsleeves, but even quiet Jessica would have none of it. Without waiting to serve in the formality of the dining room, they set plates and cutlery on the trestle table in the kitchen and began setting out the meal while demanding to know what happened.

Darley looked disgusted. "If I did not know better, I'd say there was an army troop out there this morning. After all that rain, there shouldn't have been so many footprints."

Reginald drained his teacup first, then began folding his bacon into his toast. He was all but certain there was more than one person hiding on these grounds. The bootprints looked to be of different sizes to him, and the one appeared to have an incipient hole in the sole. He bit savagely into his toast and ignored the speculations running rampant around him. O'Toole wouldn't be caught dead with a hole in his sole.

"You are being awfully quiet, Mr. Montague. What is your theory?" Marian sipped carefully at her tea. The dark circles beneath her eyes reflected her sleepless night.

He tried not to look at her. Generally, he didn't see women until well into the afternoon, when they were elegantly gowned and coiffed and prepared for the day. Lady Marian had not taken the time to do more than tie her hair back in a ribbon, and its dark waves seemed strangely thick and luxuriant for one so slender. She was gowned only in some frail muslin that apparently had little beneath it to conceal her natural shape. He was having a devil of a time keeping his eyes from straying to discover just how natural that shape was. Instead, he focused on his breakfast.

"I have no theory. The magistrate is not here to order the roads searched. I have sent someone back to London to fetch a Runner, and another with O'Toole's description to the toll keepers. I suggest we search the house one more time in daylight. If your cousin does not put in an appearance soon, I also suggest that the ladies return to town while I remain to deal with the authorities. Short of burning the whole damned manor down, I don't know what else we can do."

"I say, Reginald, your language," Darley reminded him. He threw a worried look to Marian, but she seemed not in the least offended. Jessica was blushing, however. He patted her hand helplessly, and she gave him a shy smile of gratitude.

"We will have to organize the search better this time," Marian suggested. "If the thief is still here, he could just stay one step ahead of us and never be found. We must start at the ground floor and drive him upward until there is no where else for him to escape."

Darley gave her a look of amazement. "That is a capital idea. I wish I had thought of that earlier."

"There are many things we should have thought of earlier. I fear it is too late for any of them now. The thief has gone outside these walls. What reason is there to think that he will return?"

Lady Grace daintily poured another cup of tea. "He will need to eat again sometime," she mentioned calmly. "He has already devoured most of our nuncheon."

They all turned to stare at her. Blithely unaware of her audience's astonishment, she carefully smeared a bit of jam they had found in the larder onto her toast.

"Mama, do you mean to say that the chickens we cooked last night are gone?" Marian asked patiently.

Lady Grace looked up with surprise. "Isn't that what I just said, dear?"

Reginald scraped his chair back and went to investigate

the cold cellar. When he came back, his expression was carefully neutral. "There is naught but the bones of one fowl left. The other is gone entirely."

"Ghosts don't eat, do they?" Jessica asked fearfully.

Reginald didn't bother to give this inanity a reply, but Darley reassured her as Marian set her cup down and stood up.

"I think we need to observe a few precautions. Do you think we could hire some help from the village?" Marian turned to Mr. Montague for an answer.

"I have already looked into that. Most of the men have been hired out for the planting, but there were a couple of old fellows willing to come out for the day. We can station them with the horses. And the innkeeper thought he knew a couple of women who might come out to help for as long as we need them. No one seems to know anything of the marquess's whereabouts, but they're all curious to come look the place over. I suspect we'll have a fair company here shortly."

Both Marian and Montague waited expectantly for some sound from beyond the walls, but only Lady Grace responded.

"I suppose my Gwen has long gone to another household. She used to make the most delicious pastries," she said wistfully.

There was nothing much that could be said to that. The gentlemen went off to see to the horses while the ladies cleared away the remains of their repast. Before they were done, there was the sound of a wagon in the stable yard. Mr. Montague's new employees had arrived.

As Marian watched her mother fall into raptures over a stout old lady who was apparently the amazing Gwen come back for the sake of old times, she took charge of the bevy of young girls come to help out. As Marian set them to scrubbing the kitchen and preparing the game, she marvelled over Montague's audacity. This wasn't even his home, and he was hiring servants. If the marquess actually existed, he must think all this bustle distinctly odd when he returned.

But the new troops were swiftly organized under Mr.

Montague's direction. The men were left to clean the stables and keep guard over the horses. A pistol was left in their care to shoot as warning should anyone attempt to get away. The giggling girls were sent with dusters and mops and brooms into the various downstairs chambers with the instructions not to leave their assigned rooms without permission. If anyone entered their domains, they were to pound their buckets and yell at the top of their lungs, and everyone was to come running.

The rest of the party trudged upward in hopes the thief would attempt to escape the activity below. Reginald stationed Lady Grace at the stairs with a hunting horn and the sewing basket she insisted on. He only hesitated when it came to divide the party to search the two long wings. The ladies could not be sent off by themselves, but it would not only be improper for them to break up into pairs, but the decision as to who would go with whom was beyond his capacity.

Marian caught his dilemma at once. "It seems wasteful, but perhaps we ought all to search each wing together. Mother said she thought there might be a hidden passage on this floor. We will need to be looking for that as well as watching to see no one escapes."

Darley beamed. "Capital idea. If you will allow me?" He offered his arm for her escort.

Forcing herself to smile sweetly instead of impatiently, Marian accepted his arm and proceeded at a stately pace to the first chamber to be searched. The task of searching for a thief or his hiding place was going to be tediously time consuming if she was going to have to do it at this snail's pace, but she needed Lord Darley's approval more than ever. Without that ruby, they would soon have no home to go to when their London lease was done. She bit her lip to hide her anxiety as the others began pounding walls and doors.

Reginald sent her strained expression a look of concern, but his mind was on locating the monster of ingratitude who had stolen his pride and integrity, not to mention his fortune. There wasn't a doubt in his mind that he would have to find some way of repaying Lady Marian for her missing necklace if it should not be found. He just hadn't found any opportunity to tell her so. Perhaps after the noon meal he could separate her from the others long enough to reassure her.

The rattle of a bucket below sent the gentlemen careening down the stairs twice before the maids learned not to knock them with their mops. After the second false alarm, the search began to degenerate into a game of hide-and-seek, with the contents of the manor being "it."

Jessica discovered that some of the wardrobes still contained clothes from an earlier generation. Forgetting her fear of ghosts, she ran from room to room searching out more and more miraculous creations of hoops and petticoats and ostrich feathers.

Darley became engrossed in searching the paneling for more concealed cracks to match his earlier success, and he was soon left behind.

Reginald began mentally cataloguing the value of the artwork and bibelots ornamenting the various chambers and wondering if they could all be included on the entailment inventory.

And Marian discovered a lady's library with first editions and illustrated pages that she had difficulty leaving behind. If there were a thief to be found, he had not begun to steal all the treasures lying around waiting to be taken.

When Reginald discovered her curled in a chair scanning an illustrated version of *Gulliver's Travels*, he threw himself into a matching chair and scowled. "This is not working," he announced.

Marian reluctantly drew herself from the adventures in Lilliput back to the present. She looked around, discovering they were in a sitting room adjoining the bed chamber where her father's portrait hung and there was no one else about. In all propriety, the situation should make her uneasy, but Mr. Montague's harrassed expression did not lead her to believe she was in danger from anything except his temper.

"No, it is not," she agreed. "It is exceedingly boring looking for someone who is so obviously not here. If there is a secret passage, he could have moved half the furniture into it by now and fallen asleep. I had not realized how enormous this place is."

Since the mansion was scarcely half the size of his father's ancestral home, Reginald did not have an adequate reply. He merely sprawled in the chair and continued scowling at her. "I will see that you are repaid for every shilling that the necklace was worth." He hadn't meant to announce the fact so coldly, but it had been on his mind for too long and he wished to be rid of it. He wasn't even certain how he meant to carry out his promise. He might have to give in to his father's wishes and marry an heiress to scrape together that kind of blunt.

Marian simply looked at him with that dark-eyed expression that made Reginald want to haul her into his arms and kiss her until he melted away her false façade.

"That is generous of you, of course," she said slowly, "but entirely unnecessary. I risked the necklace every time I wore it. I risked it by taking it to the jewelers'. You did nothing that I did not ask you to do. You could scarcely have foreseen that it would be stolen."

Yes, he could have. She didn't know he had a thief for valet, but he knew. Reginald wasn't in a mood for arguing with her about it. "I'll speak to your solicitor. We'll make some arrangement. I'll not have you marrying Darley just to pay the bills."

"I don't suppose anyone has ever told you that you are an odious tyrant." Marian closed the book and rose from the chair. She kept her voice pleasant, fearing Lord Darley would enter at any moment.

He drew himself out of his chair and blocked her path. "And you are a sharp-tongued witch. That does not change anything. You will have the funds as soon as I am able to collect them."

He was too close, but to retreat would be a sign of surrender. Marian held her place and glared up at him. She was of an average height and had not ever considered herself small before, but he made her feel helpless. She did not like the sensation at all. It was quite unnerving to have this man glaring down at her as if she were a gnat he could swat. But something in his eyes told her it wasn't swatting that he had in mind. She clenched her fingers into fists and tried not to retreat. "You will remove yourself, sir."

The tension and frustration of the day had been too much

for him. Reginald knew full well the danger of rosy lips and slender curves, even when they were armored with a mind and tongue equal to his own. He could think of no other action other than to reach for her. A brief wish to shake her passed through his mind, but it wasn't Reginald's mind in control now. His fingers clasped her arms and pulled her to him.

Marian felt the harshness of his lips across hers before she fully registered what he meant to do. She was twenty-two years old and could count the number of times she had been kissed on the fingers of one hand, and not one of those times had in any way resembled the ferocity of Montague's kiss. She could taste the experience on his lips, in the way they molded to hers, forcing her to relent and kiss him back. She shuddered as she did just that.

He was hard and warm and his fingers were strong as they held her to him. She feared there would be bruises where his hands held her, but she couldn't bring herself to pull away. Her hands came to rest on his chest, and she realized vaguely that she wasn't wearing gloves. "How improper" murmured through her head, while her mouth grew soft and moist and parted slightly at his insistence.

The sound of Jessica calling her name brought them both abruptly back to the moment. Reginald dropped her arms, and Marian backed away, and they both stared at each other as if lightning had struck between them. Jessica's arrival forced them to turn away.

"Look at this! Do you think I might be introduced at court in this?" She swirled around in a gold velvet cloak with a gold band of ostrich feathers wrapped about her hair.

Marian slid her hand over her cheek, tucking her hair behind her ears, tentatively touching the place where a rough beard had chafed her. She didn't look at Montague as she watched her sister's posturing. "It is rather—" she stumbled for words—"quaint," she managed. Her insides were still shaking. She needed to sit down and recover herself, but she couldn't let him see what he had done to her. She didn't want to appear an inexperienced young miss. She would brush this off as if nothing had ever happened. Nothing *had* happened. It was just the strain they were all under.

"Montague, where the hell are you? Come here, would you? I want you to look at something." Darley stumbled into the room and stopped. Uncertainly, he glanced to his friend's stiff posture, to Jessica's pretty smile of welcome, to Marian's nervous fiddling at her hair. With a shrug, he went back to his original intent. "There's something behind this wall. I just can't find how to get at it."

He crossed the small sitting room and knocked at the far wall. The sound was oddly hollow. "See that? It shouldn't sound like that." He went to another wall and knocked. The resulting sound was more of a thud. "That's the way a solid wall sounds. There's something back there, I tell you."

Marian gratefully turned her attention to this new discovery. She pounded high and low on the wall, getting the same hollow sound as Darley. She tried it on either side of the same wall, with no difference. Reginald left the sitting room and his steps could be heard in the room adjoining. Soon his knock could be heard on the wall on the other side.

"Still hollow!" he called. "And this is the end of the hall. If there's a passage, it can't go any farther."

They all immediately descended on the pretty bedchamber to renew their exploration.

Behind the wall, the marquess unfolded his lengthy frame and crept back the way he had come earlier. It would be a damned nuisance losing his hiding place, but he had other things to think about right now.

Michael had said the Lady Marian was soon to be pledged to the wealthy Lord Darley. From all he could tell, the viscount was the usual pleasant British fool. He had no particular objection to the match. But it hadn't been Darley in that sitting room when all went silent.

The eighth marquess of Effingham had the distinct feeling that his little cousin had just been thoroughly kissed by a man with whom she had moments before been trading insults. And if Michael's information was correct, that "odious tyrant" and cynical aristocrat was little more than a shopkeeper and not the wealthy lord the ladies needed.

It made his head hurt to think about it.

Fifteen

The marquess removed his boots and crept quietly up the servants' stairs to their quarters. He glanced down the bare hallway of closed doors, then decided on the nearest one. Michael wouldn't waste steps going to the end of an empty corridor.

He swung the door open quickly and stepped in, pushing it closed with his heel. Had his gaze been steel, it would have pierced the occupant through the heart.

Instead, the auburn-haired man on the narrow bed merely threw another card in his hat, wriggled his wrist, and flung a coin at the man glaring at him. The marquess caught the coin and shoved it in his pocket without looking at it.

"I ought to wring your neck." The look in his eyes was murderous, enough to make anyone believe he meant to carry out the threat. The scarred cheek twitched furiously as he spoke.

"You'll disturb your guests," the other man replied calmly, gathering his scattered cards with a wave of his hand.

"They've all taken a break for something they're calling 'nuncheon' but which smells very much like roasted game and apple pies. I'm damned well going to starve, thanks to you."

"Tarts. They call them tarts here. Pies contain meat." O'Toole crossed his legs blithely, tailor-fashion. "You could go down and join them. They're only looking for me."

The marquess grabbed a straight-backed chair and straddled it. His expression wasn't any more pleasant. "Fine idea. I'll go down and terrorize the ladies, have the damned hot-headed gentlemen call me out, and spill my blood on foreign soil. What else have I got to do today?"

The irrepressible O'Toole grinned. "You're all cock-a-hoop about nothing, as they say here. Your fair visage ain't nothing to expire over. Lady Marian will no doubt pin you to your chair and interrogate you over hot coals, but the other two will twitter and offer you tea. Scary thought, ain't it?"

The marquess rubbed idly at his mutilated face. "It isn't your Lady Marian I'm wary of, it's that other damned bastard, the stuck-up fellow who looks down his nose all the time. He's already putting two and two together, and it's his cash on the line if the ruby doesn't show up. I heard him offering to pay for it."

O'Toole looked impressed. "I didn't think he had it in him. From all I can tell, he lives pretty modestly by London standards."

The marquess crossed his arms over the back of the chair. "He's arrogant enough to bankrupt himself trying. When all this started, I just thought we'd be removing a bauble no one would miss. Now we're losing ladies their homes and bankrupting noble aristocrats. I don't like it."

"Gavin, your soft heart is showing. Besides, the ladies can't lose their home and Montague lose his blunt both. It's one or the other. Once we sell the necklace and get things righted around here, you can ask the ladies to come stay."

The marquess scowled, drawing the scars into a formidable mask. "It's not going to be that easy. That blasted Marian has all the gall of every Lawrence ever born. She's determined to throw herself away on the viscount and save the family fortune. And I think your friend Montague is likely to tear a few people apart to prevent it. The situation is getting downright nasty out there."

O'Toole gave a fascinated whistle. "And here I thought the British were a cold lot. I'm damned glad Mother had the sense to find someone besides a Lawrence to father me."

The marquess stood up quickly and kicked the chair

aside, bunching his fists as he did so. "Say that again and
I'll beat you into a shadow on the wall. You're a Lawrence,
just some hideous throwback, that's all. I'd suggest you put
that active brain of yours to finding some way out of this
mess, or I'm going to have to give the necklace back."

He turned and strode out of the room, leaving his
younger brother to grin after him.

His brother, the marquess, wasn't such a bad lot,
O'Toole mused to himself. Perhaps Gavin had killed a few
men in the latest war between Britain and her former
colonies and wouldn't be looked on all that friendly in
these parts, but he hadn't bothered to kill his closest living
relative yet. Considering the temptation Michael had offered frequently enough, that was saying a good deal about
the marquess's character.

"If it doesn't rain again, the roads will be clear enough
for the ladies to go back to London. There will be enough
light if we hurry." Reginald wiped his hands on his napkin
and sat back in his chair as if he were the head of their odd
household.

Marian managed a pleasant smile. "We have hired the
servants for at least a day's work. We cannot leave them
unsupervised."

Reginald gave her a sharp look. "And tomorrow there
will be some other excuse not to leave. You will wish to
wait for the marquess to be certain he is well, or to make
your apologies for intruding, or half a dozen other damned
excuses. I say we leave now before anything else happens."

One of the new maids came to clear away the dishes, but
Lady Grace spoke as if she were not there. "You really
must mind your language, Mr. Montague. I had to remind
the squire quite frequently. Single gentlemen often fall into
bad habits, you know."

Since this was not at all to the point and misdirected his
intentions, Reginald scowled and looked to Darley to pick
up the notion again. His friend was so lost in thought that
he did not appear to notice there was a conversation going
on.

Reginald stifled an exclamation of disgust. The damned

hidden passage had yet to be discovered and explored. He wasn't going to get Darley out of here any time soon, and he had hoped to send the viscount back with the ladies. He could see when he was overruled. He didn't even have to look to Marian to see her triumph.

"I suppose we must search a little longer, then, but we are all leaving here on the morrow. I will speak to the help and see if any wish to stay until then." He waited patiently for Lady Grace to lead the way from the table so he might get about his business. Reginald wasn't accustomed to having ladies in the house, but he remembered his upbringing when it was necessary.

Lady Grace gave him an approving smile and rose from her chair, indicating that her daughters follow. Reginald felt as if he had just been given a motherly pat on the back. He hadn't known any such damned thing since he had been in leading strings, and then it had most likely been from a nursery maid. His mother had seldom noticed his existence when she had been around, and she had left his father when he was little more than a lad. He had scarcely been aware of her existence by the time she died. Motherly pats weren't anything he expected.

Shrugging off the odd feeling caused by that approving smile, Reginald went in search of the old woman who had made herself head of the household servants. Lady Grace would no doubt wish to have the woman's pastries for breakfast on the morrow.

They congregated in the upstairs hall a short time later to resume their search for the passage. Marian had pinned her hair up before the meal, and now she was wearing a more appropriate afternoon gown that concealed most of her figure in loose folds. Now that he had been made aware of her, though, Reginald could not forget the willowy slenderness of her waist nor pretend he did not see the long-legged grace with which she walked. He clenched his teeth and tried to keep his mind on the subject at hand.

"We will need to find the length of the passage and position look-outs all along the way so our thief cannot escape if he is hiding in it."

"There are no doubt stairs to the first floor. We cannot

possibly guard all exits," Marian replied thoughtfully, her gaze following the length of the various halls.

"The house is not old enough to warrant a warren of old passages like some." Darley did not realize he was correcting a lady. He was too lost in this new game to remember that he was actually talking to a female. He, too, was following the length of the hall and determining the passage's possible path. "I think the original owner simply had some eccentric tastes. It would have been costly to build in hidden staircases."

"It does not appear to me as if cost ever deterred any of the Effinghams," Reginald replied cynically, "but I think we can begin with one of us standing here and watching down the hall where we know one end is, and the rest of us starting down at the end of this other hall and working our way around."

They applied themselves more seriously this time, now that they had some evidence that there might actually be a hiding place. Discovering that the hollow wall actually began in the master suite occupying the entire north end of the manor, they quickly examined all the rooms in between to determine that it passed behind all of them, then set about looking for exits. Lady Grace stood at the stairway as before and watched with mild interest, calling encouragement.

Possessing more patience than the others, Darley was the one to discover the door concealed between the fireplace and the windows in the sitting room of the master suite. The ladies came running at his call, and they cheered as the hidden door silently opened. Then they grew silent at the prospect of someone entering that unlit hole.

"I think it might be dangerous," Jessica whispered, standing back from the cold draft of air coming from behind the wall. "I wish you would not go in."

Marian tried not to give her sister an impatient look, but she could tell she was not entirely successful by the flicker of amusement she caught in Mr. Montague's eyes. She managed to hold her tongue, however, and allow the gentlemen to make the decision, not doubting for a moment that they would ignore Jessica's admonitions.

"I think it would be best if we found another exit before exploring the passage," Montague advised.

"We're more apt to find it from within the passage," Darley argued.

"Perhaps we could follow on this side while you explored the other," Marian suggested, attempting to disguise her impatience with this argument. She wished to grab a lantern and descend into the darkness right now to see if it harbored a despicable thief. "You could knock on the walls as you go and we would answer as to which room you're nearest."

This suggestion was eventually adopted, with Darley being given the honor of exploring the passage, since he had discovered the door. Both gentlemen carried pistols but neither thought there would be need of them. The thief was no doubt long gone.

Montague guarded the doors into the hall while Jessica and Marian rushed in and out of the chambers communicating with Darley behind the walls. If the thief left the passage by some route and attempted to leave by way of the hall, Reginald meant to catch him.

By the time they reached the final sitting room at the end of the east hall, everyone was thoroughly disappointed. Darley had reported no hidden treasures, not even a skeleton or an old sword behind the walls, and still no other exits had been found. When he thumped against the final length of the wall and the sound came from within the wardrobe, even Montague joined them in searching for the door.

It was scarcely a minute's work from there to discover the latch that unfastened the door, and Darley stepped out. He dusted himself off as he stepped from the wardrobe, but there wasn't the amount of webs and dust that could be expected from a long-deserted passage. He exchanged glances with Reginald but didn't say anything aloud in order to protect the ladies. The passage must have been used recently.

Marian caught the glance and tried to interpret it, but her mother rushed in and exclaimed excitedly over the hidden door, examining it front and back while rattling off conjectures on its purpose. The gentlemen could very well guess the purpose, but they didn't mention the possibility to the dowager. For all they knew, her late husband could have kept a mistress in this room.

Marian waited for her mother to quit prattling before asking, "How could Mr. O'Toole have known about this passage?"

Reginald managed to look uncomfortable. "He claimed to have worked for the old marquess. I wasn't certain whether to believe him or not. I suppose I should have believed him."

Lady Grace looked surprised. "He did not look old enough to work for George. George has been dead nearly twenty years, after all. Mr. O'Toole couldn't have been more than a child then. I should think I would have remembered him."

Silence reigned momentarily. Montague was the first to break it. "Is it possible he may have worked for the new marquess?"

Everyone turned to Lady Grace, who shrugged her delicate shoulders. "It is possible, but I have been told he has been here only a very short while. He is an American, you know. They had to go back to the heirs of the fifth marquess to find a descendant." It had been her failure to provide a son that had resulted in that search. She had never been bitter about being turned from her husband's home upon his death. She had only been upset about the brief amount of time she had been given to do her duty.

"O'Toole didn't sound American," Montague said more to himself than any other.

"I can't think of any good English servant speaking as he did," Marian reminded him. "He was above all insulting. I cannot understand why you engaged him in the first place."

As of this moment, neither could Reginald. Darley, however, interrupted his thoughts.

"O'Toole insulted you?" he asked with a hint of outrage.

That had let the cat out of the bag. Marian bit her tongue and glanced helplessly at Mr. Montague. She could not very well explain the contretemps that had led her to exchange words with his valet.

Reginald gave her a closed look from beneath his lashes and lazily explained, "He also acted as my groom. I asked him to take the ladies to some lecture or another and they had a difference of opinion. He was appropriately dealt with for the incident."

The question was quickly dropped as Marian swept from the room declaring as she went, "I have had enough of this nonsense. I think it is time we searched the third floor. Who is to guard the stairs?"

By the time they reached the servants' quarters, O'Toole, his hat, and his cards had vanished. All that remained in his place was the carcass of one chicken.

With frustration and disappointment, the small party searched the remaining rooms, pounded all the walls, and wished the valet to the devil. When their search was complete, they were tired, filthy, irritable, and hungry. It didn't take a second request when Lady Grace called them down to wash for dinner. The ladies went one way, and the gentlemen, the other.

Feeling thoroughly wretched, Marian discarded her filthy gown as soon as she entered her chamber and quickly washed herself off in the bowl provided. The ruby was lost, Darley had not proposed, and the elusive marquess was obviously bankrupt. The entire journey had been a complete disaster. She did not see how matters could get any worse.

She did her very best not to even think about Mr. Montague's kiss. If she allowed herself such an indulgence, she would lose sight of all her goals. She could not be swayed from her purpose by a kiss that made her soul ache.

She closed her eyes and tried not to remember Mr. Montague's hands upon her, nor the firm feel of his chest beneath her palms, nor how it felt to be held so close while a man's mouth devoured hers. It would not do at all to think these things.

But the moment she saw his tall, elegantly garbed form standing in the hall waiting to escort them into the salon, her heart began to pound, and she greatly feared he would hear the commotion it was making. She refused his arm, tilting her chin proudly as she entered the salon without his aid.

Sixteen

Reginald sipped at the claret some enterprising person had found in the wine cellar and watched, disgruntled, as Marian turned her rapt attention to Darley's repetition of the day's adventures. She was hanging on to every one of his friend's words as if they were pearls of wisdom, when even Reginald was forced to admit they were little more than self-serving paeans to himself. He knew Darley's faults intimately and had never been irritated with them before, but was now.

She was staging this show for his benefit, Reginald knew. She was simpering like an idiot to show him she and Darley would suit beautifully. After that kiss today, he damned well knew otherwise, but he was at a loss as to how to prevent the inevitable. Darley was so thoroughly blinded by her act that the viscount would be calling on the marquess to make his offer right now if the dratted man could be found.

Reginald would have to appeal to the lady herself. She knew precisely what she was doing. She wasn't blinded by anything but her damned need to save her family. She could let Darley off the hook gently, if she chose. He would have to force her to so choose.

He bided his time. The ladies rose and left the gentlemen to their claret. Darley eagerly followed them shortly afterward. Reginald finished his wine, then found his way to the library instead of joining the others. It would drive Marian crazy not knowing where he was or what he was up to. He was beginning to understand her nature very well. And she understood his. She would look for him here first.

He wasn't disappointed. When Marian arrived, she carried a candle and a book she had borrowed earlier from the shelves. They both knew it was highly improper to meet like this, but it was rather difficult not to be in each other's pockets all the time when the party was so small. No one would suspect collusion except the parties themselves.

She didn't even bother to act surprised when she found him examining the shelves. "Most of the selections are quite boring," she informed him.

Reginald tried not to turn and look at her, but the temptation was too strong. She had dressed for dinner in an appropriately low-cut gown that had kept him on the edge of his seat all evening. He had dined for years with ladies wearing less and had only given them a second glance when attracting attention had clearly been their purpose. He had also seen ladies with more assets to display than this one. He could see no earthly reason why he should suddenly be so fascinated with a woman who held him in contempt, but his gaze wandered unerringly to the soft swell of ivory breasts in candlelight. Since he still held an open book in his hand, he hoped she would think his eyes were on it.

He forced his gaze to lift to her face. She was watching him with suspicion, but she really was too innocent to know what he was thinking. Reginald wondered what it would be like to teach her the power of her femininity, but he had a strange reluctance to teach her something she would only use on others.

He answered politely, "Boring, perhaps, but some are quite valuable. This one, for example. There is only one other known copy in existence." He held out the book for her perusal.

It was in Greek. She looked at it with disappointment. "It is in very poor condition."

"The entire library will be in very poor condition if changes are not wrought soon. There is damp in the walls, and without fires in the winter, I daresay the pages are becoming very brittle. I have a mind to seek your cousin out and make a bid for the collection." Except that he would

have no money with which to make a bid once he repaid
the ladies the cost of their necklace. Reginald kept that to
himself.

"Obviously, it would do better in the hands of someone
prepared to take care of it, but I should think you would
find very few buyers for as large a collection as this. Did
you think to acquire it all for yourself?"

She had the mind of a shopkeeper. Reginald tried to remember his purpose here. "That is not to the point. I have
decided we must return to town in the morning. I will begin
transferring funds to your man of business as soon as the
banks open. I know you did not wish to sell the necklace,
but I think it can be arranged so that your mother believes
the copy is the real thing. Once you have the worth of the
necklace, you need not worry about funds for quite some
while. I can advise you on how to invest them, if you wish.
They should bring in more than adequate income for as
long as you like and even provide dowries, if that is your
wish. You need not go fishing for wealthy husbands any
longer."

There had been ample opportunity for Marian to consider
his earlier offer, but her answer had not changed. As much
as she craved the excuse he offered, she could not accept it.
Pride would not allow her to take such an immense sum
from any gentleman, and certainly not from this one. She
shook her head vehemently. "No, I cannot accept that. You
cannot be made to pay for a favor that I asked of you. I
know you think me a vulgar fortune-hunter, but please do
not insult me in this way."

Furious, Reginald slammed the book back on the shelf.
"I am offering you and your sister an opportunity to seek
affection instead of wealth. I would not have my friend suffer for your greed. Obviously, Darley is worth a great deal
more than your necklace and he is titled, as well. Are you
so greedy that you would make his life miserable in return
for what he can do for you?"

"I have no intention of making his life miserable!" Marian's voice raised an octave, and she glared at him. "He
likes me, even if you do not. Why can you not see that he is
happy and leave him be?"

"He is not happy!" Reginald roared. "He has a harpy of a mother and two for sisters. They tell him what to do night and day, and he is too good a fellow to say them nay. You will only add to his long list of nags and make his life hell. I will do everything within my power to prevent that happening!"

"Is that why you are forever tempting my temper? Do you think to expose me as a shrew and make him take a disgust of me? How very considerate a friend you are! Did you hope he would come upon us when you kissed me today? Is that what that was all about? I have wondered, you know, but I am not a complete fool."

She was practically standing beneath his chin, daring him to admit the truth, and he could not admit it even to himself. Without a single coherent, logical thought, Reginald halted her tongue by putting his arms around her and clamping his mouth to hers.

He felt her start of surprise. Her hands pushed ineffectively at his arms. But her mouth was an unwilling victim that he tortured unmercifully until he felt her surrender. He would teach her there were more pleasant things to do with her tongue than wield it in anger.

Reginald had not meant things to go so far, but once she was in his arms, he could not seem to set her aside. Her lips learned his lessons quickly, eagerly. Her hands began to cling to his arms rather than push. She resisted the persuasion of his tongue at first, but as her breaths came rapidly, she could no longer fight him. He felt the shock of his invasion ripple through her, and it drew him closer to taste more. He had never experienced a woman as innocent as this one. The pleasure of her response was greater than he could ever have imagined. He craved more, and his hand slid naturally up her waist, to the curve of her breast that had tempted him all evening.

She sighed against his mouth. Her breath was sweet and intoxicating, and Reginald pressed his hand upward that last little inch until his thumb rubbed the pebbly crest of her breast beneath layers of thin cloth. The jolt of shock rushing through her at his touch caused an equal throbbing in his loins, and he could not have separated himself from her

now had he wanted. He pressed his kiss deeper and
thrummed her sensitive nipple carefully, until she was
melting in his hands. She had no defenses against him, and
he wanted it that way.

The little capped sleeve slid easily from her shoulder. He
knew just where to find the ties of her chemise. Reginald
lifted her breast from its concealment just as he lifted her
from the floor to bring her to the leather couch behind him.
Marian clutched desperately at his neck as she lost her toe-
hold to reality, but she sank gratefully into his lap when he
sat down and wrapped her in his arms. If her head was
spinning as much as his, they both needed to sit down.

The lamplight was dim, but Reginald used its small illumination to admire the breast he had freed from confine-
ment. His fingers smoothed the skin and played a tune upon
the crest that had her wriggling with small cries against his
already aroused flesh. It was time to put a stop to this, he
knew, but not without one more kiss. He could not remember when he had acquired more pleasure by the simplest of
sight and touches. He could not release the moment completely just yet.

That was his mistake. Had he set her aside then, allowed
her to whip him with her tongue, no one would have intruded. But the protracted silence after the earlier explosion
had aroused too much curiosity. Unfortunately, Reginald's
mind wasn't on anyone but Marian at the moment.

A small hand grabbed Darley's arm as he clenched his
fist and prepared to enter the library. He had only the dim
light of one lamp to shatter his illusions, but he had heard
enough of the earlier argument to understand what was
happening behind that chair back now. The hand closing
around his arm caught him by surprise.

He looked down into the terrified expression of Miss
Oglethorp. The hall was much better lit than the library,
and light danced off her golden curls as she turned a pleading gaze to him.

"Please, don't," she whispered. "It is all my fault. I was
supposed to be the one to make a great match, but I have

been much too timid. Marian means only to take care of me."

That was an extremely odd way of looking at what was happening in there. Darley couldn't see the other couple in the distance very well, but it hadn't precisely looked like a wrestling match when Montague had lifted the lady from her feet. He needed to move quickly, but he couldn't just ignore Miss Oglethorp's pleas. Her timidity had caused him to overlook her more than once, but in these last days he had come to understand and respect her a little better. One did not completely ignore a lady's requests.

"I am not blaming Marian. I blame Montague. Go back to your mother. We will be there directly," he whispered, trying to keep one eye on what was happening in the library.

"But you heard what they said. Let me go in there. Marian never meant to hurt anybody, I know it."

Her voice was breathless and hushed and Darley wished he could shove her aside, but she was the only voice of reason in a vacuum of pain. He was having difficulty sorting his feelings out. His very best friend was making love to the woman he wished to marry—in order to protect him. He wanted to kill them both, but he wanted to weep for the loss of what he thought he'd had. He was being torn in two, but violence presently had the upper hand. He could cry when he was done with them.

But he could do nothing in front of Jessica. "I will do nothing to harm your sister. It is Montague I mean to kill. He has done this deliberately."

A look of alarm flashed across her face. "You cannot! You will have to leave the country. Please, do not. We will think of something. There must be some other way."

"Before he ruins your sister completely? I think not," But a plan was already forming in his head, one that almost made him chuckle if he were not hurting so badly. Montague had never wished to marry. His friend had frequently pronounced he had no desire to have his independence crippled by a woman. He was just about to have his words thrown in his face.

To Darley's surprise, just as he pushed his way past Jessica and stepped into the room, an unfamiliar voice spoke from the distant wall by the fireplace. Both figures on the couch leapt apart at the sound.

"I thought perhaps I ought to put in an appearance so you could make your offer before the fact instead of after," the strange voice said dryly.

All eyes turned to the far shadows where a tall, lanky male figure leaned against a shelf, twirling the large world globe at his fingertips.

Reginald recovered first, leaning over Marian and adjusting the sleeve of her gown discreetly, returning her to the couch while keeping his eye on the stranger. He felt her shivering uncontrollably, and he kept his arm around her, even though his own heart was pounding madly—more from nervousness than fear. The situation looked very bad.

"I don't believe we have been introduced," he answered coldly, refraining from using so much as a "sir" to this stranger who had walked in on them like this.

The man gave the globe one last twirl and stepped forward to light a lamp on a desk. The flare of fire gave a twisted shadow to his face, and Marian gasped and sank farther into his arms. Reginald held her protectively while knowing his best choice was to put all the distance in the room between them.

The light of this new lamp flickered over a tall form garbed in a loose coat without tails, trousers that did not pull taut over his legs, and a pair of boots that looked as if they had seen better decades. Nonetheless, he stood there in perfect arrogance, arms crossed over his broad chest, as if he were the marquess himself.

Marian gasped as her gaze reached the shadows of his face. He *was* the marquess himself. The face was almost exactly the same as the man in the portrait that was her father, only her father would have been nearing fifty now and this man could scarcely be thirty, the same age as the man in the portrait twenty years ago.

A twisted version of a smile crooked his lips as he watched Marian's recognition. "Very good, little cousin. I have been admiring your intelligence, although I have cause to doubt it under current circumstances. The man you are clinging to is a rascal who needs to be shown how to behave." He bent his head in Montague's direction. "I believe your customs here are similar to ours, but as I have no friends in this country, I request that we dispense with seconds. Would you prefer pistols or swords?"

The gasps from the doorway behind them had Marian and Montague swiveling their heads in a different direction. With a reassuring pat, Reginald stood up and faced this new audience.

Darley finally broke free from Jessica's grasp and marched into the room, his face a mask of anger. "If anyone challenges the bastard, it will be me. Marian, leave the room, and take your sister with you."

Jessica darted between the two men and placed her hands on her hips. "Stop it. This is silly."

As an argument, it left much to be desired, but as a deterrent, her action worked. Darley halted, and Marian had time to recover herself sufficiently to rise, although she kept her arms wrapped around herself as if fearing she would shatter at any moment.

Although sensing her approach, Montague kept his eyes on Darley. "It would be better if you went to your room, Lady Marian. I'm quite capable of dealing with this."

"No doubt," she said dryly behind him. "But entertainment here has been lacking until now. I do not wish to leave just when it is becoming interesting."

Reginald wanted to laugh. He could almost see her expression as she spoke. He might be fighting for his life within hours, but Marian's irreverent tones made it all seem quite reasonable. He just feared his laughter would stir Darley to greater lengths.

The man behind him had no such fears. The marquess's chuckle came closer as he walked up to this little tableau. "I am beginning to think I like my little cousin too much to saddle her with a loose screw like you, Montague. Where I come from, we don't always wait until dawn to level these things out. There's a set of pistols over the mantel. Let's just check them out now, shall we?"

"Who in hell are you?" Unaccustomed to being ignored quite so obviously, Darley shoved Jessica behind him. He would have done the same with Marian could he have reached her, but she was currently standing between Montague and the stranger, glaring at them both.

"Lord Darley, I believe I ought to introduce you to my cousin, the Marquess of Effingham. Unfortunately, I cannot give you his name since he has not seen fit to introduce himself to his family, but I think we could settle on something obvious, like Bumble-headed Ninnyhammer."

Marian's scathing tone brought another smile to the stranger's face. He made a slight bow to the surprised company, "Gavin Arinmede Lawrence, Eighth Marquess of Effingham and all that other rot, at your service, sirs." He straightened, and his smile was gone. "And now you will all get out of here while I straighten out this ruffian."

He grabbed Reginald by the coat collar, jerked him backward, and slammed a fist into his jaw.

Seventeen

As dramatic action, the punch was quite credible, Marian decided as she shook off Darley's hand. But Montague wasn't completely cooperative. Instead of staggering backward and falling when the marquess released his collar, Reginald lunged forward, slammed his fist into her cousin's abdomen, and sent his attacker into the bookshelves. Marian was forced to sidestep hurriedly.

She would have been forced to leave just to remove Jessica from danger had not Reginald immediately stepped back, dusted himself off, and halted the fight before it really started. Taking his cue from the Englishman, the American marquess straightened and shoved his hands in his pockets.

"Not bad from a spineless womanizer. Shall we move on to pistols now?"

Marian lost her patience. "That is quite enough! You have no right to come in here after twenty years and make claims to a family you have never bothered to know. I am quite capable of looking after myself, and I will thank you not to interfere. For my mother's sake, I ask that we be allowed to remain the night. We will be gone in the morning and you need not concern yourself over us any more."

For the proper dramatic exit, she ought to grab Jessica's arm and sweep out of the room, but drama and intelligence weren't always related. Marian knew better than to leave until she had the promise of the men that this would go no further. From their resounding silence, she could see that she had more work to do.

The marquess lifted a mocking eyebrow. "You may stay the night. Now get out of here so we may continue our conversation in private."

"Conversation? Is that what you call it in America? Your drawing rooms must be *vastly* amusing of an evening." Unable to rely on any of the gentlemen at the moment, Marian glanced over her shoulder to her sister. "Jessica, can you climb up over that mantel and retrieve the pistols? Then we can leave the gentlemen to their 'conversation'." She drawled the last word in imitation of the marquess.

As Jessica obediently drew a heavy Jacobean chair toward the mantel, Darley stepped back into the picture. "This has gone entirely too far. Jessica, leave that chair alone before you hurt yourself. Sir," he glanced at the marquess, "the insult has been to the lady I wish to marry. It is my place to call Montague out."

Reginald gave a gutteral groan, threw up his hands, and crossed the library to pull Jessica down from her precarious perch. She had apparently decided her sister had the right of it, and he wasn't one to argue in this case. She squealed when he lifted her down to the floor, but she made no protest as he reached for the pistols and put them in her hands.

"Take them to your mother. And take your damned sister with you, if you can. I promise not to kill anybody if you do."

Marian noted Montague was speaking to her sister but not to her. That was a pretty kettle of fish after what he had done, but she wasn't going to quibble with his tactics for the moment. She just wanted the situation defused and her questions answered.

She turned to the damnable marquess. He really didn't seem particularly angry. In actuality, she thought he was laughing at all of them. His eyebrows quirked as he caught her gaze, and he waited to hear what she had to say next. Marian wondered if her father had been that annoying. She shouldn't wonder that her mother would have wished him to an early grave, if so.

"I think you should present yourself to my mother, sir. She has been most apprehensive of this visit. We'll promise not to tell her you've been lurking in the woodwork if you'll promise to behave."

He grinned, a wide grin that went from ear to ear, although drawn up badly at one corner because of his scars. He looked to the other men to see if they were as appreciative of her challenge as he was. Lord Darley still seemed furious and perhaps a bit confused. Montague shrugged his shoulders as he came back across the room, escorting Jessica and her tightly clenched pistols.

"She'll jaw you to death if you don't," Reginald informed him coolly.

The marquess stopped smiling. His hand went to the scarred side of his face. "I'll not upset the lady unduly. It would be better if I remained an invalid outside this room. If you ladies will excuse us, I think we gentlemen can settle things amicably without you." He took a firm grip on Marian's arm and pushed her toward the door.

She grabbed a bookshelf and refused to go farther. "Unhand me, at once, sir! There is nothing to be 'settled' that does not concern me."

Reginald stood back out of the way, crossing his arms and looking to the appalled viscount for action. "Well, old friend, there's the woman you wish to make wife. Control her, if you will."

When the marquess attempted to pry Marian's hands from the bookshelf, she stamped on his toes and smacked his hands, then darted out of his way. Hands defiantly on her hips, she glared at all three men. "I don't need any of you!"

She swung around and walked out the door—right into her mother's arms.

All three men cringed at the polite, lady-like tones coming from the hall. "Why, whatever is going on here, Marian? I do hope it is proper. You are looking flushed, dear."

The marquess was already trying to blend in with the bookshelves when Lady Grace sailed into the library. She went pale at the sight of Jessica attempting to hide the pistols behind her back, and accusing blue eyes circled the room. When they came upon the stranger hiding in the shadows, she straightened and headed straight for him.

She frowned as he made a polite bow. "You are undoubt-edly a Lawrence, sir, even the scars cannot hide it. If you are anything like that reprehensible old man who was your grandfather, I can see why you might try to disguise your-self, but it won't do. Introduce yourself, and explain all this faradiddle at once."

Jessica and Marian stared at their mother with awe. They had never seen the Marchioness of Effingham in action. The Lady Grace had always been a fey, pampered lady who smiled indulgently and allowed her husband to make the decisions. Squire Oglethorp had reveled in his role and in-dulged her slightest wish. She had never, ever lifted her voice to anyone. They couldn't believe what they were hearing now.

Unaware of the lady's true nature, the marquess hastened to do as bid, introducing himself formally and making a po-lite—if slightly rusty—bow over her hand. When she seemed undaunted by his scarred visage, he relaxed visibly.

"Matters are at a pretty pass, madam, and I cannot promise to rectify them any time soon, but I wish you to know that you and your daughters are always welcome in this house. It is more yours than it will ever be mine."

"Very well said. We will discuss 'matters, 'as you style them, in the morning. This has been a very trying day. I suggest that we all retire now." With an imperial wave, she gestured for her daughters to follow her from the room.

Marian hung back long enough to give Reginald a steely look that he could interpret any way he liked.

He preferred to interpret it as a challenge. He waited until the ladies were gone before boldly turning to the mar-quess with the accusation that had just leapt to mind. "Cir-cumstances require that I offer to wed Marian, but if you will just return the necklace, Effingham, I think we can all get out of this relatively unscathed."

Reginald dodged Darley's furious punch, walked past the stunned marquess, and helped himself to the nearly empty brandy decanter on the far table.

The marquess glanced to the hapless viscount. "Back home, someone would have put a bullet between his eyes long ago."

"That's what being civilized does for us," Darley answered grumpily. "One cannot live on an island for long and not try to get along with the other inhabitants or we would kill each other off."

The marquess chuckled. "I like you, Darley. Or do I call you 'my lord' or some other such nonsense? I haven't quite got the hang of this title business yet."

The viscount looked vaguely irritated as he continued staring at Reginald, who was now pouring two other glasses of brandy. "You rank higher than me. You can call me anything you damned well wish. 'Cousin-in-law' was what I had in mind."

Gavin Lawrence shook his head. "That won't do, and we both know it. I like you too much to give you to my cousin. She'll make life hell for you. We Lawrences are a stubborn, arrogant lot. What about the other one? Miss Jessica? She seems to be quite attractive, and obedient, I noticed, much more so than her sister."

Darley sent him a look of loathing. "Affections cannot be manipulated so easily. Miss Oglethorp is entirely too young to know her mind yet."

Reginald returned carrying the brandy. "Then begin your assault in the morning and teach her. I wager she'll come around soon enough. Once she knows her mother and sister are taken care of, Marian will be free to find someone more suited to her temperament."

Darley scowled and took a deep drink of the brandy offered. "That's bloody rot." He set the glass aside. "And if I cannot have her, you must offer for her. After what we all witnessed here tonight, there is no better solution."

The marquess sipped his brandy slowly and allowed Reginald to speak first.

"There are a thousand better solutions. I do not have the wealth she requires. You know perfectly well why I cannot offer for her. She is the daughter of a bloody marquess, for heaven's sake! She could pursue Devonshire if she wished."

The marquess cleared his throat, distracting the attention of the two combatants. "I think the lady has made her choice, and Mr. Montague has sealed his fate by encouraging her. I'll have your offer now, Montague, or your head at dawn."

Reginald drained his glass and set it aside, turning to glare at Marian's cousin. "She'll refuse me, and rightly so. You would do better to inspect my background before offering Lady Marian as a sacrifice to your American morals. We can keep what happened here to ourselves. There is no need for it to be mentioned elsewhere." The muscle over his jaw tightened. "And if you'll persuade that thieving valet of yours to return the necklace, she will have all the dowry she needs to attract a suitor more worthy to her station."

The marquess shrugged beneath his loosely tailored coat. "Even if I knew where the necklace was, it belongs to the estate and not to Lady Marian. And I have thoroughly investigated your circumstances, Montague. That shop of yours is doing quite well. You have paid off a monstrous debt in a few short years. You are in a position to keep my cousin quite comfortably."

The two Englishmen stared at the American as if he had grown two horns and a tail. Reginald's face had turned pale, and his jaw tightened until it seemed immovable. Darley was the first to recover.

"That is privileged information, sir. You should not have access to it. But since you do, you must surely see why Reginald cannot marry Lady Marian. She would be appalled to discover he is a shopkeeper. As much as I would like to see him brought to justice, we must consider the lady's position."

The marquess no longer looked amused. "What a damned bunch of hypocrites! I suppose you would have the timid Jessica marry this arrogant bastard because she is the daughter of a country squire and more suited to a shopkeeper? You all have bats in your belfries." He turned to Reginald. "I'll have your offer or your head. Which will it be?"

Stiffly, Reginald nodded his head once. "Your permission to ask the Lady Marian for her hand, sir?"

The marquess grinned broadly again and slapped him on the back. "Well done! We'll discuss the settlements in the morning after you pop the question to her." He turned hopefully to Darley. "I don't suppose you'll want to take the other one, would you? I can see that Lady Grace is kept off your hands."

Darley looked glum. "I'm not much of one for the ladies. Marian's the only one as has ever listened to me. I'll wait for her answer to Reginald's proposal."

Reginald cursed and wished there were more brandy. For Marian's sake, he needed to persuade her not to accept his offer. For Darley's sake, he needed to persuade her that she must accept his offer.

What a bloody rotten fix he found himself in now.

Hearing Jessica's breathing even into that of sleep, Marian climbed out of bed and went to the window. A light rain had started to fall again, and she could see very little through the darkness other than the row of evergreens swaying on the lawn. She would have seen very little more had the moon been shining brightly. Her mind was elsewhere than the front park of the manor.

Her thoughts were on the way Reginald Montague had kissed her. Worse yet, they were on the way he had touched her. Her breast burned through her heavy nightgown with just the memory of what he had done. She should be red with shame and embarrassment, but it was curiosity that held her firmly in its clutches. She wanted to know more of those kinds of touches. She had a vague notion that they led to the forbidden, but she had been certain what had happened tonight *was* the forbidden. She could not imagine what could be more dangerous and shameful than what she had already done.

She was not a silly young miss. She knew Montague would have to offer for her. She did not know why he had done what he had if he had not meant to offer for her, but she knew that hadn't been his intention. Reginald Montague was not one to marry where he must. But she hadn't thought him one to toy with innocent misses either. She was beginning to suspect that there was a great deal more to the gentleman that she did not know, but she would find out the hard way if she must marry him.

She wrapped her arms around herself and tried to keep from shuddering. When she had thought of marrying Darley, it had only been the wealth and comfort that he could offer that she had considered openly. She had chosen a gentle man who did not drink heavily and would not be abusive, because even in the country she had seen what could happen to wives if they did not marry the proper sort of man. But she had not thought beyond that.

Her mind was feverishly thinking beyond that now. She was quite certain that what Reginald Montague had done to her in the library this evening had more than a little to do with what happened between husbands and wives. She had not really given the physical act of marriage any thought at all. No one had mentioned it to her at any time. It was not a topic that was discussed among gentlewomen, particularly unmarried ones. She had received vague impressions from her reading that men did something to women that eventually caused them to bear children. Even though she had lived in the country, she had never quite learned the process by which hens had chickens or cats had kittens. The squire had kept them very protected, after all. She just hadn't realized how protected until confronted with her own ignorance.

Surely what she and Mr. Montague had done would not lead to children. That did not make any sense that she could see. The sensations that she had felt then, the ones she felt now, left her to believe there was something more, something that might have happened had they not been interrupted. She ought to be hideously frightened, but she was terribly curious instead. She wanted to know where those sensations led.

And she could not apply them to Lord Darley. Try as hard as she might, she could not imagine kissing Lord Darley and feeling the way she felt now. Perhaps that wasn't necessary when one was married. Perhaps she need only let him do what he wished with her and everything would be quite as she had expected it to be. But that wasn't enough any longer. She needed to know what she would be missing.

That thought frightened her as no other had. She couldn't

find out what she would be missing without ruining herself. She would have to marry Mr. Montague to find out where his kisses led.

It would serve him right if she accepted his offer. Lord Darley would never offer for her now. She could never accept Mr. Montague's cash for the lost necklace. She and her family would have to return penniless to the farm and pray for some means of finding the money to pay the debts. Unless she married Montague.

Marian felt as if her insides were on fire as she considered that notion. Flickers of flames danced in places she could not even think about. And she had yet to consider Montague's wrath at being forced unwillingly into marriage.

She closed her eyes and leaned her fevered brow against the cool pane of glass and prayed that he would not murder her in her sleep.

Eighteen

L ady Grace, if I might, I would like to speak with Lady Marian in the salon," Reginald said stiffly upon finding the ladies leaving the breakfast room. There was no sign of the ephemeral marquess. It was as if he had never been. Reginald knew better.

Lady Grace made a slight nod and departed in the direction of her chambers, leaving Marian to stand awkwardly in the hall, avoiding his look. Reginald caught her arm and steered her firmly toward the salon that had recently been draped in Holland covers. A watery sunshine came through the newly cleaned windows to illuminate the stately, old-fashioned furniture.

He dropped her arm once they were in the room. She still would not face him. Her back was stiff and uncompromising, but the thin muslin did not disguise the soft swell of her hips and derrière. Reginald did not often find himself admiring the posterior portions of a lady, but knowing how close he was to possessing the right to touch her, he could not help himself—and the thought was making the rest of his thinking fuzzy.

Reginald tried to raise his mind to a more serious level, but Marian chose that moment to walk toward the window. The sunlight filtered right through that bit of gauze and muslin, revealing a clear outline of what lay beneath, and his thoughts fell in tatters once again. Just last night he'd had the opportunity to learn some of the soft swells of flesh he saw silhouetted there now. He found himself mentally stripping the clothes from her back.

Appalled, Reginald closed his eyes and tried to recover his thoughts. Women never had this effect on him. He had a satisfactory mistress who relieved his physical needs in quite creative ways. He never bothered thinking about her when he wasn't in her arms. Outside of that relationship, he found ladies to be boring, on the whole. They were selfish, uneducated, small-minded, and generally did not find much pleasure in physical pursuits. He had no need to think about them. Why then, was he unable to keep his physical cravings and his mental faculties off the female in the window?

There was only one solution. He must have this over and done with at once. He'd never imagined proposing marriage. He had no easily prepared speech. He just knew his duty and had some notion of how the woman he spoke to would think. He tried to combine the two in some modicum of rationality.

"Lady Marian, I know I am not the grand match that you had imagined, but I can keep you comfortably and I think we would suit very well. If you think you might return my affections, I hope you might do me the honor of accepting my suit."

Marian heard the stiffness in his voice. He looked very well this morning, even if his cravat wasn't stiff or his waistcoat buttoned. She didn't need to turn around to see how his light-colored eyes watched her from a carved visage that could have been made of wood for all one could detect emotion in it. He didn't wish to marry her. He had made that very clear despite his words.

"I'm appreciative of the honor you do me." She had practiced the words all morning. She didn't mean them to be malicious, but when she sensed he relaxed in relief behind her, she knew she had not chosen wisely. He thought she was about to turn him away.

Marian forced herself to turn and face him. That was the least she could do, show him the same courage he was showing her. She thought she could almost see a look of genuine affection in his eyes. She was about to destroy that quickly enough.

"I'm also appreciative of the fact that you offer because

you must. That is not the way I would start out married life. Perhaps we could have a long betrothal?"

To give him credit, he did not look horribly floored by her reply. He recovered rapidly, although as she had expected, the gleam in his eye disappeared. He made a formal nod of agreement, seemed to debate the proper procedure involved in declaring his delight, and evidently decided on the obvious. He drew her into his arms and kissed her.

It wasn't quite the same as before. It was a very controlled kiss, one of possession and decision, as if once he had decided she was his, he meant to mark her. He succeeded. Marian could still feel the handprints on her back when he stepped away.

"I shall have the announcement made as soon as we return to London. You have made me a very happy man, my lady."

Marian gave him a look of annoyance. "No, I haven't. We haven't bothered in polite deceit with each other before. I see no reason to start now. You had to offer for me, and under the circumstances, I could see no choice but to accept. I am conscious of the favor you do me, and I will try very hard not to interfere in your life. In return, I trust you will not expect a great deal of me. I suspect the less we see each other, the happier we will be."

Reginald managed a small smile. "If your wretched cousin is listening through the walls again, he will undoubtedly choke on his laughter right now. Do you care to give him more to amuse him?"

"I do not see what is so amusing. I would have been happily married to Lord Darley had you not interfered. I would have the funds to pay my mother's debts had your valet not made off with my necklace. As it is, I have no other alternative but to return penniless to the country and watch our home be auctioned off. I find no amusement in those circumstances. I am doing what I must, just as you are. I was hoping we could come to some amicable agreement. If I am mistaken, please tell me."

His face went cold and tight. "I am not in the least interested in a modern marriage. If I am to be saddled with a wife, it will be to a wife who belongs to me alone. You will find among my other disagreeable habits, I tend to be very possessive of what little I own."

Marian scowled and returned to the window. "You do not own me, nor will you ever. I am prepared to respect you, even to obey you if your commands are rational, but I am not prepared to turn myself into a doorstop for your convenience."

Reginald felt his fingers curling into fists and wondered how often he would wish to feel them around her throat. "I am not asking you to be a doorstop. I am asking you to be my wife. *My* wife, not anyone else's. That means even if you find yourself enamored of some other exquisite, that you remain loyal to me. Is that clear enough?"

Marian turned to face him again, her expression one of surprise. "I am not exactly certain. What precisely am I suppose to do with some other 'exquisite' if I find myself enamored of him? Run off to Gretna Green? Since I will be married to you, that hardly seems feasible."

Stunned, Reginald took a moment to gather thoughts that had just been blasted to the four winds. She was an intelligent woman. He knew that. She was twenty-two years of age and well-read. Of course, she had not lived in the sophisticated world of society, but surely even in the country. . .

Nothing was certain when it came to Lady Marian Lawrence. She seemed genuinely curious. Reginald raked his hand through his hair and tried to imagine explaining what he had thought her capable of doing when she in all probability did not even know what he meant to do to her once they were wed. He didn't think even his versatile tongue could explain. He shook his head in surrender.

"Never mind. We will have this conversation after we have been married for a while. Just be warned that I will not share you with another man."

A gleam of enlightenment reached her eyes. Reginald would have been relieved had he not been distracted once again by the sight of her silhouette in the sunlight. He would have to put shades on all his windows if he meant to remain a sane man. He was beginning to think a long betrothal would not be a wise idea.

"Did you really think I was capable of kissing another man? Or doing what we did last night?" Her cheeks burned as she asked this, but Marian was determined to keep this relationship on an honest basis. That was the least she could do for him after all these weeks of deceit. She was almost relieved that it was over.

Reginald didn't need to be reminded of what they had done last night. His mind couldn't go beyond that at the moment. He took a tentative step in her direction, his hands itching to reach for the breasts so temptingly displayed beneath that flimsy material. "I am not the only man in the world who knows how to kiss," he responded dryly. It was a wonder she did not see the direction of his gaze and run for shelter.

Instead, she stepped forward until he need only lift his hand to have her. "Kissing with other men isn't nearly as pleasant as kissing with you," she murmured.

He couldn't help it. She had wide lips, lips really too wide for her face, but he could imagine a dozen things she could do with those lips, all of them pleasant. They were moist and red as summer strawberries. Tasting them was absolutely required.

This time, the kiss was not nearly so controlled as earlier. Reginald collected her in his arms, pressed her tight against his length, and took her mouth with an intensity that had them both fevered in seconds. Their tongues were already discovering the places remembered from prior explorations when the salon door exploded open.

"Dammit, Montague! Can you not keep your hands off her until the vows are said? I will recommend to the Lady Grace that an early date be set." Darley stopped behind a carved mahogany chair and curled his fingers around the back.

Reginald gently returned the lady to her feet. His eyes didn't stray from her as he answered his friend. "I was just thinking the same myself. How about you, my dear? Shall we make this a short betrothal?"

She looked up at him with alarm. "We scarcely know each other," she whispered.

Reginald shrugged. "We'll learn quicker once we're

married. I think we'd best take the news to your mother, then set about our departure. I'll not be content until I have my back to this place."

The harsh, arrogant Montague was back, but his hand was still wrapped around hers, and his grip was tender. Marian contemplated this contradiction as she allowed him to drag her from the room. She was terrified of having bound herself to a man who held half the world in contempt, but some other part of her, some hidden private part of her, craved to know his affection. She hoped with time that the hidden part would overcome the terrified part.

They found Lady Grace in her sitting room, sharing tea with the scar-faced marquess. The other man stood when they entered the room, then returned to his seat when Marian was seated.

"May I extend my felicitations?" he asked, raising his brow.

Reginald ignored him, turning to Lady Grace instead. "Lady Marian has consented to take my hand in marriage, madam. I hope we have your approval."

Marian's mother looked to her daughter to confirm that everything was as it should be and, reassured by the stunned look she found there, she smiled pleasantly. "Of course, Mr. Montague. Marian has ever had a mind of her own. I would not think to question it at this late date."

"Then with your permission, madam, I would like us to return to town after nuncheon. We would both prefer to make this a short betrothal, and there are things I must do in preparation."

The marquess intruded at this point. "I don't see the hurry. The ladies have only just arrived and I am just beginning to make their acquaintance."

Reginald gave him an impatient look. "And you are enjoying the service at the expense of myself and Darley. You have the ruby now. Pay for the servants yourself. We will be leaving this afternoon."

"The ruby?" Lady Grace looked up expectantly. "Has it been found? I certainly hope so. Marian's father meant it to be part of her dowry."

The marquess bowed politely in her direction. "We have

yet to discuss the settlements, my lady. The ruby, however, wherever it is, is part of the estate."

Lady Grace blinked in surprise. "No. No, I am quite certain it is not. I would never have taken it otherwise. George gave it to me quite explicitly when Marian was born, saying it was mine until our daughter wed. But the point is moot, is it not? The necklace is gone. I am sorry, for I could have wished Marian to have something of her own when she went into marriage."

The marquess appeared to be losing his patience. "I could have wished the same, my lady, but the point is that the entailment inventory lists all prior jewelry. It is quite obvious from the portraits in the gallery that the necklace has been in the family for a long period of time. A valuable piece like that would go a long way toward restoring this estate. You would be assured a home for a lifetime were I to turn this into a profitable estate again."

Montague quietly interfered in the escalating argument. He had seen the look now on Lady Grace's face on her daughter before. He did not wish to hear what would come next. "That necklace would save Lady Grace's home and give her an income for life. There are more valuables in this blasted mausoleum than she could collect in a lifetime. Sell some of them if you are in need of funds."

The marquess turned him a wary look. "I think we need to leave the ladies alone. They will have no interest in our discussion of business and settlements. If you will excuse us?" He stood up and bowed to the dowager.

Marian wondered what would happen if she told them both to take a flying leap off the nearest cliff. She had as much interest in settlements as they did. It was her life they were dictating. Since it was quite obvious that her cousin could not provide anything for her, she had hoped that Montague might be persuaded to settle an allowance on her. She wasn't at all certain that the American would even think about that. He must, or there would be nothing for her mother and sister if he decided to abandon the estate and return home.

Montague must have seen the rebellion in her eyes. He

caught her hand, raised it to his lips, and murmured "Trust me," before releasing her.

It was the first command he had given her. They were fatal last words if she had ever heard them, but she had promised to try to obey.

Marian looked resigned as she watched them depart. She had promised to trust a man who had lost her only valuable and who had seduced her away from his best friend. What was the phrase Darley had told her the American had used? She had "bats in her belfry."

Darley had retired to the stable to nurse his aching heart. He hadn't really believed Reginald would do this to him, but he had seen the way Lady Marian had looked at his friend after she had been so thoroughly kissed. There wasn't any way he could pretend she was anything else but enamored of a man who was by all accounts a good deal more dashing and handsome than Darley could ever hope to be. He would have to go in and wish her well as soon as he could force his tongue around the words.

Perhaps it wasn't his heart that had been hurt so much as his pride. He had thought he had caught a rare diamond, and he had been feeling very good about himself. There were other wealthier and better looking gentlemen out there who Marian could have set her cap for, but she had chosen him. She had listened to his ramblings with interest, and had made him feel respected and important. Now he supposed that had all been a ploy to win him.

He sighed and kicked the dirty straw. The place needed a good groom. He'd like to get his hands on that valet of Montague's. He had a feeling the scamp was somehow behind all this. He'd like to throttle the thief.

Blaming someone else for his problems wouldn't solve them, however. His mother had been expecting a wedding any day. He was going to have to go back and tell her it was off. He'd rather go to Scotland and throw himself into a loch than tell her that. He had been prepared to marry Marian despite her indifference rather than face his mother without a bride. Now he didn't know what he was going to do.

He heard a cooing sound from one of the far stalls. Frowning, Darley shoved the barn doors open until a ray of sunlight cut through the center of darkness. A pigeon ought to let itself out, he thought, but there was no flutter of wings.

He followed the path of sunlight deeper into the barn. The cooing noise had become soft murmurs. Indistinct at first, they became clearer as he approached the last stall. A smile tipped his lips slightly as he leaned over the gate.

A fair-haired enchantress sat curled upon the straw, stroking a lap full of furry, playful kittens, completely oblivious to the streaks of dirt on her cheeks or the appearance of her gown as the kittens attempted to climb it. She was talking contentedly to the animals, a good deal more contentedly than he had ever heard her speak in public.

Darley cleared his throat nervously. She was beautiful and he was not. One of the reasons he had dared speak to Marian had been because she looked so much like himself. But Miss Oglethorp was the kind of shining blonde that he had never hoped to attain. But then, he had never seen a diamond of the first water sitting in a bed of straw with a lap full of kittens, either.

She gave a start of surprise at the sound he made, then looked around to see him. With a small, shy smile, she glanced back to her kittens. "Lord Darley, the marquess said I might have whichever one I wished, but how can one possibly choose? They all seem so perfect to me."

Thinking very much that there might be a moral in that dilemma somewhere, Darley crouched down beside her and picked up the tiniest, ugliest kitten clinging to her hem. "I would choose this one."

She glanced at him in surprise. "Would you? Why?"

He curled the kitten in his hand next to his lapel and listened to it purr. "Because he's the one most in need of loving."

Nineteen

That fellow Montague says the paintings are just beginning to gather value, that they'll increase in worth every year, and that the Ming vases—whatever in hell they are—are worth a fortune already. He seems to think there is a goldmine in damned gewgaws around here, if we can figure which aren't on the inventory. Do you think he really knows his stuff?"

Michael juggled three silver spoons and watched them whirl and catapult back and forth before making them disappear. He seemed more interested in his practice than in his brother. "I followed him to his shop once," he said offhandedly, pulling the spoons from various places amidst his attire. He was currently occupying the butler's quarters on the lower floor, since there was no butler. "It was packed with shiny, valuable looking things, and he was doing a steady trade. He's made his blunt knowing something."

"You're beginning to talk like a bloody damned Englishman," the marquess muttered, straddling an uncomfortable chair.

"I talk like the people around me. It's one of the tricks of the trade." Michael calmly began juggling the spoons again, only this time there were four.

"I wish you'd juggle us out of this one. Montague is convinced we have the necklace and that he can get out of marrying our cousin if we'll just return it. I don't like this business of playing lord of the manor. I want them all to just go back where they came from and leave me to the business of righting this place."

Michael shrugged and one of the spoons fell to the bed covers. He quickly scooped it up and returned it to the circle of whirling silverware. "You wanted a family, now we have one. It won't hurt to have a wealthy cousin-in-law who knows how to pawn off the family valuables, either. From what I see, he and the lady deserve each other. Our cousin could out-Lawrence you if she tried. Once she's set her mind to something, we would probably have to put a bullet through her head to stop her. Marriage to Montague is very definitely the right step. And I like your idea about the viscount and the shy one. Just think, one day we could have an earl in the family. You being a fancy marquess and all, we'll be rubbing shoulders with the whole bloody aristocracy."

The "fancy marquess" rubbed his scarred cheek and scowled. "You'll more likely be in jail if Montague has anything to say about it. How do you plan to show your face again if we don't return that blasted necklace? We could have the lawyers fight over it and make it legal."

Michael grimaced and caught the spoons in one hand. "The only ones who would profit then would be the lawyers. I'm not much for moving in society, anyway. Maybe I'll abscond to the states and sell the necklace there."

"You'll bloody well stay here and help me out for a change. We're not street beggars anymore. Give back the necklace and figure out some way of getting yourself back in circulation. I'm going to start selling off anything not on the inventory."

Gavin removed himself from the chair and stalked toward the door, leaving his red-headed brother multiplying spoons and producing forks.

"I must return to London, Marian. If you and your family wish to stay here, that is your choice, but I cannot. Among other things, I must see that your man of business has the funds to pay those notes you owe. If you will give me his direction, I will make that one of my first tasks."

Marian felt a sinking sensation in the pit of her stomach as she turned to look at the man she meant to marry. Reginald's words made it all too clear that he had already come to think of her as his responsibility, and he meant to deal with her problems alone, without need of her help. She wasn't certain she liked that idea at all. It made her feel like a schoolgirl again. Or was it the idea of belonging to this man that she didn't like?

"I cannot ask that of you," she murmured, staring down at the faded carpet at her feet. "I will sell the rest of the squire's library. It is his home we are attempting to save. It only seems fair."

The only person who would give her a fair price for the books was him, but Montague refrained from reminding her of that. She thought him a collector, and that Jacobs had purchased the last manuscript. She didn't know he would have to turn around and sell her precious library to make a profit so they could live. He would not be able to explain if he bought her library and then she couldn't find it in his home when he brought her there. This was beginning to get too complicated for words. He needed to keep things simple.

"That is a trifle foolish," he reminded her. "You could not get what you deserved out of those books unless I bought them. Wouldn't it be simpler if I just paid the debt and we kept the books in my library?"

Marian appeared taken aback by the notion, but then her eyes began to gleam as she understood. Reginald felt the full force of her smile as it fell on him, and he felt oddly warm inside, odd because it was not the heat of desire but something else entirely.

"Then it would be a fair exchange of sorts, would it not? Except that I still get to keep the books but you are out the money." She puzzled over that. "I still feel as if you are coming out on the wrong end."

Reginald smiled and tilted her chin until she looked at him again. "I will not only have the pleasure of sharing ownership of your books, but I will be getting my sister and mother-in-law out of my hair. It will be much better if they have a house of their own to go to. Mine is none too large,

and I would prefer to have my wife to myself. I don't feel
slighted in the least."

Marian's cheeks burned under the warmth of his gaze.
He was scarcely touching her, yet he was doing that to her
again—making her feel all hot and wiggly inside. The notion of marriage to this man was looming larger and larger,
like some giant obstacle she must cross. She tried not to
gulp as she stood still beneath his hold.

"I don't suppose my cousin was able to make much of a
settlement on you. All I seem to be bringing to this marriage is my family. Do you think I might be of some use to
you in some manner? I know how to run a household, but
that seems scarcely enough."

Reginald shook his head and brushed his thumb across
her lips. "You really don't know, do you?" He brushed his
lips where his thumb had been, and she quivered slightly.
He raised his head again, and a flicker of amusement
reached his eyes. "I can see where you might save me from
one of my extravagances. I'll let you know if I can think of
any others."

Reginald remembered that wide-eyed dewy look well
after he was down the road. Lady Marian Lawrence would
definitely save him his most expensive indulgence—his
mistress, Madelyn. Reginald didn't think he would have
any trouble adapting to this one pleasure of having a wife.
Lady Marian had his blood racing hotter than any opera actress he'd ever seen, and he wasn't adverse to teaching her
what a mistress ought to know. Perhaps other men thought
ladies were only for getting an heir. Perhaps other ladies
thought they only must do their duty to get an heir. He was
of a different mind, and he thought Lady Marian might be
the same. If he must marry, he was glad that it was to
someone he could bed as readily as his mistress.

Reginald sighed as he thought of Madelyn. She was
going to throw a tantrum when he gave her her congé. He
was going to have to give her a very expensive gift to ease
the parting. That would have to be the first thing he did
upon returning to London. He didn't wish to imagine what
would happen should Marian discover he kept a mistress.

Theirs was going to be a difficult enough marriage as it was.

If marriage there must be. He was still more than certain that the marquess and O'Toole were working together to hide the necklace. Perhaps the first thing he ought to do when he returned to town was to visit the dealers he knew so well to determine if anyone had tried to sell the ruby. He'd have them nab the thief if he showed up anywhere in London. Once the necklace was back in his hands, he might have the power to release Marian from this vow they were neither willing to take.

Of course, if he were released from his betrothal after he had disposed of Madelyn, he would have to go to the trouble of finding another mistress. That would be a damnable nuisance. At the moment, he had little enough interest in Madelyn. He definitely couldn't summon much interest in finding someone new. He was much more interested in having Marian.

At that startling thought, Reginald spurred his horse to a gallop and rode into London in a brown study unconducive to communication of any sort. The idea that he might possibly prefer marrying Marian to taking a mistress was a bite he was having great difficulty swallowing.

"Lord Darley! I thought you had left for town with Mr. Montague." Marian entered the dining room and found the viscount already there, conversing with her mother and sister. The marquess was again nowhere to be found.

Darley looked up with a small frown between his eyes. "I am not presently speaking to the cad. Besides, we have not yet found the necklace, and I am convinced it and that blasted valet are still about. I mean to do more exploring, and I don't think you ladies ought to be left unprotected while a thief is still on the grounds."

Neither Lady Grace nor Jessica objected to the fallacy in this explanation, but Marian couldn't refrain from reminding him. "Our cousin is about somewhere. We aren't entirely unprotected."

Darley scowled as he pulled out a chair for her. "He's as much a rascal as that valet. I don't trust him."

Marian looked to the walls and waited vainly for the

choked laughter she was certain she had heard more than once. Perhaps she was imagining things. After all, they had only found one passage behind the walls, and that was in the other wing.

"We thank you for your care, sir," Lady Grace murmured when it became obvious that Marian would not. "You have been more than gracious under the circumstances."

Darley took his seat and threw a brief glance to Jessica, catching a shy smile on her face before she returned her gaze to her plate. She was too young, he decided for the millionth time that day. But then, so was he. A man shouldn't have to think about marriage until he was thirty-five, not for another good six years. But in six years, Jessica would surely be snatched up by someone bolder than he, and he would be back to looking at simpering misses half his age.

Dash it all, there was no escape from this marriage trap. Morosely, he examined the plate of food he had chosen and wished he had followed Reginald. It had all been much simpler when Lady Marian was leading the way.

Marian was set upon doing just that now. Wielding her fork, she mentioned casually, "I am sensible of the fact that you wish to come to know our new cousin better, Mother, but as we could not cancel our gowns with the modiste, we are due back for fittings shortly. That is, unless you have decided we should not go to the ball?"

She was perfectly aware that now that her mother and sister were back in the country, they were not disposed to readily return to town. Their brief fling had been more than adequate to satisfy their curiosity and craving for company. But the problems that had sent them to town in the first place had not been adequately resolved, and they could not be while remaining on this bankrupt estate. Since Marian had failed to make a triumphant marriage, it was now Jessica's fate to find a husband of her own. That couldn't be done while chasing ghosts in the walls.

Besides, Marian was not yet ready to trust Montague out of her sight. He could have gone haring off to town with the necklace in his pocket for all she knew. She didn't think he would, but she had learned not to trust so easily these last weeks. If they were truly to be married, it would be better to be seen together after the announcement. It probably wouldn't do to let him gallivant around London behaving as if he were still unattached. If she must marry Montague, then she meant it to be a very real marriage.

"Uh-oh, Marian's got that look in her eyes," Jessica whispered in an aside to Darley. "That means we might as well agree now or she will never let it go."

Caught by surprise by this admission, Darley looked up in time to see the resigned look on Lady Grace's face and the determined one on Marian's. He was beginning to understand who ran this family. He felt a little quiver of relief at the thought of Reginald instead of himself running up against this stubborn determination every day of his life. He ought to be ashamed of the thought, but he wasn't.

"I suppose you are right, dear. Perhaps we could persuade the marquess to accompany us. He really must be introduced to society."

The elusive nobleman appeared as if summoned by the sound of his name. He strode into the room in rolled up shirt-sleeves with the smell of the stable still on him, and when the ladies didn't appear to take offense, he pulled out a chair and made himself at home.

"This marquess doesn't need any such thing," he said as if he had been included in the conversation all along. He watched with interest as a maid hurried to pour tea in his cup. He would have preferred something stronger, but he was thirsty enough not to argue. He drained the cup while dishes were passed to him so he might fill his plate. "I have enough on my hands without having to meet a bunch of gussied-up snobs."

"They're not all snobs, dear," Lady Grace said as she wrinkled her nose in thought. "But they can be frightfully judgmental, I suppose. It would be better if you could appear in the proper clothes. Perhaps Lord Darley and Mr. Montague could help you there."

Gavin glanced up to see if she were serious, then looked to his young cousin to see how she was taking this monstrous suggestion. Marian was fighting a smile and hiding behind her teacup. At least she had the sense to understand that his clothes were the least of his worries. He rubbed his cheek unconsciously and returned to eating.

"Personally, I think Lord Effingham is much more effective as a phantom," Marian murmured with some amusement. "We could host house parties and insist that the guests must bring their own servants and food as the price of admission. All we need do is go back to London and gossip about our Gothic visit with missing jewels and haunted passages and ghosts, and all society will wish to visit for the excitement, hoping they will be the first to see the phantom marquess. It would be as diverting as Vauxhall. We could charge admission, I'm certain."

"Obviously, you are in dire need of entertainment, Lady Marian," Gavin growled. "Shall I wear a black cape and lurk in shadows to keep the company thrilled?"

"Ohh, please don't," Jessica hastened to answer. "That would be much too frightening. I don't like masquerades. At least, I think I don't. I have never been to one, actually, but lurking in shadows sounds most unpleasant."

Marian almost giggled and hastily sipped her soup as Lord Darley leaned over to pat her sister's hand and reassure her no one would lurk in any shadows when he was around. She looked up and caught her cousin's eye. There was a glint of something there that made her quickly look back to Jessica and then to Darley. Her eyes widened as she noticed the slight flush on her sister's cheeks.

When she looked back to the marquess, he was calmly devouring his food.

How odd. She had the distinct impression that the marquess was feeling very satisfied with himself about something, and that something seemed to have to do with the new color in her sister's cheeks.

Twenty

Reginald cursed as he struggled into his coat without the help of the wretched O'Toole. He had too quickly grown accustomed to the services of a valet, a result of his own expensive upbringing, he realized. He trusted Marian's taste didn't tend to be as expensive as his own or between them they would be in dire trouble quickly.

That was a ridiculous thing to think, and showed the unstable state of his mind lately. He wished he had a well-furnished town house, an elegant carriage, and an unlimited budget for fancy gowns for her, but he knew only too well the limits of his means. Had this been a love match, he might have felt more comfortable with that knowledge. As it was, he feared he was going to be a dreadful disappointment to a woman who had hoped to marry money.

This train of thought led back to the blasted necklace. He had agreed to settle a comfortable allowance on Marian for her own use, but the amount would be much more comfortable should the necklace be found and sold. He was quite aware that Marian would use her allowance to provide for her family, and that if the necklace came to her, she would sell it without a qualm to help them. He had no objections to that if the necklace rightfully belonged to her. The damned marquess could obtain his funds elsewhere.

But first he had to find the necklace, which meant finding O'Toole. So far, his search of London's dealers had yielded nothing. He hoped the man wasn't foolish enough to go elsewhere to sell the thing. He'd never get half the price anywhere else but London. But then, O'Toole might fear getting caught if he tried to sell it in London and prefer to take a lesser price. Reginald would gladly give him the difference for the opportunity to wring his neck.

Deciding his coat was as straight as it was going to get, he checked his image in the mirror, gave his cravat one last tuck, and picked up his hat and stick on the way out the door. The announcement of his impending marriage had appeared in the newssheets just today. He needed to play the part of happy fellow as he made the rounds of his clubs tonight.

Reginald found himself wishing for Darley's company after the first round of congratulations. The betting had been running heavily in the viscount's favor of late, and there were those who were looking at Reginald with suspicion and a trace of disapproval. His intention never to marry had been widely known. Suddenly announcing a betrothal to a woman without a shilling who had been known to favor Darley was causing gossip in all corners. Only Darley would appreciate the subtleties of this quagmire.

Reginald suffered through the first round of drinks with what he considered to be great aplomb. Offers to take Madelyn off his hands he referred to the female in question. She had thrown a rather valuable crystal vase at his head when he gave her notice. He didn't think she would take any of his suggestions when it came to her next lover. He also didn't believe Marian would be properly appreciative of the sacrifices he was making for her. All things considering, he was feeling particularly put upon.

It wasn't until he walked into White's and found his brother waiting for him that he knew the evening was going to plummet from low to lower.

Charles, Viscount Witham, gestured an invitation with his port glass. "Thought you'd be around this evening. Sit, Reggie. Tell me what you've been doing with yourself lately."

It was bloody unlikely that he would tell his family precisely what he had been doing, but Reginald knew the reference was to the announcement in the paper. It was just his luck that Charles had trotted out of his country home across the breadth of England just in time to read that announcement. Reginald took the seat and the glass offered.

"Don't play sly with me, Charley. You saw the paper, else you'd not be here. If you want to meet her, you'll have to travel up to Hertfordshire to Effingham's Gothic relic. You'll need to bring your own servants, though. He's not got a penny to squander on one." There, that ought to tell his brother everything he wished to know without getting too personal with Marian's history. Reginald disliked talking about her behind her back. He preferred that she be by his side while he introduced her to his family. That was another thought that caught him by surprise, and he took a hefty swallow of his wine.

"You could have had any heiress in the kingdom, yet you settled for a penniless bluestocking? I had not thought you a romantic, brother mine."

Older than Reginald by some five years, Charles did not have the same dramatic looks as his younger brother. His hair, always thin and of a lighter color, had begun to recede slightly. He wasn't quite so tall nor as athletically built as Reginald, but there was a quiet handsomeness in the way he held himself that marked him of a superior nature. His speech was no different. Refined and elegant, he did not raise his voice or even use sarcasm. His question hit its mark all the same.

Reginald tried not to wince. "Where did you hear that she was a bluestocking?" was the only reply that he could make.

Charles smiled slightly. "I left my card at the lady's house, of course. It was the only proper thing to do. While I was doing so, my groom had a long chat with hers. Seems the lady enjoys Hatchards and museums and scientific as well as literary lectures. I cannot think of another soul in our circle who is half so well educated."

Reginald wondered if there was enough wine in the bottle to get him through this night. He didn't think so. Perhaps he ought to go back to Hertfordshire. He enjoyed being roasted by Marian a great deal more than by his peers. That was probably because he could spend most of the time imagining other uses for her tongue and wondering how best to win her into his arms. Her tongue might be tart, but by Jove, the rest of her was as sweet as any he had ever sampled.

His thoughts were interrupted by a laugh from across the table.

"Smitten good, are you? You aren't even listening to me. I didn't think I'd live to see the day when the mighty Reginald was brought down by a pretty face. I'm itching to meet the lady. When will she be back in town?"

Reginald shrugged. "Devonshire's ball is in two days' time. I daresay she'll return for that." He struggled with his conscience, wondering how much he ought to say to Charles. His brother knew him too well to believe he had actually fallen for any woman, bluestocking, penniless, or not. But he found it difficult mentioning the actual circumstances of his unplanned betrothal. Charles didn't seem to be questioning too hard yet. Perhaps it could be glossed over.

"If she's not an heiress, how do you intend to support her? I find it hard to believe Effingham even permitted your addresses."

That was cutting to the bone. Reginald grimaced and filled his glass. "You'll have to meet Effingham to understand. He's an American and a recluse. He's inherited a deteriorating estate and no funds. I imagine he's simply interested in seeing that he doesn't have any relatives encroaching on what little he does have."

Charles made an uncommunicative grunt. "So you have seen the man. I wondered. The town is agog with rumors, you realize. No one was even certain he existed."

"He exists, all right." He was the reason for this damned marriage, but Reginald didn't say that aloud. There was another thing or three he held against the marquess. "As I said, he's American. He doesn't know our ways and isn't much interested in learning, apparently. He's been badly scarred, by a rapier it appears. I imagine he was in the war. He has a military bent to him. Combined with the fact that he hasn't a shilling for entertaining, I can understand why he stays out of society."

"Then I suppose it will be up to us to introduce the lady

and your betrothal. Harriet has been wishing to come in for the Season, but she's breeding again and I didn't wish her to travel. I suppose the weather has improved enough the roads shouldn't be too difficult for her now."

Reginald gave his brother a sour look. "Congratulations. You mentioned nothing of the blessed event when I was there last month. Starting your own dynasty, are you?"

Charles shrugged carelessly, but there was a gleam of pride in his eyes. "She says she wants a pack of 'em. Damned inconvenient, if you ask me, but I can't think of any way to stop her. She'd kill me if I set up a mistress."

Suddenly imagining Marian growing round with his child, Reginald reached for his glass again. He'd never given children a thought. The idea made him weak in the knees now. Had Marian given any thought to carrying his child? Of course, she had. Women always thought of these things. They had to. They were the ones who had to bear the burden. By agreeing to marry him, she agreed to bear his children. Devil take it, but his lust was aroused at just the thought. He was going to turn into one randy bounder before this was over.

"Lost you again, didn't I?" Charles inquired genially. "I can remember before I married Harriet, I went around with a third leg for months. Hits you like that sometimes. Never thought it would hit *you* though. You always come across as a deuced cold fellow, little brother. I still haven't figured out how you've set yourself up so well without father's help. He swears it's that racing stable of yours, but I've watched the odds. You can't make a living that way."

Reginald sighed. It always came around to that. He'd burn in hell before he'd tell his family he was a shopkeeper. He wasn't certain how he was going to tell Marian either, but he was still having a hard time dealing with even the idea of Marian. He took another swallow of wine.

"The stable takes care of itself. I've been lucky. You may tell father not to worry. We won't come begging at his doorstep. I've set aside funds for Marian's welfare in case anything happens to me. If we could just find her damned necklace, she'd have an additional income to fall back on, but the thief's been too clever for me." Reginald glared at his wine glass. The port must be stronger than he had thought for him to blurt that out. He seldom mentioned anything that troubled him to anyone, and he had a good head for wine. He'd better leave the rest of the blasted bottle alone.

Charles refilled his glass. "Necklace? The lady's jewels have been stolen? Why didn't she call Bow Street?"

Now he was in for it. Cautiously, Reginald outlined the bare details of the theft, leaving out the reasons for the copy but including his suspicions about his valet and the marquess. Charles appeared fascinated.

"So, you end up offering for the lady to make up for the loss of her dowry, eh? Very noble of you."

Reginald slammed his glass down. "No, I did not. I offered to reimburse her for the necklace. That is neither here nor there. I am marrying Marian because she is all that I could ever ask in a wife. We will rub along very well together." He found himself believing this quite thoroughly. Maybe he ought to stock up on a case of this port. He glared at the glass again. He hated port.

Charles sat back, satisfied. "Just wanted to make certain you weren't doing something foolish that we could get you out of before any permanent damage was done. Marriage is a lifetime sentence, Reggie. You don't want to go into it with your eyes closed. Didn't think you'd do anything bumble-headed, but where women are concerned, men can be damned blind. Father will tell you that. He's been worried you'd do something foolish if the tide started going against you. I knew he'd want me to ask. Maybe we ought to settle the cost of that necklace on her as a betrothal gift since you feel responsible for its theft. Seems to me there ought to be a few other baubles in the vault that she might wear, too. Harriet is fair and can't wear the colored things."

His head was beginning to feel rather light. Reginald found himself nodding foolishly, thinking how well Marian would look in the family jewels. He didn't think even his father possessed a ruby to match the one lost, but Marian wouldn't mind that. He'd like her to know that her husband's family wasn't impoverished, even if her husband was. He wanted her to feel like she would be taken care of in any event, unlike her mother. He was glad Charley was an understanding sort. Reginald closed his eyes and tried to remember the path of his thoughts, but they had gone wandering.

Charles laughed. "Think it's time we took you home, old boy. You never were much of a port drinker. Bet you had a bottle of brandy before you even got here. Never mix your alcohol, that's what I always say."

Reginald allowed himself to be pulled from the chair and led home like a drunken schoolboy. He felt like a drunken schoolboy. He was about to be married and he had never before given the state of marriage a thought. He could be a father by this time next year, and he'd known the potential mother for all of four weeks, at best. His mind flickered from images of Marian lying naked in his bed, to children screaming up and down the stairs, to chattering women in his parlor. He was about to be very, very sick.

Charles held his head as his younger brother cast up his accounts in the gutter, then hired a hack to take them the rest of the way home.

The viscount wasn't in the least surprised when an auburn-haired servant ran down the stairs of Reginald's town house to help carry his master in. The surprise came when Reginald looked up to see who it was, gave a cry of rage, and launched into the smaller man with two fists. It wasn't like Reginald to take advantage of his greater size.

It took two nightwatchmen and the secretary, Jasper, as well as the viscount to pry Reginald off the man now identified as his valet. Charles nodded approvingly as Jasper paid off the watch and closed the door firmly behind them. These things were better kept in the family.

Reginald continued to glare at the man lying on the parquet floor, holding a handkerchief to his nose and bleeding from cracked lips. "Where in hell is it, you miserable excuse of a lying, thieving . . . "

He seemed on the edge of launching himself at the smaller man again, and Jasper and Charles grabbed his arms.

The man on the floor gasped for breath as he answered. "A man can't visit his dear old parents for two days without

being treated like a mangy dog. That's what I get for falling
onto sad days. My father always told me never to lower
myself to begging. Lord knows, I tried to hold myself
proud, but a man can only stand so much, you know. Here
I've turned your wardrobe into a thing of beauty, a thing to
be admired by Brummell himself, and what do I get in return, I ask? He wrinkles his linens and muddies his boots
and comes home with his coats covered in filth, then complains to me about it. I'll not have it anymore. I'll go back
to begging in the streets before I do this again. I'll—"

Charles kicked him lightly in the ribs. "Shut up, you
wretch." He looked at Reginald, who appeared little the
worse for wear although a trifle wild-eyed. Charles kept a
firm grip on his brother's arm. "I suppose you're going to
tell me this is the valet who made off with the necklace?"

"Damned right, and I'm going to beat every miserable
little diamond out of him if I have to bring them out
through his nose." Reginald launched himself forward, only
to be jerked back again by two firm holds.

The man on the floor sat up, dabbing daintily at his nose,
which did not seem to be in serious disrepair. "Now I'm accused of being a thief, I suppose. Damned suspicious lot,
you are. I just went to visit the old folks. They live right
there in the village. Had a little too much of the hair of the
dog, you know, and they put me up for the night. Had to
make my way back here alone when I found I'd been left
behind. Not the way a man ought to act to his personal servant, if you ask me, but then, no one ever asks me."

"Rightly so," Charles said sourly. "You talk too damned
much. My brother says you absconded with a lady's necklace. Unless you want to end up in Newgate, you'd better
put that fast tongue to better uses."

O'Toole made a show of dragging himself from the floor
and scraping a low bow. "My pardon, your lordship. I
didn't recognize your worthy self." He grabbed the handkerchief to his nose again to keep a fresh spurt of blood
from staining his shirt. "I do not steal necklaces, my lord.
They are not at all suitable for my attire." The words came
muffled through the cloth. "I may occasionally borrow a
shirt stud or two, but I always return them. And I have

never so much as touched a watch. I can assure you, I have no necklace on me."

Reginald made a threatening noise and Charles was tempted to allow him to go for the fellow's throat. It would do the rascal good to turn purple for a while, but it wouldn't solve the puzzle of the lady's necklace. The viscount lifted an eyebrow at the somewhat bewildered secretary. The man had obviously been in his bed when the commotion erupted. He had trousers pulled on backward over his nightshirt.

"You'd best call the watch back. Let him try his tongue in Newgate for a while, then maybe he'll be a little more forthcoming."

The valet shuddered visibly. "No, no, sirs, please do not do that to me. I am innocent. I am a cherished only child. I would never survive such a place. If you are looking for a necklace, perhaps you want the one I found in Mr. Montague's coat pocket when I cleaned it. Blue fustian of the finest quality, and he brought it home covered in filth. Cobwebs! I have never seen the like in all my born days. There's no accounting for what the aristocracy will do."

Reginald went still. His eyes were murderous as he glared at his valet. "O'Toole, produce that necklace at once!"

O'Toole looked at him with green-eyed innocence. "Why, it is on your desk just as it was before we left, sir. I'm sure I wouldn't know what to do with anything so valuable as that. It seemed odd to me, sir, but I'm not one to question my betters."

Reginald was halfway up the stairs before the last of these declarations was out of his valet's mouth.

Twenty-one

"That the genuine article?" Charles asked, watching his brother hold the stones to the lamplight and examine them thoroughly.

Reginald made a dissatisfied noise and reached in his desk for his glass to better examine the stones. "It is the original," he agreed coldly.

"Then what is the problem? Admit you made a mistake, give the poor fellow a bonus, and return the necklace to your lady." Charles watched with bewilderment as his younger brother scowled. Reginald had been stubborn and independent as a boy, but he had always readily admitted his mistakes.

"The five largest diamonds are paste. The bastard's had them replaced." Reginald set his glass back in the drawer and clenched the necklace as if he would murder it.

Charles whistled. "We'd best call the watch, then. He'll remember where they are once he's spent a night in Newgate."

Reginald frowned thoughtfully. "No, let him think we're fooled. He could have hidden those stones anywhere. He could have sold them already. We have no proof of anything. I still firmly believe he's working with Effingham. I want to catch him at it."

"I don't know how you plan to do that." Puzzled, Charles looked at the necklace for himself. He could see no difference between the glittering bits.

Feeling quite weary and more than out of sorts, Reginald made a gesture of dismissal. "I don't know yet either, but I will find a way. Take the damned thing with you. I'll not give the scoundrel another chance at it." He rubbed his hand over his eyes. "Wait. I'll have to take it back to Marian." He had cost her the advantageous marriage with Darley; he would not take away her only other alternative. He wondered if she would use the return of the necklace to call off their betrothal. His head ached too much to think about the other aches that thought engendered.

Charles slid the necklace into his pocket. "I'll be around to get you tomorrow. We'll go to see the ladies together. If they are going to the ball, they will be back then. It always takes ladies days to prepare for an occasion like that."

Not Marian, Reginald knew, but he didn't say it aloud. He wanted to say that Marian was different. Marian didn't waste time primping and painting and adorning herself and deciding between this ribbon and that. Marian would be plotting to wring O'Toole's neck or to sell the Effingham library or to find her sister a husband. Marian wasn't like any other lady he knew, but Charles wouldn't appreciate her finer qualities. Reginald kept them to himself, as he kept his own secrets.

He just nodded in agreement and watched his brother leave with the necklace in his pocket.

He didn't even have to yell for O'Toole before the ever-efficient valet appeared to help him off with his coat. At least the thieving bastard had the sense to hold his tongue.

When the butler came up to inform Marian that Mr. Montague and Lord Witham were below, she almost panicked—not because she couldn't remember any Lord Witham, but because she feared Mr. Montague had come to beg out of their betrothal. Having had a day or two to reconsider, he might have realized what a bad arrangement he had made.

Surely he wouldn't do anything like that in front of another man. A Lord somebody-or-another wouldn't be a solicitor. Reginald had just brought a friend to lend him support since he and Darley were no longer speaking. She would have to find some way to repair that damage.

Since Jessica and Lady Grace were still recuperating

from their journey, Marian called Lily to act as chaperone
and waited nervously for the gentlemen. Her gaze went instantly to Mr. Montague when he entered. He looked splendid in his chocolate-brown frock coat and fawn trousers
with his Hessians polished to a high shine, but there was a
smudge of color under his eyes and a crease upon his brow
that spoke of an uneasy night. She felt her heart lurch when
he bent over her hand.

"You do not look as if you slept well, sir," she murmured
quietly, for his ears alone, as he straightened.

A trace of a familiar wicked smile touched his lips. "I
thought only of you while you were gone."

That was the Montague she knew. With a slight blush
staining her cheeks, Marian jerked her hand away and
turned her interest to his guest. He was very distinguished
looking, and there was a trace of something familiar in his
face. She tried not to stare too boldly.

"Lady Marian, may I introduce my brother, Charles?
Charles, my betrothed."

Of course, she had forgotten. Mr. Montague was the son
of an earl, but not the heir. It stood to reason that he had an
older brother. She just hadn't considered his family, since
he seldom spoke of them. She tried not to bite her lip as the
viscount bowed over her hand. He really was quite formi-
dably dignified. She felt like a schoolroom miss.

"My pleasure, sir," she managed to murmur, wishing her
mother were here to help. Darley was a viscount, but he
hadn't made her nervous as this man did. For all that mattered, her cousin was a marquess, but he didn't have the
kind of presence that demanded respect and dignity. Marian
sent a helpless look to Mr. Montague.

Reginald took a seat beside her and propped his arm
along the back of the sofa as if he belonged here and as if
she belonged to him. Which she did, she admitted uneasily
to herself. She had given him every right to think of her as
his. He crossed one booted leg over the other and watched
his brother settle into a chair across from them. Marian
very much thought her betrothed was hiding a grin that
probably deserved an elbow to the ribs, but she played the
demure miss as well as she could.

"I'm glad to have this opportunity to meet some of Mr. Montague's family, sir. He speaks of you often." She kept her eyes modestly on the rug between them.

Charles leisurely lifted a doubting gaze in his brother's direction. "Why do I find that hard to believe? Reggie would prefer to believe that we don't exist except when it pleases him."

Reginald caressed a curl at the back of Marian's neck and leaned toward her familiarly. "Hadn't you ought to call me by name now, my dear? We would not wish to give my brother the wrong impression."

He was laughing at her, she could tell. He knew she was putting on the same act for his brother as she had these past weeks for all society. She really ought to open her mouth and let out all those things she really wished to say, but she wouldn't jeopardize her chances another time. She didn't wish his family to take offense at her and talk him out of this marriage. And he knew it, the dastardly toad.

She turned a sweetly admiring smile in his direction. "I didn't wish your brother to think me too familiar, Reginald. I am sure Lord Witham is much too proper to behave as you do."

Charles chuckled. "I think I am beginning to see the attraction, Reggie. All these years you've been cleverly ripping people to pieces in front of their faces without their ever knowing, and now you've found a female with as much wit as you. You needn't be polite for my sake, Lady Marian. The rogue needs to be taken down a peg or two, and that's a fact."

Marian turned a real smile to her guest. "Would you care for some tea, my lord? We could discuss your brother's faults over scones, if you'd like." With a nod, she sent Lily to fetch the tray.

Reginald growled softly near her ear at the insult and tugged on the curl in his possession, but when the maid was gone, his voice was pleasant. "We have a surprise for you, my dear. Charles, the necklace, if you will."

Marian looked up in surprise as the viscount stood and presented her with a velvet pouch. He seemed to be watching her curiously, but she forgot that as she opened the pouch and saw the glitter of her ruby. She gave a cry of delight and drew the necklace through her fingers. "My mother's necklace! You have found it. Where? Did you catch the thief?" She turned excitedly to Reginald.

He smiled at her excitement, admiring the way it made her eyes dance. He also liked the way she automatically assumed he was the one responsible for returning the jewel, even though it was his brother who had presented it to her. He could do worse than Lady Marian Lawrence, Reginald decided. If one had to have a wife, it ought to be one who believed in one's worth.

His smile disappeared as he answered. "O'Toole returned last night with some story about finding it in my coat pocket. You and I know that the necklace in my pocket was the copy, but I have no proof of his guilt." He hesitated, wondering if he ought to mention the missing diamonds. If the marquess was involved, it would disturb family relations. But if she discovered they were fakes, she might blame him for the theft. He glanced to Charles for advice.

Charles shook his head. "We have no way of knowing who was responsible for the theft. You'd best give the lady the whole truth. Since the necklace was in your hands at the time, I think we can safely offer to replace the missing pieces."

Marian looked questioningly back and forth to the two men.

Reginald was the one to explain about the missing diamonds and O'Toole's wild explanations of his whereabouts. Marian looked at the necklace again but could see no difference in it, but then, she couldn't tell the fake from the original, either. She slid the jewel back into its pouch and closed it.

"Perhaps, if my cousin is responsible, we should say nothing to Mama. It does not hurt to share a little of what we have. He was not greedy. He gave us back the most valuable part." She looked to the viscount. "I really don't think it's necessary to replace anything. The necklace was to be part of my dowry. It seems foolish for Reginald to have to replace what would have been his anyway."

Charles gave her an approving look. "The family is bound to do something in honor of your betrothal. You and Reginald may decide how you wish it settled. In the meantime, we will wish to have a dinner and perhaps some dancing in your honor. When my wife arrives, I will have her call so the two of you may make the arrangements." He rose as if to depart.

"You have not had your tea, sir. Would you not care to stay to refresh yourself?"

Charles sent his brother a quick glance. "I have another engagement, but I suspect Reggie might stay for a scone or two. I trust your maid will be prompt if I leave now? I wouldn't wish to leave you alone with him for long, not the way he's looking at you right now."

Marian looked up at Reginald in surprise but didn't see anything there that hadn't been there before. Charles chuckled and walked out, leaving the two lovers to work it out between themselves.

"You are learning very quickly, my dear. I might come to miss hearing your brutally honest truths, but I suppose the sugar-coated kind will go farther in keeping harmony among family." Reginald leaned over and touched his lips to hers.

Marian hadn't been prepared for that. She had little or no experience with men. She couldn't tell what they were thinking from one minute to the next. She particularly couldn't tell what this one was thinking because he kept everything hidden behind a stoic façade that would give credit to a marble statue. But his mouth had no resemblance to marble at all. She gave a sigh of contentment as his lips slowly administered to hers.

A tingle of excitement was just beginning to build when the rattle of a tray outside the door forced them back to a more respectable distance. Marian heard Mr. Montague—Reginald—give a frustrated moan as he sat back, and she stole a peek at his expression. He wasn't exactly looking cold at the moment.

Lady Grace followed the tray in. She looked as if she had only just arisen and had dressed only because they had guests instead of remaining in her usual dishabille until she had been served her morning chocolate. She hid a yawn behind a discreet hand, and smiled at Mr. Montague.

"You are early, sir. Eagerness in a suitor is recommended. I understand I have missed your brother?"

Reginald rose from the sofa to bow over the lady's hand and to escort her to a chair. He took his place beside Marian again but refrained from his more possessive pose of earlier. "There will be time for you to meet all my family shortly. My sister-in-law will be arriving soon, and no doubt my father will accompany her. I trust your journey was not too uncomfortable?"

"No, the weather was fine. The hours were long, however." She dismissed the maid and poured the tea.

Marian leaned forward and laid the velvet pouch upon the tray. "Mama, Mr. Montague has found our necklace. It was apparently only lost instead of stolen."

Reginald showed no emotion at this version of the story. He sipped his tea and watched Lady Grace exclaim over the return of her one piece of jewelry. It was more than obvious that the necklace's only value to the lady was in its memories.

He tilted a look at the demure miss beside him. They needed to talk. "Is it too early to ask you for a drive in the park? I thought we might stop by a jeweler and choose a betrothal gift, since I failed to have one available earlier."

Marian sent him a look of surprise from beneath her lashes, but she answered calmly enough. "The park would be lovely. Mama, would it be all right?"

Lady Grace dismissed them with a wave of her hand.

When they were within Reginald's curricle—without O'Toole as groom—Marian turned a questioning glance to her betrothed's suddenly grim expression.

"There is some other problem that you have failed to mention?" she asked, trying to ignore the annoying feeling of unease roiling in her stomach. He had played the part of attentive suitor much too well. She feared now was the time he pulled the rug from under her feet.

"I placed the announcement of our betrothal in the papers before the necklace was returned. All of London knows of our plans to wed. Now that you have your necklace back and don't need me any more, I would appreciate it if you waited a while to change your mind about our marriage. I have no wish to be a laughingstock."

Marian gaped at him in surprise. "Are you hoping that I will end our betrothal?"

Grimly, Montague smacked the whip over the horse's heads and turned them through the park gates. "That's plain speaking. I suppose I deserve that. This honesty business becomes a trifle difficult, doesn't it?"

Marian sat back against the squabs and stared out at the lovely green of the trees. Her expression didn't reveal any appreciation of the scenery. "The necklace was ever only a temporary measure. I must marry so my mother need not worry about my support for years to come. If you are truly opposed to this marriage, then we must end the betrothal now and pray that no word of our . . . indiscretion . . . leaks out. We can only afford this one Season. I will need to find another suitor before it ends."

Montague gave her a hard stare, but she didn't meet his gaze. "I only wished to give you the opportunity to end the betrothal if that was what you wished. I have not changed my mind in the least." He sent the horses into a trot that had pedestrians dodging to the grass.

Marian clutched her gloved hands in her lap. He was only doing the honorable thing. She ought to release him from his promise after all he had done for her. That was evidently what he had expected. She closed her eyes and tried to force the words to her tongue, but they wouldn't come.

She wanted to marry Reginald Montague.

Twenty-two

They did not appear the affectionate couple searching for a betrothal gift when they entered the jeweler's. Montague stiffly surveyed the cases until he found a display of brooches. Marian slowly followed in his footsteps and stood behind him as he examined the available wares. When he dismissed the selection and turned to the rings, she remained where she was, looking wistfully at the brooches. This was not at all what she had in mind for a peaceful marriage.

"This one is quite pretty," she said softly, trying to diffuse some of his anger. "It is like the ivory one we once saw. It would look very well on several of my morning gowns."

Reginald gave it a second look and turned away. "I wish to give you something you will wear when we go out together, not something no one will ever see."

Marian's shoulders drooped. She was tired of fighting. She had chosen her course; she must stay with it. She just wished she had chosen an easier one. Reginald Montague was going to be a hard man to please.

She glanced around at the rings. He had the tray with the most expensive selections, and she shuddered at the waste of wealth displayed there. She turned to a more modest display and pointed out a small gold band with a single garnet. "Something like this is very elegant."

He scarcely gave it a second glance. "Society would think me a niggardly fellow to give you something so small."

With an exclamation of disgust, Marian gave up. She had offered all the compromise she could. If he was determined to stand on his end and never move toward the middle, there was little she could do about it. She turned around and stalked out.

"Damn." Reginald turned to the startled jeweler. "Give me the ivory brooch and the garnet ring." His gaze caught on a display of necklaces, lighting on a delicately contrived design of emerald and diamonds—one that would suit his betrothed's subtle tastes and his own preferences. "And have that delivered to this address." He passed the man his card and the address and gathered up the jeweler's boxes the clerk had produced. The name on the card was scarcely needed to cause the man to nod respectfully. He knew Reginald Montague on sight.

He had spent far more than he had meant to, yet she had asked for far less. He must be out of his mind, Reginald fumed, as he looked up and down the street to find his runaway bride. Had she asked for garish diamonds, he would have laughed and bought her garnets. So she had asked for garnets and he had bought her diamonds. He was quite simply losing whatever control he might ever have maintained.

He found her gazing in the bay window of "Aristotle's Antiquities," and he groaned. Whyever had he brought her to this street when there were jewelers all over town?

"I wonder if he has sold my manuscript?" she asked calmly as he hurried to catch up with her. "He doesn't display his books."

"The covers fade and dry out in sunlight. The crystal and the gems look much better in the windows. Collectors know to ask for the books." He produced the box with the brooch. "You have excellent taste, you know. The artisan who carved this is very talented."

She opened the box and gave the contents a look of surprise. She touched the gently unfolding rose carved in ivory. "Thank you," she murmured in a choked voice. There were tears in her eyes when she finally looked up to him.

Reginald felt a jerk of some unwanted emotion at the sight. He wanted to drag her off the street and kiss away those sparkling crystals, and at the same time, his stomach clenched as he realized what a bastard he'd been. All she had wanted was this simple gift, something meaningful between them. And all he had wanted was to show off his latest acquisition. Gad, but he was a rotten bounder.

Sheepishly, he pulled the box from his other pocket. "Your ruby will outshine it by a mile, but I do want you to wear something that shows you belong to me. I've already told you I'm a very possessive fellow."

Marian clenched the box with the ring in her fingers and searched his face. "I am trying very hard not to make this too difficult for you, Reginald. If I were a better person, I suppose I would release you from your promise, but I'm a coward. I'm afraid I will never find anyone else I like so well. Is that terribly wrong of me?"

Instead of answering, he slid the ring from its satin bed, removed her glove, and tried it on her finger. "It's a little loose. Shall I have it adjusted?"

Her fingers curled possessively around the tiny band. "No, I do not want to take it off. I shall just have to grow into it."

Finally, he smiled, a gentle smile that did not look comfortable on his harsh features. "Not growing romantical on me, are you, my sweet? I'm not very good at that kind of thing, you know. I'm still trying to think of something to say in response to knowing you like me. I had thought you held me in great contempt."

"And so I ought." She pulled her hand out of his grasp and carefully donned her glove. "You think me foolish and romantical and probably wish me to the devil, when I know very well that I will make you a very good wife. If I did not think that, I would never agree to this marriage. And since everyone has made it plain that you are not inclined to be attached to any woman at all, I feel quite certain I am not hurting your chances of finding lasting affection. I'm not at all certain that you are capable of lasting affection. I will settle for respect."

Amusement danced in his eyes as Reginald offered her his arm. "You already have that, my lady. I can think of no other woman in the world who could have managed an offer from me. We will discover some way to make this arrangement work."

Arrangement. Marian kept her sigh to herself. It would have been very nice if she could expect tender looks and soft words more often, but she supposed she ought to be content that he had at least attempted them when presenting her with his betrothal gifts. It was not as if they had a love-match. They had an arrangement.

She tried not to scowl. He made her sound like a bunch of flowers.

"Oh my, Marian, you look so dashing! I wish I could hope for some of your flair someday." Jessica looked wistfully at her sister's image in the mirror as she straightened the sash at Marian's waist.

Marian studied her image critically. Lily had swept her dark hair up in a dazzling array of smooth waves and loose curls entwined with a ribbon made of threads of gold. The ribbon complimented the ornate gold tussie mussie that had arrived bearing three tiny wine-red rosebuds from Reginald which she now wore pinned on the ivory sash at her waist. She had chosen a gown of paper-thin ivory silk with a net of fine gold for her first appearance at a ducal ball, knowing it would accent her one piece of jewelry, the ruby necklace.

However, the low bodice of the gown left such a vast expanse of flesh exposed, Marian feared no one would even notice the necklace. The gowns Lily had made for her had always been modest. This one that the modiste had made exposed more than she thought remotely decent. Marian flushed at the thought of Reginald looking at her there, as he couldn't help but do. The stays the modiste had insisted on pushed her up so that he could scarcely miss the display.

"Dashing" was scarcely the word Marian would have chosen to describe the result, but Jessica was always polite. She could scarcely say "lovely," for Marian didn't have the face for that. Her lips were naturally red and her eyes were too dark and her skin closer to tawny than creamy. She might be called "striking." She would never be called lovely.

But right now Marian felt quite indecent. Surreptitiously, she pulled at the tiny bodice, but it was made to fit snugly just where it was. She wiggled her shoulders to see if the tiny sleeves would cover more, but she succeeded only in dislodging her flowers. Jessica helped her put them back, and Marian surrendered. Maybe she would feel better if she didn't look at herself.

She turned her critical gaze on Jessica. Her sister was everything that a lady should be. Her gown was more modest, as was fitting for a young girl. She was more slender than Marian, and the little flounce of pale-blue silk adorning her snow-white bodice flattered her young curves. A slight train of the pale blue flowed down her back, enhancing her tiny waist and slight stature. With her golden hair and blue eyes, she looked a fairy princess from a storybook, and Marian hugged her fiercely.

"You are beautiful, Jessie. All the men will fall at your feet. Even the duke will have to ask for introductions. Just remember to keep smiling and nod at everything a man says, and you will do wonderfully."

Jessica's smile faltered. "Lord Darley is the only gentleman who has asked if I will be attending. Do you think he will ask me to dance? I would hate to be a wallflower all evening."

"You will dance every dance except the ones you choose to sit out. I am sure of it. Let us see how mama is doing."

If nothing else, Jessica would dance every dance because all society was consumed with curiosity about the marquess and about Marian's and Montague's marriage announcement and they would descend on anyone with information, but Marian didn't intend to say that. She was learning to hold her tongue very well. If curiosity is what it took to make society see what a lovely person Jessica was, then so be it.

They arrived at the residence of the Duke of Devonshire in a crush of other carriages, all of them more elegant than their own. Again, Marian had to wonder why they had received their invitations, but the cards were duly accepted at the door and they were issued inside with the usual announcement just as if they were the duchesses or marchionesses around them. A "Lady Grace" and a "Lady Marian" among the Countesses of This and That was scarcely to be noticed, but several heads did turn as they descended into the ballroom.

Several of Lady Grace's friends hurried to offer their congratulations on the impending nuptials. One or two of Marian's erstwhile suitors came to jest that she had not given them sufficient time and to sign her card for dances. Lord Darley hurried to attend them before his mother could sail up and offer reproaches for taking a lesser man. To show he suffered no harm, he took one of Marian's waltzes, then put his name down for two of Jessica's dances. She was immediately radiant, and the brilliance of her smile attracted several other young men to sign her card. Darley scowled at them all, and continued to stand with the ladies as the room began to fill.

It was almost time for the first dance, and Marian began to watch the newcomers nervously. She had saved the first dance for Reginald, but he had yet to make an appearance. Of course, in that crush of carriages outside, he could be stuck halfway down the street.

When the footman finally announced Charles, Viscount Witham, and Mr. Reginald Montague, Marian gulped a sigh of relief and distracted several young men in the immediate vicinity. Unaware of the direction of their interest, she watched eagerly as Reginald descended into the ballroom. She knew the exact moment he found her, even though a smile never crossed his face. Her heart pounded a little fiercer as he set a straight path in her direction. Others must have been watching, too. It seemed as if the path opened through the crowd between them.

The music was already starting when he reached them. He must have said something appropriate to Lady Grace, and Lord Witham no doubt made some greeting also, but Marian heard nothing. She only felt the heat of Reginald's gaze and the crush of his hand around hers as he led her to the dance floor without even asking.

The opening dance was a quadrille, as was the custom. It left little opportunity for more than an occasional comment, but Marian was aware of Montague's gaze following her throughout the steps, never once leaving her despite the formation of the dancers. She was beginning to wonder if her clothes had suddenly become transparent, but only in the eyes of her betrothed. No one else seemed to pay her any extreme attention. She felt the color rising between her breasts, but she met his stare as calmly as she could.

When the dance ended, Reginald did not immediately return her to her mother as was proper. He pulled her to one side, out of the crush, and touched the flowers at her waist. "I had not thought about where you would wear them, but if I had seen that gown, I would have thought of nothing else. I can see a more appropriate gift would be a jewel that would dangle here." His gaze dropped to the place he had in mind.

Marian blushed deeper. "You are being unseemly," she whispered, but not in protest. His words and his looks were making her tingle like his kisses had earlier. She was much too aware of what the gown did not cover.

"That damned gown is unseemly," he muttered hoarsely. "Haven't you a shawl or something you might use to cover it up?"

She stiffened. "It is no more unseemly than the ones the other ladies are wearing. I had it made by a very fashionable modiste. I thought you would be pleased to see me rigged out properly."

"I'd be pleased if I were the only man in the room. I can feel them all breathing down my neck right now, just waiting for me to get out of the way so they can see you. I don't like sharing." He grabbed her dance card and glanced over it, then deliberately threw it into a potted palm.

He held out his hand. "I will take you back to your mother and explain that I do not intend to share you this evening. She may inform your disappointed suitors."

Bemused, Marian allowed Reginald to drag her back in the direction of her family. She wasn't at all certain how to take his reaction to her gown. She had hoped he would find her attractive. Did he consider her shameless instead? And what right did he have to throw away her dance card? She liked dancing. She wanted to kick and protest, but she was all too conscious of the eyes watching them. Lord Witham was still standing with her mother.

"I believe I see a scene approaching," the viscount murmured as they watched the couple emerge from the potted palms. Marian's growing rebellion was not easily hidden. The black look on Reginald's face was the real surprise. His brother never openly expressed any emotion.

"Oh dear, I hope Marian has not been too hasty. Sometimes she is not overly cautious with her words." Lady Grace twisted her gloved hands and glanced toward her younger daughter to make certain she was safely in Darley's care and out of hearing before returning her attention to the approaching storm.

Witham looked amused at his companion's understatement. He was more than certain that Lady Marian had a way with words that rivaled his brothers's. He didn't think words were the problem here. He glanced at the young lady's revealing gown and bit back a smile. She had hidden herself very well indeed the morning he had met her. Reginald was undoubtedly in a state of agony Charles could not wish on any man, but the viscount wasn't about to try to explain that to Lady Grace or her daughter.

"Madam, if you will, explain to Lady Marian's other partners that I do not intend to allow my betrothed out of my sight this evening. Unless they wish to dance with me, they will have to find other partners for their dances." Reginald spoke stiffly, keeping his eyes correctly on the woman to whom he was speaking rather than the irate one behind him.

Charles chuckled as the stunned Lady Grace sought an appropriate reply. "Don't suppose it is the necklace that has you distracted, is it, little brother? When did you say you meant to set the date?"

Marian tried to shake off Reginald's imprisoning hand. "Never, if I have aught to say about it. He is being beastly unreasonable."

Reginald pulled her up beside him and glared down at her. "Next time, I will go with you to the modiste. I'll not have my wife . . . " A frown formed between his eyes as he bent his head closer over her and stared quizzically and quite immodestly at her bosom.

Marian raised her free hand to push him away, but Charles caught it with a warning shake of his head. He gave a discreet cough. "Reggie, you are going at it a little too far."

Reginald caught Marian's necklace between his fingers and lifted it enough to catch the light from a bracket of candles on the wall. The duke had chosen not to use gaslights, which would blacken his new wall hangings, and the room was entirely illuminated by smoking candles and discreetly placed lamps. It made for a romantic setting, but not good lighting.

Reginald dropped the necklace and frowned at Marian. "I did not bring that back with me. I left it at Arinmede. Why did you choose to wear it tonight?"

Marian stared at him. "Are you all about in your head? You brought this to me just yesterday."

Reginald's jaw muscles went grim and taut as he raised his gaze to his brother. "He's done it again. That miserable cur has done it again. This time, when I get my hands on him . . . " He turned away and started toward the stairs, his fingers clenched into fists.

Although Lady Grace had no clue to what was going on, Marian and Charles exchanged worried glances. While Charles made hasty excuses to her mother, Marian raced after Reginald.

If her necklace had been stolen again, she meant to slit the thief's throat personally and save Reginald the trouble.

Twenty-three

Charles caught up to Marian in a few quick steps. Catching her arm, he tried to halt her progress toward the door. "You cannot go with him. We are making a scene. Smile and go find your next partner. Reggie and I will take care of this."

Marian gave a blinding smile, patted his coat sleeve lovingly, picked up the skirt of her gown, and continued on up the steps. Heads turned as she passed, and hands went up to cover whispers. The duke himself departed the reception line and stopped to inquire if anything was wrong. Marian offered him the same blinding smile and hurried on.

Charles murmured something about a sudden illness in the family and ran after her. He wasn't a man who often cursed, but a few pithy phrases were coming to mind.

Marian caught up to Reginald at the door, where he had summoned his brother's carriage. He scarcely noticed her arrival. Charles had brought him, but Reginald was wishing he'd had O'Toole drive. He wanted his hands around the valet's neck right now.

"I'm going with you," Marian announced beside him.

He wasn't going to take the time to argue. The carriage came around, and he was already running down the steps to claim it. Marian ran after him, and Reginald remembered his manners in time to practically throw her in. He leaped in after her, and Charles had to grab the door and propel himself inside before he was left behind.

"This is insane, both of you. Lady Marian's reputation will be ruined. You cannot go about chasing criminals in the middle of the night. It is not done. I'll call Bow Street. They'll take care of the character until we can get to him. The two of you need to get back in there and settle the gossip."

"You may return Lady Marian and settle the gossip. I intend to wring the necklace out of O'Toole's throat. He has played me for a fool one too many times."

Marian scarcely noticed the luxury of the viscount's velvet-lined carriage. She caught Reginald's hand between her own and wound her fingers between his, needing the reassurance of his touch. "I don't understand. How could he have switched them? I have kept the necklace on me since you brought it back."

Reginald shot her a quick gaze, his mind instantly imagining that string of jewels resting between her breasts as she slept and beneath her gowns as she went through the day. He almost choked on the mental image he summoned. If it hadn't been for his rage at O'Toole and the presence of his brother . . .

He jerked his thoughts back to the moment. "O'Toole was still in the hall when you went down last night?" He turned to Charles with the question.

The viscount considered the question. "Yes. He was leaning against the newel post holding a handkerchief to his nose while Jasper kept him under guard. Then you yelled for him to come up."

"I suppose he brushed past you as you left." Reginald sounded resigned.

"As a matter of fact, I believe he did. I thought he was weak and staggering slightly. He isn't a large man, you know. Your assault no doubt caused him some pain."

"Balderdash." Reginald would have sat back and crossed his arms over his chest, but Marian's fingers were soundly entwined with his. He squeezed her hand instead. "He picked your pocket. He must have found the copy and brought it with him. Damn, but what did he hope to accomplish?"

"He either hoped that once you returned the original to me you would not notice it again, or he meant to give himself a little extra time to escape England." Marian frowned.

"I'm not so certain that he is working with my cousin, Reginald. I truly believe Lord Effingham must have made him bring back the necklace."

"Then Lord Effingham can make him produce it again. I mean to bind and gag the monster of ingratitude and deliver him to your cousin's doorstep." After I strangle him, Reginald added to himself. It wouldn't do to allow the lady to know the extent of his rage. It was entirely a matter of personal pride now. No man—particularly a skinny, red-haired valet—was going to get the better of him.

The journey through damp city streets was a short one. They rode it in relative silence, each with their own separate thoughts. Reginald worried over what he would do should O'Toole not be where he left him. Marian prayed there would be no violence. And Charles tried to conceive a scheme to stop the scandal before it started. None of them had any great hope of being successful.

Reginald was out the door and ordering Marian to stay where she was before the carriage wheels scarcely stopped rolling. Marian was on his heels before Charles could halt her. With a resigned look, the viscount leisurely strode after them, reviewing the fastest sources for obtaining a special license. Ladies other than wives simply did not follow gentlemen into their homes. He would have to remember to impress that upon his own daughters as they grew up.

Jasper came out of his employer's downstairs study when the front door slammed open. The secretary struggled for some semblance of stoicism as his employer—rigged out in evening breeches and frock coat—dashed up the stairs as if his heels were on fire. He rubbed his eyes in disbelief as a goddess in frail silk and gold netting ran after him. But when the dignified viscount trailed in, shrugged, and followed them up the stairs, Jasper turned around and went back to the study where a decanter of brandy always waited.

By the time Marian located Reginald's bedchamber, Reginald had his valet by the throat and dangling a foot off the floor. O'Toole appeared in danger of turning a virulent purple, which didn't go at all well with his reddish auburn hair.

"Reginald, you will never discover anything if you kill him," Marian said prosaically. "I don't suppose you have any rope or anything we can use to tie him up?"

The valet made a strangling noise and gazed at her wildly.

Charles strolled into the room in time to hear Marian's question. He chuckled at the valet's panicky look. "I believe in the colonies they call it 'stringing' him up, my lady. One binds a rope around the thief's neck and flings it over the branch of a tree. The result is quite as satisfactory as a gibbet, I believe."

Marian gave him a curious look but responded instantly to Reginald's order.

"Take the sheets off the bed. They'll do. I'll mummify him."

O'Toole gasped for breath as he was lowered into a chair and his arms jerked behind the chair back. "I trust I get a bonus for playing these kinds of games, my lords," he protested mildly.

"Oh, certainly, O'Toole." Reginald pulled the sheet Marian handed him around the valet's chest and knotted it firmly in back. "Give me the other, Marian. I'll bind his feet too." To O'Toole, he responded, "Transportation to Australia sounds a sufficient bonus to me, unless you prefer a brief sojourn with the Navy. I understand Americans are a little peeved with our treatment of seamen, but you do seem to fit in quite well over here. I'm sure you'd enjoy the sea air."

"I'm not much of a sailor, sir. I'll forego the pleasure, if you don't mind. If you could explain the goal of this game, sir, I might play it a little better."

"The goal?" Reginald appeared to consider this as he jerked the second sheet around the chair and his valet's legs and bound them all together securely. "The goal, my good man, is to teach you not to play with things that don't belong to you. The faster you return the lady's necklace, the sooner you may expect to be released, although I don't promise you will enjoy your freedom anytime in the near future."

"That being the case, sir, I would rather decline the game. I don't have need of any bonus at the moment."

Reginald smiled grimly as he checked his handiwork. "You're a cool customer, I'll give you that, O'Toole." He turned to Charles. "I say we send Jasper for the marquess. Tell him we have his servant here and mean to hand him over to the authorities if the necklace doesn't appear within the next twenty-four hours. Does that seem reasonable to you?"

Marian frowned. "What if Mr. O'Toole doesn't work for my cousin?"

Reginald shrugged. "Then he had better come up with the necklace's whereabouts on his own, hadn't he?" He brushed off his hands and started for the door.

"Wait a minute!" O'Toole called after him.

Reginald turned and lifted a quizzical brow.

O'Toole glanced to Marian. "The lady's wearing the necklace. What is it I'm supposed to produce?"

Reginald smiled coldly. "The genuine one. Good-night, O'Toole."

He walked out, leaving the valet cursing and struggling against the sheets. Marian and Charles hurried to follow him.

Downstairs, Reginald gave orders to his secretary to search out the marquess, and a servant was sent to find the watch to keep a guard on the house. Satisfied that all was done that could be, Reginald turned to Marian with a frown.

"Well, now that we have scandalized the entire *ton* all at once, what should we do for an encore? Do you wish to return to the ball?"

"Are you going to let me dance?" she demanded.

"Of course." Reginald caught her hand and pulled her toward the door. "With me only, unless you mean to change that gown."

"I will not change my gown. I paid a fortune for this gown. I mean to wear it every chance I get." Marian hurried down the steps after him.

"Then resign yourself to dancing with me for the rest of your life. I have no intention of watching grown men drool over you as they guide you around the dance floor." Reginald held out his hand to assist her into the waiting carriage.

Marian ignored it and climbed in by herself. "Only children drool. And if there are only children at these affairs, I have no wish to attend them."

Behind them, Charles rolled his eyes and pulled out his watch. He wished Harriet was here. He needed to hear a few sensible words to keep him steady and on course, else he was likely to say something he shouldn't. He wondered if he had ever been so young as to bicker like this when what he actually meant to do was to haul the young lady in his arms and kiss her mouth shut.

Reginald was struggling with just that urge even though Marian went silent once Charles entered the carriage. The heady scent of the roses he had given her drifted around him, combining with the softer scent of the lemon juice she must have used on her tresses for this occasion. He wanted to bury his face in her hair and pull her against him and forget everything but the joy of making her his. He knew he had gone beyond rationality but he no longer cared. What was done was done, and he meant to make the best of it. He was quite certain that bedding Marian would be the best thing that had ever happened to him.

Reginald gave a grimace of distaste as the carriage returned to Devonshire House. His thoughts were far from the glittering panoply of guests inside. He wondered if Marian felt the same. He sensed her reluctance as he helped her out.

Charles was the one to break their silence. "We will have to enter together so it is known that the lady was not alone with you all this time. I told Devonshire there was a sudden illness. Perhaps the lady's maid?"

"You had best give the truth to Marian's mother. Their maid is a veritable part of the family. She would be concerned if you tell her the lie." Reginald's voice had returned to the cold and impersonal as he escorted Marian into the house.

"I trust you are prepared to marry quickly, then. Lady Grace will not look kindly on this escapade, even with my accompaniment."

Marian gripped Reginald's arm tighter and gave his taut features a look of concern. "I'm sorry. I only wished to keep you from doing something you would regret later."

Reginald managed a grim smile as he glanced down at her. "You will be the one who is sorry for ever having anything to do with me. And I shan't tell you that you succeeded

in your quest; it will only lead to more impetuousness on
your part. But I fully intended to strangle O'Toole."

Marian gave him an uncertain smile as they made their
way up to the ballroom. She wasn't entirely certain of all
the innuendoes behind his words. Reginald was capable of
many layers of communicating. What was she going to regret and why? Was he sorry that she had prevented him
from strangling his valet? Was he prone to acts of violence
when enraged? Should she return with him after the ball to
prevent him from murdering the poor man?

The prospect of marrying a murderer kept Marian so bemused as they entered the ballroom that she was scarcely
aware of the heads turning at their entrance. She smiled politely at the duke as he came forward to express his concern, allowed Lord Witham to make their explanations, and
asked to be led to the ladies' retiring room so she might repair herself. She needed time to gather her courage before
facing the crowd again. Or facing Reginald. She wasn't
certain which.

When she came out, only Reginald waited for her. His
brother must have headed off her mother and sister and
their questions. She couldn't read the expression in his eyes
as he watched her approach, but remembering his opinion
of her gown, she felt certain he was looking at her bosom.
She lowered her gaze and tried not to blush.

"I thought you might like some punch and then a stroll
on the balcony before returning to the ballroom. It is quite
stifling in there." Reginald took her hand on his arm and
led her properly toward the refreshment room.

"It can't be proper to stroll on the balcony," she murmured as he produced a cup of punch for each of them.
"Haven't we created enough scandal for one evening?"

"We might as well start out as we mean to go on. Since
we have already announced our betrothal, they will just
think we are overly romantical. Of course, everyone will be
counting the months until our first child is born, but that is
common enough."

Marian gave him a scandalized look, but Reginald's expression was quite calm as he led her toward the doors to
the outside. Their first child? She had barely thought as far

as their wedding day, and he was already considering children. The notion sent a fascinating thrill through her as she stepped out into the coolness of the evening.

"I don't wish to be thought fast," she protested as the door closed behind them. "It leads gentlemen to assume things that aren't proper."

Reginald snorted. "That gown leads them to assume a great many things that aren't proper. I think I'll lock you in the house when we are married."

"I am growing tired of this argument," Marian answered peevishly. "I have excellent taste and this gown is no worse than any other I have seen tonight. If you really mean to be a possessive tyrant, I will rethink this betrothal at once."

Reginald pulled her firmly into his arms. "Too late. The deed is done. Neither of our families will allow us to cry off now. You sealed your fate tonight, my dear. Try not to protest too vigorously as we march up the aisle."

His mouth closed over hers before she could even begin her protests.

Marian began to remember why she wanted this marriage. She liked the possessiveness of Reginald's mouth on hers, the heat of him as he claimed her, the thrill of his hands as they held her. There were other things she liked and admired about this man also, but they escaped her when he held her like this, as did everything else. Her hands slid to his shoulders and clung there as their mouths came together with intoxicating fires. She was entirely too aware of his hard body as he pressed her against him.

They were neither of them aware of their audience until a dark figure lounging against a far rail asserted himself.

"And here I thought it was my dramatic cape that you wished to admire, cousin. When are you going to learn to keep away from this mongrel fellow?"

The caped figure stepped into the patterns of light from the ballroom window. A hood hid his face in shadow, and only a glimmer of white linen could be seen through the folds of cloth as he propped his arms akimbo on his hips. But neither Marian or Reginald had any doubts as to his identity.

The Marquess of Effingham had come to London.

Twenty-four

Reginald gently but firmly put Marian behind him. "Relation or no, I am growing tired of your intrusion into what is none of your affair. Unless you have come to return Marian's necklace and the missing diamonds, you would do better to make yourself scarce."

Behind him, Marian gasped. Reginald felt her moving to interfere, but he stopped her with his arm, keeping her at a safe distance from the American.

Hidden behind the folds of his cape, the marquess's expression couldn't readily be determined, but there was a hint of amusement in his voice as he replied. "You have a very good eye. The diamonds were needed. They will be replaced as soon as I can generate a flow of cash from the estate. In truth, I did not think the ladies would miss them until I was able to replace them. So you have caught me out in this. But I sent Michael back with the necklace. I still believe it to be mine, but I could not wish to unduly upset the ladies. Michael is generally obedient to a direct order. Is that not the necklace my cousin is wearing?"

Marian's fingers gently closed around Reginald's arm. He liked the feel of them there, and he didn't protest when she stepped to his side. Somehow, the fact that she clung to him was reassuring.

"That is the copy that your blasted valet ferreted from its hiding place. Undoubtedly he thought to rob us both. He returned the original to my keeping, then replaced it before it reached Marian's hands, probably thinking I would not notice it once she was wearing it." Reginald didn't mention that he almost hadn't, distracted as he had been by Marian's more natural assets.

The marquess gave a sigh of exasperation. "I will wring his neck this time. I have warned him often enough that his light fingers were going to get him into trouble. You are only half-right. Michael won't steal from me. He has a warped sense of justice developed over years I won't bore you by describing. He is probably waiting to see if you will discover the switch, and if you don't, he will feel quite comfortable in returning the original to me. His loyalty is commendable, even if his morals aren't. I will see that the necklace is returned."

"Oh dear, do you think we ought—" Marian's question was interrupted by the arrival of the duke and Reginald's brother. The plight of the valet was momentarily forgotten as the two new arrivals discovered the cloaked figure in the shadows.

"Ahh, you are chaperoned. Lady Grace was growing concerned." The duke sent Marian and Reginald a laughing glance, then turned his attention back to the man in the shadows. "Have I had the pleasure?"

"Effingham. I believe your invitation was open?" The voice behind the hood was gruff.

Delight crossed the young duke's face. "Effingham! I should have known you would be here to look out for your cousin's interests. I don't suppose you have time to discuss those artifacts you mentioned in your letters? Or if we could meet at my club tomorrow . . . ?"

Charles grimaced and turned to the young couple he had come seeking. "The two of you had better make an appearance in the ballroom before the gossips have you half way to Scotland. Lady Grace is beginning to lose that beautiful patience of hers."

"Oh, but we must tell the marquess—"

Reginald caught Marian's arm. "We don't need to tell the marquess anything. He hasn't proven he can be trusted any more than his valet." He started moving toward the ballroom doors.

Unimpeded by the British etiquette of dealing with a duke, the marquess abruptly ended his conversation to step in front of them, halting their progress. "Why is it I get the impression the lady has been trying to tell me something?"

"Because the lady is of a more pleasant temperament than I am. Considering the scolds she is capable of giving, I never thought to say that, but the truth will out. If you will excuse us, the lady has yet to dance with me this evening." Reginald started around the caped figure blocking his way.

Charles coughed discreetly behind them. "I say, Reggie, you might at least make a proper introduction before you leave me out here."

Reginald scowled. "Gavin Lawrence, Marquess of Effingham; Charles Montague, Viscount Witham. Now, if you'll excuse us—"

Since the marquess was again moving to block their escape, Charles tried to smooth the social waters. "Effingham! I was hoping we would have a chance to meet before the nuptials. Where are you staying? I would like to pay my addresses on the morrow, if I could."

There was a note of harassment in the American's voice as he tried to fend off a duke and a viscount determined to do their duties while keeping an eye on the young couple who looked decidedly guilty of something. "I'm only here for the evening to look in on my cousin. Marian, if you would, I'd like to have a word with you."

Marian sent Reginald a questioning look. Pleased that she turned to him for his opinion rather than giving in to her cousin, Reginald managed an almost conciliatory reply. "He will come to no harm where he is. I will hand him over to your cousin as soon as I have the necklace in my hands again, I promise."

The duke and the viscount looked vaguely bemused when the marquess grabbed for Reginald's cravat at this seemingly irrelevant comment.

"Where is he, Montague? What have you done to him? He's not much of a brother, but he's the only one I've got. I'll deal with him, not you."

Reginald caught the man's wrists at his throat and twisted. A popping noise of bone rubbing bone forced the marquess to jerk from his captor's grasp and curl his hands into a fist. Before he could throw the punch, the duke and Charles caught his arms.

"Reginald is a damned stubborn independent bastard. If hitting him would do any good, I would have done so long ago, but it only makes him worse," Charles spoke consolingly, holding the marquess's arm in a firm grip. "Lady Marian, if you would, please tell your cousin what he wants to know before someone gets hurt."

"You always did play dirty, brother mine. It's unfair to ask my betrothed to go against my wishes. It puts her in a damned awkward position, and you know it." Reginald straightened his cravat and glared at the hooded figure still prepared to attack him once unrestrained. "I didn't realize the wretch was your brother. He doesn't exactly have the family resemblance."

The marquess relaxed somewhat warily at this reasonable tone. "Fortunately for him, he resembles our mother instead of the damned dark hot-tempered Lawrences. Excuse me, Marian, you are the exception that makes the rule. It is good to know that the blood runs to beauty in the ladies of the family. Now, what have you done with Michael?"

Thoroughly unsettled that she had still another cousin, one who was a thief and a valet, Marian glanced quickly to Reginald for reassurance. At his nod, she admitted, "We tied him up until Reginald could get back to him."

The marquess uttered a curse that Marian had never heard before, shook off his captors' hands, and started for the ballroom door. "Tied him up! Damnation, the house will no doubt be in flames, or flying off on the wings of pigeons before I get there. Tied him up!" He continued muttering and cursing as he threw open the doors and plowed his way through the glittering company, his black cloak flapping behind him.

The sight of this Gothic phantom striding through the room, muttering madly, sent the ladies shrieking and gentlemen backing out of his way. The marquess seemed completely unaware of the chaos erupting around him. Still hooded, he stalked through the room, trailing the duke and the others behind him.

As it became apparent that Reginald and Marian meant to follow in his path, Charles hastened to intervene. "I'll go with him. You two stay here. You've caused enough scandal for one evening. Someone has to stay and explain this scene to the satisfaction of the gossips."

He gestured, and they became aware of the staring faces all around them. Lady Grace was attempting to get through the crowd to her daughter, Jessica and Darley were waiting hesitantly near the steps for some signal to indicate what they should do, and the rest of the guests were whispering and staring at the caped phantom now striding briskly up the stairs to the exit.

Reginald gave a resigned grimace. "Hurry, then. Don't let him out of your sight until you have the necklace in hand. Jasper will help you."

Charles turned quickly on his heels and rushed after the departing marquess, giving a word of explanation to the duke as he left.

Marian just clung to Reginald's hand and shook her head. "It's not worth it. None of this is worth it. I could wish I had never set eyes on the thing. His brother?" She turned incredulous eyes to her escort.

He ought to be frustrated by his inability to follow the action, but Reginald found himself staring down into her bewildered face and wishing they were back out on the balcony again. As people began to cluster around them with a dozen questions, the musicians struck up a waltz. He squeezed Marian's fingers between his own. "My dance, I believe?"

Eyes widening, Marian glanced around them. Her family and Darley had nearly caught up with them. Lady Jersey was already patting her on the shoulder and offering to lead her to a retiring room to recover. Lady Agatha had caught Reginald's right arm and was pelting him with questions. Several of both of their acquaintances were adding their observations as to the identity of the mysterious cloaked figure, the ladies admiring his physique while the men protested his rudeness and speculated about his dangerousness. And Reginald wanted to dance?

That sounded fine to her. She slid her fingers around his arm. "Lead on, MacDuff," she purposely misquoted.

" 'And damned be him that first cries, "Hold, enough!" ' " Reginald murmured as he steered her unapologetically through the curious crowd.

Thrilled beyond speaking that he knew the reference, Marian merely floated into his arms when Reginald held them out at the dance floor. Gaze fastened on his face, she scarcely cared where her feet were as he guided them skillfully into the crowd. The knowledge that she had actually found a man who knew Shakespeare held her rapt as he swirled her in circles around the room. Eventually, however, she became aware of the heat of Reginald's hand at her back and the warmth of the gaze he was returning, and she began to blush.

"I didn't mean to stare," she murmured helplessly.

"That's quite all right, as long as you are not staring at a piece of grape between my teeth."

"I cannot imagine you ever having a piece of grape between your teeth."

His eyes danced. "Straw, then. Braying jackasses most likely keep straw between their teeth."

Marian's lips twitched with the effort to hold her smile. "You will never forgive me for that, will you?"

"Ummm, maybe in a thousand years, give or take a hundred or so. Do you think once we are married my life might return to some order again, or is it your intention for us always to live amidst chaos?"

Marian felt a nervous palpitation of the heart at the way Reginald was looking at her. She still had not quite grasped the reality of marrying this man. They scarcely knew each other. Yet she knew the pressing intimacy of his mouth against hers, and the way it made her feel, and she could think of no other man with whom she would share it. Shortly, they could be sharing their meals together, living in the same house . . . she blushed when she came to the idea of sleeping in the same bed together. Surely not.

"I would like to know what thought led to that charming bit of color in your cheeks, but perhaps I am better off not knowing. The dance has ended. Do you think if we stand here like this long enough, they will take pity on us and begin another?"

She was still in Reginald's arms in the middle of the dance floor while all others around them broke up to return to their various places among the guests. Marian discreetly stepped from his embrace and tried not to stare at him again.

"We had best go back to my mother. We have no doubt made a sufficient spectacle of ourselves for one night."

"I have never had any particular desire to attract attention, but I find myself caring little if we do. Darley is heading this way and I mean to tell him no if he thinks to draw you away from me." Reginald held her hand firmly clasped in his.

"What has come over you?" Unable to help herself, Marian turned her gaze back up to Reginald's starkly handsome face. The determined jut of his jaw made her heart leap. The stiffly arrogant man she had first met was rapidly becoming someone she liked and understood much too well.

Reginald had the grace to return her an uncertain smile. "I don't know. I think it must be that gown. I have this strange urge to ask your mother for a bill of sale so I might take you home with me."

Marian didn't know whether to laugh or scold at this reluctantly given admission. Darley's arrival interfered with either.

"I have been nominated to drag the pair of you off the dance floor before you can make utter cakes of yourselves. You would be doing me a great favor if you can make some show of complying to my authoritative orders."

Reginald quickly masked a look of frustration and irritation and, offering his arm, escorted Marian in the direction of her mother. "How are we to ever come to know each other if we cannot be left alone for even two minutes?" he asked rhetorically, for no one bothered to explain.

"Lady Grace can be quite a tartar when she gets her dander up. You're about to be raked over the coals, or I miss my guess," Darley said genially.

"Perhaps I ought to go see how Charles is faring," Reginald mused as they drew closer to the lady in question.

"Craven," Marian murmured as they came to stand in front of her mother. She wished she could bottle the look that Reginald gave her in return. It contained a confused frustration that she thought never to see in him and would no doubt never see again. It was good to know there were a few things that the lofty Reginald Montague could not deal with entirely on his own.

"Mama, did you know that the marquess has a brother, and that he has been serving as Reginald's valet all this time?" A direct attack usually served to divert Lady Grace's intentions.

Surprise lifted her eyebrows, but Lady Grace still maintained a frosty look as she kept her gaze on her daughter's betrothed. "Then we shall have to invite him to the wedding, I suppose. You are not planning a long betrothal, I trust?"

"I don't think there will be any difficulty obtaining a special license, my lady. I would like Marian to meet the rest of my family, of course, but you may set the date at any time you wish," Reginald answered a trifle stiffly.

"Very good. I think the first of the month will suit. We would not wish anyone to think there is need for haste."

Before Lady Grace could say more, she was distracted by a cry from her younger daughter. Jessica was looking to the entrance, where a small crowd of people gathered. Many of the guests had drifted off to the supper table since the musicians had retired, but a few stragglers like themselves had found some new entertainment.

"He had a dove, Mama. It flew away. Did you see it?" Delighted by the show, Jessica was already drifting in the direction of this new distraction.

Marian looked to see what her sister saw, but she could only discern a small crowd of people laughing and watching something in their center. Taller than she and better able to see above heads, Reginald was frowning slightly at whatever spectacle was there. She tugged on his hand. "What is it?"

Offering an arm to Lady Grace while Darley hurried after Jessica, Reginald led them toward the stairs and the lingering company. Perhaps the duke had arranged some form of entertainment for the supper break. Marian was in no hurry to join the crowd at the banqueting tables. She hurried to keep up with Reginald.

His frown deepened as they drew closer, and he made no apologies as he pushed his way through the onlookers. Marian clung to his arm rather than be left behind. She was beginning to think perhaps this wasn't some innocent entertainment after all, judging just by Reginald's frown. She scanned the crowd for the source of their interest.

A man in black beaver hat and tails similar to those of all the male guests stood at ease near a pillar pulling a string of colorful scarves from his coat pocket. At Marian's approach, he smiled broadly, swept off his hat, and bowed low. When he stood upright again, his hand held a bouquet of flowers he held out to her.

Astonished, Marian looked up to see his face before accepting the offering. His smile widened with her eyes.

Michael O'Toole, the valet. Her cousin.

Twenty-five

Marian clutched the bouquet of flowers and laid a restraining hand on Reginald's arm. She didn't know how Mr. O'Toole had escaped the bonds holding him. There hadn't been time for the marquess and Charles to free him. But he was her cousin, and he hadn't run away when given the opportunity. The marquess had said Michael had his own sense of justice, and something told her that this particular cousin could not be judged by ordinary standards. She waited to see what he would do next.

Casually elegant in his formal clothes, O'Toole—as she knew him—leaned against the pillar, put his hand in a pocket suspiciously large for evening wear, and produced a second bouquet of flowers. He handed them gently to Jessica instead of flourishing them, as if aware that any extravagant gestures would frighten her. Jessica made a coo of delight and eagerly shared the gift with the ladies around her.

While part of the crowd was distracted with Jessica and her prize, O'Toole straightened, opened his coat as if to look for something inside, and a flock of doves suddenly took wing all around them, sending the majority of the onlookers stepping backward and out of the way. Under cover of this commotion, O'Toole bowed to Lady Grace, reached into her elaborately coiffed hair, and came away with a tiny enameled box which he held out for her.

Lady Grace released Reginald's arm to accept the gift wonderingly, patting her hair as if to ascertain there were no further surprises to be found there. Pleased with the box itself, she made no haste to look for the opening. O'Toole solved the problem for her, snapping his fingers with a quick wave that caused the box to pop open.

By this time, the crowd was drifting back, and they gaped and tittered while Lady Grace drew out a delicate necklace of pale sapphires. Or at least, Marian thought they were sapphires. They could have been paste and she wouldn't know, but she couldn't be so rude as to question a gift. Her mother smiled as if they were a treasure of diamonds, and that was all that mattered. O'Toole bent gracefully and kissed the lady's hand when she thanked him.

With a wink at Marian, he swung away from her and back to the completely amazed Jessica. Marian didn't dare take her eyes off him to look at Reginald to see how he was taking this. The son of an earl might not appreciate having a street magician for cousin-in-law, but even Reginald would have to admit that Mr. O'Toole was a rather elegant magician. Also, a light-fingered one, she would have to remember. Her eyes narrowed as he reached for Darley's pockets.

Darley, too, was suspicious of the move, and he attempted to step out of O'Toole's reach. Ostrich and peacock feathers suddenly began erupting from the coiffures and pockets of the ladies and gentlemen all around him, and poor Darley was caught up in the excitement and the crush as the guests laughed and grabbed for the frivolous favors. Before the viscount could escape, O'Toole produced a box from behind Darley's ear, and Darley was protesting and grabbing for the prize.

"It was intended for the lady, was it not?" O'Toole asked smoothly, bowing and presenting it to Jessica.

"Not yet, you idiot!" Darley vehemently protested, but his gaze was anxious as Jessica took the tiny box in her fingers.

When she looked up to him and offered to give the box back, Darley shook his head. "I meant to wait and do it proper," he said stiffly. He sent an uncertain look to Marian and Reginald, then returned his attention to Jessica. "I found it in a shop, and I knew it was perfect for you, and I realized I very much wanted you to have it." He swallowed uneasily as Jessica gazed up at him with wide blue eyes.

O'Toole was busily distracting the crowd with gold watches appearing in ladies' bosoms and silver coins in gentlemen's ears.

Relieved that he was no longer the center of attention, Darley said softly, "I know I cannot properly give it to a lady who is not my wife, but I thought . . . If you would think about it . . . I mean, I can wait until you are ready . . . "

Astonished but evidently pleased, Jessica opened the box. Nestled in the satin was a delicate ring in the shape of a silver rose with a beautifully cut diamond in its center. Not much of a talker at the best of times, Jessica could only stare wordlessly at the ring, then back to Darley until tears rimmed her eyes. Her lips tried to form the words, but nothing came out, and Darley hastened to reassure her.

"You don't have to say anything, Miss Oglethorp. Just keep it until you're ready." Darley closed his hand around the one holding the ring. He threw an anxious look back at Reginald. "I only just bought the damned thing. How'd he know I had it?"

As if sensing he was being discussed behind his back, O'Toole turned around, planted a white gardenia behind Jessica's ear to bring her quivering lip to a smile, and finally turned his attention to Reginald.

Marian noted that Jessica and Darley continued to hold hands while they watched to see what the irrepressible O'Toole would do next. She dared a hasty glance to Reginald's face, but his expression was imperturbable as he met his former valet's look. The gleam in her cousin's eyes was more than mischievous, and Marian felt a nervous quiver or two of her own. She remembered quite clearly the marquess's admonitions about flying houses. At this moment, she was more than convinced that Michael O'Toole could float the ballroom off the ground if he desired.

"The lady's necklace is too easy," O'Toole murmured, idly producing a few coins from nowhere and juggling them back and forth while looking Reginald up and down.

"She wears it now. Perhaps one more suitable to her tastes?" he asked, as if to himself.

Reginald glanced hastily to Marian's throat. The ruby glittered in the light of the branch of candles on the pillar. He was momentarily distracted by the creamy hills rising around it, but he blinked and focused his attention on the jewel. It looked decidedly real in this light. A flush of pink was beginning to color the skin beneath the jewel, and Reginald reluctantly looked away from this fascinating display. He turned his attention back to O'Toole in time to see the man juggle a necklace along with the coins in his hands.

A slow rage began to rise as Reginald recognized the delicately fashioned emerald necklace he had purchased for Marian's wedding gift. He had locked the piece up in his desk drawer as soon as it had arrived. If the blasted thief had stolen the stones from this . . .

O'Toole grinned as if reading his mind. With a wave of his hands, the coins disappeared and the necklace once more lay in the box in which it had arrived. He bowed and presented it to Marian. "Your betrothed is as deceptive an illusion as I am, but his gift to you is the genuine article. He thinks to disguise the real gift with these jewels, but I think you are wise enough to discover the truth. Please accept my apologies for any distress I have caused you, my lady." He sent Reginald a wicked look. "But I don't apologize for any I have caused your betrothed. Keep him on a short rope, cuz." He turned quickly back to the amusement of the crowd.

Marian glanced uncertainly from the lovely emeralds in her hands to Reginald's stoic expression. "Are they yours?" She held the box reluctantly out to him. In the general run of things, she wasn't enamored with jewelry, but this was the most exquisitely wrought confection she had ever laid eyes on. She couldn't help a second longing glance to the glittering stones.

Reginald's expression relaxed slightly. "I had meant to give them to you on our wedding day. I wanted you to have something of your own, and not the family heirlooms. Does it suit?"

Marian's eyes widened as she lowered her hand and allowed herself the pleasure of examining the necklace with more care. "It's a piece of art," she murmured, fascinated by the play of light on the stones. "I never thought jewelry could be so beautiful."

"It can never be more beautiful than your eyes right now. I have been foolish to think my collections were all the beauty I need." Reginald closed the box in her hand, forcing her to look up to him.

Marian didn't have time to interpret the look in his eyes, only to know that it disturbed a tidal wave of sorts in her insides before an explosion of noise behind them distracted their attention.

Puffs of smoke rose upward from the center of the crowd, and an exotic scent vaguely like that of the gardenia Jessica had been given filled the air. Reginald closed Marian firmly in his embrace, pulling her back against him as the crowd stepped away in cries of astonishment. All eyes searched in vain for the elegantly garbed magician who had stood there just moments before. He had vanished into thin air.

Reginald growled in disbelief and would have moved to search the area had not still another sight caught his eye. Closing his fingers firmly around the hand in which Marian clutched her necklace, he glanced to a figure just being announced at the entrance. He stiffened and adjusted Marian to a more proper position at his side.

Shaken by O'Toole's disappearance, Marian gazed up at Reginald, questioning this sudden placement. Her gaze followed his to the entrance, and she sucked in a sharp breath.

The man standing at the top of the stairs had the same proudly erect stance and arrogant features as the man at her side, only aged by years Reginald had not yet lived. Studied closer, the features were perhaps not the same. The older man's nose was sharper and longer, his mouth thinner, but the resemblance was there just the same. Marian shivered slightly in anticipation of the scene to come. There wasn't a doubt in her mind that the new arrival was the Earl of Mellon, Reginald's father.

"Damn," Reginald muttered under his breath. "Between

us, we seem to have an overabundance of relations to entertain the crowd tonight."

Marian began to giggle, probably more with nervous hysteria than amusement. "If he pulls flowers out of his coat, I shall faint immediately."

"So shall I," Reginald answered grimly.

Apparently locating his prey, the earl steered a straight course toward his younger son. With whispers of scandal, the crowd moved out of his path. Not one among them regretted missing their suppers for this fascinating entertainment.

The Earl of Mellon came to a halt before the unlucky pair. Marian gripped her bouquet and her necklace nervously, but he dismissed her with a glance. He reserved his glare for Reginald.

"You will explain the chaos I found on your doorstep when I came to call."

Reginald remained icily aloof. "Good evening, sir. It is a pleasure to see you again, too."

The earl scowled. "Don't give me that lie. You'd rather I disappeared like that other scoundrel just did. I'll make the lady's acquaintance, if you will, and then I will know what is going on. Not only is Devonshire's ballroom overrun with pigeons and silly idiots and smoke, but your place is teeming with females of ill repute and a rather noisy melee of mongrels. It seems all of London has gone mad, and I would know if it is contagious."

Marian began to giggle again. She couldn't help it. It was all much too improbable. Reginald looked as if he would choke. The earl—despite his harsh face—seemed fairly mazed. And she could almost hear Michael O'Toole's laughter ringing from the rafters. The Phantom and the Magician: her father's family would soon set all London on its ears.

Lady Grace finally appeared at their side, and as Reginald struggled with all the introductions, the earl's face softened somewhat. He bowed low over the lady's hand when all was said and done.

"Grace, it has been a thousand years. How is it we have not met in all that time?"

Marian's mother smiled thoughtfully. "We neither of us were much for society, sir. It is good to see you again."

Marian and Reginald watched in astonishment as their respective parents exchanged light badinage about her name and his title and an old argument over who should be called what. Shaking his head in astonishment, Reginald gently eased Marian away from the reunion.

"I'm not in any hurry to return home and discover the chaos my father complains about. With any luck, Charley and your cousin will set the house back to rights without my help. Do you think we might retreat to the balcony and learn to know each other a little better?"

Reginald's eyes gleamed knowingly as he looked down at her, and Marian tried not to blush. She had a good idea of what he considered getting to "know" her, but they were betrothed. Wasn't she obliged to obey his wishes?

She glanced up at him through a curtain of lashes. "Are you certain that is wise? What if we take each other into dislike before the wedding?"

"My lady, at the moment I am trying to calculate how I can put your whole damned family on the market and sell them as rare objects. But you, I would keep. Come along, I would see what I have won by my immeasurable patience."

Marian nearly ran to keep up with him as he dragged her through the ballroom rapidly filling with guests returning from supper. "Patience?" she inquired indignantly. "I have not seen you exude one iota of that virtue at any time. You have yet to win anything, sir."

Reginald swung open the door and pulled her out, closing it firmly behind him, shutting out the noise and the people and the music. Dragging her from the light, he circled her waist with his arms. "Then I have my task cut out for me, don't I? Where shall I start?"

Before she could offer any of the opinions so obviously ready to burst from her lips, Reginald leaned over and caught them with his mouth.

It was the best way in the world to silence her, and he enjoyed it immensely.

Twenty-six

The sun sparkled against the bay windows of the shops as they strolled past. Marian was aware of the bustle of people around them, of the expensive fashions and laughing chatter of the society she was coming to know. She liked the smell of meat pies coming from the stalls on the street corner. She enjoyed the variety of objects displayed for her perusal in the windows. But most of all, she loved walking beside this proud man who made heads turn whether he was frowning or laughing.

He was frowning now, and she quailed a bit inside at the expression. He had arrived this afternoon quite unexpectedly, made her excuses to her family, and appropriated her company without asking her permission. She had much rather be in Reginald's company than her mother's, but she was still rather uncertain of his moods. These past weeks had been a whirlwind of activity from which they had stolen every possible moment for themselves, but there still hadn't been enough time. The wedding was only a week away, and the only time they'd had alone together had been measured in minutes of every day.

Reginald hadn't said he loved her, but Marian had never expected that. He'd given her beautiful compliments, and that had been much more than she had anticipated. He had taught her passion with their stolen kisses, and she had no fear of their wedding night. Her betrothed had been more than gentle, more than she had ever dared hope, while still conveying his very real desire for her. She lay in bed at night with her heart thumping in longing for his presence beside her. No, she was more than ready to be his wife. That wasn't the reason for her qualms today.

Her qualms had more to do with Reginald's dangerous quiet since he had swept her from the house. He no longer had a groom to ride behind them in the curricle, and they had been used to talking incessantly and holding hands when they traveled together. There had been none of that today. He had merely driven them to this street, handed the reins of his horses to some street urchin he seemed familiar with, and handed her down to the cobblestones. His grim expression was beginning to frighten her.

Refusing to admit to fear, Marian exclaimed in delight at the display in the windows of Aristotle's Emporium. "Look, Reginald! It looks just like a miniature of the entrance hall of Arinmede! However did they make the stained glass so tiny? Isn't it marvelous? The sun sets off all the colors just as it does at the manor. I've never seen anything so exquisite."

Reginald stopped stiffly in front of the window to allow her to admire the artisan's handiwork. "Your cousin has talented hands. It's about time he applied them to something useful," he said gruffly, not daring to touch her.

But he didn't refuse her hand when she slid it into his palm, Marian felt his fingers tighten around hers, and she dared turn him an expectant look. Jessica would have been terrified by his stern demeanor, but she knew Reginald had a habit of hiding himself behind that expression and his cynical attitude. And she loved the man he tried to hide. She smiled and watched his gaze grow wary.

"Surely you don't mean the marquess? Gavin might set a regiment of soldiers in line with a single word, but he could never make anything so exquisite as this. And if it is Michael's doing, how do you know it? I think it would be easier to catch a leprechaun than to catch Michael."

"He fancies himself Irish," Reginald hedged, not yet certain how to breach his news. "That's why he calls himself O'Toole instead of Lawrence."

Marian made a moue of distaste. "You need not be polite with me, you know, Reginald. It's not as if I haven't questioned Gavin thoroughly on the subject. He is as evasive as you, but it does not take a great mind to see that Michael doesn't believe he shares the same father as Gavin. I shall ferret out the entire story sometime, but it is of little account. Their mother was married to my great-uncle or whatever when Michael was born, so his name is Lawrence no matter what he believes."

Reginald almost managed a smile, but his eyes were still wary as he watched her. "His birth does not matter to you? You would claim a thief and a street magician for family even if he may not be related?"

Marian shrugged and turned back to the fascinating display in the window. "I understand they led hard lives after their parents died. I don't think Michael is really bad, he just has a different set of values than we do. And if Gavin claims him as brother, that is enough for me. I've never had the privilege of cousins before. I'm rather enjoying the sensation. They are my protection against your avalanche of relations."

"I trust no one in my family has been hurtful to you?" Reginald's thumb moved back and forth across her wrist as he continued to hold her hand.

"No, they have been lovely. Your sister-in-law is a delight, and I am dying to meet your nephew, and all the others have been more than proper. I do adore your brother. I wish I had been there when you returned home after the duke's ball. The way Lord Witham tells the story raises terrible images. I cannot believe Michael could have created such chaos so quickly. Were some of the ladies really undressed? Your brother does not say so, but there is this gleam in his eye . . . "

Reginald finally grinned and squeezed her fingers. "I shall never tell, and you are above all naughty to ask. Suffice it to say that Michael will be paying for that episode for a long time to come." The grin slipped away. "That is not why I brought you here today."

Marian turned her gaze up to him. "I've been waiting for you to tell me. Am I supposed to beguile you out of whatever it is that is bothering you?"

He winced. "No, witch, I would rather not be twisted between your manipulative little hands. I'll take your honesty any day. I only wish I'd had the courage to give you the same from the start. Now we are so thoroughly embroiled I see little way out, and I fear you will despise me for the rest of our days."

Startled, Marian removed her hand from his, only to place it on his arm instead. "Are you feeling quite well? I thought we had come to some understanding over these last weeks. I like you too well to ever despise you. Surely you know that." She paled a little and removed her hand. "Unless you have found someone else, someone you can truly love. Is that why you wish out?"

With a muttered curse, Reginald grabbed her waist and hauled her toward the door. "That might be easier for all concerned, but no. It is not I who wishes out of this arrangement. You are the one who will be sorry. I have debated every possible way of not telling you, hoping you will never know, hoping if nothing else I can make you so enamored of me that you will not care, but I cannot do that to you. I've come to love you too damned much to deceive you like that. You will have to know the truth before it is too late for you to cry off."

Head spinning with the impossibility of that one little phrase, Marian ignored all the surrounding words and allowed herself to be shoved through the door of the emporium. The boy behind the counter looked up from waiting on a customer to give them a respectful nod of greeting. Jacobs came hurrying out at the sound of the door, then shrugged and returned to the back at the sight of them. Marian thought it rather odd that he did not wait on them, but she was too confused by Reginald and his behavior to question anyone else's.

Holding her waist tightly in his arm, he steered her toward the back of the store. Marian began to resist. "Where are we going?" she whispered. "We can't go back there."

"We can do anything we like in here." Reginald grabbed up a crystal paperweight and lobbed it at a marble statue. His throw nicked the crystal, sending it bouncing against the Turkish carpet, while nearly toppling the statue. Marian held her breath, waiting for it to fall, waiting for someone to come out screaming at this desecration. The boy raised

an inquiring eyebrow, his customer slinked out the door
and away from the madman, but no one protested Reginald's reckless destruction.

"Reginald, what are you doing?" Aghast, Marian
watched as her betrothed helped himself to a selection of
leather bound books from behind the counter. She clasped
them to her when he dumped them in her arms, fearful he
would throw them like the paperweight if she gave them
back.

Once her hands were otherwise occupied, he set himself
to decorating her with every exquisite jewel his eye caught
on in the display case. He placed a glittering tiara on her
hair, adorned her ears with diamond bobs, wrapped golden
necklaces around her throat, and clasped a jeweled band
around her wrist. Marian struggled desperately with the precious volumes in her hands, returning them to the shelves
before he made her into a walking display of valuables.

"Reginald, stop this at once!" she commanded with a
hiss when he enveloped her in a cloth of gold cloak that
looked vaguely familiar.

"Why should I?" he asked disinterestedly. "They belong
to me." He adjusted the cloak. "Or your cousin, in the case of
this item. He has generously allowed me to sell his posses-
sions on consignment, so I needn't come up with the cash to
buy them all. My commission will keep us very comfortably
for many years if I am successful in selling them."

It was the way he said it more than his words that made
Marian stop and listen to what he was really trying to say.
She fingered the costly bracelet on her wrist and looked
with interest at the fascinating variety of titles on the shelf
in front of her. Her gaze drifted back to the miniature in the
window, and with a swirl of her golden cloak, she stalked
behind the counter and through the doorway she had
thought only for the shopkeeper.

The room beyond was a fascinating assortment of books
and maps and antiquities too delicate to be left unattended
in the main display area. An open staircase led to another
story, and glancing over her shoulder at Reginald's blank
expression, she daringly started up it as if she owned the
place. He made no objection.

The cloak swirled around her as she ascended the stairs and entered what was evidently a large work space. Old wood covered this floor rather than valuable carpet. Shelving littered with odd bits of hardware and tools, legs off old tables and chairs, heads of crumbling statues, and any number of oddities collecting dust filled the walls. Beneath a gabled window on one end of the room sat a table cluttered with myriad bits and pieces of metal and fabric and glass— and her cousin Michael.

He glanced up, startled, at her entrance. He seemed to be working on a replica of the exterior of Arinmede Manor, but Marian gave him little notice. She stalked to the far end of the work area where she had spied a door with a glass transom. Michael watched without expression as Reginald raced up the stairs after his cousin, following her with a dangerous look in his eyes as he crossed the room. Only after they disappeared into the far room and slammed the door did he grin and return to his work.

Marian swung around, swirling her cloak with a dramatic ripple as Reginald followed her into his office. With a theatrical gesture, she unfastened the cloak and let it fall to the floor. She stepped over it, dropping a bracelet on its gleaming folds. Unfastening necklaces and earbobs and bracelets and letting them fall as they would, she approached her betrothed.

Gold and jewels littered the path she made toward him. Reginald remained frozen where he was, unheeding of the fortune in valuables scattering across the floor, his gaze focused entirely on the woman in the center of these treasures. His eyes narrowed dangerously as Marian reached him and placed both hands on his chest.

"Are you going to make love to me now?" she whispered huskily.

His body responded as she meant it to, but Reginald was made of sterner stuff. He held himself stiff and unresponsive, not touching her. "You don't understand yet, do you?" He swung his arm. "This is my office. This is my shop. I own this place. This is how I earn my living. I, my dear, am a shopkeeper."

"And I, my bumble-headed ninnyhammer, will be a shopkeeper's wife." Marian slid her hands over his shirt, beneath his habitually unfastened waistcoat. She really was quite fascinated with the feel of him beneath the fine cloth, and the scent of him. Reginald had a fascinating scent of male flesh and a lime fragrance and occasionally the musty odor of old books. She could recognize him in the dark just from his scent, she was certain.

His hands slid reluctantly to her waist, attempting to hold her away. "Is a bumble-headed ninnyhammer better than a braying jackass?" he asked inquisitively, just for the record.

"Not better, just more endearing."

She leaned into him, and Reginald didn't stop her. She felt good cuddled against his chest, her head tucked under his chin. He warmed his arms by wrapping them around her back. "You aren't paying attention, my love," he reminded her. "If society finds out what I do, we will be ruined. We will be scorned by family and friends, cut from all entertainments, mocked by all around us. This is what I would bring you to if we married. I'm not a wealthy man, Marian. You must consider what you are doing before you make that fatal step. You are the daughter of a marquess. You can do much better than me."

She sighed and played with a button on his shirt. "You buy and sell books and things?" She felt him nod. "I buy and sell books and things, too. So does Gavin. I much rather buy than sell, but one has to live. I don't see any difference."

His hands stroked her back. "You and Gavin sell the occasional oddity when you need funds. You don't make a habit of acquiring things to sell for profit. There is a distinct difference, my dear."

"I could make a habit of it," she said thoughtfully. "It could be very challenging. Just the other day I heard Lady Agatha wish for an old lorgnette she once owned. I saw one that would be just perfect for her in a Covent Garden stall. I could buy it from that vendor and sell it to Lady Agatha for easily twice as much as I bought it. I think it would be rather amusing."

Reginald ran his hand into her hair and dug his fingers deeply into her thick coiffure. He tilted her head back until she met his eyes. "I love you even if you are insane. You will not go down to Covent Garden to buy Lady Agatha a lorgnette. Is that clearly understood?"

"Even if I do love you enough to be classified insane, I will not let you bully me, Mr. Montague. If I wish to sell Lady Agatha a lorgnette, I shall. And no amount of kissing will make me change my mind."

"No amount?" His eyes gleamed as he studied her.

"No amount," she answered firmly.

He lowered his head and found her deliciously full lips. "If I kiss you enough, will you love me more?" he murmured against them.

"Insanely," she agreed as his mouth closed over hers.

In the work area beyond, Michael whistled a happy tune and polished a piece of glass for a tiny mullioned window. He lifted an eyebrow at the sound of a piece of furniture in the office bumping against a wall.

The old sofa in there was none too comfortable. He'd give them another window or two before intruding. After all, he had no desire to end up back on the streets again. These London streets were damned damp even at the best of times.

And illusion held little comfort when compared to the genuine emotion he saw between those two lovers. He rather imagined his little cousin was a true original, one who didn't mind being a shopkeeper's wife. He wouldn't mind finding a woman like that for himself one day, a real woman, not an illusion.

But in the meantime, he found it extremely amusing to sit back and watch this pairing of the noble marquess's daughter with a man who made his own living. He rather liked to think that he was partially responsible for the sounds of love emanating from that room right now—he and the ruby necklace, anyway.

Whistling, he snapped his fingers and produced a tiny gem to install in the miniature desk drawer waiting for its place in the manor. Ruby red sparkled in the sunlight from the window, and the magician grinned.

Now that Montague possessed the genuine article, he wouldn't miss this piece of glass.

Allison Lane

"A FORMIDABLE TALENT...
MS. LANE NEVER FAILS TO
DELIVER THE GOODS."
—*ROMANTIC TIMES*

BIRDS OF A FEATHER
0-451-19825-5
When a plain, bespectacled young woman keeps meeting the handsome Lord Wylie, she feels she is not up to his caliber. A great arbiter of fashion for London society, Lord Wylie was reputed to be more interseted in the cut of his clothes than the feelings of others, as the young woman bore witness to. Degraded by him in public, she could nevertheless forget his dashing demeanor. It will take a public scandal, and a private passion, to bring them together...

S556